CENTRAL
INTELLIGENCE
AGENCY

Extracts from a CIA Report titled: The Berlin Tunnel*

*https//www.CIA/gov/library/center for the study of intelligence/books and monographs/On the Front Line of the Cold War/ Documents on the Intelligence War in Berlin, 1946-1961. Document V—the Berlin Tunnel

No single operation more typifies Berlin's importance as a strategic intelligence base than the construction of the Berlin Tunnel. Probably one of the most ambitious operations undertaken by the CIA in the 1950s, it succeeded despite the fact that the KGB knew about the operation even before construction of the tunnel began!

The genesis of the tunnel operation lay in Berlin's location in Europe and its prewar status as the capital of a militarily and economically dominant Germany. The largest city on the Continent, Berlin lay at the center of a vast network of transportation and communications lines that extended from Western France to deep into Soviet Russia and Eastern Europe. This was still true in the 1950s; Soviet telephone and telegraph communications between Moscow, Warsaw, and Bucharest wererouted through Berlin....This became became a factor of crucial importance beginning in 1951 when the Soviets began to shift from wireless communications to encrypted landlines for almost all military traffic....encrypted messages as well as nonsecure voice communications.

Thus was born the idea of tunneling into the Soviet sector of Berlin to tap into Soviet military communications [known to insiders as Operation Gold]....By August 1953, detailed plans for the tunnel were completed, and a proposal was drawn up for approval by DCI Allen Dulles. After much discussion, this was obtained on 20 January 1954.

Having learned the location of the underground cables used by the Soviets from an agent inside the East Berlin post office, the Altglienicke district was selected as the best site for a cable tap...The tunnel itself was completed a year later, at the end of February 1955, and the taps were in place and operating shortly thereafter.

In all, about 40,000 hours of telephone conversations were recorded, along with 6,000,000 hours of teletype traffic. Most of the useful information dealt with Soviet orders of battle and force dispositions—information that was invaluable in the days before reconnaissance satellites....Unfortunately, the whole operation was blown even before the DCI approved the project. On 22 October 1953, US intelligence officers briefed a British Secret Intelligence Service (SIS) audience that included KGB mole, George Blake.

Although the KGB was aware of the potential importance of the tap, its first priority was to protect Blake. Early in 1956, the Soviets developed a plan whereby the tap would be "accidentally" discovered....On the night of 21-22 April 1956, a special signal corps team....penetrated the tunnel in the full glare of a well-organized publicity coup.

> The above extract describes the first time that US Intelligence Agencies built a tunnel into Soviet-controlled East Berlin. This is a fictional account of the building of a second tunnel in 1960-1961 during the period of the closing of the Berlin Wall and the Berlin Crisis.

THE SETTING OF
THE TUNNEL

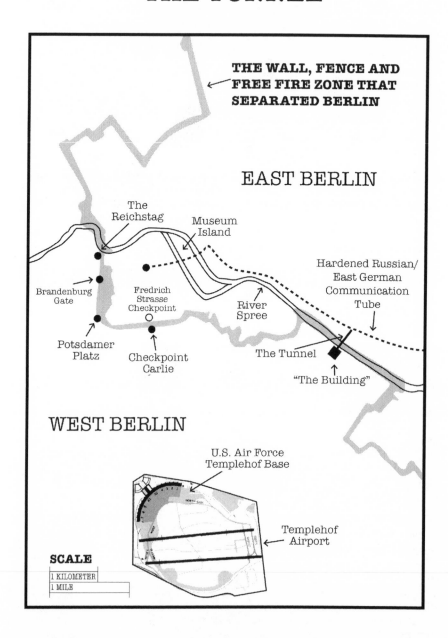

THE WALL, FENCE AND
FREE FIRE ZONE THAT
SEPARATED BERLIN

EAST BERLIN

The
Reichstag

Museum
Island

Hardened Russian/
East German
Communication
Tube

Brandenburg
Gate

Fredrich
Strasse
Checkpoint

River
Spree

Potsdamer
Platz

Checkpoint
Carlie

The Tunnel

"The Building"

WEST BERLIN

U.S. Air Force
Templehof Base

Templehof
Airport

SCALE

1 KILOMETER
1 MILE

THE BERLIN TUNNEL

A COLD WAR THRILLER

BY

ROGER L. LILES

The Berlin Tunnel—A Cold War Thriller

First Edition
Copyright © 2018 Roger Liles

Paperback ISBN: 978-1-947392-27-4
Hardcover ISBN: 978-1-947392-28-1

"In the long history of the world, only a few generations have been granted the role of defending freedom in its hour of maximum danger."

John F Kennedy's Inaugural Address
—January 20, 1961

AUTHOR'S NOTES:

As the citation from President Kennedy's inaugural address states, the world in the early 1960's was a perilous place. The Russians possessed the hydrogen bomb. Both the U.S.A and U.S.S.R. had settled on a policy of Mutual Assured Destruction (MAD)—if you strike us with nuclear weapons, we will retaliate in kind. Everyone realized that both Russia and America, perhaps even the whole world, would cease to exist if an all-out nuclear war occurred.

In reaction, Americans built fallout shelters in their backyards, confident that Armageddon was imminent. The communists dominated most of Europe and Asia. The space race was on—spectacular Russian feats contrasted with a string of failures on the part of the U.S.A.

By 1960, the Warsaw Pact countries enjoyed a five-to-one advantage in conventional forces in Europe. President Dwight Eisenhower frequently declared that, if the Russians attacked Western Europe, he'd employ tactical nuclear weapons to prevent them from overrunning our allies and American forces stationed in Europe.

Since 1958, the Russians repeatedly threatened to sign a separate peace treaty with the East Germans. Such a treaty would recognize East Germany's right to incorporate all of Berlin into a sovereign country. The Russians, utilizing the United Nations and other international forums, inflamed world opinion in support of this planned action. Their saber rattling threatened a crisis, even war, if the West did not capitulate on this issue.

Since the two million West Berliners relied on the two-way flow of virtually everything, the constant communist threat of another Berlin Blockade was especially compelling.

In the mid-1950s, the American CIA and British Secret Intelligence Service (MI-6) dug a tunnel and tapped into a buried communication cable located in East Berlin. The frontispiece of this novel contains a one-page excerpt from a CIA report, which describes that monumental feat. More details about that Berlin Tunnel—PROJECT GOLD/STOPWATCH—are available on the internet.

As far as the author can determine, a second tunnel was never built in Berlin during the Cold War. I'm sure that, at many levels of the American government, it was contemplated. You can almost hear someone say, "All that valuable intelligence is readily available, if only…"

This is a fictionalized account of how a second tunnel might have been built by the Americans. It is based on real events and seeks to recall a time—1960/1961—and a place, a divided Berlin before, during, and after the dramatic events that surrounded the closing of the Wall and the Berlin Crisis.

The conditions and events that occurred on both sides of the Iron Curtain, and which divided Berlin, are faithfully recreated. The characters are the product of the author's imagination. The leaders of this period are quoted, and one is included in the story as a character for dramatic purposes.

DEDICATION

This book is dedicated to the estimated fifty million American citizen soldiers who, like Cincinnatus, selflessly served their country in the fight against Communism between the conclusion of World War II and the end of the Cold War. As a result of their efforts, the communist grip on the countries of Eastern Europe and the Soviet Union ended in the last decade of the twentieth century.

Those Cold War warriors, and the individuals who served in the "Hot Wars" in Korea and Vietnam, deserve the recognition often withheld when they returned home after their service.

Finally, this book is dedicated to those American servicemen and women 'who gave the last full measure' in death or disability during this period.

PROLOGUE

Robert
April 14, 2010

MY QUEST INTENSIFIED after an internet search revealed that after fifty years, the code word LUMAR had been declassified. In the months that followed, I spent time each day on Google as I searched for additional information.

My eleven-year-old grandson Jonathan recently helped me set up a Google Alert to automatically inform me when someone posted something new. My search terms included Berlin Tunnel, U.S. Air Force, and, of course, Project LUMAR.

Following my regular routine, after lunch I checked my email account. Startled, I discovered my first alert. When I opened the URL and the subject document, a familiar page jumped out at me from my computer screen. Shocked, I pushed back my chair and sat frozen in place. I finally caught my breath, and shouted, "Well, I'll be damned!"

Anna rushed from her nearby potting studio, gasping, "Are you okay, *leibchen*?"

"Come here! Come around so you can see what I've found!"

"I thought you were having another heart attack or something."

"No! No!" I pointed. "Look! Look here! The construction plan I wrote in Berlin almost fifty years ago. It's on the internet!"

She moved behind me, smoothed an errant tuft of my thinning gray hair into place. She put both hands on my shoulders, bending forward for a better view.

I felt her stiffen. She moved her hands to my throat, pretending to choke me. "So is this what you've hidden from me all these years!"

Knowing I'd opened an old wound, I turned to face her. "There was a reason I couldn't tell you. An important reason."

"What might that be?"

"I signed a non-disclosure agreement with the American government." I raised my hands in mock surrender. "I could have gone to prison for thirty years for the unauthorized disclosure of information about Project LUMAR, the program I managed."

Her face softened. She put her arms around me. "Robbie, if you'd told me about that agreement, I wouldn't have pressed you so hard for information or been so hurt that you wouldn't trust me."

"I was even ordered not to tell anyone about the non-disclosure agreement," I explained. I felt both relieved and exhilarated that, at last, I could share this secret with Anna, my wife and best friend of almost fifty years.

I'd suppressed thoughts about the Top Secret construction program in Berlin, but the old visceral reaction persisted. Perhaps this once highly classified information could still be used by our former enemies, although they no longer existed. East Germany and their Secret Police, the Stasi, as well as the Soviet Union and its KGB, had passed into the history books many years earlier.

Anna kissed the top of my head. "From the start of our relationship, I knew you were hiding something important, but I trusted you and believed you would tell me one day. I helped you with the charade, didn't I?"

"Yes, despite everything that happened to you—to both of us, you helped to preserve my cover. I wouldn't have succeeded without your support every step of the way, Anna." I stood to give her a heartfelt hug and kiss.

"So now that this information is on the internet, you can tell me everything. I've always wanted to know the complete story."

Anna deserved to know why she'd been the target of Stasi harassment and torture. I positioned her chair next to mine. "Let's read this report together. Then you'll finally learn what my construction crew and I were doing in Berlin." Holding her hand to reassure her, I continued. "See the original classifications on the top and bottom of my plan? **TOP SECRET**

RESTRICTED DISTRIBUTION/US EYES ONLY and the caveat **PROJECT LUMAR."**

"All of those lines have been crossed out," she observed. "What does that mean?"

"First, twenty years ago, the document was reclassified to **SECRET.** You can see that word was also lined through and dated. Last year, a large rubber stamp was used to declare the document I generated officially **UNCLASSIFIED**."

"Early in our relationship, I realized that those communist bastards in the Stasi were making every effort to uncover your secret. My distinct impression was that you, Scott, Mark, and Kurt were dedicated to whatever you were doing. Because I trusted you, I hid my disappointment at being kept in the dark and did my best to help every step of the way."

"Yes, you did! There was an excellent reason I couldn't tell you or anyone what I was doing. If one of the thousands of communist spies who entered West Berlin every day, or their myriad operatives at every level of German society, heard just one word, the whole game would have been over. The communists would have enjoyed another major victory."

"What one word, for heaven's sake?" she asked, clearly intrigued.

"TUNNEL. Upon hearing that one word, the Russians and East Germans would have immediately begun a concerted search on both sides of the border between East and West Berlin. They would have discovered where we were digging and then used every means, including force, to sabotage my project."

"I knew there was a tunnel!" Anna insisted. "During family reunions, our nieces and nephews still talk about your amazing tunnel. But you always avoid those conversations. You've even refused to confirm such a structure existed. Finally, you'll be able to share the part you played in the building of that tunnel."

"Yes…Yes, I can!" So many memorable events, I realized. The closing of the Berlin Wall, the Berlin Crisis, and the Tunnel. Memories of those fifteen months came rushing back, as if they'd happened only yesterday. Now, I could share it all with Anna. "Where should I start? The day I arrived in Berlin. Let's see it was October….October 11, 1960….As the aircraft began its descent…."

PART ONE

"We will bury you!"

Threat made against the United States and her
Allies by Russian Premier Nikita Khrushchev
while banging his shoe on the rostrum at a
meeting of the United Nations General Assembly
—October 12, 1960

CHAPTER 1

Tuesday, October 11, 1960

THE PAN AMERICAN DC-6B aircraft descended through the cloud cover on its approach to Tempelhof Airport. Through my window seat forward of the rotating propellers, I saw farmland, forests, and lakes. Then, an ugly, wide ribbon of barren earth with a long row of guard towers resting between two barbed-wire fences came into view. The sight sent shivers up and down my spine.

"Welcome to Berlin," I whispered to myself. Passing over this communist-built barrier meant I was now in West Berlin, an island of freedom 110 miles inside a totalitarian sea.

I'd hoped to see the world while serving my country. With my usual bad luck, my first duty station had been March Air Force Base, just eighty-three miles from my parents' home in Pacific Palisades, California.

My luck hadn't improved. Now I was assigned to what was widely recognized as the front lines of an ongoing battle of wills between two superpowers over the fate of mankind on this planet—Tempelhof Air Force Base in the divided city of Berlin.

Having only dozed off for a few minutes at a time during three flights and two lengthy layovers, I was exhausted. I craved food, a warm shower, and a bed. With my destination beneath me, I perked up, anxious to experience my new duty station and first foreign city. My sleep cycle was messed up because of the time difference, so I didn't expect to sleep right away.

The aircraft made its final approach to Tempelhof. It parked under a massive canopy designed to protect passengers from the steady rain. At the bottom of the movable metal stairs, I was greeted by two fellow American Air Force officers. We exchanged salutes. A slender man of medium height with dark hair and a bright, friendly smile greeted me, "Welcome to West Berlin, Captain Kerr. I'm Colonel Mark Powell."

"Glad to meet you, sir," I replied, shaking his offered hand.

"And this is Captain Scott Taylor."

The lanky, red-headed captain greeted me with a grin and a firm grip. "Welcome to Berlin." Turning, he pointed. "Our base occupies the ground through sixth floors of the north end of this building. Commercial aviation occupies the other half of the building."

"We'll get you settled in your temporary quarters, get acquainted over lunch at the Officer's Club, and then attend a short meeting. How does that sound?" the colonel asked. With his unwrinkled brow and jet-black hair, he looked much too young to be a Lieutenant Colonel.

"Food sounds good. It'll help me stay awake for a few more hours."

Mark Powell explained over lunch, "Tempelhof was the main Berlin airport in the 1930s. Back then, this was one of the twenty largest buildings in the world…"

"—It's a huge, almost mile-long semi-circle," Scott interjected in a slow Texas drawl. "It was one of Hitler's pet projects, designed to show the superiority of the German people and the Third Reich."

"During the height of the Berlin Airlift, an aircraft landed at Tempelhof every 45 seconds," Mark continued. "That mind-boggling logistical feat saved the people of Berlin and avoided another war. Imagine bringing everything a city of two million people needed here by air…"

After lunch, Scott Taylor and I passed two armed security guards at a checkpoint and made our way down a long hall into his office. His vinyl topped, gray metal desk and conference table were standard U.S. government issue. Matching grey, metal straight-back and swivel chairs were positioned around the conference table and behind his desk.

I already liked Scott because of his easy-going manner. My kind of military man—one who didn't take himself too seriously. He closed the door, then removed some papers from one of gray metal safes that lined the wall. "Please be seated."

Once we sat across from each other at the conference table, he became all business. "I'm the head of the Office of Special Investigations here in Berlin. We serve as detectives for the Air Force. Because of the project you're being assigned to manage, you've been cleared for Top Secret LUMAR information. LUMAR is the code word assigned to this highly classified, compartmentalized program. Access to any information about this program is strictly limited on a need-to-know basis. Here in Berlin, only the Wing Commander, Colonel Morgan, Colonel Powell, who's our boss, myself, and you are cleared at this time. I'll inform you when others are added to the access list. Have you understood what I've told you?"

"Yes," I replied with some trepidation. *What kind of super-secret program could they expect me to manage?*

"If you have questions about security, ask me. Colonel Powell will answer your questions about what you'll be doing. Do you have any security issues?"

"None that I can think of at this time."

"Then sign this Classified Information Non-Disclosure Agreement. If you tell an unauthorized person anything about this project, you'll be prosecuted. The current statutes call for thirty years in a military prison. You'll essentially be locked up, and they'll throw away the key." His sober facial expression left no doubt that I should take his admonition seriously.

I'd taken an oath to protect and defend the United States with my life. Although I felt apprehension over the task I would be expected to manage, I took the offered pen and signed the intimidating document.

"Your cover while you're here in Berlin is that you're the new chief of the Berlin weather station at Tempelhof. Here is a USAF manual on weather forecasting—study it and be prepared to use the correct terminology when describing what you do. We'll discuss this more next week."

He directed me to follow him across the hall where I was photographed. The photo was laminated into my security badge, then attached to a chain which went around my neck.

Templehof Air Force Base

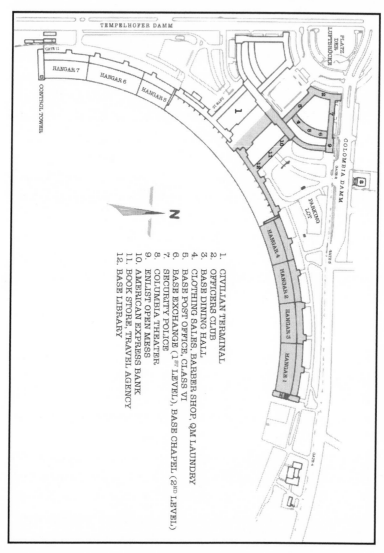

1. CIVILIAN TERMINAL
2. OFFICERS CLUB
3. BASE DINING HALL
4. CLOTHING SALES, BARBER SHOP, QM LAUNDRY
5. BASE POST OFFICE, CLASS VI
6. BASE EXCHANGE (1ST LEVEL), BASE CHAPEL (2ND LEVEL)
7. SECURITY POLICE
8. COLUMBIA THEATER
9. ENLIST OPEN MESS
10. AMERICAN EXPRESS BANK
11. BOOK STORE, TRAVEL AGENCY
12. BASE LIBRARY

Scott instructed, "When you enter this Special Security Area, hold your badge up beside your face so that the guard on duty can verify that your face matches the photo. Like this," he said demonstrating. "Wear the badge at all times while you're in this area."

He then escorted me to Wing Commander Colonel Glen Morgan's office. There, I met a tall, slender man with a ruddy complexion. His greeting was reserved, even aloof, but his handshake was firm. I immediately noticed the puckered scars on the left side of his face, which also covered his misshapen ear. His dark blond hair was combed to cover the scarring on his scalp. He said little, but I sensed he was assessing me, trying to determine if I would be suitable for my new assignment.

On the way toward Colonel Powell's office, I asked Scott, "Are Colonel Morgan's wounds from Korea?"

"No. WW II," Scott replied. "He has an impressive war record. He was commissioned at eighteen and flew his first combat mission over Germany before his twentieth birthday. He bailed out of his burning bomber during his 47th mission, and he spent a year and a half in a German POW camp. He's a battle-scared veteran whom you'll grow to respect. Do a good job for him, and he'll support you every step of the way."

Scott led me down the hallway. "This area contains the unit administrative offices and our main conference room."

I saw standard government-issue furnishings—light blue vinyl tile floors, tan enameled walls, and fluorescent fixtures hanging from white acoustic tile ceilings. Typewriters atop desks along with brown metal desk lamps and in/out baskets. Uniformed males of various ranks made up the office staff.

Scott paused to brief me on Lt. Colonel Powell's background. "He graduated from West Point in 1947 and requested duty with the Air Force soon after it became a separate service. Despite the fact that he never flew airplanes, he is now one of the Air Force's youngest Lieutenant Colonels. You'll find we're lucky to have Colonels Morgan and Powell as our top brass, especially given the nature of your project."

I glanced at Scott, expecting more. Just then Lt. Colonel Powell approached us. He motioned for me to follow him down a nearby hall into a windowless area with two small offices and a large conference room.

Entry into the three-room complex was controlled by a single door with a cipher lock.

"Welcome to our tank," Colonel Powell said with a sweeping arm gesture. "It's universally known as a tank, because all six walls are metal-lined. It'll be your office and primary work area as long as you're assigned to this project. Have a seat on this side of the conference table so we can both view the same things together."

I sat and listened intently.

"Currently, it's the only place where cleared individuals can discuss the LUMAR project. It's designed so that nothing said or done here can be compromised by anyone in the adjoining offices, the rest of the building, or the myriad of outsiders interested in everything that goes on here. Select either of the other smaller rooms to be your office."

I nodded, feeling overwhelmed.

"Your phone is on the desk outside of the door. Like all of the phones on the base, it's tied directly into the German telephone network. Never say anything that might be even remotely valuable to the enemy who surrounds us here. Assume they're listening to every word you utter, because they probably are." Pausing for emphasis, Colonel Powell continued, "The necessity for this level of security will become apparent as we talk."

Still unable to envision what duty I would be expected to perform, I listened intently.

"You and I have an especially important task which, if completed successfully, could thwart the Russians' intention to spread Communism to other countries."

The colonel captured my full attention with that comment.

"We relieved the man you're replacing. You're on probation until you prove you can handle the job."

I wanted to say "I have a new master's degree in civil engineering and no experience in the management of large construction programs." Instead I asked, "Why me?"

"You're here partially because you're the only one available with the required security clearance. You were initially considered because one of your professors at Cal Berkeley praised you to a senior NSA civilian. No offense, but we searched for a more senior officer with more construction project management experience. None were available."

I shook my head and smiled faintly, appreciating his candor.

"When the Cold War intensified in the mid-1950s, the communists began construction of five nuclear-hardened bunkers in East Berlin," Colonel Powell said, pointing to each in turn on a map spread out on the conference table.

"In 1958, the designers of those five facilities were ordered to connect them into a nuclear-hardened communications system," the Colonel said. "They were also instructed to reroute all important government and military communication lines via that system. Soon, an almost meter-wide metal pipe filled with communications cables was buried ten feet underground. That metal pipe connected the two communist decision makers' bunkers in central Berlin with similar facilities at Russian and East German military headquarters here and here. A trunk line runs up here to the bunker at Stasi headquarters...."

"—Stasi?"

"The East German Secret Police. Commonly known as the Stasi. They are our number one enemy here in Berlin. The Russians let them do all the dirty work—murder, torture, brainwashing—any and every bad act you can imagine. Everything that a totalitarian regime needs are their stock in trade. You'll encounter them first hand and learn to hate everything they stand for."

Colonel Powell pointed to the bottom of the map and continued, "A tunnel built here five years ago by the British Secret Service and our CIA allowed us to tap into high-level Russian and Warsaw Pact communication lines. Unfortunately, it was exposed by the Russians about a year after it became operational. The voluminous amount of extremely valuable information gleaned from that source has prompted our leaders to build a new tunnel into East Berlin. You and I have been tasked with its construction. We'll not only be tapping into the lines that connect those bunkers—we'll also access communication links between Berlin, the rest of the Warsaw Pact and Russia. Your job is to manage that project."

Stunned, I said, "If that red line on the map is the border and the blue line is the route of the pipe between each of the bunkers, it's quite a long distance from West Berlin."

"It is, except right here." He indicated a spot on the map. "Where the border is the River Spree. The buried pipe is only about 1400 feet from a vacant apartment building that our government recently purchased to house the western terminus of the tunnel. The plan is to start the tunnel inside that building, go under the river, and come up beneath the pipe on the other side."

"I have questions."

"I'll try to answer them."

"What are my duties?"

"Program manager for the construction of the tunnel and the Signals Exploitation Center. You'll plan and supervise the entire construction effort."

"Isn't that your job?"

"No. I'm the Deputy Commander of Detachment 2 of the 6910th Security Wing, which is the Air Force Signals Intelligence Collection Unit here at Tempelhof. I have a large number of other duties, and I'm not an engineer. I'll be available to assist you to work within the military system."

"What'd my predecessor do to get relieved?"

"He feared mistakes, wanted me to make all of the decisions, and drank too much. He was a potential security risk."

"Do we know precisely where the pipe is buried?"

"No. It was buried two years ago, and the decision to exploit it is recent. One of our operatives traced its route on a map with a ballpoint pen. Here is a copy of the map he marked up."

Looking at the map and its scale, I remarked, "This map covers a large area. The line showing the pipe's possible route must be thirty, forty, perhaps even fifty feet wide, so we only have an idea about the route of the pipe."

"That's true."

"Do we know what obstructions are between the building and the tube?"

"On this table is a set of public works drawings from the late 1930s. They show the location of the subway, storm drains, sewage pipes, underground electrical conduits, and certain other obstructions in that immediate area. Unfortunately, they haven't been updated since 1945."

"Does it show building foundations?"

"Unfortunately, no."

"Let me summarize," I said, trying hard to keep an amused tone out of my voice. "We are going to excavate a fourteen-hundred-foot-long tunnel under a wide, deep river into East Berlin, bisect a one-meter wide pipe without actually knowing where it's located while also avoiding unknown obstructions that are probably in our path."

Mark snickered at my description. "It's even worse than that. While building the tunnel, we are also going to need to keep a paranoid, totalitarian East German regime and the three million civilians of Berlin, plus our closest allies, from discovering what we are doing."

"Sir... Colonel Powell, if you'll forgive me, my favorite professor in graduate school said, 'Almost anything is possible given enough time and money, but many things are improbable.' I think this project falls into the latter category. In fact, it's highly improbable."

The Colonel nodded his agreement. He even smiled. "I don't disagree. But Captain Kerr, your job is to figure out how to accomplish the highly improbable."

Feeling overwhelmed, I said, "Sir...I'm probably not the right man for this job. I do have bachelor and master's degrees in civil engineering, but I've only worked under the direct supervision of experienced people. We relied on local contractors to perform most of the work. My experience is as a contracts administrator for the construction of aircraft hangars and the paving of runways, not as development manager for a tunnel."

"For now, Captain, this is your responsibility. Thirty-four experienced construction workers will arrive in early January to start work. You have almost three months to prepare to direct their activities. Is that clear?"

In officer's training, we learned there were only three acceptable responses to an order from a superior officer. Yes, sir—No, sir—No excuse, sir. I chose the only reasonable response. "Yes, Sir."

"One more thing you need to know. By September of next year, the tunnel must be finished and preliminary operation of the Signals Exploitation Center must begin."

"Eleven months from now! Why?"

"The East German and Russian leaders are committed to signing a separate World War II peace treaty in October or November of next year. Their objective is to negate the four-power control of Berlin. This action will cause a confrontation between the Russians and us, which might well lead to war."

"Obviously advanced information on their intentions would be exceeding valuable," I remarked, staring in disbelief at the Colonel. "Um…That's a lot of responsibility on our shoulders."

"Yes, it is, Captain."

I cringed. *Doing all this in less than a year is unrealistic. I'm responsible for the whole thing. My God!*

"Be here in the tank early Friday. The combination of the cipher lock is 3192. Find an apartment as soon as you can. Captain Taylor has agreed to give you a tour of Berlin on Saturday."

"Yes. Sir." I responded, still feeling confused.

As we left the tank, he added, "Always make sure this door is secure before you leave the area. I expect a debriefing on your progress every Friday at 1300 in the tank." He escorted me to a nearby stairway, shook my hand, smiled, and walked away.

His words rang in my ears. *"You're the only one available."* But if I fail, I thought, what happens to the world?

Feet of Tunnel Completed: 0   Days until Deadline: 351

CHAPTER 2

Wednesday, October 12, 1960

THE SUNLIGHT THAT pierced the thin curtains of my drab Bachelor Officer Quarters (BOQ) room awakened me three times. Hunger finally forced me into the shower at 2 p.m. My body remained on California time, but I was half a world away in Berlin, Germany.

As I dressed, the knot in the pit of my stomach returned. I was on a very dangerous island of freedom, far behind enemy lines, and my new job was probably impossible.

The elevator stopped on the ground floor, and I walked out into an open courtyard. Overcast skies were visible between the tall buildings that made up Tempelhof Air Force Base. The air felt cool and crisp.

After I took a wrong turn, I passed several base support facilities, including the bookstore, and ended up on an aircraft parking ramp. Turning around, I finally found the Officers Club. The closest the chef could come to breakfast was a bowl of cereal and an egg salad sandwich. I needed to stay awake to get my body clock straightened out, so I stopped in the bookstore.

The bell attached to the door rang as I stepped into a small, high-ceilinged room with shelves arranged along three walls and in neat center rows. I immediately noticed a striking blonde with peaches and cream complexion sitting behind a desk at the entrance. To avoid staring at her, I scanned the austere décor as I approached the bestsellers table in the center of the room. I selected three volumes—*Advise and Consent* by Allen Drury,

Hawaii by James A. Michener, and *The Leopard* by Giuseppe Tomasi di Lampedusa.

When I turned around, I caught her watching me. More cute than beautiful, her violet-blue eyes were enchanting. I smiled at her.

She beamed as she asked, "May I help you?"

"I need a book to keep me awake for the next thirty hours. What do you suggest?"

When she stood, I immediately noticed that her short-sleeved sweater and matching straight skirt showed her slim waist, trim figure, and breasts to advantage.

With only the slightest trace of an accent, she answered in English, "In my experience, a poorly written or complex book requires concentration, which is one way to stay awake or to quickly fall asleep. A well-written book will keep you awake, because you want to find out what happens. Which do you want?"

"A page-turner, please."

"I have read *Hawaii,* which I thoroughly enjoyed," she advised. "It makes one want to continue, plus now I also want to visit Hawaii. *Advise and Consent* recounts US Senate confirmation hearings for a former member of the Communist Party. I do not like communists, so I will not be reading it. I read the first chapter of *The Leopard.* The book was written in Italian, and I think the translator made it difficult to understand."

Intelligent and attractive. "Do I detect a slight accent?"

"Yes, I am a native Berliner."

"My name is Robert Kerr, er…Captain Robert Kerr." I wore civilian clothes and wanted her to know I was an officer.

"My name is Anna Fischer, Miss Anna Fischer," she offered, smiling.

She looked flushed even as she sized me up.

"Why do you need to stay awake for thirty hours? It seems like a strange thing to do."

I explained my problem and concluded by stating, "I plan to stay up, drink coffee, and read this book"—I held up *Hawaii*—"until bedtime tomorrow."

"There is a café nearby that stays open 24 hours every day. I will be closing in 30 minutes, and I can show you where it is. That way, if you need coffee or food in the middle of the night, you will know where to go."

"Thank you. That's very kind of you." Our eyes met for a brief moment as I paid for the book. I sensed her interest in me. I, indeed, was intersted in her, too.

CHAPTER 3

Anna

Wednesday, October 12, 1960

I SAT ALONE at the front desk when Robert entered the bookstore that first time. Glancing up, I noted his striking appearance and long-legged stride. His tan and his sun-streaked light-brown hair indicated he spent a lot of time outdoors.

He browsed the bestseller table, his back to me. Broad shouldered and narrow-hipped, he looked athletic. When he caught me staring at him, he smiled, and his hazel eyes twinkled.

My heart beat faster. I blushed as he approached me. This was my first time to react to any man in such a positive way. When I stood, I saw he was taller than me. I could wear high heels if he asked me out on a date. Perhaps a strange thought, but I have always been self-conscious about my height.

I cleared my throat before I asked, "May I help you?" My voice sounded higher in tone than usual, reflecting the tension streaming though my entire body.

Few twenty-two-year-old women possess less experience with men than I. Though I had often resolved to allow a man into my life, I recoiled at the thought of physical contact with a man. It just brought back too many terrifying memories from the war.

When Robert remarked, "I arrived in Berlin yesterday and plan to stay up, drinking coffee, and reading a book," I surprised myself by offering to show him a nearby café.

I thought then that, if I intend to start a relationship with anyone, it should be with a man to whom I am attracted. Robert was handsome. I wondered if he might be the man to help break down the barriers I had erected as a girl.

CHAPTER 4

Robert
Wednesday, October 12, 1960

BERLIN AMAZED ME. This was the first time I had set foot outside Tempelhof. Large, modern apartment buildings lined the streets. Small shops on the ground floor offered a variety of goods and services. Bakeries, butchers, greengrocers, tobacco shops, liquor stores, cobblers, hardware stores, restaurants and bars, among others, occupied the major thoroughfare Anna and I walked down.

Late afternoon sunlight filtered through the mature trees that shaded the street. New automobiles occupied every available parking space. I don't know what I expected, but not this. Images of demolished buildings and rubble-strewn streets flashed through my mind. What I saw now could easily have been an affluent urban area in any of a vast number of American cities.

Anna's ponytail swung enticingly as we walked side by side.

"The bookstore is operated by the Post Exchange," she said. "I've worked there for almost a year now. I was recently given the job of managing the store, which involves supervising three clerks."

"You seem to enjoy it."

She smiled. "I love it."

"Your accent is very British. Did you study in England?"

"No. I have never been outside of Germany. My mother studied there. We often listen to the BBC shortwave broadcasts."

While I struggled to find another topic of discussion, Anna asked, "Would you tell me how you traveled from California to Berlin?"

"Pan American Airways has those new jet airliners—the Boeing 707. It can fly around the world in just over 48 hours."

"I've heard about jet airliners, but have not seen one. The runways at Tempelhof are too short for jet aircraft to land there. They all land at Tegel Airport over in the French Zone."

"On Sunday evening I left Los Angeles and flew by jet to New York. After a layover, I flew on the same jet to London."

"I've always wanted to visit London," she said.

"I can't say I saw much of England. Just a four-hour wait at Heathrow. Early yesterday morning, I took a DC-6 aircraft from London to Tempelhof."

Anna clasped her hands behind her back, looking at me frequently as we strolled down the sidewalk. She smiled radiantly, and then asked, "What did you do all of that time?"

"On both of the flights, the stewardesses pulled down a screen and distributed earphones, so I watched two movies—Leslie Caron in *Gigi,* and Elizabeth Taylor in *Cat on a Hot Tin Roof.*"

"Tell me, are the stewardesses as young and beautiful as everyone claims?" Anna glanced at me with a playful smile.

"They were all attractive. One even gave me her name and address, hinting she could fly to Berlin for free."

"Are you going to contact her?"

I shook my head. "She's not my type."

Anna glanced over and said, "Could I be...." she stopped mid-sentence, obviously embarrassed.

To keep the conversation going, I said, "The time goes reasonably fast—meals, movies, and a good book. It was pleasant overall."

"So, you watched the stewardess pass up and down the aisle," she teased.

"None were as attractive as you," I admitted.

Anna paused, looked at me, and shook her head as if she hadn't heard me correctly. She asked, "Could you sleep sitting up?"

"Even in coach, the seats were large and very comfortable with plenty of leg room. They recline, but not quite enough to sleep comfortably."

As we arrived at an intersection, Anna said, "And so we are at the station. See the S and U. They stand for the S Bahn, the subway, and the U Bahn is what I think you call the interurban."

"I know that bahn is the German word for train. So that makes sense."

"In Germany, major stations like this have businesses that stay open 24 hours a day. Here is the cafe I told you about. It is a good place; the food and coffee in the airplane terminal are not so good."

"Nicht sehr gut."

"Oh! You speak German!"

"I took courses in German, and I am moderately fluent. I read German much better than I speak it. My professors were Americans, and my accent is atrocious," I answered in German.

"I am impressed—you do exceptionally well," Anna replied.

An uncomfortable pause followed as I sought the correct German words to ask her to join me.

"I had better go now," she declared, and began to turn away.

I lightly touched her arm just as she started down the steps. "Excuse me, Anna—will you please join me for a cup of coffee?"

She looked back, smiling. "That would be nice; I would very much like that."

We entered a large, brightly lit room filled with marble-topped tables and bentwood, cane-seated chairs. Anna suggested a table toward the back.

When the waiter arrived, Anna spoke German. "An espresso, please."

While mentally searching for the correct German words, I failed to respond to his questioning look. I muttered, "I will have the same." I then bent forward and whispered, "What is espresso?"

"See that brass colored machine our waiter is using?" she asked. "It forces near boiling water under pressure through finely ground coffee. It is delicious. You will like it."

"Please say again, but speak more slowly."

She did, and I replied in German, "Now I understand you perfectly. I will try to remember that the word for 'pressure' is *druck*."

"See the curved glass counters along that wall; they contain cold cuts, cheeses, pastries and a variety of prepared meals. So, you can also eat here when you get hungry later."

"Looks like they also have a well-stocked bar," I observed.

"Yes," she replied, then changed the subject by stating, "Robert, I am twenty-two years old, and I studied art history at Heidelberg University for two years. Please tell me about yourself."

"I am twenty-six, have undergraduate and master's degrees in civil engineering. Thank you for slowly enunciating your words. I can understand what you are saying." I smiled and brushed the top of her hand with my fingertips. She withdrew her hand. I sensed that perhaps I was rushing things.

After a brief pause, Anna asked, "will you tell me about your life in English, if that is easier for you?"

In German, I responded, "I want to practice. Please indulge me…"

When I told her that I had attended a *hoch schule* in Los Angeles, she informed me "a school that prepares one for the university in Germany is called a gymnasium."

"Like every young American male, when I turned 18, I was required to register for the military draft. Most years thousands of young men are drafted, and many more volunteer to join a branch of our military service."

"But you're an officer."

"I wanted to serve as an officer. While in the university as an undergraduate at Stanford, I took Air Force Reserve Officer's Training Courses."

"Why did you decide to become an engineer?" Anna asked.

"Ever since I helped my grandfather Hunter construct a dairy barn when I was fourteen, I have wanted to be a builder."

"You are fortunate to have found your vocation at such a young age."

"I was lucky. My grandfather encouraged me by teaching me how to plan a project, lay it out on the ground, and how to use the correct tools to build it. So, I decided to become a civil engineer."

"You build buildings?" Anna asked.

"In America, civil engineers design, construct, and maintain roads, bridges, canals, dams, and buildings."

"Impressive," she said as she extended her hand.

I took the opportunity to touch her hand lightly. The first few times I touched her, she either flinched or pulled back. This time, she briefly, almost experimentally, clasped my hand.

"You are young to be a senior rank, like a captain. You must be good at what you do."

"Every officer who stays in the Air Force for over four years is promoted to the rank of Captain—in English, we say it is automatic. So, I am nothing special."

"You construct buildings for the military. What are you going to build here in Berlin?"

I took this chance to practice the cover story Scott had concocted. "I'm a weatherman."

"I do not understand. The American military is using a highly trained engineer to predict the weather?"

"Afraid so. They needed weathermen when I joined, so they trained me—I received six months of schooling."

"That seems strange," Anna observed, a puzzled look on her face.

Knowing I'd botched that part of our conversation, I glanced at my watch and realized I was hungry. "Anna, I hope I have not kept you from anything important. We have talked for almost two hours. Would you join me for a meal?"

"I would love to," she replied, smiling. "I know the perfect place. It is small, inexpensive, and only three blocks away."

CHAPTER 5

Wednesday, October 12, 1960

AS WE DESCENDED three steps into a cozy Italian restaurant, I turned to Anna and smiled. "It's perfect—just what I had in mind." The red and white checkered tablecloths, travel posters of Italian locals, and flickering candles in wine bottles provided the perfect atmosphere for the first of what I hoped would be many meals together.

A waiter, clad in a white apron and chef's hat took our order. He looked at me and asked, "Americano, yes?"

"Yes, I am. How did you know?"

"I'm a genius!" he replied, raising his right hand into the air for emphasis.

"Robert, it is your haircut. Only men in the American military wear their hair so short here in Germany."

In broken English, the waiter stated, "We hab de besta pizza in Berlin und Americano vino. Wha kinda of pizza you vant?"

After we both studied the menu, I turned to Anna and suggested, "How about three meat—ham, salami and pepperoni pizza with extra cheese?"

"That sounds wonderful."

"What kind of American wine do you have?"

"Coca-Cola, of course," the waiter replied, laughing at his own joke.

Laughing, I asked Anna, "I think we would like real wine, correct?"

"Yes. I do not share your American craving for Coca-Cola."

"I know little about European wines. Will you help me select a wine?"

After some genial banter between the three of us about which wines they served, we settled on a half carafe of the house Chianti.

The rich, alluring fragrance of the cheese, sauce, toppings and freshly baked dough wafted over us as the next table was served.

"Anna, I'm glad we came here. You made an excellent choice." Touching her hand lightly, I smiled. "Now is your turn to tell me about yourself. You are obviously well educated, and you attended university, but you did not finish?"

"My whole family has not been as fortunate as yours—two wars, the Nazis, and now the communists."

Clasping both of her hands, I encouraged, "Anna, I know it was probably bad, but if you are willing to tell me, I'm genuinely interested in knowing about you and your family."

"Ok, but I will relate this part in English to make sure you understand everything. Although my parents lived in East Berlin, I attended a gymnasium in West Berlin. I finished at the top of my class and was admitted to the University of Heidelberg in West Germany."

"I'm impressed. Heidelberg is a very prestigious university."

"University tuition is free for those who live in the West, so I officially immigrated when I was 18. I was still required to pay for books, accommodations, food, and transportation. The East Mark/West Mark exchange rate is so bad, my family could provide me with little support."

"Go on."

"A nearby family paid me to housekeep and babysit for them. I shared a room with another girl, and we cooked our meals on an electric hot plate. Last year, my family's financial circumstances worsened. I was forced to leave the university."

"That's unfortunate."

"In Europe, the university only takes three years, so I was desperate to finish my last year, but that was not to be."

"So, you returned to Berlin."

"Yes, I wanted to be near my family. During my interview for the bookstore position, I was told that only West Berlin residents were eligible to apply. I now live in one small room with the bath down the hall here in the West."

She seemed to want to say more but she stopped, as if hesitating to share some troubling family or personal matters. After long moments of silence between us, she looked relieved when our pizza arrived.

After the first bite, I observed, "This is delicious. The thin crust is done to perfection."

While we ate, she explained how the subways and interurban system worked. "One can go virtually anywhere in either East or West Berlin on the subway. It is an excellent system."

"No one stops you from travel into East Berlin?" I asked.

"Travel is unrestricted between the two areas of Berlin—it is part of the Four Power Agreement on Berlin signed after the war."

After we shared a dessert of spumoni ice cream, we walked to the subway station. I offered my arm. As she turned toward me, my arm accidentally brushed against her breast. She quickly pulled away.

"Sorry," I apologized, "that was an accident."

She hesitated, then smiled and latched onto my arm.

At the subway stairs, I offered, "It is not very late. May I see you safely to your door?"

"No, thank you. Women are perfectly safe on the streets of Berlin at any hour—day or night."

I took her hand, kissed it lightly and said, "Thank you for helping me to stay awake."

To my surprise—and delight—she hugged me and pressed her lips to the side of my neck. I smiled and touched her cheek, staring into her eyes for several seconds. She eased away, and I watched as she descended the stairs to the subway. Still smiling, she looked back and waved to me from the bottom of the steps.

CHAPTER 6

Wednesday-Thursday, October 12-13, 1960

WHEN I ARRIVED back at my BOQ room, I looked at my watch—only 20 hours until I could go to bed. I had to report for duty at 0800 on Friday, so I needed to stay awake.

First, I went to the gym on the sixth floor, did an hour of calisthenics, and then took a shower. Only eighteen hours to go.

The rest of the night I sat at the desk. I tried to stay awake by reading, but I struggled to concentrate on the book. All I could see was Anna's face. Those striking violet-blue eyes. The hair tucked behind her ears, those inviting ears with the tiny pearl studs. The perfect teeth and effervescent smile. The reserved, yet endearing way she tilted her head a little to the left as she responded to my questions and comments. Maybe Berlin wouldn't be such a bad place after all. Now I had an excellent reason to stay.

Hours later, I still sat in the desk chair. My forehead rested on the book and my back ached. The clock on the end table read 6:55. It had to be morning, so I still had fourteen hours to go. I decided I needed to get out of that room, because the only other option was bed and sleep.

When I exited the elevator, I buttoned my coat because it was cold and still dark. I wondered if it might just be evening, then remembered that sunrise occurred at around 7:30 a.m. in Berlin this time of year.

A stack of *Stars and Stripes* newspapers covered a corner of the cashier's desk at the Officer's Club. I noticed the headline, which occupied almost the entire space above the fold.

WE WILL
BURY YOU

—Khrushchev

I purchased a copy. As I scanned the front page, I realized that for Americans stationed overseas, this newspaper provided a vital link to events happening at home and around the world. I didn't like what this headline portended.

At a little after 4 p.m., I went to the bookstore. I didn't see Anna. When I asked for her, the clerk indicated the small office in the back. I knocked on the door.

"Come in."

As she rose to greet me, I was again attracted by her winsome smile and almost forgot what my excuse for going to the bookstore was, but finally blurted out, "I've managed to stay awake, but I'm fading fast. I'll probably go to sleep after a beer and hamburger at the Officer's Club. I need your help—I looked at two nearby apartments on the base housing office list. Neither was acceptable."

"I'm not surprised," Anna replied, a little bemused. "We Germans always increase the price for Americans, because you seem to have so much money. Do you have the list with you?"

"Yes, right here."

"I will need to study this and consider your options. Perhaps you could return tomorrow."

"Gladly! I don't want anything too far away from the base. Perhaps you would be willing to show me Berlin. We could go out and have another meal, my treat."

She smiled, "I accept your invitation."

"At 5 p.m. tomorrow, here?"

"Yes, that would be best."

We stood close together as we talked. I took Anna's right hand and was contemplating kissing it or her when a knock sounded on the door. She gestured for me to follow her into the bookstore. Not wanting to interfere with her work, I walked toward the exit. I looked back at her. She waved furtively and smiled.

CHAPTER 7

Friday, October 14, 1960

AFTER SLEEPING SOUNDLY, I arrived at the tank a few minutes before 0800.

Colonel Powell greeted me. "Let's go upstairs to our Signals Intelligence Collections Center. I can show you the types of information we'll be collecting at the signals exploitation site in the building at the end of our tunnel."

Surreal accurately describes all that he showed me.

"The men in this room are plotting the movement of Russian and East European Air Forces on these giant maps of the surrounding area. All of this information is broadcast over the air using wireless media, which we intercept with the antennas on the roof of this building." He gestured to the next area. "These are manual Morse intercept operators. This rather archaic form of communications is used by the vast majority of Soviet and Warsaw Pact forces, because it is reliable, effective and relatively inexpensive."

In another area, Mark said, "The individuals with headphones are linguists. They listen to Russian, East German, Polish and Czechoslovakian wireless conversations."

Moving into the largest of the four rooms, he explained, "The men in this room intercept teletype signals. They print out the information and linguists translate it. Sometimes the messages are encrypted. Then, the cryptologists try to break the code, either here or back at NSA."

"So, we can determine everything the communists are doing by listening in on their communications with each other. Amazing!"

"Exactly. Our military forces have always excelled, because personnel at all levels exercise individual initiative to solve problems on the spot. Communists are taught to follow orders blindly and to seek guidance from superiors before acting. So, we know what they are going to do long before their subordinates act. That's a huge advantage."

Once back in the tank, Mark said, "At this point in time, almost ninety percent of the useful intelligence information we and our allies have is derived from intercept sites like the one we just toured. We have sites like this surrounding the communist world."

Perplexed, I asked, "Why tap into buried cables, especially with vast amounts of information available from broadcasts that travel through the air?"

"The communist countries are switching from broadcast mode, which we can intercept, to buried landlines. They intend to deny us as much information as possible."

"Makes sense."

"I told you there was another tunnel. I want you to review a detailed report on that program. I'll return at 1500 this afternoon. We'll discuss what you've read."

He handed me a forty-four-page joint CIA/British MI6 report on the 1953 to 1956 Berlin Tunnel and excused himself. It was codeword classified:

TOP SECRET / LIMITED DISTRIBUTION
GOLD/STOPWATCH—US/UK EYES ONLY

I carefully read the entire report, and even went back and reread the description of the construction of the tunnel.

At the appointed time, Colonel Powell returned, took off his coat and rolled up his sleeves. "When only the two of us are working together in this area, call me Mark. I'll call you Robert."

"Thank you, sir. I like working informally. Let me summarize what I've read, in case I missed something important."

"Sounds good."

"Our CIA and the British Secret Intelligence Service built a large warehouse with an exceptionally deep basement. A two-meter boring machine dug the tunnel, while a trailing structure called a tunnel shield supported the surrounding soil. Cast-iron curved plates were then installed to serve as the tunnel's top and sides. That tunnel was 1480 feet long, coincidentally almost the same length ours will be."

"That tunnel was located 15 miles south of here in a part of the American Zone that's a sparsely populated forest," Mark explained. "Since then, the East Germans patrol most of the border using devices designed to detect underground excavations."

"Interesting. I assume that's part of the reason our tunnel entrance is in an urban area and will go under a river," I observed.

"Exactly," Mark replied.

"To continue, it took them eight months to build the warehouse. Then another ten months from the time they started tunneling until the first successful tap of Soviet communications. An impressive feat made much easier by the fact the tunnel started and ended at a shallow depth and the underground cable location was accurately known to be under a paved road. We have a daunting task. We must excavate under a deep, wide river and find an imprecisely located target."

"Your predecessor decided to solve that problem by digging a deep pit and installing an elevator. He proposed to begin tunneling operations sixty feet below street level."

"Mark, supporting the soil around a sixty-foot deep pit is a difficult engineering feat. It requires experienced people."

"Your team of thirty-four men from the Army Corp of Engineers will report for duty in three months."

"Have they ever built a pit and tunnel?"

"Soon, you'll visit Washington D.C. so those in charge of this project can meet you and approve your plans. You can determine the building skills of your staff during that trip. Let's discuss the tunneling operation itself."

I nodded. "Good idea. That'll help me prepare for my trip to the States."

"You'll find that the two-meter boring machine used to dig the first tunnel is very similar to the three-meter wide one we've purchased. Our system will be equipped with two small outrigger boring heads, which will allow our tunnel to have a flat bottom. It's also equipped with an automatic soil removal subsystem, and a mechanical erector which places the concrete tunnel lining components in place."

"Tunnel lining components?"

"Two round sections form the top, and four straight sections form the sides and flat bottom of the tunnel. We purchased ten sets of molds. Your predecessor wanted them made off-site and trucked into the building in covered trucks."

"Makes sense, I guess."

"We've been assigned the largest hanger on the base for this project. The Tunnel Boring Machine will be flown in and stored there. Everyone calls this machine a TBM, instead of constantly saying Tunnel Boring Machine. It'll be delivered to Rhein-Main Air Base next week. We've arranged for a huge, new propeller-driven aircraft called the Pregnant Guppy to fly it here in two weeks."

"Why don't you just bring the TBM into Berlin by rail or truck?"

"The East Germans and Russians carefully examine all of the cargo that comes into Berlin. The Stasi and KGB would be informed that such a device was on its way. Spies of every form would trail it to the building, and the game would be over."

"I have two questions. First, how do we get the TBM from the hangar to the building?"

"That's one of your jobs, and it won't be easy. All of our activities on this base are constantly monitored by the Russians and East Germans."

"Another thorny problem—just what I need! Why'd they encase the cables in a metal tube? Usually, communications cables are just buried in the ground."

"Through a clandestine source, we determined that the communications cables are housed in a galvanized iron pipe. Part of their initial efforts to harden their communications against the effects of the electromagnetic pulses created during nuclear explosions. Known as EMP, these pulses cause current and voltage surges, which apparently destroy, damage, or render inoperable electronic and communications devices."

"I studied EMP in the Air Force Civil Engineering training course, so I understand what the Russians are trying to do."

"Fortunately, tapping into the tube is not our problem. NSA has a trained staff to undertake that part of the process once we dig the tunnel and expose its outer surface."

Mark glanced at his watch and shrugged into his coat. "Please spend the rest of the day studying the tunnel boring equipment documentation and the plans for the building." He handed me the stack of manuals and drawings.

"You have orientation on Monday. I'll see you Tuesday at 0800." He shook my hand. "We're scheduled for a tunnel kickoff meeting with our Commanding General, Richard Harrison, here in this tank next Wednesday. You'll find him to be an excellent commanding officer."

Nothing I'd learned allayed my fear that I was on a fool's errand. My completion deadline was several months shorter then the previous endeavor. As well, the project would be far more complex in execution than the first tunnel.

The hours passed as I pondered the situation. Concentrating on the intricacies of the project became impossible, as my thoughts kept returning to Anna. We hadn't yet gone out on our first real date, yet I believed the attraction between us was mutual. Now I had an incentive to stay in Berlin, despite the seemingly impossible assignment I'd been given.

CHAPTER 8

Friday, October 14, 1960

ANNA WAS IN her office when I arrived for our date. I knocked on the door. When I entered, she was standing beside the desk. I could tell she had taken special care with her appearance—her long hair was arranged in a neat bun and her attire feminine and flirty.

"Anna, you look stunning, but it is cold outside. You will freeze."

"Oh, I have a sweater and a coat. Unfortunately, I have not found any apartments for us to look at, but next Saturday we will find one for sure."

"I can wait until then."

"I have a couple of errands I need to run. Would you mind?"

"Of course not."

"Great, I can show you the best parts of Berlin before we eat. Do you like to dance?"

"Yes, I love to dance."

"Then I may know a perfect place for your introduction to Germany."

I helped her into her sweater and coat, thinking that it was a shame to cover her lovely figure.

As we walked to the Tempelhof subway station, I asked, "Is it always this cold in mid-October?"

This is just the start of our weather which will not be good again until spring. Sometimes, we go weeks without seeing the sun even once."

As we stood on the platform to wait for a train, I asked, "Where are we going?"

"Kurfurstendamm. It is the heart of West Berlin, much like the Champs Elysees in Paris or Times Square in New York. You'll see."

One train change later, we stood on a broad, partially tree-lined boulevard that separated two solid lines of brightly lit, multi-storied businesses. The gloomy, damp night instantly transformed into an inviting haven of flashing neon signs, and closely spaced, bright street lamps.

The expensive, larger shops and hotels were interspersed with block after block of small specialty shops, bookstores, restaurants, cinemas, nightclubs, cafes, and bars. The scarcity of architecturally distinct structures reflected the haste with which the area had been rebuilt during the fifteen years since the war.

Seeing my amazement as crowds of people rushed every which way, Anna told me, "It is Friday evening, so everyone is preparing for the weekend. Almost all Berliners come here at least once a week to shop, dine, or be entertained."

Taking my hand, Anna led me two blocks down the street to a ruin. "This is all that is left of the Neo-Romanesque Protestant Church where the Emperors of Germany worshiped—it is called the Kaiser Wilhelm Memorial Church."

"It must have been an impressive structure at one time."

"Yes, but in November of 1943, a British air raid on Berlin destroyed all except this." She waved her hand upward. "It is being preserved as a memorial to those who died in the World War Two."

I studied what remained. "The damaged roof of the bell tower and entry hall are open to the elements."

"Yes, and the windows and front doors have not been replaced, but the clock in the tower works—defying the worst that man could inflict on it."

Pointing, she explained, "That figure of Christ was salvaged from the church altar." After pausing for a minute before of the statue, Anna turned to me. "Now we shall do our shopping."

First, she led me down a side street into a chocolate shop. Once inside, she said, "Herr Schultz, please help me select all of papa and mama's favorites."

After much banter between them, the proprietor placed a dozen sweets into a box and placed it in a paper bag with a handle. He also offered us each a truffle which I complimented by saying, *"Das ist köstlich,"* (That is delicious).

As we left, Herr Schultz half-bowed. "Fraulein Fischer, please give your father my kindest regards. Thank you for shopping here. Have a good night."

We walked to a coffee and tea emporium, and later, a bookstore. Each proprietor respectfully addressed Anna as Fraulein Fischer and each one asked to be remembered by members of her family.

"We are finished shopping. Now we can have fun. I would suggest we go to the Hofbrauhaus. You will like it—it is very German."

During our time together, Anna and I switched between English and German. I pointed out how contractions and slang would make her English sentences less formal. She noted my use of the wrong gender for German nouns. We were getting acquainted through language lessons and laughing at miscues. Mostly mine.

The Hofbrauhaus was located down two flights of stairs in a basement. Massive arches decorated with painted grapevines were supported by pillars. At one end of the hall, a band played oom-pah music. The tuba, accordion, clarinet, and trombone players soon finished a lively polka and began a slower waltz.

We were shown to a long table with bench seats that was occupied by two other couples and a family of four. Introductions were made as best we could over the loud music. Soon a waitress clad in a puffy-sleeved blouse, loose-fitting skirt, and checkered apron came over to us. Anna gave her our order.

"I hope you approve. I ordered traditional bratwurst with sauerkraut and a half liter of beer for each of us," Anna announced over the blare of the band.

Rising from the bench, I bowed deeply and, in my best German, asked, "My lovely companion, would you please honor me with this dance?"

Both Anna and I put our arms around each other, intentionally taking positions where our bodies barely touched; we smoothly moved in time with the fast waltz. Deliberately, I placed my right hand on her dress, avoiding contact with her bare back. That lovely skin was all too inviting. As we moved around the dance floor, she gradually moved closer to me.

Soon we moved as one and even managed to end with her twirling into and then out of my arms.

I bowed again. "Anna, my compliments. You expertly followed my clumsy lead."

"No, just the opposite. You are an accomplished dancer, whose lead is easy to follow."

The band announced they would take a break. We returned to our table just as our meals arrived. Now we could talk.

"Anna, please tell me about your family—everyone seems to know them."

"Tomorrow I will go to the East to visit my parents. Many things are unavailable there. So, I take gifts. I earn money in West German Marks so I can afford these trifles."

"And your family—who are they?"

"Many of the people we visited today were helped by my father and mother in one way or another. So, they give me a little discount to ensure that my family has these few luxuries," she said, gesturing to the shopping bags beneath the table.

"They certainly were deferential to you and your family. I thought you might be nobility or something."

Laughing, Anna replied, "My maternal grandfather was a minor noble-man, but all of that is over now. My father is a medical doctor, and my mother is a language professor. They are ordinary people who, over the years, have helped others in need."

After a brief silence, she added, "My family are just ordinary citizens of a country that is broken in two, divided by two political ideologies. These are not normal times for us. The difficulties we experience should not be part of anyone's daily life."

Suddenly, her chin quivered. She looked like she might cry. To comfort her, I put my arm around her bare shoulder and took her hand in mine.

She shuddered. "Robert, please remove your arm from my shoulder. It makes me uncomfortable," she said in a calm, firm tone.

Disappointment followed my surprise, but I complied, shifting so our bodies no longer touched.

Anna looked apologetic and reached for my hand. We sat there, hands clasped and communicating to each other that our relationship could grow without words. Anna's brief outburst might have been behind us, but I could not forget it. Why did she, at times, recoil from my touch, but seem loving at other times?

When the band started again, she jumped up and opened her arms wide in invitation. "Let us forget about all that bad stuff and just have fun."

For the rest of the evening, she rested her head on my shoulder during each slow dance.

Too soon the evening came to an end as we walked into the nearby subway station. Still a little concerned by her rebuff, I took her hand in mine and kissed her palm. To my surprise, I received a warm hug in return. Although I hoped for another kiss, it didn't happen.

Anna then said something in English that surprised and pleased me. "I just want you to know that many young American men who come into the bookstore have asked me out. I always refuse. You are the first American man I have talked to this way. Your willingness to learn German and your respectful attitude make me want to know you. I want to help you become truly fluent in the German language. As you know, there is much more to understanding a language than just words."

With an impish grin, she added, "Your accent does need much work." She turned and walked toward the oncoming train without looking back, leaving me a bit off-balanced.

CHAPTER 9

Saturday, October 15, 1960

LOUD BANGING ON the door woke me up. When I opened it, Scott Taylor was standing there. He wore jeans, cowboy boots, a western shirt, a Stetson hat, and a leather vest. His short military haircut, trimmed mustache and pale complexion contrasted sharply with his western attire. Holding out a bottle of beer with a mischievous glint in his eyes, he drawled, "A little of the snake that bit you last night might be appropriate this morning."

I raised my hand in refusal. "Let me get my shower and breakfast, then we can go on your tour."

"Did you have fun with the lovely Anna last evening?"

"How'd you know?"

"Word spreads fast in this tiny American village that's our little airbase. Every red-blooded man on the base has tried to get a date with that gorgeous creature. You're the first to get the time of day."

Smiling, I felt pleased Anna hadn't dated others. I attempted to deflect his comment by saying, "She wants to help me improve my German. I took her out to eat so we could talk."

"Oh, that's right, you speak and read German. When I tried my German on the beautiful Anna, all she did was laugh uproariously. I still don't understand why she'd be interested in the likes of you."

I chuckled at his expression of mock dismay. "I'm sure that with your Texas drawl, your German was almost unintelligible. No wonder Anna laughed."

An hour later, we sat in a dark-blue 1959 Chevrolet convertible sedan with side fins and green USA license plates. The sky was solid gray, and it was cold, so the top was up and the heater on.

Scott offered, "This is my car, which you can borrow if you need wheels."

"Thanks. What's with the green USA license plates?"

"They identify me as a member of the US military German occupation force. The East Germans can't interfere with our passage in all of Berlin or on the three autobahn routes between here and the West."

"Where can you go? Isn't Berlin surrounded by a fence?"

"Yes, it is," Scott replied. "I brought a map of Berlin—the American Zone of occupation is here in the south and west. Tempelhof is here," he said, tapping various spots on the map. "The British are in the west center here, and the French are in the north. The Russian Zone is here in the east."

Scott started the car. "I don't know if anyone has told you, but the Russians and East Germans have over half a million trained troops surrounding Berlin. The US Army Berlin Brigade numbers around 10,000. If we assembled all of the Army, Air Force, British, and French forces, including all of the desk jockeys like us plus the cooks and bottle washers, we would number less than 30,000."

"That doesn't make me feel safe," I admitted. "Once armed, most people like us would be more of a danger to ourselves and others on our side than the enemy."

Scott chuckled. "You're right. We'd primarily be using small arms against tanks and armored personnel carriers. Not a pleasant thought, old buddy."

"So, what you're saying is the Russians can take West Berlin anytime they want to."

"You got it, my friend," Scott replied. "It might mean World War III, but they could do it. Although there's currently free access between the two Berlins, West Berlin is encircled by a ninety-one mile-long barrier which consists of both concrete walls and barbed wire fences. Movement between East and West Berlin is controlled by eighty-one checkpoints, which the

East Germans man. At these points, they exercise control over their citizens and tourists."

"That's amazing—I had no idea."

"Over 200,000 people a year leave East Germany to settle in the West. Virtually all pass through Berlin. Once in East Berlin, they take the subway to the West. The West German Government flies five, sometimes six airplane loads of immigrants out of Berlin every day. Most aren't allowed to stay here, because the infrastructure is overloaded with the people who already live here."

"So, the people from the East are rejecting Communism with their feet, big time." I remembered Anna's words about the battle between competing ideologies.

"Those who are leaving are the trained doctors, dentists, engineers, teachers and scientists who can get good jobs in the West. In the East, it's rapidly becoming a nation of the old, infirmed, and uneducated. How much longer can a country of 19 million afford to lose its most capable citizens?" Scott asked.

"And the Russians can take Berlin at will. Perhaps it'd be healthier to be stationed elsewhere," I quipped.

"Ah, but the lovely Anna lives here. Plus, you are stuck for the next three years. Remember you agreed to serve and defend, old buddy. Most military men across the world would trade their left nut to be stationed here. Enjoy it while you can, compadre."

"My service commitment ends next April, and I intend to get out then."

"I've decided to stay in until it stops being fun, and I really like Berlin. I also understand that the inherent danger isn't for everyone."

"I haven't fired a weapon in two years," I said. "We're in the civilian branch of the military services, which is the reason I joined the Air Force."

"During orientation on Monday, you'll be issued a complete set of summer and winter camouflage fatigues and combat gear. You'll be scheduled for firearms training, using a good old US Air Force .38 caliber pistol. If war starts, you'll be expected to defend this city to the death."

We pulled up, and I saw a body of water.

Scott spoke quietly. "The building on the left is the structure which will contain the western terminus of our tunnel. The River Spree is on our right."

I looked around, trying to get my bearings. "This building must be about two miles east of Tempelhof."

"About that. The border is the near edge of the river. Here's a pair of binoculars. See the four East German Peoples' Police standing on the far shore? They are the *Volkspolizei*—VoPos in German slang."

I mentally noted two groups of uniformed young men located behind a barbed wire fence, intently surveying the river.

Scott continued, "Twenty-four hours a day, they're positioned in pairs every fifty or so feet along the entire ninety-one mile long fence and wall that surrounds West Berlin. You'll notice they're carrying AK-47's. Those weapons are loaded, and they're authorized to use them on the 'spies and saboteurs' who try to enter or leave the 'worker's paradise' by unauthorized routes."

"They do look like they mean business."

"Notice that boat flying the East German Flag, and its machine guns? They patrol the river almost continuously."

A few minutes later, we drove through the Friedrichstrasse Checkpoint into East Berlin. After only a brief delay, East German passport control personnel waved the car through as they tilted the red and white barriers up and out of the way.

"We can enter East Berlin that easily?" I asked in amazement.

"Because this vehicle has green license plates, they aren't allowed to ask for any type of identification."

We drove past uniform rows of drab, gray multi-story buildings, which Scott said contained most of the East German government agencies.

We parked to the side of a massive ruined building. A tiny car following us pulled over and parked down the street. Scott nodded his head and turned toward them, advising, "They're assigned to ensure that no one contacts us or gives us anything. They're almost certainly the Secret Police—the dreaded Stasi."

"Stasi?"

"Those bad boys apply the worst repressive tactics of the Russian's KGB and the Nazi's SS with a vigor and ruthlessness that's unique. They use every conceivable means to force their citizens to report their friends, neighbors, business associates and even relatives for the smallest infraction of their rigid communist dogma. Unfortunate individuals who're brought to their attention are subjected to the worst mental and physical torture imaginable. Many just disappear."

"What are we doing in East Berlin? Aren't we viewed as the enemy?" I sensed real danger all around us.

"The objective of our excursion into the East is for you to see the enemy and take his measure. The Russians stay in the background and allow the East Germans to harass us in any way possible. We're perfectly safe—protected by the four-power agreement on free access to all four sections of Berlin by all occupying troops. Watch and learn!"

"I hope you're right." I sighed. "I don't see any of those powers protecting us right now." Even I heard the irony in my tone of voice.

"Most of their attention is focused on East German citizens. My girlfriend, Mia, lives in the East. One of her neighbors is still in prison because his seven-year-old son reported that he called the East German leader Walter Ulbricht a dummkopf (blockhead) at the dinner table one evening. The son's teacher brainwashed the poor child with propaganda and encouraged him to report anyone who opposed the communist regime. So, he informed on his father."

"That's frightening. How can anyone live in that kind of society?"

"Nineteen million people do. You'll find that most of them are nice, ordinary people who were unfortunate enough to end up on the wrong side of a line some foreigners drew on a map at the end of the war."

Shaking my head, I again thought of Anna's remarks. It appeared that had happened to her family, too.

"Let's wave at them to show that they don't scare us." Scott swung his right arm up and down. "See the car they're driving?" Scott pointed. "It's a Trabant. The only East German production car. It has a 500cc, two-cylinder two-stroke engine whose twenty-five-horsepower engine takes twenty-one seconds to accelerate to its top speed of sixty miles per hour. The East

German joke is, it's so underpowered you can catch one by placing a piece of used chewing gum on a roadway."

I observed, "It's a sterling example of the superiority of free enterprise. Compare it to the Mercedes and BMWs built in West Germany!"

We walked around the east end of the domeless Reichstag building. Its massive charred and windowless walls, columns, and porticos still displayed pockmarked patterns of bullet and shrapnel holes.

"Hitler used the burning of this edifice as an excuse to declare martial law and become the dictator of Germany," Scott observed.

"As I remember, his own people intentionally set the fire."

As we drove past the Brandenburg Gate, Scott recited history, "This neoclassical monument was originally built in the late 1790s to celebrate peace with Napoleon. On October 27, 1806, after the victories at Iéna and Auerstädt, Napoleon rode in triumph into Berlin, passing through it. You may remember a classic World War II photo, which shows Russian soldiers raising a Soviet flag atop this Gate." He pulled over on Unter Den Linden Street. "That huge building on our right is Russia House. From there the Russians direct East German domestic and foreign policy."

"Wasn't this street one of the scenes of the East German uprising in 1953, which the Russians brutally suppressed?" I cringed at the vivid images of tanks firing on young men throwing rocks.

"It was also the scene of a victory parade. Hitler stood in the back of an open Mercedes, giving the Nazi salute to the perhaps one million people who lined this thoroughfare. He came through the Brandenburg Gate on his way to be sworn in as Chancellor of Germany. The date was January 30, 1933."

A short drive later, we arrived at a large vacant lot. "The Third Reich that Hitler claimed would last a thousand years ended here at the Fuhrer's bunker on April 30, 1945—twelve years and three months to the day after it started. Hitler committed suicide, and his body was burned at a spot just in front of us. His bunker has been sealed, but it's down there." Scott motioned to our left.

After several turns, he pointed to a nondescript building. "That's the office of Walter Ulbricht. He's the hard-line Stalinist East German leader. He's vowed to reunite Germany under a communist regime in his lifetime. His stated first target is West Berlin."

Hearing a rattling noise behind us, we turned to see the Trabant pull up. Two individuals in leather trench coats exited the vehicle. They donned fedoras and approached us. In German, one man demanded, "You have entered East Germany. Please show us your identification."

Scott responded in his Texas-twanged German, "As members of the American Occupying Forces, we refuse to recognize your authority to stop us or to otherwise impede our movements." He walked around the Stasi men, heading for his car. I followed him and climbed into the passenger side. One of the Stasi agents blocked our car with the Trabant. The other stood behind us to prevent us from moving.

Scott exited his car. In forceful-sounding German, he said, "We request that a Russian officer be summoned immediately so we can protest our illegal detention. Move your vehicle quickly, or you will be in trouble—big trouble, Herr Dieter Holburg of the Stasi!"

While Scott challenged the Stasi, I spotted a third individual using a camera to photograph the encounter.

Six-foot-four Scott towered over the five-foot-six Stasi agent. They stood toe-to-toe, as if taking each other's measure before a gunfight.

The Stasi agent pushed his homburg hat back on his head. I finally saw his face. A long scar down one cheek gave his face a permanent scowl. His flattened nose looked broken, perhaps more than once. Behind his horn-rimmed glasses, I saw the bleary eyes of a man who frequently drank too much. The thumb and forefinger of his right hand were missing, the skin around the wound was grotesquely scarred. I estimated his age to be mid-to-late forties. His physical infirmities led me to conclude he'd seen many battles in and out of uniform.

I tried to relax, but I felt a sudden compulsion to leave the scene. I exited the vehicle, deciding to walk west toward the Brandenburg Gate Checkpoint and West Berlin.

Just then, Stasi agent Holburg snapped in heavily accented English, "Captain Taylor, if you continue to show a complete disregard for the sovereignty of the DDR, we will take firm action against you. I will personally make you suffer. Now go away and stay away!" He pointed west with his crippled hand.

On the way back to the West, Scott told me, "I've had several run-ins with Herr Holburg. He's one of their best agents, and he's relentless once he decides someone's trying to do something that could be detrimental to East Germany."

Once we reached the West, Scott grinned and shouted, "Man alive, that was more fun than riding a bucking bronco, partner! It'll give those pukes in East Germany something to think about."

"Aren't we going to get in trouble for our little joy ride? Those guys took photos of us."

Scott shook his head. "Our access to Berlin is guaranteed by the Four Powers Treaty signed by the victors in 1945. No World War II peace treaty will be possible until the Cold War ends. The Russians want East Germany to be recognized as an independent country and we'll never allow that, so it's a stalemate. Until something changes, we've got Herr Holburg and his kind by the short hairs. His superiors will know little or nothing about our altercation today, because he failed to intimidate us into complying with his requests."

"I hope you're correct," I said, still feeling uneasy. "Why does Holburg know you?"

"I've had several run-ins with him. When the men who work upstairs in Tempelhof get into trouble in the East, I have to extract them."

"Why do the men who work upstairs even want to go to East Berlin? Isn't it dangerous for them?"

"Everything is much less expensive over there. Preventing red-blooded American men from exercising their God-given right to free pussy and cheap beer is an impossible task. Even on an E-3's meager salary, our lowest ranking troops can live like kings in the East with an apartment and a girl-friend, who may be a Stasi agent or informant. She rents an apartment for them and they play house. My job is impossible."

"In a way, you can't blame them. What you've described would be tempting for any young man."

"I only really get involved when they get in trouble in the East."

"So, we just broke a rule you're supposed to enforce!"

"Because of my job, I have a special dispensation, which I extended to you today."

CHAPTER 10

Saturday, October 15, 1960

OVER LUNCH, WE talked about the two Berlins.

"After the war, the destruction from bombing and shelling was virtually the same in most parts of the city," Scott said. "Rebuilding is nearly complete in West Berlin. Few vacant lots exist and there are even fewer damaged buildings."

"The newspapers often have articles on the 'West German economic miracle,' but to see it first hand is incredible," I replied. "Everyone seems to live in new and modern apartments, and many have automobiles."

"Today on our tour of the East, we only traversed the showplace areas the communist leaders want the world to see. Elsewhere, in East Berlin, a good part of the destruction still remains."

"Really!"

"Yes. The Russians claimed most German industrial and manufacturing facilities as reparations for the destruction Germany wrought on them during the war. Virtually every factory in Berlin was put on boxcars and moved to Russia. They took everything from lathes and bricks to toilets and telephones. As a result, virtually all of southeast Berlin in the Russian Zone is still a gigantic ruin."

Moving closer, I glanced around to assure no one could hear me as I whispered, "Isn't that where the terminus of our tunnel will be?"

"Yes."

"Tell me more," I encouraged.

"Once you get beyond the area we saw today, twisted iron protruding from broken walls and piles of rubble are familiar sights. The new structures, especially the ugly square workers' tenements, look drab, the apartments are tiny, and amenities are few. The pre-war buildings are a uniform shabby gray with slap-dab repairs, boarded-up windows, and peeling paint."

"During the short time we were in the East, I didn't see many cars," I observed.

"Private ownership of a car, even a Trabant, is rare over there. Senior Communist Party members and military elite have Russian-made, chauffeur-driven limousines. Everyone else takes public transportation—trolleys, buses, the subway, and interurban."

After lunch, we drove through the British and French sectors to their military bases. Scott gave me quick tours and described the recreational, entertainment, and dining facilities available to us. We kept running into barbed-wire barriers or walls which completely closed off streets going in random directions.

At one point, I observed, "One could get island fever living here—always running into barriers."

Scott turned onto a broad street with trolley tracks running down its middle. "This is Bernauerstrasse. Perhaps the strangest part of the crazy quilt that is the barrier which divides the two Berlins. We are driving on a street that's in the West, but the almost continuous line of buildings on the right side of the road are in the East. East Berliners exit their apartment houses—once on the sidewalk, they're in the West."

"Interesting."

"I have used this anomaly to extricate several of our errant youths from the East, without anyone knowing we were over there. That's a secret I'd prefer you not share with others. Okay, old buddy?"

"Sure." It would be several months before I learned what that comment really meant.

Our tour ended with a few beers at the Tempelhof Officers Club game room. It consisted of a semi-circular bar, a bank of slot machines, several tables large enough for poker games, a pool table, and several smaller tables with three or four club chairs around them. We wanted to talk, so we took one of the smaller tables in a quiet alcove and began by exchanging our life histories.

"I've been in the service for almost four years now," I told him. "Specialty training, then eighteen months at March Air Force Base as a subcontracts administrator. Then another eighteen months at the University of California Berkeley getting my master's degree."

"So, you're one of the lucky few who got the Air Force to pay for their education."

"It's a good deal. I got paid while going to school, and only owe them one month of additional service for every month in school. I have only a year and a half to serve, then I'm getting out. I can't wait to start working in my chosen profession as a civilian."

Scott said, "When I joined the Air Force, I was just taking care of my military obligation. I didn't want to be drafted into the Army and serve as an enlisted man. Now that I've been in for over six years, I may make it my career. I like my job, especially being stationed in Berlin."

"I can tell you're in your element here."

"Love it here. I've been contemplating marrying Mia. She was born in the East, so if we do marry, I'll probably lose my clearance and current job. Then I'd be forced to resign my commission, return to Texas, and do God only knows what!"

"Do they enforce the ban on a close relationship with a foreign national?" I asked, thinking of Anna.

"You can date them. You can sleep with them. You just can't marry them."

"Can you live together unmarried or get married and not tell them?"

"That's kind of a gray area. So far, it seems like you can live with a foreign female if you're discrete. Our bosses operate on the concept of plausible deniability—what they don't know won't hurt you."

"That's an interesting distinction. Why?"

"They know they can't turn us into a bunch of celibate monks—so we're allowed to bend the rules, but only so far."

"That makes sense. Has there ever been an exception to the marriage rule?"

"Exceptions have been made, but not for a German spouse born and raised in the East," Scott replied. "Too much potential she might be a sleeper agent or an informant for the Stasi or even the KGB. Plus, if her family is still over there, they can exert pressure on her to work for them or on you through her. Hey, you're thinking about Anna! Jeez, man, that's fast. You may want to slow down a bit."

My silence revealed the accuracy of his guess.

He looked around, then whispered, "My girlfriend lives with me, and I constantly worry that someone may make an issue of it."

CHAPTER 11

Tuesday, October 18, 1960

THAT MORNING, I was called into Colonel Morgan's office.

"You asked to see me, sir?"

"Come in and have a seat. There's something important we need to discuss. Has anyone told you that people with our clearance are forbidden to have close and continuing associations with foreign nationals?"

Not wanting to lie, I nodded. "Captain Taylor mentioned something about it."

"Well…I've been informed you had a date with Anna Fischer from the bookstore on Friday. I'm sure you understand the reason for this restriction. I know and like Anna, but there can be no exceptions. Since she was born and grew up in the East, we can't verify her true political leanings. Plus, if you continue to see her, you'll be vulnerable to coercion from the East. Every member of my staff has the same security clearance as you, and all are subject to this restriction. It's especially important you follow this restriction, because of the sensitive nature of your program. Do you understand what I'm saying?"

I answered, "Yes, sir," though knowing I was too enamored with Anna to give her up just like that. Scott had indicated that as long as we were discrete, we could still see each other. So be it.

"I'm glad you understand. If you need female companionship, there are hundreds of American nurses and school teachers here in Berlin. Find one of them to date."

CHAPTER 12

Tuesday, October 18, 1960

I LOCKED ALL of the LUMAR information in the Mosler safe so my tank could be cleaned, the floors polished and everything dusted. After the crew finished, the two U.S. Government-issue, grey vinyl topped, metal conference tables were again positioned end to end and surrounded by eight tilt-backed grey metal chairs. The setting wasn't elegant, but we had no choice. My tank was the only place in all of Europe where LUMAR information could be discussed.

Once the cleaning crew left, Mark Powell and I started to work on the briefing for the General. During a break, he said, "Colonel Morgan asked me to reiterate that, because of the sensitivity of your assignment, it's incumbent upon you to not establish a close relationship with any foreign nationals."

"Sir, I feel that I can confide in you. I really like Anna Fischer."

"You've only known her for a few days."

"I know—but we have something special already."

"Robert, let me be frank. Any relationship you establish with her could only create problems for you, Colonel Morgan and me. Before she was issued the badge, which allows her to work on the base, we did a preliminary background check on her. She was born in the East and lived there until she was eighteen. Our very cursory investigation revealed no association with communist organizations, but that doesn't mean she's not an enemy agent or an operative—one who supports the communist cause…"

"—Sir, Anna hates the communists…"

"—Every undercover agent freely spouts anti-communist rhetoric to ensure we don't suspect them of double-dealing. Sleeper agents have functioned for years and were never suspected of being anything except the role they played…"

"—But sir, I…"

"—For a minute let's assume that Anna and her entire family, who still live in the East, are what they appear to be—law-abiding citizens of an occupied city, who just happen to live on the wrong side of a line some foreigners drew on a map fifteen years ago…."

"—People here in West Berlin know and respect Anna's family. They must be wonderful people."

"That only makes the situation worse in some ways. Let's say your regard for Miss Fischer deepens, and the Stasi or KGB become interested in our little project. All they have to do is threaten Anna's family with arrest, torture or worse. Once you're committed to her, you'll be vulnerable to blackmail to free her family. These restrictions are designed to prevent this type of occurrence."

"But, sir…"

"—Enough said. We need to get back to work on this briefing. What do you think about…"

CHAPTER 13

Wednesday, October 19, 1960

EVERYONE IN BERLIN cleared for the LUMAR project—Colonel Morgan, Mark Powell, Scott Taylor, and I—greeted and shook hands with Major General Richard Harrison when he entered my tank. I was surprised that he was only five-foot-five or five-foot six-inches tall. The stars on his shoulders and his demeanor made him seem like a big man—actually he almost filled the room.

The scent of Pine-Sol and fresh floor polish pervaded the area. A ballast in one overhead fluorescent fixture must have gone bad overnight, because two bulbs flickered and buzzed.

As soon as the five of us were seated around my conference table, the General declared, "A year from now our new president, whoever that may be, will be faced with a monumental decision. He will either be forced to accept as an accomplished fact the incorporation of a reunited Berlin into East Germany, or he'll start an armed confrontation which could easily lead to World War III!"

I flinched. A somber mood permeated the room as Colonel Morgan said, "Please enlighten everyone as to the source of this information and the deadline."

"The annual meeting of the Warsaw Pact just adjourned. Russia and its satellites agreed to sign a separate World War II peace treaty with East Germany. This agreement will be negotiated over the next year, and it will be approved at their meeting next fall."

"Can they unilaterally abrogate the four-power agreements that were signed at the conclusion of World War II?" Colonel Morgan asked.

"They are attempting to throw out all of the rules that have governed our collective conduct in Europe since the war," General Harrison replied. "Perhaps equally ominous, details of new East German plans for the closure of all air, water, and ground routes into and out of Berlin have also been intercepted by our unit at Darmstadt."

None of us dared to interrupt this interchange between these two senior people. As the newest arrival and junior man present, I tried to remain calm. I thought: *Holy shit—this sounds like I'll soon be in the middle of a war! This has to be the reason for the deadline we've been given.*

"Sir, I think that we'd fight rather than...."

"—because we're outnumbered five to one in conventional forces, President Eisenhower has repeatedly stated that if the Russians attempt to overrun Western Europe, he'll have no choice but to use nuclear weapons. The question in everyone's mind is, will the next president go to war to save West Berlin?"

"Grim, sir," Mark exclaimed, his concern obvious.

General Harrison said, "I'm here to kick off the construction of a tunnel I believe will help us avoid a new war. Our leaders need solid, reliable information to base decisions on. The Russians are so secretive, the only way we can get reliable information is by reading their mail."

"What's so different now, General?" Scott boldly asked.

"Warsaw Pact wireless communications are in the process of being switched to landlines. This tunnel...our tunnel...will allow us to tap into those landlines and read virtually all high-level military, commercial, and diplomatic communication between the Warsaw Pact nations and Russia. It'll be a treasure trove of relevant information."

Colonel Morgan added, "Allowing the U.S. and her allies to anticipate and counter Russian efforts to sign those peace treaties!"

"Exactly." General Harrison stood, pointing at Mark and me. He signaled us to the front of the conference room. Once we stood next to him, he announced, "These two men are going to build a tunnel, tap into the communist's primary communications links, and help us avoid the next war."

The general took his seat at the head of the table as Mark gave the briefing I'd helped prepare. It described our preparations and provided a schedule for the construction of the tunnel. We told everyone present that the signals processing and reporting portion of Exploitation Center at the western end of the tunnel would be partially operational by September of next year.

Although very nervous, I participated in the lengthy discussions and answered questions the General directed at me. Overall, I felt pleased with my contribution to the meeting.

Feet of Tunnel Completed: 0   Days until Deadline: 347

CHAPTER 14

Thursday, October 20, 1960

ALTHOUGH I WENT to bed early, I could not sleep. My responsibilities, with their real global stakes—World War III and the destruction of Europe—kept running through my mind.

My first panic attack in five years occurred that night. I had finally fallen asleep but soon experienced a nightmare.

First, Anna and I fled for our lives as mushroom clouds filled the sky. Then, Scott and I stood side-by-side in a trench. We had our .38 caliber pistols ready to fire as VoPos with AK-47s rushed toward Tempelhof. Anna hid in the nearby bookstore. I must protect her and somehow survive, I thought as I jerked awake.

My pulse increased, and I began to gasp for breath. A full-blown panic attack. Dizzy and sweating, the tingling sensations in my extremities took over my entire conscious being.

In the past, I'd always managed to control these attacks by lying down, relaxing, breathing deeply, and thinking pleasant thoughts. I forced myself to imagine that Anna and I were back dancing to the music. Happy, wondrous times.

I slowly calmed down. Deep, controlled breathing using my diaphragm worked. My pulse rate was finally almost normal. After several minutes, I climbed out of the bed and sat in the easy chair.

My first panic attack had occurred at the age of nine. It was late June 1944. The previous week, my mother had told me that my father's unit was involved in the Normandy landings in France. I can still hear her words, "Robert you need to know that heavy German resistance has been reported with many American casualties."

The next day I saw an officer in an Army uniform and our minister walking down our street. I sensed they were going to tell us that my father was dead. I ran into the back garden and entered a hiding place I'd made in the tall hedge. Almost immediately I felt overwhelmed, could not breathe, became dizzy, and then lost consciousness. A long while later, I entered our house, seeking comfort from my mother. No one was there. Eventually, I learned that she'd gone down the street to comfort a neighbor overcome by grief. Her son had been killed in the Pacific.

A psychologist my parents consulted when I was in high school told us there are no 'known causes or sure cures' for those who suffered from panic attacks. His recommendation was for me to learn to cope with them when they occurred.

I understood why the military had rules which excluded persons who suffered from panic attacks from serving. How can one lead men into battle, or even in the building of a tunnel, if he panics when confronted by a crisis? After a sleepless night, I decided not to tell anyone of my disability—I wanted stay in Berlin, finish the tunnel, and be with Anna. This was my destiny; like my father I wanted to be a citizen soldier who served his country in time of need.

CHAPTER 15

Thursday, October 20, 1960

SCOTT ARRIVED A little early for the meeting and rang the buzzer. I admitted him into the tank. Once seated, he observed, "That was some meeting we had yesterday. I've been in this man's Air Force for six years, and I've never known a General officer to speak so frankly."

"I feel like the weight of the world is on my shoulders."

"Several of us are here to help you. Don't worry."

"I need all the help I can get."

"You really are inexperienced, buddy. You probably thought General Harrison just happened to come to Berlin to kick off the building of the tunnel. His real purpose was to determine if you could build his tunnel. You'll know soon if you passed the test."

"I had no idea. Did Colonels Morgan and Powell know, too?"

"Yes. Don't worry, compadre. You passed muster. If you do a good job for our bosses, they'll support you in every way. Remember, your performance on this project will be a direct reflection of their leadership."

"I hadn't thought about it that way."

"Believe me, this program has maximum visibility at the highest levels of our military and government."

I glanced up as someone entered the right combination in the cipher lock. I heard it click. Mark escorted an individual, whom he introduced as Kurt Altschuler. A firm handshake and warm smile complemented his erect stature. He looked like a senior corporate executive in his expensive, hand-tailored, three-piece suit, black top coat over one arm, and homburg hat in his hand.

"Since the four of us are going to be working together for the next year or so as the tunnel building program security committee, it's imperative we get to know each other," Mark said. He and Scott then described their responsibilities at Tempelhof.

Next, we all looked at Kurt, who in the deep baritone voice of a well-educated European gentleman, and with only the trace of an accent, stated, "I'm one of the CIA's Deputy Chiefs of Station here in Berlin. I was born and raised here, and consider it my home. My primary value to the program will be my ability to operate in both East and West Berlin. As problems occur, I'll help you solve them."

I introduced myself, told them of my educational qualifications and recent experience, and then bluntly said, "I need all of the help I can get. This whole task is, quite frankly, overwhelming."

Mark started us off by saying, "This morning, we'll discuss the security threat. This afternoon, we'll take a tour of what we should all refer to as 'the building.'"

Kurt took the lead. "Every activity associated with the tunnel will be of interest to the tens of thousands of spies from both sides who move freely around Berlin. The Soviet Committee for State Security, the KGB, and Soviet Military Intelligence, the GRU, have large cadres of agents here in Berlin. The East Germans have combined agencies into one organization called the Ministry for State Security, commonly known as the Stasi."

"So, what you are telling me is that thousands of people are going to watch our every move?" I clarified.

"You're not alone," Scott replied. "You've got Kurt, me, and our rather sizeable organizations to help worry about security for you. I...."

"—Scott, I think you'll agree that keeping the existence of the tunnel from the West Germans, French, and British will add a whole new layer of complexity to the problem," Mark interjected. "The West German Intelligence Service alone has thousands of undercover agents operating within Berlin and its environs...."

"—You're right," Kurt confidently interjected. "Keeping our allies from finding out about the tunnel makes hiding its existence much more difficult—but not impossible—the French and Germans will usually back off when we warn them to not be too inquisitive about our intelligence gathering activities. But it's not a matter of if the British find out about it, it's a matter of when—and they'll be pissed, as they were our partners in the last tunnel."

"There's a reason we aren't telling the British," Mark said. "Too many times, the information we provide them has been quickly given to the Soviets by the moles who have penetrated the very fabric of British intelligence."

During a pause I remarked, "I've read Berlin was a center for spies on both sides, but I had no idea of the magnitude of the activities conducted here."

"Our problems are exacerbated by the free and unlimited movement of people between East and West Berlin," Kurt warned. "Over a hundred thousand people who live in East Berlin have full or part-time jobs over here. The West German Marks they earn, and the subsidies they receive in the East, allow them to live very comfortably. Several thousand enemy agents and operatives from the East join these workers passing through the eighty-one border checkpoints each day. We and our allies send almost as many their way. Several thousand more on both sides spend their days watching their opposite numbers gather information."

"What's the distinction between an agent and an operative?" I asked.

"A spy, or more properly, an agent, is a full-time paid employee of a government organization tasked with gathering intelligence on a nation's enemies or friends. An operative is someone who, for money or because of loyalty to a cause, is willing to spy on a perceived enemy."

The conversation lagged, so I said, "Thanks for sharing your perspective with me. You're saying we need to remember to tread very lightly on the other side. Our tunnel would seem to be a provocative activity."

"Hence, it's even more important that we keep it a secret from everyone!" Kurt stated.

Scott added, "We are unlucky enough to have perhaps thirty Stasi agents who do nothing but monitor the activities at our little old Air Force base here at Tempelhof. Several of them are around every hour of the day and night."

"I want to make sure all four of us recognize that Stasi agents excel at spy craft of all forms," Kurt said, looking each of us in the eye to emphasize his point. "We must be careful not to underestimate them."

Mark closed the meeting. "Robert and I will certainly discuss every aspect of the tunnel building with the two of you to ensure we're as secure as possible. We appreciate knowing what's going on. We'll probably need to have frequent meetings, which I'll attend when I can."

"Before we adjourn, I have a question. Does anyone have any idea how we're going to secretly transport thirty-four American construction workers from their quarters here at Tempelhof to the building where the tunnel will be located every day?"

When no one responded, I continued, "I can just see the thirty Stasi agents Scott mentioned and probably more than one spy or informant from each of the numerous organizations Kurt listed, clambering over each other at the front gate. All attempting to determine who these new men are and what they are doing in Berlin?"

They glanced at each other, but no one replied to my question.

Feet of Tunnel Completed: 0   Days until Deadline: 345

CHAPTER 16

Thursday, October 20, 1960

WEARING CIVILIAN SUITS and hats, Mark, Scott and I walked out the base's front security gate, intending to walk to "the building." Kurt would meet us there.

Scott immediately determined we'd picked up a tail, saying, "We are a little behind schedule, perhaps we had better take a taxi." He herded us toward the airport terminal's taxi stand.

As soon as we climbed into a Mercedes cab, Scott said to the driver, "Take us to the Hilton Hotel." He looked back in time to see two followers get into a cab, which now trailed us. He took out a pad of paper and scribbled a note: *We're being followed by at least two people.*

After arriving at the Hilton, we followed Scott. We took an elevator to the fourth floor, descended the stairs down to the basement, and exited through a loading dock to a side street. We walked a few blocks until Scott felt sure we were no longer being followed. Then another taxi took us within four blocks of the building. We managed to arrive at the appointed time, despite our detour.

Kurt was waiting for us. By earlier agreement, the four of us silently walked around the outside of the neo-classical building. Constructed of white marble, the Ionic columns extended from the street level to the corbelled roof. The windows on each floor were positioned between the columns and surrounded by elaborately carved marble frames. The structure was capped by a decorative cast-iron parapet and a massive dome.

On the south end, I pointed to several things without verbal comment. The walkway adjacent to the western side of the Spree appeared deserted, except for us. Three sets of People's Police—VoPos were visible on the opposite shore. Storefronts on the north and west side of the building were closed for business. We went through the main entrance, down a set of stairs on the right side, and used a key to open a door. A vast basement lay before us.

Having studied a set of plans, I described the scene for my companions. "The first thing that catches your attention is the eighty-eight interior columns which go from the basement to the roof. They are spaced about eleven meters, thirty-six feet on center. They are one meter square and made out of steel-reinforced concrete. According to the original plans from 1870, they extend ten meters, about thirty-three feet, below the surface of the basement."

"It's almost like a forest of pillars!" Scott exclaimed.

"As you can see, the four-story building is rectangular—395 feet by 338 feet. The previous owner began a complete remodel of the building, so everything between the basement and the roof, except of course, the load-bearing columns and most apartments on the upper floors of the building, has been removed."

"What does load-bearing mean?" Scott asked.

"These columns and the outside walls bear the weight of the entire building. They support not only the roof, but also the interior structure—floors, walls and ceilings—everything."

"There's certainly enough room here to store a lot of the soil that will have to be removed from the tunnel."

"You're correct, Mark" I replied. "That's a significant advantage. A fleet of trucks removing soil from an existing building would be unusual and would give away what we're doing!"

I saw a German sign, which read, "Elektrisches Zimmer." Inviting everyone inside, I announced, "This building is equipped with standard German 50 Hz, 400-amp, four-wire service. It looks to have been replaced recently—probably the initial step in the remodeling process. That means we've sufficient electrical power to support all of our construction efforts and the Exploitation Center when it's built."

As we walked toward the east end of the building, I told my companions, "When we were outside, I noticed the visible deterioration of the south-east end of the building."

"I also noticed some large cracks around some of the windows," Mark observed.

"A note on the plans for the remodel, which were recently approved by the Berlin Building Department, call for substantial repairs to that end of the building. It was severely damaged by allied bombs in 1944, and hasty repairs were done in 1946 to satisfy the demand for housing. We'll need vehicle access to this basement, so a roll-up door and ramp down to the basement are a must at that end of the building."

"I'll go to the building department this afternoon. Perhaps no additional approvals will be required for a temporary installation," Kurt volunteered.

"Let's take a look at the southeast corner, which is where my predecessor decided we should place our elevator shaft."

After we reached the corner, I stated, "His concept was to build a shaft perhaps sixty feet deep in this area and install an elevator. Everything would go up and down to our tunnel entrance in it. As you can see, several of the columns in this area were hastily repaired in 1946 with cement and bricks. The structural integrity in this area is questionable, so we'll have to keep that in mind with every step we take."

"Would you define structural integrity?" Scott asked.

"In layman's terms, it means the building might fall down. See the cracks in this column and the next one over, plus those running up and down that outside wall and around those windows? Those mean something has moved, which isn't a good thing!"

"Kurt, can we get a German structural engineering firm to do an assessment of that end of the building?" Mark asked.

"I'll look into it and get back to you."

I asked, "Mark, you've indicated the Army Corps of Engineers is sending all of their people with top-secret, code-word security clearances to build the tunnel. Do we know exactly how many men?"

"Thirty-four enlisted men."

"Do any of them speak German?"

"I doubt it."

"I've calculated we need at least sixty-two men to complete the tunnel within the allotted time, because we'll operate day and swing shifts."

"I'll start working on getting more people," Mark offered.

"A large number of them need to speak German like a native."

"Why?" The others asked in unison.

"Since we are right in the middle of a residential area, it's inevitable for our construction crew to interface with the local residents and others as they move around Berlin," I informed them. "The men who are going to man the security checkpoint at the front door, the roll-up door, and truck drivers need to speak German without a noticeable accent. Remember, everything has to go in and out of here by truck."

Scott gasped, pointing out, "Very few foreign-born individuals are ever granted top-secret clearances."

"Someone should have thought about this before now," Mark observed.

Kurt nodded his agreement. "Everything I've seen and heard today gives me pause. The structure is unsafe, and a large part of our workforce needs to speak German like a native. I hope solutions to both problems can be found quickly, or I may conclude we were a bit hasty in buying this building."

Feet of Tunnel Completed: 0   Days until Deadline: 343

CHAPTER 17

Friday, October 21, 1960

THE NEXT MORNING, at my request, Scott dropped by.

"I've got two things we need to discuss. First, both Colonel Morgan and Mark have leaned on me to stop dating Anna. Can you help me?"

"They also talked to me about your situation," Scott said. "I explained they had four options: send you back to the states, continue to harass you until you comply with that requirement, exercise some form of judicial authority to get you to conform, or accept the situation and hope nothing comes of it. They then asked me to leave so they could determine a course of action."

"You've been here for a while. What do you think they'll do?"

"They don't have anyone to replace you—so you've got them by the balls. Just relax and hope neither Anna nor her family creates problems for you, old buddy. What's your other topic of discussion?"

"One of those Stasi agents who followed us yesterday was Dieter Holburg."

"Yes, I know. That's bad. Somehow he has decided you're here for something he should know about."

"What are we going to do?"

"Don't know. Usually, we just ignore them and eventually their attention is directed at something or someone else."

"That may not work this time."

"You're right. I'll tell Mark that I'm going to give you counter-surveillance training one or two days a week until you are proficient at recognizing and losing a tail. How about Tuesdays and Thursdays?"

"Those days are as good as any."

"Don't go near the building until I tell you that you're ready!"

I nodded. "Okay."

It was at exactly 1300 when Mark entered the combination into the cipher lock and stepped into the tank. He immediately said, "This is our regular Friday meeting time. Do we have anything to discuss?"

"I've several things."

"Shoot."

"Yesterday, Kurt informed me we can install a roll-up door for as long as construction is ongoing, but it may need to be removed before we receive final occupancy approval."

"That's good. Go on."

"Sir, that brings up two things. First, building inspectors everywhere are rather aggressive, have the authority to enter a building site at any time, inspect everything, and close us down at will. We need Kurt to pull strings to withdraw our building permits so we're exempt from the entire inspection process."

"You're right. I'll make that happen. Good catch. What else?" he asked.

"Virtually all of Berlin is built on sandy, boggy soil. Here are reports on coring samples submitted by builders in the area surrounding our building."

"Where'd you get these?

"At my request, Kurt picked them up for me at the building department."

"How can this be important? It should be easier for us to dig through sand to get to our objective," Mark asked.

"Excavation in sand is difficult, because sand has no natural cohesion."

"Cohesion?"

"You've been to the beach. When you try to dig a hole in sand, it just falls back in. Even with a tunnel shield, the sand will collapse before the supporting structure can be installed. Our TBM can be equipped with a system which sprays a processed clay compound and water out the sides of the boring head to stabilize the sand. A hard surface several inches thick is formed, which prevents cave-ins and water leaks."

"I still don't understand why this is important just now," Mark said.

"It'd be best if we had the factory install the equipment instead of trying to add it ourselves."

"Make out the purchase order. I'll have our purchasing agent at Rhein-Main send it to the manufacturer before the original equipment is shipped."

"That's all for now, sir."

"Robert, I think you're doing an outstanding job. Keep it up." He shook my hand.

"I guess that means General Harrison thinks I can do the job."

"You wouldn't still be here if he or I had any doubts."

I suppressed the urge to ask Mark what he and Colonel Morgan had decided about my relationship with Anna. If you can't stand the answer, don't ask the question.

Feet of Tunnel Completed: 0   Days until Deadline: 343

CHAPTER 18

Saturday, October 22, 1960

MAKING SURREPTITIOUS CONTACT with Anna proved relatively easy. Each morning I went to the bookstore to purchase my copy of the *Stars and Stripes* newspaper. Every Thursday morning, she opened early and was by herself until 0900. This became our time to discuss our plans for what had become our regular Friday evening date.

The previous night, a Stasi agent followed us to the restaurant and movie theater. Afterward, I thought, *I'm glad the Stasi aren't reporting my activities to Colonel Morgan.*

Neither of us liked the first two apartments we saw on Saturday morning. We held hands and enjoyed clear skies and balmy temperatures as we walked to the third apartment. "This one is almost a mile north of the base. I've been told it overlooks a park and a subway station is close by," Anna said.

As the landlord escorted us up five flights of stairs, she jokingly observed, "Remember, Robert, you're an American. Everything must go up and down these steps. Are you sure you can manage?"

"I'll get much-needed exercise. Remember, I have a desk job."

Once we entered the apartment, she declared, "It is perfect! Huge and very nicely furnished."

"Anna, it rests directly under the roof. The ceiling in each room intersects the walls less than two feet from the floor. All of the furniture is located at least five feet out into each room."

"These large windows are located in alcoves all the way around the apartment. We…you will be up above the trees. See how light and airy it is up here."

"And I can hit my head every time I enter or leave one of the alcoves!"

"You'll learn to avoid them. Believe me, you'll not do any better."

In English, I divulged, "My housing allowance covers the rent, and it's vacant." Turning to the landlord, I asked in almost perfect German, "Can I rent this apartment month-to-month starting the first of November?"

In English that would put an Oxford Don to shame, he replied, "It would be my honor for you to live here. Herr Doctor Fischer is one of the finest men I have ever known. And he certainly has a lovely daughter."

After we concluded the rental agreement, I paid the first month's rent, and we walked out to the street in front of the apartment building.

"I must leave soon. I'm going to spend the night at my parent's house in the East," Anna announced. "I don't want to be late for the evening meal with them."

Unable to hide my disappointment, I protested, "I was counting on a pleasant day with you. The weather is ideal."

"I'm sorry, but I promised my parents."

After a brief hug, she kissed me on the cheek again, "I'll see you next week, Robert. Auf wiedersehen."

Before she turned to leave, I took her in my arms. We exchanged a long, caring kiss. As she slipped out of my arms, I looked up and recoiled. Dieter Holburg stood five feet away, staring at us.

Although she didn't say anything, I could tell Anna knew he was a Stasi agent—she'd grown up in the East.

CHAPTER 19

Thursday, October 27, 1960

"THE STASI KNOW we are up to something new, and they'll monitor our activities until they learn what it is," Mark announced without emotion at the start of the second meeting of the security committee.

"They follow me every time I leave the base," I advised my associates. "They also accompanied me on my night out last Friday, and Dieter Holburg followed me to my new apartment on Saturday."

"I made a big mistake taking Robert into East Berlin his first Saturday here. Now the Stasi want to know what he's doing in Berlin," Scott grumbled.

"Unfortunately, Kurt's been given a special assignment and won't return for several weeks. Perhaps he'd have some idea how we could counter the Stasi harassment," Mark said. "For now, their activities will do little harm."

"How will we prevent the spies and informants in Berlin from finding out what our sixty new arrivals are doing here?" I asked.

"For that problem, I have a solution." Scott placed a set of plans on the table. "Here's a layout of the spaces we control within Tempelhof. I suggest that everyone who goes to the tunnel building, including us, leaves Air Force controlled spaces via the airport arrivals hall!"

"How's that possible?" Mark asked.

"Here's the room we currently occupy. At the end of this hall, we'll establish a new security checkpoint, which will be manned full-time. We'll install a cipher-locked door into an existing locker room located beyond the checkpoint."

"Keep going," Mark encouraged. "I like what I'm hearing."

"Once in the dressing room, everyone changes into German clothes appropriate to the season. The hall outside that room leads down these stairs. At the end of the corridor is a door into the arrivals area. It's currently sealed. We install cipher locks on both sides of that door, and only our men will be given the combination."

"Brilliant. Airports all over the world use those cipher locks to keep passengers from entering restricted areas." Mark smiled, obviously pleased.

"Once in the arrivals hall, each man becomes just another newly arrived passenger." I said, marveling at the simplicity of Scott's plan.

"I like it," Mark agreed. "Scott, make it happen."

Feet of Tunnel Completed: 0   Days until Deadline: 336

CHAPTER 20

Friday, October 28, 1960

OUR REGULAR FRIDAY meeting between Mark and me started at 1300. When Mark didn't mention my relationship with Anna, I remained mute on that topic.

After a lengthy summation of the number of disadvantages of the elevator solution, I told him, "In conclusion, we'd miss the desired date by at least four months. I have an alternative to suggest."

"Shoot."

"The entrances to most tunnels under bodies of water start several hundred feet back from the water's edge. The top of the tunnel passes twenty to thirty feet below the bottom of the river."

"We can't do that here because we need to hide the tunnel entrance."

"Exactly. My concept would involve building a ramp along the west wall. It can be completed less than a month after the construction crew arrives. Then, we commence tunneling."

"But we're starting a lot further from our ultimate objective."

"The overall length does increase by about 360 feet."

"So, you're suggesting that all that distance, the tunnel will be inside our building between the south wall and the first row of pillars."

"That's my concept."

"How does your concept impact the overall schedule?"

"Let's review the detailed project schedule I've generated."

Ten minutes later, Mark put his index finger on the last line. "I like the fact that your plan shows that if we adopt the ramp tunnel concept, we'll be a full ten days ahead of our required date."

"That's correct. If we don't encounter any problems, we can complete the first tap into that communications tube on September 3, 1961."

"Two of your major milestones in the schedule are the installation of pressure doors. What are they, and why do we need them?"

"Every tunnel constructed under a body of water in the last century has employed air pressure to support the surrounding soil and keep water out during construction."

"Really?"

"Works every time. The last thing we want is for the River Spree to flood our tunnel anytime during construction,"

"Do we need high pressure?"

"A little over two atmospheres. Air pressure at sea level is 14.70 pounds per square inch. We'll need to maintain about 30 psi in our tunnel—perhaps a little more."

"How do we increase the pressure?"

"Put in a pressure bulkhead and use an air compressor to pump in additional air. Just like inflating a tire."

"Why two doors?"

"Two doors will allow us to maximize the construction rate. One crew removes excavated soil and replenishes tunnel support sections by opening the first door and returning that area to normal pressure levels. The second door remains closed and the second crew operates the TBM without interruption at the desired pressure level."

He nodded. "I understand. Go on."

"There's one important thing you need to know."

"What's that?"

"This added pressure creates problems for the construction crew. Moving too quickly from an area of high pressure to normal pressure can produce nitrogen gas bubbles in the body. It's commonly called the bends, which can obstruct blood flow, can also be very painful and is sometimes fatal."

"Sounds like a construction delay," Mark observed.

"Yes. Five to six hundred feet of our tunnel under the river will be constructed at higher pressure levels. We'll install a decompression chamber to slowly bring the workers back to normal surface pressures.

"So, for a significant percentage of each shift, the workers will need to be in the decompression chamber. Correct?"

"Yes. The one data point I remember off the top of my head is three hours of work at 30 psi requires almost two hours in a decompression chamber."

"Won't we be tunneling under the damaged part of the building?"

"Yes, but the tunnel will pass safely 20 feet under the lowest part of the foundation and bottom of the columns in that area."

"Looks like you have a strong case for the changes, Robert, but you don't have to convince me. You must convince two Washington bureaucrats and General Harrison. I'll arrange for you to meet with them next Tuesday."

Feet of Tunnel Completed: 0   Days until Deadline: 335

CHAPTER 21

Friday, October 28, 1960

AFTER A DELICIOUS meal at a traditional German restaurant, Anna and I walked over to Kdamm Street as some of the locals and most of the Americans called it. We reached the "The Swing Point Club," where they played recordings of the latest dance tunes from America, alternating between rock-and-roll and slow dance ballads.

I held Anna close during the *Theme from a Summer Place,* The Drifter's *Save the Last Dance for Me,* and Elvis's *It's Now or Never.* We twisted with Chubby Checker and did the bop to Elvis's *Stuck on You.* Sometime during the night, we joined a conga line for the "Bunny Hop" and the "Hokey Pokey." Neither of us were ready to quit when they closed at two a.m.

Since it was so late, I hailed a taxi. We snuggled in the back seat, indulging in restrained kisses with an experimental meeting of tongues.

As we neared her apartment, I said, "Anna, I'll be flying back to the States on Sunday. I'll only be gone a few days. When I return next Friday, we'll go out for a special meal and to a movie or dancing, whichever you would prefer."

"I'll look forward to it all week."

I told the driver, "Please wait. I want you to take me to Tempelhof Airport."

A car pulled up. A tall, thin man who had followed us the previous weekend got out.

I glanced in his direction as I escorted Anna to her apartment door. We exchanged several goodnight kisses and fervent embraces. Before I turned to leave, Anna whispered in my ear, "Why is an obvious East German Stasi agent following you?"

"I'm not sure." I shrugged and walked back to the taxi.

CHAPTER 22

Tuesday, November 1, 1960

STANDING IN THE shower that morning in the motel in Laurel, Maryland, I felt a panic attack coming on. It hit as I was reviewing my arguments for the use of the ramp to solve the tunneling problem.

By the time I toweled off, I was hyperventilating. I stretched out on the bed. *Deep breaths…use your diaphragm to bring the good air in…relax…just relax…good air in…bad air out…..*

Despite the panic attack, I managed to arrive at nearby Fort George G. Meade Army Base a few minutes early. The National Security Agency Headquarters, a nondescript two-story building, sat near a massive new headquarters building under construction. After a few minutes in the badge and identification office, I was escorted into Mr. Scherman's outer office.

A balding, overweight, friendly man in an obviously expensive suit emerged from his office. With a broad smile and firm handshake, he said, "I'm Gerald Scherman."

I followed him to a tank similar to the one at Tempelhof, where I met another individual.

"Captain Robert Kerr, this is Thomas Lane. He's here representing the CIA on this joint CIA/NSA program."

Mr. Lane offered his hand with the palm down and frowned, indicating his disdain for a lowly Air Force captain. He had a well-groomed mustache and more hair than Mr. Scherman. These guys could've been twins—middle-aged men of a similar medium height, pin-striped suits, white shirts with button-down collars, thin dark gray ties, and rotund bodies.

"Thomas, I and your Security Service commanding officer, General Harrison, are responsible for your tunneling efforts," explained Gerald Scherman. "The General is in the Far East, so only the two of us will meet with you this morning."

I'd counted on General Harrison's support. Now, somehow, I needed to convince two strangers of the merits of my plan.

"We're hoping we'll be able to talk out all the issues, reach unanimous decisions and work as a team. Do you think meeting every two to three months will be sufficient?"

"Construction is a fluid environment," I replied. "We may need to communicate more often."

Gerald Scherman said, "Couriers are available at both ends to carry voluminous written correspondence and documents back and forth...."

"—For most communications, double encrypted messages will be used," Thomas Lane interjected. "You'll be required to submit a weekly progress report to all three of us every Friday via that means."

"Where would we meet?" I asked.

"Primarily here in my tank. We might travel to Berlin on occasion," Gerald replied.

Thomas added forcefully, "Robert, we expect you to keep us informed of all problems and your progress weekly, or more frequently, as required. Anything that impedes progress must be reported to us immediately! Is that clear?"

I nodded. "Yes, sir."

"Gerald and I are the decision makers. You're the individual who implements our instructions. Is that clear?"

"Yes, sir," I replied, wondering what had happened to the 'we're a team concept' Gerald described earlier. Thomas apparently didn't agree with his previous statements. More importantly, what about General Harrison's role as a decision maker?

"You received this assignment because my good friend, Phillip Jeffers, one of your Cal professors, highly recommended you." Gerald smiled at me.

"We're concerned though. You've been in Berlin for just three weeks and you're already changing things we thought were settled," Thomas thundered.

Using the plans and other documents couriered to D.C. over the previous weekend, I spent the next hour providing the rationale for the ramp tunnel option.

When I explained the need for pressure doors, Thomas again became combative. "This is the first we've heard of this need to keep water out while we dig under that river. You're telling us that this will dramatically slow progress and increase the number of needed personnel. Why are we just learning about this now?"

"Sir, you'd have to ask my predecessor."

"How many people will you need?" Thomas demanded.

"I've completed a time and motion study, using the excavation rate of our TBM. I believe that at least sixty-two individuals with substantial construction experience will be required."

"What's a time and motion study?" Gerald asked.

"It's a new method which determines how long it takes to perform individual tasks. Then the tasks are aggregated, and the number of men required to perform a program, in this case building the tunnel, is determined."

Thomas glowered at me, but I continued, "As many as possible should speak German, with at least fifteen who have no discernable accent!"

"Why? Again, young man, this is the first we've heard of that requirement!" Thomas exclaimed.

"Before I became involved, it was decided to build the tunnel in a very densely populated urban area. Native German-speaking workers will be needed to perform all of the tasks that require interfacing with the local population both around the building and in Berlin itself. This is essential if we have a chance to hide this construction project in plain sight."

In a friendly tone, Gerald asked, "Why sixty-two?"

"To have any chance of meeting your construction deadline, we'll need two shifts running the Tunnel Boring Machine (TBM) up to sixteen hours a day. Here's a breakdown of my current plan." I handed several sheets of paper to Gerald Scherman.

Thomas stood and shouted, "We're acting as if this **kid** has the job and we plan to blindly follow his lead by building the ramp tunnel and then just hope for the best!"

I kept my facial expression neutral as Thomas Lane stomped around the room.

I wondered, *What I had done to warrant his obvious displeasure.*

"How old are you?" Thomas asked me in the condescending tone one would use with a misbehaving child.

"Twenty-six." I quickly lost respect for this pompous ass.

"Do you have any construction experience?"

"A year and a half at March Air Force Base, building hangers and runways."

"Wasn't that as a sub-contracts administrator, not a hands-on construction manager?"

"I was also responsible for directing the efforts of twenty-three people, who performed maintenance and repairs of the entire base infrastructure."

"Supervising the replacement of toilets in the Officer's Club is a far cry from being responsible for the construction of the United States most critical intelligence collection facility while trying to meet what you've characterized today as an 'impossible deadline'!"

I declined to dignify that personal rebuke with a response.

"Neither Gerald nor I are engineers, so I am very troubled by the prospect of allowing you to be solely responsible for this construction project," Thomas barked, shaking his index finger at me in a hostile manner.

Gerald pointed out the obvious. "Thomas, you know Robert is the only individual with the right clearance who was available in time to meet our deadline."

"We should immediately explore alternatives!"

Standing, Gerald approached Thomas, his demeanor and gestures designed to be calming. "I know you are concerned that failure of the tunneling project will affect your next promotion, but you must be reasonable. Let's take this discussion to my office. It's not Captain Kerr's fault he was the only choice available."

I was astonished by their exchange. Thomas Lane voiced the same fears I harbored, but I detested his belligerent grandstanding.

When the two men returned, Gerald carried a metal case, which measured perhaps one foot by three feet by eight inches. "Put all of the material you need to describe your plan in here. It is a classified document courier case; the combination is 24-34-17. A staff car's waiting to take you to Army Corp of Engineering Headquarters in Washington, D.C."

I stood and placed the materials on the table into the courier case. I'd do almost anything to get away from Thomas Lane, who sat in a nearby chair and glared at me.

Gerald continued, "Colonel George Stevens will meet you there. Tell him everything you've told us. He's fully cleared for this project and has twenty-seven years of civil engineering experience. If you can convince him that the ramp in the location you've selected is the correct choice, then the matter will be settled."

Thomas added, "At least, for now."

I didn't bother with a reply, although I nodded at Gerald Scherman as I departed.

Feet of Tunnel Completed: 0   Days until Deadline: 331

CHAPTER 23

Tuesday, November 1, 1960

COLONEL GEORGE STEVENS, whose uniform displayed an impressive collection of ribbons, had gray, thinning hair, and a welcoming countenance. He'd arranged for a catered lunch. To begin the meeting Colonel Stevens said, "Meet Senior Master Sergeant Neal Loring. He will lead the Corp of Engineers team, which will arrive in Berlin in January."

Sergeant Loring's firm, two-handed handshake was welcoming. He was short with broad shoulders and the ramrod-straight military bearing of a career soldier. His appearance spoke volumes—immaculate uniform, very short haircut, thin mustache precisely located in the middle of his broad lip, and jutting chin.

"Captain Kerr, as I understand it, what Mr. Scherman and Mr. Lane expect from us is to validate or reject your concept for the building of the tunnel. Correct?" Colonel Stevens asked.

"Yes, sir." I then gave the same briefing I'd just presented to Gerald and Thomas. For this audience, I used more technical terms and provided significantly greater details. In return, I received more penetrating questions. Most I fielded without difficulty.

After my briefing, the Colonel said, "That all makes sense. What you're suggesting is a conventional tunnel, which would begin at the bottom of a ramp. Tell me about it. First, why?"

I provided a lengthy explaination, concluding with the comment, "We don't have to worry about the structural integrity of the southeast end of the building—we'll be twenty feet below it when the tunnel reaches that point."

An hour later, the colonel stood to stretch his legs "If you want a job after you get out of the Air Force, come see me. I'd hire you in a minute. Your plan to install two pressure doors to maximize the construction rate is clever. I'll have to remember that one."

"Thank you, sir. I appreciate your validation of my concept."

As I put away my materials, the Colonel approached to shake my hand. "Captain, I have another meeting now. You have my full endorsement, and I'll inform our friends at Fort Meade of that fact."

"Thank you, sir."

"And Captain, I hope you've taken the admonitions of your superiors to heart. I believe your tunnel is the most important construction project the United States government has undertaken recently."

"That's what everyone keeps telling me."

"Since 1945, the Russians have won on virtually every front. We desperately need the intelligence this tunnel will provide to reverse that course of events. It's the reason I've assigned my best people, led by Sergeant Loring here, to help you. Make this pipe dream a reality. We're relying on you!" He smiled, patting me on the back.

"Sergeant Loring," he added, "immediately determine if any of your men can speak German. Most can operate any machines or vehicles you can name and do any construction job."

I shook the Sergeant's hand. "I'm genuinely glad you'll be leading the team, and I'm looking forward to working with you."

"Thank you, sir. Together, we'll crack this nut."

"All of your men will be required to look like Germans while on this assignment. Tell them to start letting their hair grow out now. No GI buzz cuts or white side walls. Be sure their superiors don't give them a hard time over that in the interim."

"I'll make sure they understand the importance of this request, sir."

Informing Anna by telephone that my return would be delayed for a week proved difficult. Several military operators refused to connect a personal call, and long-distance calls were prohibitively expensive. Finally, the best I could manage was when an individual who identified himself as the manager of the Post Exchange at Tempelhof agreed to tell her of my change of plans.

My itinerary took me to six cities, eight business firms, and a tour of two tunnels that were currently under construction. When I boarded my flight back to Europe, I felt certain that my ramp tunnel was the correct solution for the task I'd been assigned. I couldn't wait to get back to Anna.

Feet of Tunnel Completed: 0   Days until Deadline: 331

CHAPTER 24

Friday, November 11, 1960

AFTER I ARRIVED back at Tempelhof early Friday morning, I went immediately to the bookstore. After being told that Anna was on a break and would return shortly, the clerk said, "I believe she anticipated your return **last** Friday, and she was disappointed when you did not show up for your date."

Oh, shit! She apparently hadn't gotten my message about my delayed return. *What could I do to make amends? I know—that little shop in the airport terminal.*

A few minutes later, I returned to the bookstore. The bell over the door rang as I entered. Anna stood directly before me. The surprised look on her face was followed by a brief smile and then a scowl. She turned her back on me, walked into her office, and slammed the door.

Although I expected her to be angry, the intensity of her reaction gave me pause. The clerk at the front desk gave me a questioning look. I had to leave or face up to Anna's displeasure. I hadn't heard the lock on her office door click shut. Without knocking, I tried the lever, pushed open the door, and stepped inside. Extending the giant bouquet of red roses I hid behind my back, I pleaded in English, "Please forgive me. I tried very hard to let you know my return was delayed."

She frowned, turned her back to me and moved toward the back door. I stepped into her path and switched to German. Soon she giggled as she faced me and declared, "Your German is worse when you get excited and try to use the familiar form. We must work on that. I forgive you. I was just worried something terrible had happened to you."

Putting my arms around her waist, I whispered in her ear, "I had a rather special night planned. Supper at the Zum Hugenotten Restaurant in the Intercontinental Hotel and dancing at the bar on the roof of the hotel until dawn. Remember I need to stay awake until tomorrow evening."

She clasped my face with her hands and kissed me. "The entire evening sounds wonderful."

"I'll even pick you up in Cinderella's carriage or perhaps a taxi—depending on what I can find. I'll be there at…say 7:30." After a hug and another long kiss, I walked out, throwing a thumbs up to the nosy clerk.

Anna wore a light blue shimmering silk, full-skirted dress with puffy sleeves.

"Wow! You're a knockout!" I proclaimed as I fell to the floor.

She dropped to her knees, sure I'd fainted. I took her in my arms and began to passionately kiss her. She finally pulled back. "You are going to mess up my makeup, and my dress will get wrinkled. Get up, silly clown."

I stood, helped her to her feet, gave her a light kiss, bowed and then announced, "Your chariot awaits, my princess."

The maitre d' assisted Anna into her ornately carved chair. The French Provencial style table was covered with crisp white linen, crystal glasses, fine china, flickering candles inside of a heavy cut-glass holder, and a fresh flower centerpiece.

She took my hand, squeezed it, and whispered, "If you were trying to impress a girl, you have certainly succeeded." We both marveled at the scene. High ceilings adorned with large crystal chandeliers complemented the walls covered with intricate molding, dark red-flocked wallpaper, cut-glass sconces, and antique étagères and sideboards.

I squeezed back. "Am I forgiven?"

"Yes, I was primarily concerned that something had happened to you or you did not really care for me."

"I care for you more than you know!" I announced, clasping her outstretched hands.

Our meal proved memorable—excellent wine and food, exceptional service and a posh setting. We were together, laughing, flirting and holding hands.

CHAPTER 25

Anna

Friday, November 11, 1960

THE VIEW OF the lights of Berlin from our table in the rooftop bar was spectacular. I especially remember Robert observing, "One can certainly see the dividing line between the two Berlins. Bright lights on this side and relative darkness over in the East. It's almost as if there's no human activity on the other side of the line that divides this city."

We sipped champagne and danced until the orchestra stopped playing. We followed our taxi ride to his apartment with a glass of wine on his worn couch. For the first time, I let a man hold me and kiss me passionately. I followed his lead, returning his kisses with abandon. Our lips fused and our tongues explored. Soon we were both breathing heavily. Then, he stroked my breast and cupped it with his hand. I froze, flashing back to an alley when I was only seven years old. Fright gripped me. I pushed him away.

Looking shocked, he anxiously asked, "What is wrong, Anna darling. Have I hurt you in some way?"

I shook my head, still shaken by the flashback. "Robert, it's not you, it's me."

"I don't understand."

"It isn't something that's easy for me to talk about."

"I'm a good listener and our relationship means everything to me. Tell me, please Anna." He used his fingertip to gently tilt my head up so he could see my face.

"I'll try," I said swallowing hard. "I was just seven years old in March 1945, which was when the Russians surrounded Berlin. They cut off all avenues of escape. My family, like most others, was trapped. As several million people waited for the inevitable Russian attack, food supplies rapidly dwindled. Because I was so young, I was frightened and confused."

"Our home was in northeast Berlin, away from the government, railroad and factory targets of central and southern Berlin. This meant that most of the late 19th-century, gray stone homes in our neighborhood were spared the devastation. Soon, Russian shells started to fall all around us. Our electric and gas service stopped. We hid in the cellar, seldom venturing out, because the shelling was intermittent and often started without warning.

"I will never forget when one night my mother told us we had no more bread. We ate cabbage soup in the morning and potato soup in the evening. Each day for the next several weeks, my fifteen-year-old sister, Sophia, and I ventured out to collect boards from the back fence. We started the fire so mama could prepare our meals in a black pot that hung on the hook over the fireplace. I had difficulty sleeping because I was hungry, terribly hungry. Everyone's portions grew steadily smaller."

I blinked back tears. "We knew our defenders had failed to keep the Russians out when the guns finally fell silent. Papa went out on a reconnaissance mission, but soon returned and told us, 'Russian troops are looting occupied houses across the street at gunpoint. I will reopen the surgery. Perhaps they will respect the property of a healer.' Amazingly, they didn't touch our house. In fact, Russian soldiers soon lined up outside his surgery as Papa treated their numerous infirmities. In return, they gave us a little food, some wine, and vodka. My father continued to treat our neighbors and strangers for numerous maladies, including wounds inflicted by the Russians, but his medical supplies were rapidly depleted. He shook his head as he whispered to my mother frequently about the number of women who had been violated. I only vaguely knew what that meant.

"By mid-May, the five of us had not eaten for a few days. Some of my father's German patients paid him in then-worthless Reichsmarks. His requests for food went unheeded. The only time I heard my father curse was when he returned home from a fruitless search for food, saying, 'Those

God-damned Russians. They have intentionally stopped food supplies from reaching Berlin. Revenge on all of us for the war that madman Hitler caused.' One night, Sophia awakened me. She said 'I cannot sleep. I'm too hungry. Come with me. We'll find food in the Schaffers' house. They fled Berlin in February with their daughter, Gisela. There were cabbages, turnips, hams, and large rounds of wurst in their basement.' I told her, 'Someone will already have taken that food.'

"Sophia said the food was well hidden behind a false wall. I dressed and followed her out the back door. As we moved through the shadows of a moonlit night in the alley, I heard 'frau, komm' (woman, come), then closer 'ah, fraulein, komm' (young woman, come) in a lustful tone. Five massive Russian shock troops surrounded us. Their strange, filthy faces still haunt me in my sleep. They were apparently from Central Asia." I began to cry, tried but failed to regain my composure and ended up weeping uncontrollably, "They violated Sophia. Papa had to repair her…."

"Anna, it's all right." Robert said. "I don't need to know all of the details now….let me dry your tears….please…please stop now…"

Unable to see through my tears, I blurted out, "She was a virgin and…. she had to have an abortion…."

Robert shook his head as if to clear it, handed me his handkerchief, and said, "Use this to blow your nose and dry your tears."

When I finished, he pulled me to my feet and embraced me. We stood this way for a long time. He then lightly kissed my lips. "It is too late for you to return to your apartment, darling. You take the bed, I have to stay awake all night, anyway."

After several minutes of back and forth on where I should sleep, Robert said something I'll always remember. "I care for you and want nothing to harm our relationship, so you take the bed. I'll join you briefly, because I want to hold you and reassure you that you're safe with me."

I wore a tight corset. It went from the midriff to the top of the thigh. I could not sleep in it, so I asked Robert for a pair of his pajamas. I changed in his bathroom and then got under the covers in his bed. In a few minutes, he joined me similarly dressed. I snuggled into his arms and fell asleep. He woke me up when he left the bed later. Nothing happened—beyond a kiss on the top of my head.

The next morning Robert came into the room, sat on the bed and announced, "It's after 10 a.m., party girl. Time to face the world." After kissing my cheek, he declared, "Anna, you're very precious to me. I'm absolutely willing to wait until you're ready. Until then, I would like to make you part of my life."

I melted into his arms—we'd committed to having a future together.

CHAPTER 26

Robert
Monday, November 14, 1960

AS A RESULT of my trip to Washington D.C., I was required to prepare and send a weekly status report on the tunneling program to the three decision makers.

TOP SECRET LUMAR—RESTRICTED
DISTRIBUTION—US EYES ONLY

Memorandum #1 from Captain Robert Kerr   Berlin,November 14, 1960

After leaving Fort Meade last week, I issued purchase orders for the following equipment and supplies:

1. Ninety-eight (98) fifty-five-gallon drums of Bentonite, a highly absorbent clay derived from weathered volcanic ash. When mixed with water and injected into our Berlin sand, it should form a hard surface which water can't easily penetrate. Our Bosch TBM head has a 360-degree slurry-coat injection nozzle system, so our equipment is capable of supporting its use. Once dry, it will support the sand long enough for our erector to place sections of the tunnel structure into position.

2. Ten (10) battery-powered mining tractors and twenty-two (22) mining carts (14 designed for soil removal and 8 for equipment

transport). Six (6) electric personnel transport vehicles. All ordered from Caterpillar in Peoria, Illinois.

3. Two (2) pressure doors designed for a 3-meter tunnel; five (5) air compressors with automatic feedback loops and one (1) prefabricated 20-man decompression chamber from the US subsidiary of Booth Industries of Britain. They will be taken from stock in the UK and trucked to Rhein-Main AFB next week. This equipment can then be transported with the tunneling equipment to Berlin via the Pregnant Guppy.

4. Miscellaneous electrical and hydraulic tools from Milwaukee Power Tools Company, located in the city of the same name. List attached.

I also visited Bechtel in San Francisco where I interned for two summers while an undergraduate. They took me on tours of two California tunnel construction projects. One was located beneath a river. I was able to talk with project managers, construction supervisors, and tunnel boring machine operators. I now feel more confident this project can be successfully completed.

Signed,

Robert T. Kerr, Captain USAF

**TOP SECRET LUMAR—RESTRICTED
DISTRIBUTION—US EYES ONLY**

Feet of Tunnel Completed: 0   Days until Deadline: 318

CHAPTER 27

Anna

THURSDAY, NOVEMBER 17, 1960

TODAY AFTER WORK, Robert and I left the base, holding hands for the first time. The sun had set over an hour earlier, but there was no wind, the temperature was moderate, and we were warmly dressed. The street lights provided an inviting path to our destination, a nearby restaurant. We passed a small park, and I led him to a well-lit bench. "I want to finish my description of that night, so you will understand why I fear the touch of men, all men, including Papa, my brother and….even you. I'll tell it in English to ensure you understand it all. Once I've told you, then we need never talk about it again."

I took both of his hands into mine, looked him straight in the eye. Intent on remaining calm, I began to explain what happened "that night."

"The five giant Russian monsters surrounded Sophia and me. First, they searched us, then ripped off our clothes. They made comments to each other, but we did not understand what they said. They had not bathed for weeks or even months—the stench they gave off made me nauseous. They were filthy, and they all had long scraggly beards and hair.

"One of the men groped me, digging his rough hands into the flesh between my legs. He made a comment, and they all laughed uproariously. I tried to run away, but he grabbed my hair with one hand and placed his free arm around my neck."

I bit my lip as my chin quivered. I fought off the urge to burst into tears, but managed to continue, knowing I needed Robert to understand. "One grabbed me when I tried to run away. I wanted to get help. The other four shoved Sophia down onto the muddy, cobblestoned street. I tried to look away, but my captor used his iron grip to ensure I watched them rape my beloved sister. She whimpered but did not resist. She seemed to sense they would have beaten or killed her had she struggled. Soon, blood covered Sophia's lower body.

"By this point, I was crying so hard I could barely see. I struggled and cried for help. The man holding me placed his arm over my nose and mouth. I could not breathe and went limp. He took his arm away. I became cold, very cold.

"All the while, jovial banter was being exchanged between our captors. Next, they turned Sophia over and spread her legs wide. Now the man who had been holding me took his huge penis out of his pants, flashed it toward me and made me touch it. He then knelt down and inserted it into Sophia's anus. Her loud scream so frightened me, I hid my face in the foul garment of the Russian who caught me as I again tried to run away. After the last man finished with Sophia, he took his limp penis in his hand and approached me, making another comment which elicited mirth from the others.... I was shoved to the ground, sure my turn was next. The five soldiers sauntered down the street, as if nothing had happened."

I again felt the cold terror of that night. I began to weep. Robert took me in his arms. We sat in silence for a long time. Then I looked up into his face.

Sadness clouded his features as he rasped, "Anna, I can't imagine how much you suffered over the years—you were so young—traumatized by evil no one should be forced to witness or experience." He brushed my tears from my cheeks and kissed me tenderly.

I muttered, "I want to tell you all about it, so...."

He waited patiently until I mustered the strength to continue. "For some minutes after they left, Sophia and I just clung to each other weeping, unable to move. I finally crawled over to our discarded clothes and helped Sophia to dress. I began to sob. Sophia tried to comfort me and she eventually got me dressed. My torn clothes only partially covered me. I felt nauseous and almost fainted. It seemed to take forever as we struggled to our feet and supported each other down that deserted alley. Once we entered our home, my screams for help brought my family down the stairs. Between sobs, Sophia told them, 'Papa, some Russian soldiers hurt me badly.' "

" 'No. Not that, not my sweetheart!' Mama shrieked, knowing she had been raped. Turning to me, she asked, 'Did they also hurt you?' 'Not like that!' I replied. Taking Sophia in his arms Papa shouted 'Those bastards! How could they...my innocent, lovely girl...' Turning to me, he asked, 'Why did you two go outside?'

" 'We thought the Schaffer's left some food behind...' Sophia murmured before she fainted into Papa's arms. Papa shook her vigorously. She revived somewhat, and over time they got her down the stairs into the examining room. Helmuth was told to go back to bed."

Almost afraid to recount this part of that night, I winced but went on, "Once Sophia was undressed and on the examination table, Papa said, 'You must take her hands. I have neither antiseptic nor painkillers. Sorry, Sophia, my dear.' He gave her a piece of gauze, telling her, 'Bite down on this because everything I do will hurt you. Put your feet in the stirrups and slide as far toward me as possible.' The electricity had been off for weeks. All we had were kerosene lamps. Mama held the lamp for Papa. He spent several minutes examining Sophia's vagina and anus, suturing tears. Each time the needle entered her flesh she flinched and squeezed my hands hard, but never cried out. He next closed several cuts on her lower abdomen, which he said were 'caused by something sharp worn by one of the men.' Papa attempted to comfort my sister by saying, 'Sophia, darling, you are severely bruised and will be sore for a few days, but will be okay.' "

"At the time I was happy at Papa's reassuring words. Then, I began to cry. Mama took me in her arms to comfort me. Papa found a bite that one of the Russians had inflicted on Sophia's neck. He used vodka to sterilize that wound. Mama stood her in a tub and washed her. Once Sophia was propped up in bed, Mama went out and soon returned with broth from a neighbor. Papa kept an eye on all of her wounds for several days to make sure she developed no infection. Four weeks later, he performed an abortion on Sophia.

"One night a few weeks later, I heard my parents talking. Mama said,

'Only those barbaric Russians would use organized rape of women as revenge.' Papa replied, 'My associates at the hospital and I have performed several thousand abortions on those victims, and many have one or more venereal diseases. The black-market price of that new drug, penicillin, is beyond the means of those poor women. Our other treatments are not very effective.' "

I looked at Robert. "It was only when I was much older that I understood exactly what my parents were saying. As you know, being touched by a man causes me severe anxiety. That night of dancing with you was the first time I hadn't panicked at having a man's arms around me."

"What about your sister? Is she all right?" Robert asked.

I nodded. "Within three years, Sophia married and now has three children. We never discuss that night. As far as I can tell, she's been able to block it out or otherwise cope with it. I was the one who suffered as I was growing up. I felt raped in repeated nightmares and flashbacks."

Taking me in his arms, Robert whispered, "Anna, I'm surprised you were able to recount such a harrowing experience without breaking down. You're very brave."

"I knew I had to tell you. I've frequently rehearsed in my mind what I would say. I'm happy you now know it all. It's a big relief."

"Please, remember you're safe with me. I promise to never do anything to cause you distress. If you ever feel even the least bit uncomfortable, tell me—I'll immediately stop whatever's bothering you."

I snuggled into his arms. We sat there in silence knowing we had passed another significant milestone in our developing relationship.

CHAPTER 28

Robert
Thursday, November 24, 1960

"HOW IN THE world does one have Thanksgiving in Berlin?" I'd asked Scott the previous week.

"All the Officers Clubs put on lavish spreads, but the best is at the main club in Clay Compound. All the brass and civilian VIPs will be there. Advanced reservations are required, and they've been booked up for weeks."

"Doesn't sound like a fun place for the likes of us, even if we could get in!"

"It's a mid-afternoon sit-down meal here at the Tempelhof Club for us, I'm afraid."

"Why don't we have a party?"

"Neither Mia nor I can boil water, and takeout pizza isn't really appropriate for this particular holiday."

"Anna is an excellent cook. She wants to do a combined Thanksgiving Dinner and housewarming for my new apartment, and you're invited."

Two friends from the base agreed to come to the party; one married to an American girl, the other asked if Anna could arrange a blind date for him with one of her friends. Everyone had the day off because they worked for American companies or on the base.

On Monday, I bought a turkey at the commissary, only to be confronted by the tiny refrigerator in my apartment. "It'll never fit," I said to Anna.

In English, Anna said, "It's frozen, and we must let it "unfreeze" in the refrigerator. If we leave it out, it'll spoil."

"Anna, darling, the correct word in English is 'defrost.' "

"That doesn't make any sense, frost is moisture that forms outside in the winter, isn't it?"

"I know. English has many words and phrases that make no sense. Whereas German is so precise and exact." Laughing and taking her in my arms. "A good example is that refrigerator is kuhlscharnk, cool cabinet in German, a very descriptive word. I have no idea where we English got the word refrigerator."

Anna smiled. "This is what we'll do—take everything out of the refrigerator, put the turkey in, put as much back as possible, and cook everything else for supper this evening."

Of course, Anna's solution worked perfectly.

By the time our guests arrived Thanksgiving Day, dinner was in the oven. We suggested a game of couple's team English-German Scrabble—words could be made in either language. We had a rousing time, five Americans and three Germans challenging each other on words in both languages while consuming copious amounts of good German white wine and beer.

From time to time, Anna or I popped into the kitchen to check on the meal.

Dinner went exceptionally well as the turkey was done to perfection and the pumpkin pie (Anna's first) was only a little over-done.

Later, we divided into two teams and played charades.

After our guests departed, Anna hugged me and exclaimed, "I so wanted your holiday to be like it is in America. You're so far away from family on this special day."

"Anna, darling, I feel like my home and family are here in this room. Your meal was as good as any I ever ate at home. Thank you."

We went to bed together, Anna falling asleep almost immediately. I avoided touching her, as I didn't want ruin our budding relationship

CHAPTER 29

Friday, November 25, 1960

I awoke with a start and soon realized that Anna was sleeping on her side and her hand rested on my shoulder. She was touching me in this intimate setting—that was good. We both had this Friday after Thanksgiving off. I got up, determined to let her sleep in. A few hours later I kissed her forehead and served her breakfast in bed.

Later, we walked hand-in-hand to the Dahlem Museum, which Anna explained "houses almost exclusively European old-masters paintings. This collection was divided after the war and about half of our finest works are now in the East, on Museum Island."

"What happened to these works of art during the war?" I asked.

"What's here was hidden in an old salt mine in Bavaria. Unfortunately, all of the largest works, which were some of the finest, were stored in a nearby bomb shelter. Despite being underground and supposedly safe, all of them were destroyed in a fire-bomb raid toward the end of the war."

Her facial expression revealed she felt the loss at a personal level. "That's unfortunate," I said, touching Anna's arm.

"Let's see the magnificent works that survived," she replied in an effort to lighten the mood.

Walking into a nearby gallery, Anna said, "Ah so, here is one of the best. Jan Vermeer's *The Glass of Wine*. See how the light entering the room through the window illuminates a scene where a young woman shares a glass of wine with a young man. Vermeer just hints at the relationship between them. Get close and see the minute details displayed in this relatively small painting. He mastered…."

For the next several hours, Anna took me from one painting to the next. She provided spellbinding explanations of the lives of the artists, why each painting was an important work, and how they were produced and authenticated. Late in the day, she said, "And now we come to one of my favorites—Pieter Brugel's *Dutch Proverbs*. It was painted in an era when few could read, so this was a visual morality lesson. Let's see how many of the hundred proverbs we can find these tiny figures performing…."

On the way back to my apartment, we stopped at a restaurant for supper. During the meal, I thanked Anna for the wonderful day, especially her detailed descriptions of the works of art. She clearly cared about art, and I had a greater appreciation of her desire to complete her art history studies.

"First the Nazis and now the communists want to control and subvert the natural human desire to express ourselves through art. That is why it is so important for me to study and understand this creative desire. Robert, I must complete my education and help promote the freedom of expression that is our human right."

I smiled, nodded my agreement and tenderly caressed Anna's hand, not wanting to spoil the mood with words.

CHAPTER 30

Saturday, November 26, 1961

THE NEXT MORNING Anna gave me a present—*Komplettes Menschliches Sex-Handbuch*—The Complete Human Sex Manual. "When I was at Heidelberg, I had some therapy sessions. The psychologist recommended I use a sex education book like this with a man I liked to overcome my phobia."

I was speechless, so she added, "If I'm ever going to get over my fear of men, you'll have to be patient with me. We'll read this manual—it'll be therapy for me, and you might even learn a thing or two."

We sat there fully clothed and began to read and discuss the manual together. The glossary had to be consulted to explain many of the terms used in the descriptions of physiology, foreplay, stimulation and sexual positions.

For the next month and a half, our love grew as we explored each other's bodies and learned how to please each other, remaining chaste in the process.

CHAPTER 31

Monday, November 28, 1960

AFTER GREETING SCOTT in my tank, I groused, "I spent most of the last two days in my apartment. Every time I looked out the window facing the street, one or more Stasi agents were standing on the curb. Even through that snow storm, they were always there. They certainly are dedicated."

"So, you really need counter-surveillance training. My Special Investigations Officers training course included Counter Surveillance. Because I was coming to Berlin, I was provided with a refresher course on the same subject at the CIA Training Center at Quantico, Virginia."

"Impressive credentials."

"Virtually all surveillance and counter-surveillance involve human interaction. People are both more vulnerable to another person's actions and more capable of reacting creatively to being monitored."

"That certainly makes sense."

"What we are going to cover today are just the basics, which are known in the spy business by the acronym SELCH."

Laughing, I repeated, "SELCH. Okay. Enlighten me."

"The 'S' stands for **Situational awareness**. The 'E' stands for **Evasion**."
I nodded.

"Remember when we headed over to the building the first time? I exercised the first two; I saw a Stasi agent, realized we were being followed and went to the Hilton to take evasive action."

"Got it. That's straightforward."

"A significant percentage of your encounters will be solved by the intelligent use of those first two tactics."

"I understand. How about the other three letters?"

The 'L' is a little more difficult—**Leave a location or area without being seen or followed."**

"I suspect this one is simple in theory, but harder in fact. These guys seem to have the ability to latch on to me."

"You're right, but we'll practice this one—training is required. "C" stands for **Conceal your identity**. Both L and C involve some sort of deception. Having your construction crew come and go through the airport arrivals hall and then blend into the millions of Berliners heading to and from work is an excellent example of these two."

"With your help, we're already employing four of the five counter-surveillance techniques. Interesting," I observed.

"The 'H' is **Hide your presence or intentions."**

"I know, we're already doing this by hiding our tunnel construction efforts."

"You got it, good buddy. At first, I thought this was an oversimplification of the myriad of encounters one has in the spy game. After more than two years here, I have yet to find anything that isn't covered by these five counter-surveillance techniques."

"I agree; it seems oversimplified."

"Do you recall in our first security meeting, I indicated that there are perhaps thirty Stasi agents who do nothing but monitor our activities at the base?"

"Yes, of course."

Scott spread out twenty-one candid photos and said, "The men in these pictures, and probably a number we've not yet identified, are assigned to provide full-time surveillance of our little Air Force base. They work rotating shifts so at least two or three of them are always here."

"What about the guys who were standing outside of my apartment."

"I bet if you look closely, they're some of this lot. Most of them live in the East and come over here every day by subway. I'll leave these photos here. Memorize their appearance and start immediately looking for them."

"That seems like a logical thing to do."

"If known, their names are written on the back of their photo. Otherwise, they are given a number."

"I definitely saw number eight outside of my apartment several times."

"Keep a detailed written record of each sighting—who, where, when and what they did…"

"—Then I give it back to you for your files, I assume."

"You got it, old buddy. Eventually, you'll even be able to pick them out of a crowd. After you observe what they do, then you'll start seeing them talk to others or see similar surveillance tactics. Detecting these guys will become second nature."

"Isn't that Dieter Holburg?"

"Yes, last week our sources reported he's been given full responsibility for surveillance of the base and you. He's a high-level agent. Congratulations, the enemy is interested in you!"

"That's not a distinction I want or need. What're we going to do?"

"I think it's time for a little concealment—if we can convince them you're head of the weather station here, perhaps they'll lose interest. Let me think about it for a while longer."

"That sounds difficult to me, but…"

"—I have an idea, but I need to mull it over before we implement it. Here are two of my surveillance/counter surveillance training manuals. Study them when you get a chance."

"You indicated we're going to meet here Tuesday and Thursday mornings for one hour until I'm a trained spy."

"Yes, and after a while, we'll go out on real training exercises. You'll soon be as proficient as James Bond."

"Are they going to start sending beautiful spies to lure me into compromising positions?"

"You'll be immune to their ploy because you have Anna! Remember!"

"Hope so! However, it'd be fun to resist the temptation."

We both laughed as Scott left the tank.

Feet of Tunnel Completed: 0   Days until Deadline: 303

CHAPTER 32

Friday, December 2, 1960

EARLY THIS MORNING, I was again called to Colonel Morgan's office. "I thought we had an agreement that you'd stop seeing Miss Fischer. I saw you leave the base with her last week, hand-in-hand."

"Well, sir. I'm seeing her and intend to continue. If you decide to make an issue of my relationship with her, I'll understand. I consider this to be a personal matter, which shouldn't be within the purview of my superiors."

It was clear the Colonel hadn't expected my reply. He declared, "Captain, I believe you're mistaken if you believe this is the end of this matter! Your words are very close to insubordination, which is punishable under the Uniform Code of Military Justice. I don't want to mar your unblemished record, but I will if you persist in refusing my order! You're excused!"

At my weekly meeting with Mark that afternoon in my tank, he urged me, "Robert, please reconsider your decision to defy Colonel Morgan's order about dating Miss Fischer. We need you to help us dig this all-important tunnel. Colonel Morgan is a terrific guy, who's only trying to do his job. He'll have you sent back to the States if we can't resolve this matter."

"You and Mr. Scherman have both told me that I'm the only qualified person available to manage this project. Sending me back to the States won't accomplish any of our objectives. Can't the Colonel just accept that Anna and I are very close and want to be together?"

"He's indicated he's about to revoke your security clearance which means you'll immediately be shipped back to the States. I'll reiterate your position to Colonel Morgan. Don't assume this discussion closes this matter. With that said, do we have any tunnel-related matters to discuss?"

"I want you to evaluate a few ideas. They'll help us solve a variety of real and potential problems," I responded, hoping my technical prowess would dispel the tension between us and convince the Colonel to keep me on this job.

"Enlighten me."

"You may recall that I showed you a report from the Berlin building department, indicating that the entire west bank of the River Spree in our area is high-grade sand sufficiently free of impurities to be used for construction."

"Yes, I recall that conversation."

"You'll also remember that my predecessor wanted us to have the tunnel's structural sections built outside and trucked into the building."

"Yes."

"Even the dumbest spy will figure out what we are doing when thousands of cement tunnel sections are delivered to an existing building. To remodel our building, we should be hauling in much different materials."

"What's the solution?"

"Make the sections in our basement. There's plenty of room."

"Won't we still be hauling in a vast amount of material?"

"Not necessarily. When I built runways at March Field, we used a rock crusher to reduce the concrete slabs into aggregate, which we reused. This reduces the cost of trucking and materials."

"How does that work for this application?"

"We should be able to mix the crushed concrete from the basement slab with the sand we excavate from the hole for the ramp and tunnel. Add cement and water, and the result would be new concrete for the retaining walls, ramp, and tunnel's structural sections."

"I can see the advantage!"

"Concrete is over 50 percent aggregate, 35 percent sand, and only 15 percent cement. Imagine the cost and time savings of only having to haul a few truckloads of cement to build a significant part of the ramp and tunnel."

"Plus, and perhaps most importantly, the outside world, in particular the 'Reds' (communists) from across the river, would have less chance to determine what we're doing here," Mark offered.

"You understand my thought processes."

"That's brilliant! What'll we do when we run out of aggregate from the basement floor?" Mark asked.

"Here in Berlin, I see trucks hauling rubble away from building sites all the time. We'd have our truckers pick up the right kind of rubble, cover the truck bed with tarpaulin, take it to the building, and use that to continue our operations."

"Again, Robert, this sounds like the correct solution to me. Anything else we need to discuss?"

"I just need to remind you that on Monday I leave for London. I'm visiting the Deptford Tunnel, primarily to see the pressure doors we ordered installed and in use."

"Have a safe trip," Mark told me as he exited the tank.

Each day during this period was filled with counter-surveillance training and planning for when construction actually commenced. I worried outsiders would discover the tunnel. Avoiding negative thoughts was hard until I thought of Anna. She became my anchor in a turbulent sea of self-doubt.

Feet of Tunnel Completed: 0   Days until Deadline: 299

CHAPTER 33

Friday, December 2, 1960

IT HAPPENED SLOWLY. Anna spent more and more time in my apartment. Soon her possessions started to occupy more cupboard, shelf, and drawer space. Tonight, as we lay in another chaste embrace, I whispered in her ear, "Why don't you move in with me? You can save the cost of your room."

I was surprised when she replied, "Only if you allow me to share the cost of this apartment. I won't be a kept woman!"

Our back and forth discussion took almost an hour. It became heated, until I finally conceded, "Okay, you win. You'll rent the bedroom from me, and I'll be allowed to occupy your bed as long as I please you."

It took us two trips on the subway to transport all of her possessions to my apartment.

That week I'd received a package from my parents. It contained home-made cookies and a note addressing me as Robbie. Seeing the note, Anna beamed. "Robbie, I like that name. That's what I'll call you."

After some discussion, I persuaded her to only use that name when we were alone.

CHAPTER 34

Thursday, December 8, 1960

AFTER MY FLIGHT from London, I briefly dropped by the office. Mark told me, "the decision-making triumvirate—Harrison, Scherman, and Lane—will be here next Wednesday to give final approval for the tunnel building project."

I told Mark of my unpleasant encounters with Thomas Lane.

"He sounds like a real asshole to me," he commented.

Next, we discussed the briefings we'd give to the VIPs during the upcoming meeting. Since Mark had tasked me with preparing and presenting most of the material, I decided I still had my job.

I studied the personnel list Mark gave me and began to extract what I considered to be the pertinent information.

- Of the thirty-four members of the Army Corp of Engineering team, only four were rated as proficient in German, but all had substantial construction experience. They were scheduled to arrive on January 11, 1961, via military transport and in uniform. Before they arrived, their distinctive Army Corps of Engineers insignia would be replaced with various infantry division badges. They'd be transported to the Replacement Depot in buses. There they would change into civilian clothes, exit McNair Barracks, and enter Tempelhof via the arrival-hall cipher-lock entrance one at a time over a thirty-six-hour period.

- All fifteen of the Air Force reservists from Fort Meade were proficient in German but were American born. In civilian life, five were truck drivers, and four worked in construction. Their arrival dates stretched from January 2 through January 11, 1961, all would arrive via commercial aircraft, and be just another new arrival at Tempelhof Air Force Base.

- Thirteen individuals from the Navy Seabees made up the remainder of the construction crew. A cover letter explained: "Nine of these men grew up in the international city of Gdansk between the two world wars. As refugees before and after the war, they immigrated to the United States. German is their first language. Every effort is being made to grant Top Secret and LUMAR program access to all nine as soon as possible."

All thirteen of the Navy Seabees had worked on a variety of projects scattered all over the world. Since they would be the only US Navy enlisted personnel in Berlin, they would fly via three different commercial aircraft in civilian clothes, arriving here on the fourth of January. They would gather at the Hilton Hotel where Kurt, Scott and I would meet them. We would then provide them instructions on entering the base through the Tempelhof arrivals hall.

Overall, I was pleased. The vast majority were experienced construction workers, and many of them spoke German. My only concern: would the nine Seabees be granted clearances that would allow them to actually work on the tunnel?

Later in the day, Kurt Altschuler dropped by my office. A month earlier I'd handed him a stack of paper, saying, "We need you to acquire all of the construction equipment and supplies on this list from local sources. I've provided specification sheets or other data to ensure we get what we need. New or used doesn't make any difference, as long as they're serviceable."

Today, I asked him, "How are you coming on gathering the equipment from my list?"

"I think we got everything, including the electric cement mixers, hydraulic concrete pumps with conventional and shotcrete nozzles, dump trucks, flatbed trucks, and everything else on the list. The one exception is a hydraulic rock crusher, and it should be delivered next week. We've acquired the assets and name of a defunct construction company, which includes ware-houses and a paved parking area. We've been collecting the equipment there."

"Where is this facility located?"

"Perhaps three miles southwest of our tunnel building in an area of similar businesses."

After his visit, I released a giant sigh of relief. Everything was finally ready to go. The men were scheduled to arrive at the same time as the last of the equipment. Construction could start in early January 1961.

When a program of this magnitude transitioned from the planning to the actual construction phase, mistakes caused significant delays, so I repeatedly reviewed everything.

That afternoon Scott came into the tank. "Old buddy, grab the nameplate off of your desk and follow me."

We entered an office near the roof on the sixth floor. An airman pho-tographer waited for us with a Graflex camera. Following Scott's instruc-tions, he took photos of me at a desk with weather maps in the background and on the roof surrounded by weather instruments.

The photographer assured Scott, "I'll have proofs of all the photos in two hours. Pick the ones you want. Tomorrow morning, the six 8 by 10 framed photos you want will be ready. They'll be date stamped on the back, October 25, 1960, per your request."

Once back in my office, I asked, "What was all that about?"

"The cover and deception begins," he announced, making strange ges-tures with his hands and arms.

"What the hell are you doing?"

"This is a cloak, see covering my lower face with my arm, and I have a dagger in my hand. See...see...cloak and dagger!"

"That money I gave you for acting lessons was totally wasted." We both laughed.

Feet of Tunnel Completed: 0   Days until Deadline: 293

CHAPTER 35

Friday, December 9, 1960

SCOTT ENTERED THE tank with a sly grin on his face. I couldn't help laughing aloud, thinking that he looked like a red-headed weasel who had just caught its favorite prey.

"What's up?"

"Mia and I will meet you and Anna at the Grossbritannien Pub this evening at 5:30, and we'll start our camouflage campaign on your behalf against the Stasi." He was chortling as he exited the tank.

Anna and I led the parade, which consisted of at least the three Stasi agents I could recognize and perhaps others from various other organizations, to the pub, a building with an ornately scrolled black and gold exterior and etched windows. Two signs in front listed the 'Pub Grub on Offer' in German and English. The entrance at the apex of the building led us to a large brass and polished wood bar.

Scott had sold the proprietor on an idea to increase his after-work business. He'd post my five-day weather forecast on a blackboard, and we'd accept bets on its accuracy. Because Berlin weather was so capricious, we expected to lose money but to win by drawing everyone's attention to my 'real profession.'

'Weatherman' photos of me were attached to a poster above the bar.

Scott whistled loudly and then read the sign aloud, "Expert American Weatherman will accept beer bets on the accuracy of his weather forecasts."

His Texas-drawled German was intelligible enough that a line soon formed by those desiring to place a wager. We accepted bets on the amounts and types of precipitation, overcast or any sunshine, and high/low temperature.

Among the first to bet against us was Anna, who encouraged others by shouting loud enough for most of the patrons to hear, "Robert here is my boyfriend. Every time he tells me it is not going to rain, it does."

The patrons clapped, whistled and catcalled.

Scott said, "That is unfair. She has an unfair advantage—she knows him." Uproarious laughter and banter followed this remark.

A while later, at his urging, Mia pointed at Scott. "This one is my friend. He likes to throw his money away on lost causes, like Robert here. I'll bet there will be no sunshine the next five days. A sure bet."

That first week we lost ninety-seven dollars. But several Stasi agents placed bets. And they seemed to especially enjoy their beers.

Later Scott told me about his other steps to validate my weatherman cover. "From now on, several times a day, the Armed Forces Network weather forecast will be attributed to you by name. The Who's Who poster just inside of the front gate at the base now identifies you as the commander of the Berlin USAF weather station."

CHAPTER 36

Saturday, December 10, 1960

ANNA AND I spent several hours that morning studying the sex book. We had gotten to the chapter near the back on sexual dysfunction. It described how various physiological and psychological conditions could affect one's ability to enjoy a healthy sexual relationship.

In the middle of the chapter, Anna suddenly exclaimed, "Remember when you touched my shoulder and caused me great distress? I no longer fear your touch. In fact, just the opposite; it's now electric. I think I'm ready for us to see, feel, and touch each other undressed."

Hugging her, I promised, "Remember, I'll never do anything you don't want. You must always feel safe with me."

She melted into my arms. We sat fully clothed on the couch kissing and caressing each other with great ardor for a long time. I murmured, "We could start now."

Equally breathless, she replied, "I could stay in your arms forever, but promised my parents I'd be home by 5 p.m., so I need to leave soon, Robbie."

"Will you return after lunch tomorrow as usual?"

"Yes, we can spend a leisurely afternoon in bed, reviewing the beginning chapters on how to please your mate. Would you like that?"

"Yes, Anna. I'm anxious to satisfy you in every way I can."

CHAPTER 37

Wednesday, December 14, 1960

AT THE CONCLUSION of my briefing, Thomas Lane stood, banged his fist on Colonel Morgan's conference table, and snarled, "Are we just going to rubber stamp young Captain Kerr's ramp plan? Before he arrived, the tunnel was over 400 feet shorter and required half the workforce! Plus, we'd have reached our objective months earlier!"

Even though I had feared another confrontation with Thomas, I was still surprised by his vehemence. Pausing, then looking over to General Harrison, he continued, "Richard, did anyone ever inform you of this change?"

I sat down, gripping the arms of my chair.

Looking around the room at the other participants in the meeting—Colonel Morgan, Gerald, Mark, Scott, and Kurt—the general pondered his reply. Then, he calmly said, "Gerald sent me a memorandum outlining the issues and stating that the two of you concurred with the decision of the Army Corp of Engineers. That seemed to settle the matter."

"I wasn't convinced at the time, and…"

"—Thomas, you've had two months to raise your concerns. Why now?" Gerald asked.

"As the glossy sales job Colonel Powell and the young captain unfolded, I became less comfortable with that decision!"

"Please voice your concerns now," General Harrison requested.

"The justification this young captain gave to change direction was flimsy at best." He pointed his finger at me.

How could this nitwit not see that, given all the variables, including an unstable building, the ramp tunnel was the only viable solution? And how did I get so high on his shit list? It didn't seem to matter if what I suggested made sense. If I suggested it, he opposed it! But why?

Despite my inner confidence, tension again formed in my diaphragm and around my heart. Now wasn't the right time for another attack. *Deep breaths...more deep breaths.....good...okay...*

"We have no idea what this young captain told Colonel Stevens to convince him to make the decision he did. None of us were there," Thomas persisted, again stabbing his index finger in my direction.

Breathing was becoming more difficult. *You can't have an attack here under any circumstance. That would end everything.*

Gerald rose to his feet and calmly stated, "Colonel Morgan, I believe you indicated we'd have lunch at the Officer's Club at about this time. Why don't we recess and go there now? If I could make a telephone call on the way, perhaps we can straighten this out."

The others left. Once alone, I lay down on one of the conference tables and started my deep breathing exercises. The attack came. I eventually recovered, but it was too late for me to join the others for lunch.

Upon hearing the cipher lock click, I stood in time to see Mark enter. He said, "We missed you at lunch."

"I thought I could use the time to prepare arguments to refute Thomas's contentions this afternoon."

"Robert, you aren't familiar with the games some Washington bureaucrats play. It's called 'covering your ass.' "

"How so?"

"It works like this. He writes a series of Memos for the Record, stating when and how he was repeatedly overruled by other members of a decision-making group. If the project fails, he hauls out the memoranda to prove he professionally executed his responsibilities. His mantra will be: 'This failure wasn't my fault. Those other guys were wrong.' "

"Oh, I see. And if the project is a success, he destroys the memos and claims 'the success is due solely to my brilliant management of every aspect of the project' even though he was seldom within 5,000 miles of it."

"You understand. Thomas needs a scapegoat, and you're it for this project. Don't take it personally!"

"Somehow I sense that he genuinely dislikes me." *Maybe it's that he perceives me as young and competent; he'll never be anything but a middle-aged, third-rate hack.*

"Here's the nine-page memorandum Colonel Stevens generated after his meeting with Captain Kerr. It clearly indicates what the Captain told him and the reason the Colonel made his decision in favor of the ramp tunnel."

With a sigh of relief, I looked Thomas in the eye—he looked back with casual disregard. *He's still got something he plans to use against me.*

"I would suggest everyone else leave the conference room while Richard, Thomas and I review the document and discuss its contents," Gerald requested.

After Scott, Kurt and I adjourned with Mark to his office, I remarked, "Having never seen the memo, I had no idea what it contains. Hope it settles this issue once and for all. There's no time for a change in direction."

Mark observed, "Sometimes committees make dumb decisions, Robert. General Harrison will hopefully succeed in convincing them of the correct course of action."

We were called back into the conference room and Gerald announced, "It's the unanimous decision of the steering committee that we will pursue the ramp entrance to the tunnel. We would like to thank Captain Kerr for his untiring efforts."

"Captain Kerr, please present the charts you prepared for our afternoon session," Colonel Morgan said.

At the conclusion of my presentation, Thomas stood, a smarmy smile on his face, and announced, "The CIA has received numerous reports that young Captain Kerr, here, is living with an East German woman. This is in direct violation of directives on close personal contact with foreign nationals by those with his security clearance."

I staggered as if shot as I moved back to my chair.

General Harrison looked at me. "Is this true?"

I cleared my dry throat and replied, "Anna Fischer was born in East Berlin, now is a West German citizen. She works in the base bookstore downstairs. And yes, we live together."

Colonel Morgan whispered something to Mark, who sat beside him.

Kurt Altschuler stood, went to the front of the room, and waved his arms to silence everyone. In his commanding baritone voice, he said, "Will everyone except Thomas Lane, General Harrison, Gerald Scherman, and, of course, Colonel Morgan, please leave the area."

Halfway out the door, I turned and surprised everyone one, including myself, when I said "I don't want anyone in this room to misunderstand my intentions. I vow unequivocally that I'll give up my security clearance and stop working on your god-dammed tunnel before I give up Anna Fischer!"

That day I learned my hatred of Thomas Lane was a more powerful emotion than fear of danger or failure. Not once did any of the symptoms of another panic attack appear.

Thirty minutes later, we were asked to return to the conference room.

General Harrison addressed the group, "Mr. Altschuler explained that he, Colonel Powell, Captain Taylor, and Captain Kerr have formed a tunnel security committee. He described the activities they have undertaken and that are planned to hide the existence of the tunnel. Captain Kerr's is at the core of those efforts. Thus, his continued presence in Berlin is essential! Part of that cover will be his continued close relationship with Miss Fischer."

A shiver went down my back, elation at being vindicated followed by relief—I could stay in Berlin and be with Anna.

"All of us here agree that hiding the existence of the tunnel from the rest of the world is essential to our national defense. Your cover..."

"—General, if I could interject," Kurt insisted, again acting like the senior man present, "All of the enemy spies who operate in Berlin work on the assumption that those individuals forbidden to both travel to East Berlin and have a close association with German nationals, have access to the highest-level information they seek. A weatherman should know little of interest to them and, hence, would be allowed to live with a woman born in East and travel into East Berlin if he so desired."

Colonel Morgan added, "He'd also be able to move around Berlin free from the harassment of being followed that most of us experience frequently."

"You've all brought up good points," General Harrison observed as he continued. "So, Captain Kerr you'll be expected to not only stay with Miss Fischer, but also to find good reasons to enter the East on occasion."

"Anna has asked me to join her family for Christmas Eve and Christmas day. So now I can accept."

"Perfect," the General concluded. "Captain Kerr, you'll be expected to call either Colonel Morgan or Lieutenant Colonel Powell a few minutes before you depart for East Berlin, telling them your estimated return time. You'll call again to report your safe return. If you don't call, we'll begin raising hell with the Russians within an hour of your expected time of return. Is that clear?"

"I understand, sir." I smiled, happy with what seemed to be a win-win solution for me, and glanced briefly at Thomas, who obviously still did not agree with the decision and clearly didn't like being overruled.

Feet of Tunnel Completed: 0   Days until Deadline: 287

CHAPTER 38

Saturday, December 24, 1960

In the taxi on the way to the subway station, I took Anna's hand. "I'm looking forward to meeting your father—half of Berlin seems to think they're beholden to him."

"They do owe him. When the war ended, my father helped establish an organization to assist the defeated men with medical care and civilian clothes so they wouldn't be taken to the POW camps run by the Russians."

"Those soldiers' families certainly appreciated his help."

"They did. By May 1945, most of Berlin was just a pile of rubble. My father worked twenty hours a day, treating people medically and organizing the northern half of the district of Lichtenberg. With the help of others, water service returned, the streets were cleared, people moved out of basements and rat-infested hovels."

"No wonder people show such respect for your father. He must have touched many lives."

"Soon the cadres of German communists descended on Berlin like a plague. With Russian assistance, they took control of the entire city. They appointed block and apartment house wardens to spy on people."

"What about the Allies?"

"It was several months before the British, French and Americans arrived to take control of what's now West Berlin. In the interim, local leaders like my father were harassed and even arrested by the communists. My father was released with a stern warning. Following that, he spent all of his free time at the POW camps on the outskirts of the city, treating wounded German soldiers who were dying by the thousands."

Anna began to choke up. I put my arm around her to comfort her. "Those must have been terrible times for everyone, including you."

"My parents sheltered me, and except for the assault on my sister, I had a relatively happy childhood. Eventually, the POWs, who included my older brother Fredrich, were marched to Russia and put into forced labor camps…"

"—I read about that, some didn't return until 1948."

"Yes. Many of those men are in such ill health even today, they can't work. Fredrich's heart is damaged."

Once on the subway train, I requested, "Now tell me about your mother."

"Oh! My mother is a professor at Humboldt University, which is located in the old administrative center of Berlin—known as Mitte. Before the war, it was known as Berlin University. In 1929, she met my father, who was completing his medical training in Berlin at Saint Hedwig Hospital. It was apparently love at first sight, and they have been inseparable ever since. She was awarded her Doctorate in Linguistics in 1930, the same year my sister Sophia was born. She teaches foreign languages—French and English primarily. She's a gourmet cook and, as you will see, runs her large household with a loving but firm hand. Papa defers to her on most matters."

"Let me see—Sophia is the oldest."

"Yes, and her three children are Stephen, age twelve, almost thirteen— Angelica, age nine—and Hans, age seven. They share the second floor and third floors with my parents. Stephen rides the subway to attend a gymnasium here in the West. Everyone wants him to go to a university in the West."

"Fredrich, the next in age, is unmarried and has no children."

"Correct. He sleeps in a small apartment on the ground floor. Helmuth, the next in age, and his wife, Johanna—have two children, Ludwig, age six and Andrea, age four."

"His family also lives with your parents?"

"Yes, Helmuth didn't do well in his studies and failed the test which would have allowed him to get into the gymnasium. He refuses to join the

Communist Party, so he does menial labor. Both he and Johanna work, but don't earn enough to get their own apartment. They stay in the attic of my parent's home."

"What of Sophia's husband."

Anna hesitated, she seemed uncomfortable. "Derrik . . . .Is in prison."

"Really! What did he do?"

"He's an engineer like you. He worked at the East Berlin Public Works Department. He reported a conspiracy to use substandard materials in the construction of state-owned apartments. It turned out numerous officials high in the Communist Party were skimming the money and shipping it to bank accounts in Switzerland. They had him prosecuted and sent to prison for three years."

Anna clasped my arm. "Robert! The next stop is ours! We need to get the suitcases next to the door, so we can shift them on the platform before the train leaves."

Once off the train, we accepted the offer of two East Berliners to carry our luggage for whatever tip we were willing to pay.

CHAPTER 39

Saturday, December 24, 1960

A LITTLE BEFORE noon, we approached a sizeable four-story-tall row house, which sat in the middle of a block. A brass sign on the black cast-iron fence directed patients to Doctor Fischer's surgery located on the lower floor. Holiday wreaths decorated the two front doors at the top of ten stone steps. The exposed gray stone structure looked like a typical 1870s New York row house.

The front door sprang open, and a distinguished man in his mid-fifties, who I assumed was Anna's father, greeted us. "Robert, please come in. All Anna ever talks about when she visits is you." He stepped aside to allow us to enter. "You are so far from home, consider our home to be your home."

"Thank you, sir...."

"Please call me Bernard."

As we entered the house, the smell of delicious food and a fir tree filled the air.

Bernard wore a suit that looked a little worn. His ample girth strained the confining vest and his thinning gray hair surrounded a ruddy pate. His intelligent, penetrating eyes were topped by bushy eyebrows. A sizeable rosy nose supported thick tortoiseshell glasses. When he talked, he looked over the rims of his glasses at you.

Anna's mother came into the entryway, wearing an apron. She gave me a prolonged hug, a kiss on the cheek, and instructed, "Call me Emma. No formality with us. Today, we will treat you to a traditional German Christmas Eve. First, we decorate the tree. Then we eat, open presents and attend Mass at the neighborhood Lutheran Church. How does that sound?"

"Wonderful," I replied.

Her once-fashionable best dress showed frequent use. Her large breasts sagged above her round obviously corseted middle.

After being introduced around, Fredrich handed me a glass of beer. "Please, join us in the decoration of the tree."

The large fir tree filled one corner of the high-ceilinged living room. With every member of the family helping, it was soon covered with family heirloom decorations—many of carved wood. Finally, the children were allowed to light the real wax candles on the lower branches while the adults lit the upper ones.

I stood behind Anna as we admired the tree. Putting my arms around her waist, I whispered into her ear, "That is the most beautiful Christmas tree I've ever seen. The real flickering candles give the whole room a fairy-tale beauty."

I had to remind myself that this ordinary, loving family lived in a communist city. Outside freedom might be stifled by totalitarian propaganda and mind control, but in this small haven of sanity, love reigned.

Emma entered the room to announce, "Dinner is ready. Please, there is just enough room for all of us at the table."

After everyone was seated, Emma turned to me. "Robert, it is a tradition that today we serve the fish called carp along with potato salad, boiled potatoes, cucumber salad and lemon slices. Thanks to Robert, today we have large real lemon slices, and everyone will have a large orange from California. And for dessert, chocolate cake."

During the meal, the banter among the members of the Fischer family was in the high German I had learned at the university. I understood most of their conversation, despite the fact they talked fast and often talked over each other. When I failed to catch something, I just smiled.

One of the things that impressed me was the children felt free to enter the conversations and express their opinions.

Sophia's oldest son, Stephen, asked me, "You are an Air Force Officer. Do you fly?"

"In der Amerikanischen Luftwaffe, fliege ich einen Schreibtisch, (In the

American Air Force, I fly an office desk).” This was my standard reply when people asked me if I flew. It allowed me to hide what I really did. They all laughed, but Bernard especially seemed to enjoy the joke.

"Anna told us you are a weatherman. Is that correct?" Emma asked.

"Yes, I determine if it is safe for American military aircraft to take off and land at Tempelhof Airport. Perhaps not the best use for my university education as an engineer, but in the military one learns to adjust to their requirements. It is an easy job which I have learned to like."

Nine-year-old Angelica, whose pigtails bounced as she talked, joined in. "Anna says you live near Hollywood. Do you know anyone famous like Paul Newman or Elvis Presley?"

"No, I am afraid not. Fifteen million people live in or near Los Angeles."

"Amazing. That is almost the same number as live in all of East Germany, including East Berlin," Stephen observed.

Little four-year-old Andrea's long blond hair was cut in bangs. Her flashing blue eyes showed a budding intellect. She picked up her orange. "Thank you for the orange. Did you grow it?"

"No, but when I was your age, I could walk out into my backyard and pick one anytime I wanted."

After eating the main course, I raised my voice and delivered a carefully thought out statement, *"Emma, Dies ist eine ausgezeichnete Mahlzeit—der fisch war köstlich* (This is an excellent meal—the fish was delicious)." Emma beamed with delight as everyone else complimented her on the excellent dinner. Then I thanked them all for sharing their Christmas with me.

Bernard rose and proposed a toast, "May the Fischer family always be all together for these important holidays."

"Prost." Clinking of glasses around the table.

"We need especially to welcome Robert from America to our celebration. We have this excellent Mosel white wine due to his largess."

"Prost."

Soon the family gathered in the living room, and the presents were opened. Anna had spent almost a month carefully selecting each gift. Her efforts were rewarded with hugs for Anna and either hugs or handshakes for me.

For Andrea, Anna's favorite, she had selected a Barbie doll with several different outfits. The child was so excited, she was speechless. Then, she hugged and kissed Anna. Next, she crawled up into my lap, gave me a hug, and said, "I like you. Are you going to marry Anna? She really likes you and needs a husband."

Speechless, I looked around the room as everyone laughed. I took Anna's hand in mine. "Anna is very precious to me. If we decide to marry, you will be the first person we will tell. Is that okay?"

"Okay." She giggled.

CHAPTER 40

Saturday, December 24, 1960

MOST OF THE family left to visit in-laws. Only five of us sat around the table for the evening meal. Midway through supper, I turned to Emma and Bernard. "Why do you continue to stay here in the East?"

"This part of Berlin, this neighborhood, this street, and this structure are our home, right, Emma?"

"Yes, we have owned this house for over twenty years."

"But you no longer really own this house," Anna said gently. "The communists can confiscate it when any member of the Fischer family displeases them."

Bernard frowned at her comment. "For many years, I have been on the Board of Directors of Saint Hedwig's hospital. Before the war, it was widely recognized as the best hospital in Germany. Our fellow citizens who live in the East deserve the quality medical care that it and I can provide."

"Couldn't you just as easily help people in the West?" I asked.

"Yes, but there are so few doctors left in the East. The need is great here, not so much over there."

"They pay you very little here, Papa," Anna observed. "That should tell you what the communists think about your dedicated service."

Emma interjected, "Many of my fellow professors at Humboldt University have immigrated West. They now teach at the Free University they established there. I decided to stay, because the people of East Berlin also deserve a quality educational institution."

"Mama, you are constantly grousing about the communist interference in academic affairs!" Anna said emphatically.

"Despite the education commissar's effort for us to be a mouthpiece for their propaganda, we have managed to maintain our academic excellence and independence to a great extent."

"You see," Bernard added, "we have decided that if all of the good people leave East Berlin, the communists will have won. We do not want that to happen. It is a form of defiance on our part. We may be naïve to think the best people must stand up for what is right, but that is how Emma and I have decided to live our lives."

"The communist bureaucrats only occasionally interfere with our day-to-day lives or operations at work," Emma said. "We know and are willing to live within the political boundaries they have established."

"Life is good, so why change?" Bernard concluded. "If another war comes, we are no safer on one side of the border than the other."

CHAPTER 41

Sunday, December 25, 1960

AFTER CHURCH SERVICES that Sunday morning, Bernard shared his father's life with me. "After he was ordained in 1917, Gunther volunteered to be a chaplain for a new division of men being recruited in Saxony. They spent much of the war fighting the Russians, but they were eventually sent to the Western Front."

"World War I was such an unfortunate tragedy for both sides."

"Then, at the relatively young age of forty-five, he was given one of the largest Lutheran congregations in Saxony—Halle's Saint Michael's Church. On the Sunday after the famous Crystal Night, he preached the first of many sermons that eventually earned him two years in prison."

"As I remember, on Crystal Night, store windows of Jewish shops were broken, Jewish homes and apartments were destroyed, and synagogues were demolished and set on fire."

"That is correct. When few other people protested, Hitler decided the German citizenry would acquiesce to his persecution of the Jews, so he authorized an escalation in the level of atrocities."

"Your father is, indeed, a brave man."

"I was in the congregation several months later when he delivered the sermon that got him sent to prison. He described how during the Great War the Jewish soldiers in his unit fought as valiantly as any Lutheran or Catholic. At the end of his sermon, Gunther pointed his finger at a senior uniformed SS officer in the congregation and revealed, 'Only three Jewish soldiers in my unit survived the war. All three were among the German citizens who were arrested and shipped to concentration camps from here last week!' ”

"No wonder they sent him to prison," I observed. "The Nazis never accepted criticism of any form."

"He was finally released in 1941 when Hitler and the Nazis were in control of most of Western Europe—they no longer feared the truth."

"He survived? I hope to meet him one day to shake his hand."

"Yes, and today from his church in Halle, he continues to fight the corrupt communist regime that controls us. A Lutheran youth movement he helped establish is designed to counter the communist Young Pioneers. It is gaining ground in many places here in the East."

Emma entered the room, sat on the arm of the overstuffed chair that Bernard occupied, and said, "Robert, I need to tell you of my parents. My father was a minor nobleman, who owned a large estate. When the Russians arrived in early 1945, they occupied my parent's manor house and then burned it to the ground as they moved toward Berlin. Soon after the war, the East German government confiscated their land and incorporated it into collective farms. Today they live in a tiny apartment in Dresden on the small pittance the East German state pays 'non-contributing' retirees. They are in failing health. We help them as much as we can, but…."

She sighed and stood. "Today we have a traditional German Christmas dinner. Goose—one-half is stuffed with apples, dates, chestnuts, and onions—the other half is stuffed with ground beef mixed with bread cubes. It is accompanied by red cabbage, dumplings, and gravy made from the drippings. Everything is as it has been in Germany for hundreds of years."

After dinner, Anna and I stood near the front door and said our goodbyes. The doorbell rang. Nearest to the door, I said, "I will get it." I felt the floor drop out from under me as I looked into the face of Dieter Holburg.

I'm vulnerable here—mustn't panic—calm down—deep breaths—now!

Bernard, sensing my distress, moved in front of me. "Yes, may I help you?"

"Ah, Herr Doctor Fischer. My name is Dieter Holburg." He held out his hand which Bernard ignored.

He sneered, "I am actually here to see Captain Kerr of the United

States Air Force. It is a private matter." With a sweep of his hand, he stated, "If he would join me outside, that would be best."

This brief delay had allowed me to steady my breathing and regain my composure to some degree. I asked, "What do you want?"

"This matter will be best handled between the two of us outside."

I reluctantly followed Dieter across the street, where a Stasi agent I recognized as number 13 stood on the curb behind the little Trabant. Dieter opened the door. "We could sit in my car and have the privacy this matter requires."

Determined to resist whatever he had in mind, I exclaimed, "You know the speech that my friend Captain Taylor gave you a few months ago—I can repeat it, or you can tell me what you want—do so now, or I'm going back to Doctor Fischer's house." I crossed my arms over my chest so that he couldn't see my shaking hands.

"Maybe you would like to talk at the local police station or in my office at Stasi Headquarters?"

"Look. We both know you do not want the shit storm that would occur if you try to arrest me. Tell me what this is about or leave."

"Here are photographs I would like you to tell me about."

He spread out numerous telephoto images of Scott and me in the hangar as the Pregnant Guppy aircraft rolled into position so the doors could be closed.

I laughed. "I'm standing beside an airplane."

"Tell me more."

"Captain Taylor and I are standing beside an airplane."

"Don't play games with me. Why did this odd-shaped plane arrive in Berlin at 23:17 last Sunday evening, and what was inside of it?"

"How long were you in the military, Herr Holburg?"

"From 1938 to 1946. Why?"

"Did you spend much time on the front lines?"

"Yes, from the siege of Stalingrad to Berlin."

Pausing, I thought, he's a dedicated communist who fought with the Russians against the Nazis. This ploy may just work. "How many times did your superior officers tell you to do something?"

"Too many to count."

"How many times did they tell you everything about what was going on?"

"Never."

"Okay, my boss Colonel Powell is on leave in the United States. Before he left, he ordered Captain Taylor and me to meet that strange shaped aircraft and sign for the cargo. The invoice for the shipment did not say what it was or where it came from or who sent it. All blank. It was described as fifteen wooden crates of various sizes. That is what I signed for. As a weatherman, I know less than you probably do about all of the things the United States Air Force does at Tempelhof Airport."

I turned, my legs rubbery and my gate was a bit unsteady. I managed to march lock-step across the street, up the steps, and through the Fischer's front door before I collapsed.

Anna caught me before I hit the floor. Together, she and Bernard helped me down to his surgery via the back stairs.

"It's a heart attack. I'll give him a shot of digitalis."

"I am having a panic attack," I gasped.

"Then a mild sedative will do the trick," Bernard decided.

Fifteen minutes after I felt a prick in my arm, I was back to normal.

Glancing down at my watch, I almost had another attack. I had just over thirty minutes to get back over the border and call Colonel Morgan about my safe return.

"Anna, I have a critical phone call I forgot to make. We must leave immediately." Hurried goodbyes were said.

At the subway station, we had just eighteen minutes until my deadline. Anna looked at me strangely, but she supported me, saying, "We'll go straight through to Potsdamer Platz station. It's in the West. There are phone booths there. The holiday subway schedule says the next train won't arrive for nine more minutes. Sit down and relax—we'll make it."

Ignoring her assurances, I paced back and forth, checking my watch every few seconds. Finally, I felt the air being pushed forward as the train entered the station.

"Robert, relax. You'll have another problem if you don't just sit down."

I fidgeted in my seat for the six-minute transit. Anna handed me a coin and took charge of the luggage. I ran to the phone booths. All were occupied except one, and it had an out-of-order sign on it. I paced, watching each booth for any movement, and rechecked my watch. Finally, one became vacant.

My hand shook as I forced the coin into the slot, dialed the number, and waited. "Come on, come on—answer the damn phone," I muttered.

Finally, I heard a familiar voice. "Colonel Morgan speaking."

"Sir, this is Captain Kerr. My visit was enjoyable, and I have returned." My voice sounded surprisingly calm.

"Thank you, Captain. I'll see you in the office in the morning."

Once we returned to our apartment, Anna confronted me. "That encounter with that Stasi agent on my parent's doorstep has convinced me you aren't a weatherman. What do you really do?"

"Anna, what I do is very important to the defense of both our countries. That's all I can tell you. You'll just have to trust me on this one matter."

CHAPTER 42

Thursday, December 29, 1960-Tuesday, January 3, 1961

MY CHRISTMAS PRESENT to Anna was a six-day vacation to London. During the long bus ride from Heathrow, she squeezed my arm and whispered words I'd waited so long to hear. "I'm ready for us to make real love this evening."

Once we reached the rented apartment, I let her set the pace, careful not to rush her. It was more beautiful than I could have imagined. All those weeks of pretend lovemaking actually paid big rewards. I knew what pleased her, and she knew what pleased me.

"We've become one, darling. I love you," I told her at the conclusion of our first coupling.

We lay in a post-coital embrace for several minutes before she kissed me and whispered, "Robbie, that's the first time you stated you love me—I love you too, darling man—Ich liebe dich!"

The warm rosy glow in the early hours of the next morning was followed by many couplings over the next five days and nights. We were so enamored with each other, we were in bed making love when the New Year 1961 arrived. It was a good thing we couldn't foretell the future, as neither of us was prepared for most of what happened to us in that momentous year. The attention of the entire world was often focused on Berlin, and Anna and I were at the very center of events that daily made headlines in newspapers around the world.

PART TWO

"Berlin is the testicles of the West.
When I want the West to scream, I squeeze on Berlin."

Nikita Khrushchev, 1961

CHAPTER 43

Thursday, January 5, 1961

"DURING YESTERDAY'S EXCITEMENT, I never got a chance to introduce myself. I'm Captain Robert Kerr, the Chief Engineer for this construction program. You've all signed the appropriate paperwork, so we can tell you that the Cold War may well be won or lost due to the efforts of those assigned to this program."

I leaned in and paused for effect. "We are going to tunnel under the River Spree and tap into a major communist communications system. By reading their messages and listening to their phone conversations, our government will hopefully foil their efforts to continue the spread of Communism into Western Europe."

I had the undivided attention of the twelve Seabees who'd arrived the previous day, and eight Air Force enlisted men who'd arrived over the past week.

"The existence of the tunnel and its purpose are classified beyond Top Secret. We're relying on each of you to support our goal of hiding our construction program from the world. As most of you experienced yesterday, the communists are out there waiting to pounce—one casual remark, one unguarded moment, or one untoward action by you could compromise this entire project. Remember, think before you speak or act!"

I continued, "If you reveal anything about any aspect of this construction project, you'll be prosecuted under the espionage laws. The prison sentence for each infraction is a maximum of **thirty years!** Is that clear?"

They answered with a resounding, "Yes sir!" I pointed my finger at each of the twenty sober-faced individuals who looked back at me.

"Yesterday, one of us almost handed the communists a major victory. We all must be constantly vigilant—Berlin is a city awash in communist spies and operatives. The objective of this two-day orientation session is to make you understand one fact—if the enemy finds out about our efforts, they'll do everything possible to deny us this crucial source of information. Lieutenant Colonel Powell, my boss and our immediate senior officer here in Berlin, has a few opening remarks he'd like to deliver before this training session really gets underway."

"Thank you, Captain Kerr. First, I'd like to...."

During Colonel Powell's speech, I reflected on the events of the previous day....

Feet of Tunnel Completed: 0   Days until Deadline: 261

CHAPTER 44

Wednesday, January 4, 1961

KURT DROVE A black CIA Mercedes sedan with German license plates. Scott and I were passengers, wearing civilian clothes. Thirteen Seabees were scheduled to arrive at Tegel Airport aboard three different commercial jet aircraft. Once everyone gathered in a Hilton Hotel room, we planned to provide them instructions on how to get into Tempelhof Air Force Base through the arrival-hall cipher lock.

As our car descended into the main underground parking garage, Kurt snapped, "What the hell! That man's a KGB operative! He's shaking hands with a senior Stasi agent. They call him the professor." With considerable effort, he maneuvered the car out of the parking garage and onto a busy thoroughfare

"This can't be just a coincidence. We've been compromised," Scott announced.

"I'll pull over at that tobacco shop," Kurt explained, pointing. "It'll have a pay phone. I'll call my counter-surveillance team. It'll take us time to gather and execute the plan I have in mind, but in the interim here's what we'll do…"

In less than an hour, a CIA-owned slab-sided black delivery van pulled into the entrance of the Hilton service garage. Kurt, Scott, and I were hiding in the back.

"The Hilton Hotel's Head of Security, a retired U.S. Army Military Police Major named Bobby Shores, will help us every way he can. He's one of us, a real trooper," Scott said.

After introductions, Mr. Shores assured us, "I've personally verified that your thirteen men are assembled and waiting in Suite 1107. I've devised the perfect ruse to get our two young Captains here into that suite."

Ten minutes later, Scott and I were under two food delivery carts covered with tablecloths as bellhops wheeled us to our destination.

A knock and the announcement, "Zimmerservice—Room Service." A door opened. "We didn't order room service, but as long as it's here, we might as well eat," someone said.

Once the bellhops had departed, I crawled out of my hiding place and immediately held up a cardboard sign: *Don't say anything—the room is probably bugged.* I moved the sign around so all could see it.

The room went from boisterous comradery to silence, until a big beefy man behind me suggested, "Dig in. Then we'll take a tour of the town."

Turning the card over, I wrote: *I'm Captain Kerr.*

Taking my pen, the big man replied: *Chief Weber. Senior NCO here.*

I scribbled: *The commies surround us. Help's on the way.*

Meanwhile, Scott locked and dead bolted the door, closed all of the curtains and began to look for listening devices.

Fifteen minutes later, three knocks, a pause, followed by three more knocks. Scott let a man into the room that neither of us knew.

Scott, Chief Weber, and I followed him into the bathroom. He turned on the shower and instructed, "Call me Jerry. The place is crawling with bad guys. Kurt's working on a diversion, but we must be patient. Several of them appear to be armed." Opening a briefcase, he handed each of us .38 caliber handguns and shoulder holsters, which we put on.

Holy shit. *"Are we expecting a shootout?"* I murmured under my breath.

Scott and I wore three-piece civilian suits. I briefly wondered if it was legal for us to be armed while out of uniform and off the base. Since the shower was still running, I asked, "Can we use these guns?"

"Berlin is still legally a conquered enemy city. In each zone of occupation, the senior military commander is the ultimate authority. He can command elected German officials to take whatever action is required to maintain order. We work for him. So, to answer your question, here in the American Zone we can carry these weapons in order to protect American interests."

"What about our opposite numbers out there?"

"Russian officials can move freely through Berlin and carry arms. Those East German Stasi guys can legally come over to our zone, but they have no authority, and by our regulations they shouldn't be armed."

Leaving the shower on, Jerry got out a walkie-talkie. He pulled a three-foot-long telescoping antenna out of the large oblong box. "Ranger one to base. Over."

"Base."

"In position, ready for action."

"Roger. Stand by for instructions. Reinforcements expected in thirty minutes."

"I'd better go out and let my men know what's happening," the Chief advised me in a gravelly deep voice with a foreign accent. He quickly returned. "One of my men, Hans Jelnicky tried to leave, but others restrained him."

Taking a pair of handcuffs out of his briefcase, Jerry handed them to the Chief, who understood. "I'll make sure he stays here."

"Scott, do you understand what's happening?" I asked. "The East Germans have one of the finest hotels in West Berlin surrounded. Why are they threatening an armed confrontation?"

"The only thing I can think of is that this guy...Jelnicky...spilled his guts to someone."

"He doesn't know about our objective."

"No, but he does know that thirteen Seabees were given Top Secret clearances and assigned to work on a highly-classified construction project in West Berlin. Once they learned that much, finding details would immediately become a Stasi and KGB high priority."

"Unfortunately, you're probably right," I agreed. "But wouldn't attacking us in this hotel cause an international incident?"

"If Kurt hadn't been with us and recognized the KGB and Stasi agents, they might have learned about our little construction project and put a stop to it with little fuss. After determining the location of the cipher-locked door today, next week they could follow someone to the building. Game, set, match, just like that."

Jerry received a message. "Rover One, there may be a change of plans. Standby." He turned the shower off, waited a few minutes, then turned it back on, as if several men were taking turns in the shower.

No panic attack so far. Not even fast breathing. Amazing.

Forty minutes later, Kurt knocked on the door, pushed in a delivery cart, and joined us in the bathroom. "We're ready to leave. All of us will move from here to the service elevator at the end of the hall, down to the service garage and out that exit into two unmarked panel trucks."

"What about the bad guys?" I asked.

"The Berlin Police have forced them to leave the hotel, but they're waiting on the streets," Kurt replied. "Due to the Four Powers agreements, they actually have every right to be in this hotel and out there. They aren't supposed to be carrying arms, but they are. Regrettably, the police have decided not to press that matter at this point in time. Chief, are any of your guys proficient with firearms?"

"Yes, two in particular. Kowalski and Nowak. They fought in the Korean War."

"There are two grease guns and a couple of bandoliers of ammunition under the cart I brought into the room. They need to load their weapons. One of those two will lead the way, and the other will cover our rear."

"Where are we going?" Scott asked.

"Do you have a suggestion?"

"Let's go to U.S. Military Police Headquarters at McNair Barracks," he recommended. "We'll be safe there, and they have facilities which will allow us to determine what happened."

"Perfect. Jerry, use your walkie-talkie to tell everyone our destination."

We formed a line—Nowak led the group, followed by several Seabees, the Chief with his weapon pointed at the ceiling, Jelnicky in handcuffs between two senior NCOs, Scott with his gun pointing down, me, the rest of the Seabees, and then Kowalski.

Scott turned to me. "Old buddy, it's show time. Get your weapon out and try not to shoot yourself in the foot. Even more important, don't shoot me!"

"Don't worry; I know how to use this weapon. During marksmanship training in ROTC, I qualified as a small arms expert. How about you?"

"Get ready, Wyatt Earp. A showdown may await us."

Slowly, all eighteen of us made our way down the hallway. A guest opened the door beside me and cried, "Dorothy, get down. It looks like World War III has started in the hall!" The door slammed shut.

Deep breathing...from the diaphragm...don't panic now...not here... not now!

Everything went smoothly, and I remained calm.

Once in the basement, Kurt took charge of assigning people to various roles. "These cargo vans have no seats in the back, so most of us will stand or sit on the floor. My men will drive. Captain Taylor, you're the armed, front seat passenger in the lead van; you'll provide driving directions to McNair Barracks. Jerry, communications through your walkie-talkie, lead van. Nowak, you protect the lead van from the back window."

With a glance, Kurt commanded, "Captain Kerr, passenger seat, second van. The Chief, Kowalski, and I will take Jelnicky in the trailing van." He looked at the remaining eight men, "Four of you get in the back of each van."

Seven people were crammed like sardines into the back of the two vans and had to stand. Kurt clutched the second walkie-talkie and took a position at the back window of the trailing van, leaving no doubt about his role in our escapade.

The driver made a right turn. I heard someone groan and looked back. People struggled to keep their balance.

Jerry reported, "At the top of the parking garage ramp, a car is blocking the street to the left. To the right three individuals have seen us and taken positions with their hands inside their coats, their other hands out, palms up, to stop us. What should we do?"

Into the walkie-talkie, Kurt shouted, "Van one, gun the motor immediately! They want us to surrender Jelnicky."

The driver ahead of us hit the accelerator. I heard groans and whispering as everyone in the back of my van bounced around. Jerry reported from the lead vehicle, "We hit one of the Stasi agents. Just a glancing blow, but he'll probably be limping around for a few days."

Our convoy sped to the first corner, took a right, then a left onto a major three-lane thoroughfare. Scott said, "Go straight ahead for about a mile, then we'll take another left, so stay in this lane."

I assumed we were now safe until I heard Kurt shout, "Three vehicles are following us. They're obviously willing to take risks, perhaps even armed intervention. They desperately want to find out more about our mission and question Jelnicky in one of their prisons. Any suggestions anyone?"

From the lead van, I heard, "There's a stop light up ahead. What should I do?"

"Move into the left turn lane and execute a U-turn before reaching the intersection," Kurt instructed. "We'll try to lose them in traffic."

Both vehicles executed this maneuver, which disrupted the flow of oncoming traffic and almost caused several collisions. Those in the back lost their footing and were a jumble on the floor.

Using the open stretch of road ahead, our drivers rapidly accelerated. The three vehicles in pursuit used the corridor we'd created to stay with us.

Looking out the rear window in amazement, Kurt said, "God damn those bastards. They're still on our tail. Ideas, anyone?"

"This street leads to the British Sector," Scott advised. "Should we enter their area?"

"No. Under no circumstances," Kurt commanded. "The Limeys are very protective of their rights. There'll be hell to pay if we step on their toes."

"Tempelhof is the closest U.S. military installation. Head there. My security guys will admit us," Scott said.

I protested, "We want to avoid associating the Seabees with me or anything going on at Tempelhof."

"We need a safe place, or we'll be protecting ourselves with firearms," Kurt replied. "Shootouts in the middle of West Berlin are discouraged by our superiors—both civilian and military. I screwed up. We should have waited for an armed convoy escort."

"Tempelhof is our only choice," I conceded.

"Scott, select the route. Negotiate it as quickly as possible."

"Affirmative, Kurt. Three stop lights up, turn right and go straight for three-quarters of a mile, then a left, a sharp right, and we're home."

Our van just managed to get through a yellow light at the next intersection. The crashing sounds of an accident indicated someone behind us had not fared as well.

Kurt shouted. "We'll, I'll be damned! The first car following us just managed to avoid a collision with turning traffic, but the second vehicle was broadsided. With only one car full of men left, I don't think they'll try anything. Proceed with the plan to Tempelhof."

As Kurt predicted, the lead Stasi/KGB car followed us to the base, pulled up at the curb outside the main gate, and watched us pass through the guard post. The security guards later reported that the sedan's passengers tried to see us exit the vans.

Our vehicles entered a covered parking area within the Air Force-controlled airport building. Scott directed all eighteen of us down a corridor, up to a set of stairs, which led to the barracks area acquired for the exclusive use of my work crew.

I tried to determine what impact the day's events would have on my mission. My conclusion: *Instead of anonymity for the start of my project, we were the target of intense interest. That was bad, but not devastating. And I didn't have a panic attack.*

Feet of Tunnel Completed: 0   Days until Deadline: 262

CHAPTER 45

Wednesday, January 4, 1961

LATE THAT AFTERNOON, we gathered in the drab interrogation room at Tempelhof, which was furnished with standard issue U.S. military gray metal conference tables and chairs. Mark, Scott, Chief Weber, and I, a representative from the Judge Advocate General's Office, and a stenographer were present.

Senior Chief Petty Officer Carl Weber—a tall, broad-shouldered, massive chested man—stood out among the assembly.

"Before we interview Jelnicky, tell us about him, Chief Weber," Mark requested.

The Chief's bright, alert brown eyes took in everything despite thick, horn-rimmed bifocals. "Like me, Jelnicky was originally from Gdansk in what is today Poland. He was allowed to move to the States when an aunt agreed to adopt him after the war. He joined the Navy in 1951 during the Korean War."

"So, he's now a Second-Class Petty Officer?" Scott confirmed.

"Yes, sir. Jelnicky just turned thirty. He's recently divorced. When he returned from an unaccompanied eighteen-month assignment to Subic Bay, he found that his wife had moved in with a local contractor. In the divorce, he gave up his kids in return for no child support."

"I suspect he wasn't happy about that," Mark observed.

"He was crazy about his wife and kids. He received counseling at the base, and I thought he'd finally accepted his loss."

"Chief, he might open up if you question him," Scott suggested.

Two Air Policemen escorted the obviously chastened man into the interview room.

The Chief's calm demeanor contrasted dramatically with his cauliflower ear and many times broken nose. He cleared his throat as he approached Jelnicky, and his normal gravelly tone sounded somewhat subdued. "Hans, I guess you know you're in trouble. It'll go much easier for you if you tell us what happened."

When Jelnicky addressed him in Polish, the Chief instructed him to reply in English.

After hesitating, he responded in heavily accented English, "Chief, I was a vulnerable fool."

"Tell us how."

"When I found out I was coming to Germany, I wrote to my aunt. She replied that I should look up my only other family—a second cousin. I wrote to him at an address in West Berlin. He asked me to join his family for the Christmas holidays. I accepted."

"You were supposed to leave New York yesterday, but you've been here for eleven…twelve days. Is that correct?"

"Yes, I arrived on Christmas Eve."

"What happened to the ticket the government issued you?"

"It's in my suitcase, unused."

"What happened next?"

"I met my cousin. He indicated he'd moved to East Berlin, because it cost less to live there. I told him I'd recently been granted a high-level security clearance and didn't feel comfortable traveling into a communist-controlled area."

"Then what happened?" Chief Weber asked.

"He replied, 'You can join us for Christmas dinner in the East, what harm could that do?' I did. Once there, I met another cousin, a drop-dead gorgeous female. She insisted we were 'kissing cousins'…uh, you know…"

"Go on."

"She joined me in West Berlin the next day. To impress her, I moved from a modest pension to a nice hotel. We toured both Berlins—the nightclubs, bars, movies, restaurants, museums—had a glorious time. We also spent a lot of time in bed. We're in love. I want to be with her."

"What did you tell her about yourself?"

"That I was a Navy Seabee who'd been assigned to Berlin to work on a construction project. After much cajoling, I told her nine of us had been selected to work on the project because we were native German speakers…"

"—Go on."

"…and we could help hide the construction project from the Germans on both sides of the border."

"How did she react?"

"At first, I thought she was just curious. For the last few days, she's repeatedly pressed me for details. So, I clammed up."

"Did you tell her anything else?"

"That's all I knew! Oh, and that I'd be in Berlin for a year, perhaps even until March of next year."

"Ok. Anything else you want to tell us?"

"No, Chief. Am I in real trouble?"

"That's not for anyone in this room today to decide," Chief Weber said.

Once Jelnicky had been removed from the room, Scott informed us, "It was a classic 'honeypot' espionage sting. Gorgeous female seduces hapless dupe into telling all."

"What he told her was everything he knew," the Chief observed.

"Unfortunately, this is much more serious," Scott said. "Chief, even though you and your men were wearing suits and carrying suitcases when you arrived at the airport and again at the Hilton, the Stasi probably pegged you as American military men. We must conclude that they now have photographs of each of you. You've all been compromised."

"But we must have the native German speakers to make our construction project viable," I said in frustration.

"Perhaps there's a way…let's go upstairs," Mark suggested. "After the Chief signs some security paperwork, we'll reveal our plans. Perhaps then I can offer a solution."

Feet of Tunnel Completed: 0   Days until Deadline: 262

CHAPTER 46

Thursday and Friday, January 5-6, 1961

CHIEF WEBER WAITED for me outside of my tank when I arrived the next morning. I asked, "How'd the men take it?"

"I've good news. All of my Navy guys and three of the eight Airmen agreed to accept what's now being called the Polish Option."

"Being restricted to their quarters and the construction site for over a year won't be easy."

"I'll bet most of the other guys will select that option. If you're married, have a family, and intend to remain faithful to your wife, the Polish Option is best."

"Hope you're right. The spies here in Berlin won't be able to compromise our people if they stay on the base or are at work all of the time!"

"Everyone loved the facilities that are being provided. A large private room for each man, separate mess hall, gym and huge rec room."

"We wanted the men to stay on the base as much as possible. Having those facilities available was part of our plan."

"The per diem of $20 per day doubles most of their salaries. A four-day pass to visit anywhere in Western Europe once a month, government-paid airfare, and the first choice of leave dates were also a big incentive. These men are seldom home for special occasions like birthdays, anniversaries, family vacations......"

"It's time for me and Colonel Powell to make our introductory remarks," I said. "We've got to cram two and a half days of orientation and training into less than two full days after yesterday's excitement."

After lunch, the orientation session for the twelve Navy and eight Air Force men reconvened. Scott gave his 'Berlin is Awash with Spies' briefing. He revealed that, "Yesterday the Russians filed a formal protest claiming, Jelnicky was an East German citizen whom we'd kidnapped to make him reveal state secrets."

That got everyone's attention.

During the counter-surveillance training course, Scott said, "Those of you who selected the Polish Option will dress in German construction works clothes and go through the steam tunnels to the Tempelhof Stream Generation Plant. From there, you'll be transported to the tunnel building in the back of delivery vans with various Berlin construction-company logos on the sides. We've acquired these vehicles especially for this project."

"We'll shower and dress in our own rooms," the Chief added.

"Everyone else will dress in German suits, hats, and overcoats, exit through the cipher lock into the Tempelhof Arrivals Area and walk or take public transportation to our building, which is located about two and a half miles from here. Travel alone or in pairs. You'll change into German construction-worker clothes there."

"You'll shower at the building before you change back into your German suits," the Chief added.

"You'll also carry briefcases. In West Germany, everyone who works with his hands leaves his house in a suit with a briefcase," I injected. "They change clothes at work. All we can figure is that they don't want their neighbors to know what they do. Their briefcases must contain their lunch."

Everyone laughed.

Scott concluded his remarks by saying, "Remember when I described how to determine if you're being followed. Once you exit the arrivals hall, make several stops and go around the block to assess your situation. Only then proceed to the building where the tunnel is located. Return here rather than leading someone to that building!"

As Anna and I walked home hand in hand that Thursday evening, I was smiling and feeling jubulent, prompting her to asked, "Why are you so happy? It's raining."

"Being with you makes me happy. It makes the world a bright place." I stopped to share a lingering kiss and embrace under the umbrella as the rain splattered around us.

Happy thoughts continuously ran through my head.

All of the equipment and supplies are in Berlin. The first workers are here. Now, all I need is the courage to lead them and the knowledge to make the necessary tough decisions.

And I'm in love with a wonderful, beautiful woman!

Life is good!

The next day, the twenty men and I went over every aspect of the construction project. They appeared anxious to start work; their knowledge and enthusiasm were encouraging.

Late in the afternoon, each man was shown to his locker, where he tried on his German wardrobe and construction worker uniforms. The purchasing agent in Rhein-Main had done an excellent job of buying European-sized clothes from American measurements.

"Gather round, men. I have a few closing remarks. Our primary objective is to build the tunnel and Exploitation Center in less than nine months, while concealing its existence from the world. Our near-term goal is to begin drilling the tunnel by twenty February. I know I can count on each of you to assist Chief Weber and me in our efforts."

"Thank you, sir. You have our support," the Chief declared on behalf of everyone present.

"Men, I hate to do this on your first weekend here, but we're going to need everyone on hand to help. You're restricted to your quarters until further notice......"

To celebrate Anna's birthday that Friday, I took her to the Chez Orleans restaurant in the French Officer's Club. We enjoyed wonderful food and delicious wine. At the conclusion of our meal, I gave her a gold charm bracelet. "This is all the rage among the women of America. I selected three charms—a gold coin of Saxony from the 19th century to represent your heritage, an outline map of California with a small diamond placed in the approximate location of Los Angeles, my hometown, and a miniature Tower of Big Ben to mark our first vacation together."

"Oh, Robbie, I love it! I'll wear it always." She leaned over and gave me a kiss.

Little did we know that this gift would soon endanger our relationship.

Frequently when we were alone, Anna would whisper, "I know you're not a weatherman. Why would an engineer with degrees from two prominent universities end up working as a meteorologist?"

I always relied on some variation of, "The military is always screwed up. The Air Force didn't have many jobs for engineers when I got my commission, but because of increased flight operations, they needed lots of weathermen. So, they trained me."

She replied, "Why would a weatherman, whose job is to help military aircraft fly into Berlin, need to travel to London and to America in less than three months?"

"Training and to meet my bosses," I answered, despite how feeble the words sounded.

"You're often lost in thought, trying to find a solution to some problem. A weatherman wouldn't have to solve problems after his work day concluded. He would be finished. Are you ever going to tell me the truth?"

I ultimately dealt with the recurring question-and-answer sessions with Anna over my real job by stonewalling her. One evening when she again raised the subject, I snapped "Please just drop it." I immediately regretted my outburst as she almost teared up. But, she stopped asking.

Feet of Tunnel Completed: 0   Days until Deadline: 260

CHAPTER 47

Sunday, January 8, 1961

THE CHIEF, KURT, Mark and I occupied the lead vehicle, a Buick sedan with fog lights. Five trucks towing flatbed trailers followed us as we threaded our way through the mist. Our destination was a little-used back gate into Tempelhof Airport and Hanger 1, which was dedicated to our program.

"This fog is heaven sent," Mark said.

"Yes, we'll get the TBM and other construction equipment out of the hangar at Tempelhof just in time!" I agreed.

"That bastard Dieter Holburg and his cadre of agents can go fuck themselves." Kurt raised his middle finger in a rapid upward movement.

Those deftly enunciated words and the accompanying crude gesture from Kurt, the sophisticated European gentleman in a three-piece suit, surprised everyone and eased the tension of the moment. We all laughed.

"Their cameras and infrared sensors will be useless. We've won this round of the fight, gentlemen!" Kurt smiled broadly.

"This fog is predicted to burn off around 0900," I reported. "We have eight hours left, so no resting on our laurels just yet!"

Once inside the fenced area of the airport, I instructed the Chief. "We are now on the main runway. Take the next right turn onto the north taxiway. Follow the broad white stripe. Keep an eye on your odometer. When we've gone a mile, slow down to a crawl."

"We just passed the one-mile point, sir."

"Slower, even slower. Twenty men are out there to direct us to the hanger. Let's not run over them."

From the back seat, Kurt said, "I think I saw a flash of red on our left. Stop, I'll get out...Rover...Rover!?"

I also got out and shouted, "Rover."

"Guide." Looking to my right, I saw someone emerge from the fog. "Rover."

"Guide." When the figure got close enough, I recognized Scott.

Scott repeatedly blew a whistle. Soon men with red cone flashlights in both hands surrounded him.

Two lines of people formed and began to move. The convoy followed them into the massive hangar. The doors clanged shut.

Chief Weber directed the use of a massive aircraft-maintenance crane to lift the TBM off the ground. While using hand gestures, his loud voice commanded attention. "Alex, move that thirty-two wheeled trailer underneath this monster...just so...now a little bit forward...Jim, start lowering it...wait...okay...back up and reposition the trailer a little to the right... okay...all the way down...perfect. Now, pull forward."

A crew began to place huge, empty wooden crates around the TBM, part of our continuing effort to hide the fact that tunnel-digging equipment was even in Berlin.

The Chief continued to direct activities as the crane lifted other pieces of equipment onto the other trailers. He resembled a maestro directing an orchestra.

As we watched, I said to Mark, "The stenciled German words on the crates, boxes, and cartons being placed atop the TBM and other equipment identify the cargo on those trailers as boilers, radiators, heat exchangers and water tanks."

"Those containers look authentic," Mark replied.

"They should, they came from a couple of construction sites over in the British sector. They need to be authentic, because these trailers will be parked out in the open in our maintenance yard until the equipment and supplies on each are needed. Then, they'll be transported to our building."

"Time to put the plan into action," I shouted, "Scott, you're up, time for the decoy."

"We'll go out the main gate very slowly and make sure to get the Stasi watcher's attention," Scott told the group before he entered the lead vehicle.

The sliding doors were opened. A convoy that consisted of an Air Police car, tractor/trailer carrying only empty cartons, crates, and boxes, and two more Air Police vehicles emerged, lights flashing. It exited through the main gate onto a side street, turned left, and traveled down the main street on the west side of the airport.

Looking at my watch, I smiled. "Our timing is perfect, 0419 on a foggy, dank Sunday morning."

Kurt responded, "Usually only a few Stasi agents are on duty at this time. Hopefully, they'll follow Scott's convoy."

"Let's give them fifteen minutes as planned. Then I'll lead the real convoy out the back gate to the maintenance yard," Kurt stated.

Just before sunrise, we arrived undetected at the maintenance yard.

Feet of Tunnel Completed: 0   Days until Deadline: 258

CHAPTER 48

Tuesday, January 10, 1961

ANNA AND I apparently hadn't been followed since my confrontation with Dieter Holburg at Christmas.

Over lunch, I asked Scott, "Do you think it's time for us to cut our losses by shutting down the weather prediction, beer-betting scam?"

"Mia and I will join you and Anna for supper this evening at the pub to do just that. Then we can play bridge at my apartment."

The total bill for that little scam was $398, which Scott and I split.

While we stood at the bar to settle accounts with the bartender, Dieter Holburg approached us. In heavily accented English, he said, "Let me buy you two decadent Americans a beer." He placed a small, blue, ten West Mark bill on the bar. "I appreciate your efforts to convince me that Captain Kerr here is a weatherman. Throughout your charade the whole thing reminded me of three-day-old fish—a bit smelly."

The look of shock on my face probably revealed the truth.

"You are fortunate, my bosses insist I focus on something new. I have not given up, and I will return after I have solved this new problem," he snarled.

"I am a weatherman, no matter what you suspect," I said, probably with too much vigor.

"You played a nasty trick on me in the fog. Like that fish, I had you, but you got away," Dieter scowled at us.

I shrugged.

Scott began, "You think…"

"—Did one of my associates see the two of you at the Hilton when that major misunderstanding occurred last week?"

Both us knew then that they'd connected us to the construction project Jelnicky had revealed. The Stasi would be even more interested in our movements. I grinned, which probably confirmed his suspicions.

Dieter concluded, "Captain Taylor, I again iterate, the games you play when you cross into East Berlin will one day cost you dearly."

CHAPTER 49

Wednesday, January 11, 1961

"THE STASI ARE masters of misdirection. If Dieter Holburg says something, the opposite is usually true," Kurt stated.

"What do you think our encounter with him in the bar meant?" I asked, still shaken.

"You're probably still being followed. But the readily apparent agents, whose purpose is to intimidate, have been replaced by a cadre of Stasi trained to conduct virtually undetectable surveillance operations."

"What can I do?"

"Wear a civilian suit tomorrow. We'll determine if you're being followed and also see how well my team of counter-surveillance specialists can perform their duties."

The next morning, Kurt announced, "Robert, you're leaving here to meet one of my associates, Lorna Sanderson, at the *Pesto Restaurant,* which is just south of Potsdamer Platz. Your objective is to detect and lose any Stasi agents that are following you. Good luck."

Per his instructions, I walked at a fast pace northeast. I knew the area, because the restaurant was near our apartment and we had recently dined there.

Every few blocks, I window shopped while surveying the scene behind me. I failed to spot a tail.

I've failed Situational Awareness.

On my own initiative, I decided to walk around an entire block.

That should cause the people behind me to fall all over each other.

I was puzzled when no unusual activity became apparent. After entering a combination bar and restaurant, the Germans call a *gasthaus*, I order a beer, took a few sips, and then walked past the restroom and out the back door.

Convinced that I'd nailed Evasion and Leave without Being Followed, I headed directly to the restaurant where I met Lorna for the first time. She had a gorgeous face and striking red hair but the figure, manner, and dress of a tomboy.

During our meal, she told me, "I'm from suburban Philadelphia and graduated from Bryn Mawr two years ago." We got acquainted during a banter-filled lunch. Before we parted, she surreptitiously passed a manila envelope to me.

"This meeting will drive the Stasi to distraction, trying to figure out what you two are up to," Kurt told me earlier.

Once back at the base, he said, "They must think you're important. They're devoting five of their best to following you."

"Really! What happened?

"My simplest explanation is they used four men and one woman, who frequently traded point position in a well-choreographed effort to prevent you from recognizing any of them."

"They're very professional. I never saw them!"

"One of the secrets of their success is a new device, which consists of an earpiece that looks like a hearing aid and a small square box that fits into the breast pockets of their suits. This device transmits and receives exchanges between the agents, thus allowing them to easily coordinate their efforts."

"How do your men identify them?"

"They talk to their breast pockets!"

"I guess I'm just not cut out to be a spy. I didn't see your agents, either."

"Glad to hear it. Now let's get Scott and Mark in here to discuss what all this means."

A quick trip to their offices revealed both would be available in a few minutes.

Wanting to get to know Kurt better, I asked, "You mentioned that Berlin is your home. You're an American citizen, right?"

"I was born here and lived a short distance from here until 1933. My father was a high-ranking Christian Democrat and anti-Nazi. He was arrested, tortured, and given an option—prison or exile. We sailed out of Hamburg for New York in August of 1933."

"How old were you at the time?"

"Fifteen. Fortunately, my father's import/export business had a large office in New York City. So, we settled into relative comfort. Eventually, we all became naturalized citizens. I finished graduate business studies at Yale in 1940."

"Then the spy game?"

"I joined my father in his business. Foreign intelligence collection was a State Department responsibility during that period. I was recruited and started to make business trips to Nazi-occupied Western Europe. The game, as many call it, came naturally to me."

"So, you've been in this business for twenty years."

"I joined the Office of Strategic Services, parachuted into France in 1943, and operated with the resistance...."

CHAPTER 50

Wednesday, January 11, 1961

SCOTT JOINED US in his usual jovial mood. "What's up, partner...Oh, Kurt, Mark...this must be important."

"Have a seat. This'll take a while." Kurt then explained that my excursion had resulted in covert Stasi surveillance of my every move.

"So, Robert is still the focus of Stasi surveillance. Wonder why?" Mark asked with obvious concern.

"Their beer-bet scam, radio announcements, and all the rest were contrived," Kurt said. "Since I was away, I couldn't advise you of that fact. We must ensure that none of us is being followed when we go to the building."

"What do you recommend?" I asked. "I thought we could all go out and back through the arrivals hall with the rest of the men."

Kurt shook his head. "Scott, Mark, and I must never use the arrival halls route. We are all known entities. Second, Robert, you need to use it sparingly—once every two weeks at the most. We'll get a KY-7 scrambler telephone and install it here and in the building. You and the senior NCOs can converse on it as often as is necessary."

"The phone is a good idea, but I really need to be on site several hours each day," I replied.

"I understand," Kurt responded. "Let me think for a minute. Start going to the American Mission Building in the Zehlendorf district every workday. We want them to follow you there. In a private area of the basement, you'll get into the trunk of one of our cars with German license plates and be transported to the building."

"That isn't what James Bond does—being transported in trunks—not very dashing or brave."

"But it is very effective!" He replied with a broad smile.

CHAPTER 51

Friday, January 13, 1961

"GENTLEMEN, I'VE BEEN able to convince the Director of the CIA here in Berlin that if we don't take immediate action, our tunnel construction activities will be discovered by the Stasi within the next few weeks," Kurt announced to an emergency meeting of the security committee he called two days later.

Before anyone could ask for details, he continued, "The Stasi have the following facts or at the least have been able to make these deductions. One. Captain Robert Kerr is here in Berlin on a special assignment and is not a weatherman. Two. Thirteen Seabees, nine of who speak German have been assigned to this project, so it almost certainly involves construction of some form. We can assume they have photographs of all of the Seabees and know these men will be here for a year or more. Three. Those Seabees were transported from the Hilton to Tempelhof and have not been seen since. Four. Robert and Scott met an oversized aircraft, which flew something important into Berlin. This cargo may or may not have been removed from Hanger 1 at Tempelhof during that foggy night; or perhaps some kind of intentional misdirection occurred at that time. Five. More importantly, several of us have been working to cover up whatever is planned."

"How can we convince them that Robert is a weatherman!?" Mark asked.

"I'm sure that is now impossible. What we need to do is to get them to focus on a red herring—a massive misdirection. There is a small, US government owned and operated construction company here in Berlin, which is only staffed by German-speaking Americans. The reason they all speak German is that they rely upon German companies to provide supplies and to perform some of the work."

"How can this possibly help?" I asked.

"All of the *Bodenbau Unternehmenoden* (Boden Construction Company) employees have Top Secret Extended Background Investigation security clearances. They build, remodel, and maintain all of the sensitive American facilities throughout Berlin. The Stasi know who they are and what they do. Robert's tank, where we're sitting now, is one of the facilities they designed and installed.

He paused for a moment. "They have a variety of equipment and operate out of a warehouse and construction yard south of us. It's near the one we're using for Robert's project. We need to convince the Stasi, KGB, GRU, British M-6, French Deuxieme Bureau, and West German Intelligence Services that Robert is supervising the fabrication of a nuclear-hardened command and control bunker under Hanger 1 here at Tempelhof."

We sat there slack-jawed in amazement at his bold proposal. After almost a minute of silence, Mark demanded, "How is that possible?!"

Laughing, Kurt said, "Herr Holburg revealed to Robert that the Stasi have the capability of taking long-range telephoto images of us here at Tempelhof. They must have an apartment in one of those buildings on the south side of the airport. We'll use that knowledge to our advantage. The CIA in Berlin has a sizeable Cover and Deception Budget, plus right now the guys over at Boden are available because they are between major projects. Here is what we do, starting immediately…"

CHAPTER 52

Monday, January 16, 1961

SENIOR MASTER SERGEANT Neal Loring and the thirty-three members of his Army Corps of Engineers squad had arrived on January 11th, as scheduled. Their orientation was complete, and this would be their first scheduled work day. I was anxious to get them organized, but first I needed to support Kurt's latest scam, which would be kicked off today.

Kurt briefed the thirteen of us, who would initiate what he called the 'Bunker Subterfuge.' "Gentlemen, we've determined the Stasi surveillance post is an apartment on the sixth floor of a building on the south end of the airport. We anticipate that, in addition to still or movie cameras with telephoto lenses and telescopes, the Stasi might have an individual who is capable of reading lips when English is spoken. So, when you're on stage, say your lines and make gestures like everything is real."

Soon a panel truck arrived outside of Hanger 1. On its side were the words, **Bodenbau Unternehmenoden**. The Chief, all eleven members of his crew, and I emerged from the small door in the center of the massive rolling doors on the front of Hanger 1 at Tempelhof. I was in uniform. Everyone else wore casual work clothes—coats, sweaters, windbreakers, sweatshirts, and dungarees.

After introductions were made, I took my position facing the Stasi apartment, pointed at the hanger, and declared, "Men, we have a year to finish two nuclear-hardened bunkers. One here and the other beneath Clay Headquarters. The latter will also serve as a shelter for the senior Berlin

Mission people, whose offices are located in adjacent buildings." Fifteen minutes of verbal exchanges between those of us assembled in front of the hanger followed.

The Chief then announced each man's work assignment, using made-up last names. Then we all reentered the hanger.

The Chief, nine of his men, and I left immediately. We walked through the steam tunnels departing the base in two plumbing trucks with German Logos on the side. We arrived at the building in time to complete a full day's work on our tunnel.

Two of our men, one wearing a distinctive orange coat and the other a bright red windbreaker, emerged from the hanger with one of the Boden men, climbed into the panel truck and exited the base.

During that first day, our two men and several employees of Boden drove tractor-trailers onto the base. The bed of the first truck contained a large diamond-bladed concrete cutting tool, pneumatic power source, and jackhammers. When it arrived, the hangar doors were partially open expos-ing several crates and boxes. Our intention was to make the Stasi believe that the cargo delivered in the pregnant guppy had never left the hanger. Next, two large bulldozers, a trencher, and an articulated digger were unloaded and taken into the massive hanger before the doors were closed.

We planned that every workday several of the Seabees and the Chief or I would exit the hanger for a smoke break at odd times to provide proof that we were working inside.

In the middle of the night the next week, one of our Air Policemen caught a civilian employee of the airport as he tried to sneak into Hanger 1. He was arrested, identified as a Stasi operative, turned over to the West Berlin police and later released without being charged.

This was good news. The Stasi had taken the bait.

Our plan was for the Boden workers to cut a large chunk out of the middle of the concrete floor in the hanger and excavate the soil beneath it. Trucks would haul away the concrete and dirt. From time to time over the next several months, concrete-mixing trucks and pumping machines would cluster around Hanger 1. They would be used to fill in the hole. There would never be any structure beneath the floor of Hanger 1.

CHAPTER 53

Friday, January 27, 1961

Memorandum #10 from Captain Robert Kerr   Berlin, January 27, 1961

1. The construction rate of our work crew has exceeded my expectations. We are now eight days ahead of schedule.
2. The roll-up door and associated ramp from the street down into the basement and the wall designed to shield what goes on in the basement have been installed. In the process, the southeast end of the building has been stabilized.
3. All of our supplies and equipment have been moved from our construction yard into the basement.
4. Approximately half of the concrete slab has been removed from along the west wall.
5. Early next week we will begin excavating the ramp down to the tunnel entrance.

Signed,

Robert T. Kerr, Captain USAF

Feet of Tunnel Completed: 0   Days until Deadline: 243

CHAPTER 54

Monday, January 30, 1961

FOR THE LAST two weeks, I had been going to the building through the American Mission four days a week.

"Why do you have to go over to the American Mission every morning?" Anna asked when I told her we'd only walk to work together on Fridays.

I repeated the cover story created by Kurt. "Colonel Morgan has been asked to support the German-American Festival, which will occur here in the summer. I've turned over most of my duties to my new assistant."

"What is this festival?"

"It is an attempt to improve German-American relations at a person-to-person level by holding an American county fair here in Berlin. Something I'd expect you to support."

"Sounds to me like it's a blatant attempt to win German citizen support for your Cold War and the fight against the communists," she said sternly, then with a twinkle in her eye, added, "That's actually a pretty good idea."

Kurt greeted me in his office, which was large and furnished with Danish modern wood furniture. "Ah, Robert. Come in."

"You asked to see me?"

"I'd like to suggest that you and Lorna have lunch at least twice a week. Will that be possible?" he asked.

"I guess it's my fate to be a decoy whose task is to keep the spies entertained while the tunnel is being built. First, I have to appear outside of Hanger 1 several times a week. Now you want me to meet Lorna twice a week. Chief Weber is such an outstanding leader and manager, I can support both deception activities."

"The bad guys are convinced you are leading a super-secret construction project. So, when you're seen entering the American Mission every day and often taking a leisurely lunch with an attractive woman, they will wonder about the validity of their information."

"I'll take your word for it," I replied.

"Believe me, this is an excellent cover and deception gambit. It will drive Dieter and his bosses crazy."

This gambit would have grave and unanticipated consequences.

CHAPTER 55

Anna

Friday, February 10, 1961

ON MY WAY to pick up a few things during my lunch break, I first noticed a tan Mercedes moving along the narrow side street at the same speed I was walking. Footfalls close behind me caused me to look back just as a giant put his massive hand around my elbow. He forced me over to the curb and into the back seat of the car.

The man who had identified himself as Dieter Holburg on Christmas day was seated there.

"Ah, Fraulein Fischer, we need your help finding out what your boyfriend Robert is doing here in Berlin. Will you help us willingly, or must we force you?"

"Please release me. You have no authority here in West Berlin!"

"But as a loyal German, you must realize the Americans are intent on making our beloved country into a colony."

"No…"

"—You think that your Robert is such a wonderful man. He is seeing another woman."

"I know Robert. He loves me." I blurted without even thinking. "He wouldn't…"

"—Here are numerous photographs of your boyfriend and this gorgeous redhead. She is striking, don't you agree? You will notice that she is wearing different clothes in many of the photos. Eight times we have seen them together. Oh, in this one she appears to be kissing him on the ear. And in this one, they are obviously enjoying each other's company. Makes one wonder who the joke is on."

He forced me to look closely at each photo by grabbing my hair and turning my head toward them. "Do you and Robert enjoy your time together this much?"

Desperate to escape, I jerked on the handle of the car door and was surprised when it opened. I stumbled and almost fell getting out of the car. I rushed down the street to a major thoroughfare.

Knowing Robert loved me, I still found it difficult to get those images of them together out of my head.

CHAPTER 56

Robert

Friday-Saturday, February 10-11, 1961

EARLIER IN THE week, the first pressure door had been installed. That Friday, we spent the entire day getting the Tunnel Boring Machine into position by using a hoist and giant sling.

Once the hydraulic and Bentonite hoses were attached to the massive TBM, the entire work crew gathered as I took a bottle of champagne and broke it over the boring head. "Men, we weren't supposed to be at this point for another ten days. Each of you has worked hard, and everyone at all levels appreciates your efforts. Chief, fire it up."

The three cutting heads—one massive, and two smaller ones on each side—began to turn. Bentonite impregnated water spewed from the nozzles arranged symmetrically around the front of the tunnel shield. The hydraulic jacks engaged, and the whole boring machine slowly moved forward. Sand started flowing down the trough, up the conveyor belt, and into a trailing mining cart.

Despite the centuries of construction experience represented by those gathered around the machine, the jubilant mood resulted in a rousing cheer. "Hooray. It worked!"

All of the management team including Mark, Scott, and Colonel Morgan witnessed this momentous event. The Chief walked up to us with an invitation, "Sirs, I made arrangements for us to have a steak fry this evening. The men would like you four to join us in a victory celebration.

We'll stay up until the swing shift ends at midnight when the real party can begin."

I was surprised when even Colonel Morgan agreed to join us.

Feet of Tunnel Completed: 8   Days until Deadline: 228

CHAPTER 57

Friday, February 24, 1961

"WE GOT A big problem, sir. Better get over here as soon as possible. This is serious," the Chief revealed over the KY-7 scrambler telephone.

An hour later, he and I walked up to the end of the tunnel. The entire TBM rested at an odd angle, beyond it an open space.

"It's fallen into a large cavity, sir."

We crawled past the TBM using an opening the construction crew had dug, then jumped down onto a raised platform. I stated the obvious. "It's an old wine merchant's storage cellar. See the huge casks and racks at various levels. Looks to me as if it was dug over several centuries, new areas added at various levels as required."

"There are even a few ancient empty bottles," the Chief said picking one up. "This one has a label with the date 1735 written in old script."

"Given that the TBM is designed to move forward by pushing on previously installed tunnel sections, we're stuck. We can't move forward, and we can't move back. If the TBM falls down into that cavity on the far side, it could easily be damaged, and we might never get it out."

This kind of monumental screw up was what Thomas Lane was counting on to make him look like a big man in his superiors' eyes.

Once back in the tunnel, I began to experience a panic attack.

No way. Under no circumstance will you allow your men to see you this way, I thought, setting my jaw and clenching my fists. Somehow, I managed to blurt out, "Office...Chief...Now!"

By focusing on my breathing, I coped well enough to march lockstep to the office the Chief and I shared in the building. I bolted the door, and as the Chief stared at me in shock, I gasped, "Panic attack."

My heart rate skyrocketed. I began to tremble and gasp for breath.

"How can I help, Captain?"

"Lie down...I must lie down," I strained to say.

With his massive arms, the Chief swept everything off my desk. He then gently guided me to it and lifted my legs as he pulled his desk over to support my feet. I lay flat and began my deep breathing exercises. *Good air in...bad air out...breathe deep...again...and again!*

It took almost twenty minutes before the Chief and I could carry on a coherent conversation.

"Captain, no one could've anticipated that the cellar would be right in our path."

"That doesn't make any difference. I'll get the blame."

"Let's discuss alternatives."

"Okay. What are your thoughts?" I asked, feeling able to function.

"Raising the TBM to a horizontal position and then backing it up would involve removing several structural sections we recently installed."

"We'd have to back up a long way to take a new route that avoids the wine cellar. And..."

"—Dismantling the TBM would take a week or two," the Chief interrupted. "Then we'd need to start over on a different route after we reassembled the machine."

"By the time we implement either of those options we'd be so far behind schedule that meeting the deadline would be impossible. I..."

"—Captain, our best bet is to find some way to prop up the TBM and continue forward on the same route."

"That's impossible. The top of the TBM is about forty feet beneath the floor of the basement. It's not accessible, and it weighs eleven tons."

"If only we could get that massive A-frame and sling we used to shift the TBM into place when we began tunneling...."

"—I've got it!" I shouted, "We dig a shaft down to the wine cellar, then use that A-frame to return the TBM to its previous position and hold it in place with the sling...."

"—Then we fill the entire wine cellar with sand, using the cement pumping equipment and skip loaders," the Chief added, excited about this solution.

"It's so obvious, it should work," I observed. "How long do you think it'll take, Chief?"

"Five or six days, working 24 hours a day—maybe less," he responded.

"If we lose only a week, that would be wonderful. Get the men started," I ordered.

I remained there, observing the cutting of the slab and jackhammering of the section we needed to remove. Hunger pangs forced me to look at my watch, 2127. *You dumb shit. You had a date with Anna this evening. You were supposed to meet her outside the bookstore at five!*

Looking at my two senior NCOs, I asked, "What's your plan?"

"We'll work three shifts all weekend," Neal Loring replied. "In a few minutes, the last of the concrete slab will be removed. An 18-inch auger bit has been fitted to the back of a backhoe. Fortunately, we have numerous extensions for the auger bit. Within an hour we'll begin drilling down. We'll need to stabilize this damn Berlin sand with Bentonite as we go. That'll be our most time-consuming task. We'll have a better idea tomorrow about how long it will take us to recover."

"Chief, can I have a private moment with you?"

When we arrived in a deserted corner, he said, "Sir, your secret is safe with me. Take the weekend off, and we'll see you Monday morning."

Feet of Tunnel Completed: 158   Days until Deadline: 215

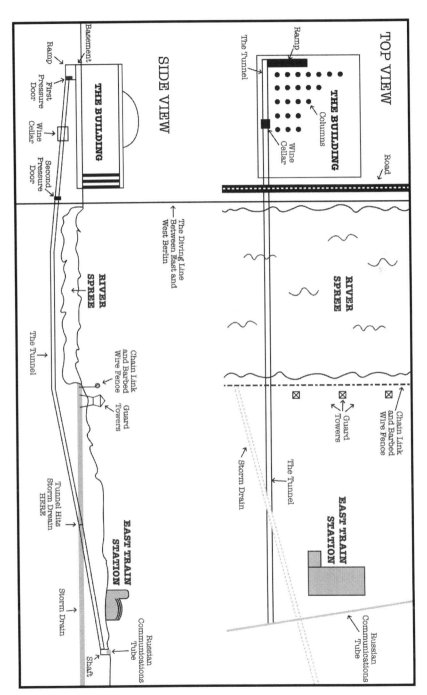

The Tunnel

TOP VIEW

THE BUILDING

Ramp

The Tunnel

Columns

Wine
Cellar

Road

SIDE VIEW

THE BUILDING

Basement

Ramp

First
Pressure
Door

Wine
Cellar

Second
Pressure
Door

RIVER
SPREE

← The Diving Line
Between East and
West Berlin

RIVER
SPREE

Chain Link
and Barbed
Wire Fence

The Tunnel

Chain Link
and Barbed
Wire Fence

Guard
Towers

Guard
Towers

Storm Drain

The Tunnel

Tunnel Hits
Storm Dream
HERE

EAST TRAIN
STATION

EAST TRAIN
STATION

Storm Drain

Russian
Communications
Tube

Shaft

Russian
Communications
Tube

Anna was in bed reading a book. She seemed to accept my excuse that I'd lost track of time at work. She warmed some leftovers. I ate, when suddenly she exploded, "If you're a weatherman, you should have very regular hours! Yet you seem to be carrying the weight of the world on your shoulders. When are you going to tell me what you really are doing in Berlin?"

"Please understand, I have responsibilities and have made commitments which sometimes will interfere with our plans. I'll make a special effort to let you know in the future when our plans must be changed."

She left the room in a huff. When I entered the bedroom, she pretended to be asleep. After I showered, I snuggled up against her. She finally relented after several minutes of cajoling and caresses. We enjoyed wonderful make-up sex until the wee hours of the morning.

CHAPTER 58

Saturday, February 25, 1961

AFTER LUNCH, ANNA left to visit her parents in East Berlin for the weekend and I returned to Tempelhof under the watchful eye of two Stasi agents. Once there, I arranged to be transported from the airport steam-generation plant to the building in the back of one of our plumbing vans.

I watched for hours as the hole down to the TBM was completed. The huge A-frame was positioned over the hole, a sling fed down and attached to the tunnel shield. The TBM was carefully hoisted back into position and held in place while a temporary support structure was built beneath it. Concurrently, five tunnel sections were removed and the TBM was carefully towed back into the tunnel. The crew then removed the sling from the hole.

I asked the Chief, "How long until we finish?"

"It'll still be towards the end of the week—maybe midday on Thursday."

As the Chief was replying to my question, I saw a three-inch flexible hose emerge into the wine cellar. Soon three men were controlling this hose as a steady flow of sand emerged. The men wore hip boots and continually shifted position to maintain their footing in the wet sand as they filled the lower sections of the immense wine cellar.

After a few minutes, I walked up to the basement of the building. There, skip loaders dumped sand into the pumping machine, Bentonite-impregnated water being added to help lubricate the sand installation. This mixture supported the immense weight of the TBM when we eventually tunneled our way through the wine cellar.

At 0400 on Sunday, I finally left the building. Despite doing little actual physical labor, I felt exhausted but also relieved that this snafu hadn't delayed our progress for long.

Feet of Tunnel Completed: 148   Days until Deadline: 214

CHAPTER 59

Anna

Wednesday, March 1, 1961

SEVERAL TIMES RECENTLY, Robert used work as an excuse for his failure to come home on time or to keep dinner dates with me. After Stasi Agent Holburg showed me the photographs of Robbie with the redhead, I'd worried he was seeing another woman.

To ensure his faithfulness, I implemented a campaign to make love to him so often, he wouldn't wind up in anyone else's arms. Last week, he came home late, disheveled, and so exhausted his lovemaking performance felt perfunctory at best.

On Sunday, I left my parents' home immediately after the noon meal. I planned to spend the afternoon in bed with Robbie. I found him still asleep when I arrived at our apartment. Although he claimed he'd worked almost all night, I doubted him. My senses of smell and sight assured me another woman had not been in the apartment. Perhaps they had made love at her place. I didn't even try to initiate a lovemaking session.

After that, finding out what was actually going on began to taunt me. I couldn't eat, sleep, or think. Somehow, I intended to determine the truth. If I saw them together, I would know. One of the Stasi photos had shown them dining at a restaurant near the American Mission. I took the afternoon off and began my quest for the truth.

To my amazement, Robert and that redhead sat at the same table in the

Restoration 1900 restaurant window. Robert was wearing his officer's uniform, and she had on a pink sweater. I watched them from across the street.

For several minutes, lively conversation went on between the two, much smiling and laughing. Robert took something out of a box and held it up, examining it. I recognized a charm bracelet similar to the one he'd given me. The one I wore on my wrist at that moment. As I touched my bracelet, I started to cry. Then, I lost my temper.

I crossed the street as he placed the bracelet on her wrist. I shook my head, as if to clear it of that hurtful image.

Entering the restaurant, I confronted them, "Robert, you told me you loved me and that you wanted to marry me. All the time you're seeing another woman! How could you?"

He jumped up as if bitten and flushed declaring, "Anna, darling, I can explain…we're business associates. We're planning the German American Festival together. Please understand!"

"Do you give all of your girlfriends charm bracelets? Careful young lady, he's a…Casanova…a lothario…he's just no good!" I shouted.

The redhead stood, moved her hand up and down to calm me down, and then pulled a chair over from an adjacent vacant table. She said, "Robert is telling you the truth. Please join us so that we can explain. Everyone in this restaurant is staring at us…Please…"

In a final fit of anger, I shouted, "You American men say that German girls are easy. Well, at least I made you work hard before I gave you my maidenhead."

"Anna can we please discuss this rationally? You've…"

"—I know what you Americans say—the four Fs—find them, feel them, fuck them and then forget them! Well, you can forget me. I'm moving out. Don't come to the bookstore and don't try to contact me!"

I half turned, paused, and then managed to open the clasp on my charm bracelet. I hurled it at Robert before I rushed out of the restaurant sobbing.

A taxi sat at the curb. I got in. As it pulled away, I looked back through tear-filled eyes. Robbie was chasing the cab down the middle of the street, waving his hands up and down.

"Fraulein, a man is chasing us! Do you want me to stop for him?"

"No! Never! Drive faster!"

CHAPTER 60

Robert
Wednesday-Saturday, March 1-5, 1961

THAT WEDNESDAY AFTER our altercation in the restaurant, I followed Anna back to our apartment. Her reaction to my presence as she packed was tempestuous; I soon realized that I was better off leaving. When I returned that night most of her possessions were gone. The rest disappeared the next day.

I approached Mark and Scott and asked them to speak to her about a reconciliation. Both failed to persuade her. She threatened to quit the bookstore position if we didn't leave her alone.

At 0800 that Friday morning, almost a week after the wine cellar accident, the day shift commenced regular tunnel-building operations. Filling the wine cellar with sand had taken nearly every grain from our colossal stockpile, but we remained eight days ahead of schedule. Our next significant milestone involved the installation of the second pressure door at the 425-foot point. At least, one aspect of my life seemed to be back on track.

Late Saturday morning I called her parents' home. I heard the conversation between Anna and her mother:

"Robert is on the telephone, and he would like to talk to you."

"Tell him I'm dead!"

"I'll say no such thing, young lady. You must talk to him."

"Never. He is a dirty, lying, cheating bastard!"

When she came back on the line, I told Emma what had happened and how I desperately wanted Anna back.

Emma left the phone off the hook, and I heard her say, "Please tell me your side of the story, sweetheart."

Anna recounted all of the details, including her encounter with the Stasi agent and the photos he showed her. This was the first I had heard of their involvement. Then, she recounted my many late nights and long absences. I didn't blame her for feeling suspicious.

"Anna, I think your Robert is an exceptional young man, who was only trying to do his job. What you thought is understandable, but I believe Robert's version of the story."

"All the times he was late getting home from work and that woman!"

"First and foremost, you cannot believe anything a Stasi agent tells you. He was intentionally trying to cause trouble in order to get you on his side."

"Maybe."

"Did you tell Robert about the Stasi photographs?"

"No."

"The redhead's name is Lorna Sanderson. They are working on a special project. It is natural for them to eat lunch together."

"What about the charm bracelet?"

"The young lady's clasp on her charm bracelet was broken. She had it repaired and the box was a jeweler's box, not a gift box. What you saw was Lorna explaining each of her charms."

"He was smiling as he put the bracelet on her wrist."

"Robert was telling the young woman that his girlfriend Anna always has a difficult time getting the clasp closed with only one hand."

"Well, I will have to think about it. Perhaps I could be wrong."

CHAPTER 61

Monday, March 6, 1961

I LOOKED AT her note again and again. "*Come home to a scrumptious dinner. All my love, Anna.*"

Frustrated that my taxi had only gotten two blocks in as many minutes, I threw a ten Mark note into the front seat, exited and started to run. Pedestrians became stationary obstructions as I sprinted to our apartment building. When I finally reached the sixth floor, I scooped Anna in my arms and carried her into the bedroom.

"Goodness, you must be glad to see me!" she said as we hurriedly undressed each other.

"There is only you. There'll only ever be you, darling—believe me!" I declared as I put the charm bracelet back on her wrist after a very passionate lovemaking reunion.

CHAPTER 62

Thursday, March 16, 1961

"DO NOT GO home—I must see you urgently—I'm in the bookstore. Anna," read a note I found outside of my office.

When I entered Anna's office, she closed and locked the door and handed me another note, *"We need to talk. Can we go upstairs?"*

Under that note I wrote, *"I'll check. Wait here."*

I found Scott in his office. Once I explained the situation, he escorted us into his office, closed the door, and asked, "Why all the mystery, Anna?"

"Robert and I are going to a play this evening, so I took the afternoon off to get my hair done. At the third-floor landing, I passed a man going down that I had never seen before. I know most of the residents of our apartment building."

"All right. What is the monumental problem?" Scott asked.

"Robbie...Robert will tell you I have an exceptional sense of smell. This man had a distinct smell, which I also detected inside of our apartment!"

"A distinct smell?" I repeated.

"Fowl tobacco smoke and cheap Romanian soap. When I was a kid, we called it stinky soap. It has a unique strong odor, and it's only available in the East."

"Go on."

"I looked to see if anything had been stolen. Down behind one of the radiators in the living room, I found a round thing that looks like a microphone. And there is at least one more in the bedroom! A cord goes from it through the wall."

"Really," Scott replied, now interested.

"That's when I came back here."

"Anna, stay right here. Robert, you come with me."

We went to Mark's office, told him what had happened, and the three of us called Kurt on the KY-7 scrambler telephone. A lengthy discussion centered on what could be done. Kurt was adamant. "Anything we do will be detected by the opposition. For now, Robert, you and Anna will need to remember the walls have ears. I'll be over tomorrow, and we can discuss other actions we can take. For now, you're stuck."

I returned to Scott's office, took her in my arms, and attempted to reassure her, "Anna, my love, our apartment has been bugged by the same people who are trying to find out what I'm doing here in Berlin. Go home, dress for the play, and I'll be home soon. Act as normal as possible."

"What happens when we want to make love?" She asked. Are we supposed to entertain them?"

"For now, we must act as normal as possible. I know it won't be easy. The walls have ears."

CHAPTER 63

Friday, March 17, 1961

EARLY THE NEXT morning, the Security Committee met in my tank. Kurt addressed the group. "The Stasi have bugged Captain Kerr's apartment. This probably means Dieter Holburg and his bosses haven't entirely accepted our gambit that Robert's crew of Navy men are building nuclear-hardened bunkers. They may have concluded we're using this hoax to hide something more important. But there is another, more ominous possibility. Someone may be leaking information to them."

"What exactly do you mean?" Mark asked with obvious concern.

"The KGB, GRU or Stasi may be exploiting a relationship with one of Robert's men to determine what he and his crew are doing here in Berlin," Kurt replied. "Let's say, that hypothetically, this guy brags to someone he's here on a super-secret assignment. They slowly, very slowly, establish a relationship with him. Then, they start to ask questions."

"Perhaps they've even gotten him into a compromising situation, and they're threatening to expose him if he doesn't spill his guts" Scott suggested. "Perhaps he's a homosexual or married, and they pump him for information with threats."

"Another possibility we must not overlook, is that they offer him money in return for information," Kurt added.

"Twenty-seven of our sixty-one men are free to leave the base on weekends," the Chief advised. "They usually go to another American military facility here in Berlin, but some go to clubs and bars. It could be anyone except the Polish option men, who are conforming to their restrictions. Of that, I'm sure. We have implemented a strict sign-out, sign-in process, which I check."

"We can speculate on what's going on, but we must take positive action now," I said. "What do you recommend, Kurt?"

He spent some time describing 'the talking to the wall' training he would conduct with Anna and me that afternoon. Then he said, "Robert, call all of the men together and reemphasize the importance of the tunnel and secrecy. Chief, you need to play detective and attempt to learn what the twenty-seven do when they leave the base."

"Brief Sergeant Loring on what's occurred," I ordered, looking at the Chief. "He's allowed to leave the base. Make him responsible for determining if we have a leak, and if so, who it is."

To close the meeting, Kurt said, "Sometimes four or even five layers of cover and deception are required to conceal someone's actual role in a sensitive activity. One of our tactics is to maintain the original cover for as long as possible. Even if the other side is convinced they are being fooled, there is always doubt that they're mistaken. With that said, Robert, for the foreseeable future, you're must maintain your weatherman cover for most of the world and hardened bunker construction lead cover for the Stasi."

That afternoon, Kurt introduced himself to Anna as Hans Zimmerman. "Fraulein, neither Robert nor I can reveal the true nature of our endeavors. We need your help to convince the people who are listening that Robert is a weatherman assigned to work on the German American Festival, a real event that will occur in June and July of this year. Your part is critical. Everything must appear to be normal in your apartment."

"That's impossible, and you know it. Once one knows that someone is listening, it is very difficult to act naturally!"

"That's why you're here. This training is critical if we are to succeed, but I do have some help for you."

"What? A new apartment where we actually sleep?" Anna snapped.

"The recording devices which are located in the basement, are sound activated, because they have limited recording capacity. We've checked, and there is enough room for you to slip one of these soundproof boxes over each microphone. After you've installed the box, close the top. Only open it when you two should be active,"

"That should help a lot," Anna responded with relief.

"Just remember, the box should be open when you are usually awake and active. Also, you're both young and sexually active. If you don't let them listen to a few of your lovemaking sessions, they'll become suspicious."

"Or we could only allow them to hear simulated sex," I suggested.

"If you agree, this evening you two will have a dinner party. Scott and his girlfriend Mia, plus Lorna and her special female friend, will visit your apartment. The main topic of discussion will be the role Robert is playing in the planning of the German-American Festival."

"Will you also give them training?" Anna asked.

"No, only you two, Scott, and Lorna will know what is going on. If you agree to host the party, Lorna and Scott are just outside and will join us. We'll rehearse each topic that must be covered."

"Before they come in, you say that Lorna is being accompanied by her special friend. Are you telling me they are a couple?" Anna queried, raising her eyebrows.

"Yes, they live together."

Anna inhaled deeply, clearly understanding that Lorna liked girls and posed no threat to her relationship with me.

CHAPTER 64

Friday, March 17, 1961

KURT'S INSTRUCTIONS ON how we should casually shape the evening's conversations were implemented. After dinner was over, we were having drinks in our living room when Lorna exclaimed, "Robert, I forgot to tell you I received word today that both Brenda Lee and Bobby Rydell will entertain at the festival. Each will bring their entire traveling show, which will include other rock-and-roll stars. She'll be here the first two weeks, and he the second two. Isn't that great?"

"What is this festival?" Anna asked on cue.

"An attempt to improve German-American relations on a person-to-person level by holding an American county fair here in Berlin," I replied.

"Anna, there will be a carnival midway, all kinds of rides, American food like hamburgers and hot dogs, beverages including beer, wine, and Coca-Cola," Lorna explained to the group and our eavesdroppers. "The exhibits will include a large tent covering the contribution Americans of German extraction have made to the world."

"Do you really believe your German guests would prefer American beer and wine over their local products?" Scott groaned.

"The American firms are providing much of the funding for the festival," I said. "They're practically giving away their products in an attempt to attract new customers."

"Hope you're also allowing some of the German beverage companies to supply something drinkable for a price."

"Afraid not. I argued for both German drinks and food—it is a German-American festival after all—but was overruled by the higher-ups," I told the group.

"Tell them they're stupid!"

"I'll try again. My exact words will be, 'Captain Taylor says you're making a huge mistake.' " I quipped, then added, "My favorite will be the tent filled with photos and memorabilia from the Berlin Airlift. Two of the C-54 transport aircraft, which actually participated in the airlift, will be on exhibit. One will be filled with coal and the other will contain food cartons from that era...."

The conversation continued until we reached the topic of how Lorna and I received this 'special' assignment. Lorna said, "I'm a special assistant to one of the diplomats at the American Mission. My regular job is not very challenging, so I jumped at the chance to help plan this festival. How about you, Robert?"

"They recently assigned another, more experienced officer to the weather office at Tempelhof. He is junior to me in rank, but he's a trained meteorologist with a degree from University of Michigan. I complained to the base commander that I had little to do, so he assigned me to the festival..."

I continued with my regular routine for the next few weeks. I took the subway to the American Mission Monday through Thursday, had lunch with Lorna at least twice a week, walked to and from Tempelhof with Anna on Friday, and appeared outside of Hanger 1 with members of my crew several times a week. I also managed to be conveyed to the building several times a week to observe firsthand the progress my crew was making on the tunnel.

One day, much to my surprise, I no longer spotted anyone following me. Several days later Kurt dispatched two of his agents to follow me. He reported, "Both the Stasi harassment squad and the covert tails have stopped."

"What does that mean?" I asked.

"We shouldn't assume that our cover and deception activities have succeeded," he said. "This is probably another gambit on their part. They want to see if you change your routine or let down your guard. Just stick to your usual routine."

Every evening when we got home, I went down to the basement to determine if the recording devices remained in place. Soon they also disappeared, but the microphones and wires stayed in place.

For the first time in six months, the Stasi appeared to be uninterested in me. The security committee discussed the matter, concluding that the bad guys knew my cover story as a weatherman was a ruse and that my real responsibilities involved the construction of two nuclear-hardened bunkers. If true, I no longer represented a subject of compelling interest to them. In actuality, they'd decided to approach the problem I presented from a different angle. During the discussions, Kurt observed, "The spy game is like a knife fight in a dark closet. You know that you're probably going to be cut-up or even killed, but you have no way of knowing when or from what direction the damaging blow will come."

CHAPTER 65

Wednesday-Thursday, April 12-13, 1961

"CHIEF, THIS DAMN tunnel isn't worth even one life. Let's retreat beyond the second pressure door and abandon this mess. The water level is rapidly increasing. It's up to my knees now."

"Sir, give me another fifteen to twenty minutes. If we don't make progress by then, you can order us to abandon ship! I'm..."

"—It looks to me as if we are in danger of having the River Spree flood our tunnel..."

"—You may be right, but stand by for a few minutes," the Chief urged.

"Okay, Chief. So far you've always been right..."

"—Sir, I need one more man to take orders and do things. Just this once, can you fill that role?"

"Order away, sir." I managed a grin and saluted him.

"First, back near the pressure door, there is a box of hardhats. Grab a few, bring them back and give them to the guys whose hardhats shorted out because they got wet. Then keep the men supplied with working lights. While at the pressure door, tell them to turn the air pump up to 50 psi. Then examine the Bentonite hose to make sure it doesn't have any kinks, monitor the water level by making a mark on the side of the tunnel, and keep me up to speed on the hose pressure readings."

After a half hour of hurried activity by the crew, the Chief said, "We may be winning."

"The water level is now stable—not increasing," I reported.

I could see that the flow rate of the incoming water was lower, and fewer of the seams between the tunnel structure sections were leaking.

The Chief shouted something over the roar in a language I didn't understand. When he saw my questioning look, he said in English and then German, "You cocksucker, we're going to lick you." He laughed with joy.

The crew manning the trowels rapidly spread the stucco-like mixture over each seam. This quick-drying mixture hardened in fifteen minutes.

As the flow stopped through the last visible seam, the drilling crew made a hole, and the Chief injected the Bentonite. "Cement that sucker tight, and we're done at this pressure level. Thanks for your help, sir."

"We've been in here so long, we are going to have to spend almost five hours in the decompression chamber, but we did it." I shook hands with the Chief and the eight-man crew.

On the way to the decompression chamber, we passed another team headed by Sergeant Loring.

The Chief and I stopped as Neal told us, "Sir, I've ordered them to decrease the pressure slowly—two psi per hour. I've arranged for a new crew to take our place every two hours. We'll keep it up all night until we are back to the earlier pressure level of 34 psi. Only then can we declare victory."

"Well done, Sergeant. I've set up a Board of Inquiry tomorrow afternoon at 2 p.m. Please be there."

"See you then, sir."

The Chief, Neal, and I gathered in my office at the building. "Okay, tell me what happened."

"The Bentonite hose flow became constricted, because it was under the wheel of one of the carts. For almost an entire shift little of that substance was sprayed into the upper half of the surface around the tunnel."

"Who was the team leader?"

"One of my best men, Master Sergeant Harding," Neal replied.

"The procedure requires continuous monitoring of the Bentonite pressure level," the Chief reminded us.

"What should we do with Harding?" I asked. "People might have died, and the whole program could have been wrecked."

"Sir, he's served with distinction for eighteen years, he'll leave for the States tomorrow, and I'll ensure that he retires at his current rank as soon as he gets his twenty in. That's punishment enough."

"Ok, Sergeant, I'll leave it at that."

"Thank you, sir."

"On the positive side, this was good training," the Chief observed. "When we try to completely depressurize the tunnel, we'll undoubtedly have more leaks."

"I put a whole week on the schedule just to cover that set of problems," I replied. "After the delay this incident has caused, we won't be at that point for another three weeks."

Suddenly, after they left, I realized that no panic attack had occurred during the events of these past two days.

I exhibited the calmness of an experienced leader—perhaps I'm finally free of that awful affliction.

Feet of Tunnel Completed: 583   Days until Deadline: 169

CHAPTER 66

Thursday, April 20, 1961

ONE OF MY recurring tasks was to maintain the tunnel's direction with very tight tolerance. I used the theodolite's telescopic sight to precisely measure the angles in the horizontal and vertical planes. Using that information, I determined where we were relative to our starting point and objective across the River Spree.

The rest of my time I spent solving problems with Chief Weber and Sergeant Loring, updating schedules, generating plans for the later phases of the program, and making appearances outside of the American Mission Building and Hanger 1 at Tempelhof. I also spent an inordinate amount of time solving myriad personnel issues that occur when a large crew worked on a major project while they are thousands of miles away from their homes and families.

Feet of Tunnel Completed: 627   Days until Deadline: 162

CHAPTER 67

Saturday, April 22, 1961

EARLY IN THE week, Anna asked if I was interested in visiting Museum Island in East Berlin that weekend. We'd spend the night at her parent's home and attended her mother's 60ᵗʰ birthday party. I agreed to go, because General Harrington made it clear he expected me to travel East on occasion as a part of my cover and deception act.

It was one of those few glorious, sunny days in Berlin that spring. When we passed by the park on the way to the local subway station, I noticed a uniquely German occurrence—nudity in public. Perhaps a hundred people relaxed in various stages of undress—most were naked.

Being an American, I, of course, gawked. Anna scolded me, "Grow up, Robbie. This is normal conduct. We Germans seldom see the sun, so when we get the opportunity, we use every second of sunlight and usually end up regretting it with bad sunburns in very private places."

I laughed, but I continued to gawk at the pink to red flesh on display.

Immediately after we passed through the checkpoint in the Stadtmitte Subway Station, I noticed our followers. After a fifteen-minute walk, we arrived at a wide pedestrian walkway on the east side of the River Spree. Anna said, "On the opposite shore is the Berliner Dom. The Protestant Church where the Kings of Germany are buried."

As we approached the bridge over the Spree, I looked down, shook my head, and stared at a gray pipe with an almost one-meter diameter, which was attached to the bridge structure with large steel clamps.

That's the communications pipe, I thought. A check revealed that our two followers remained behind us. *If it runs from Russia House and East German government offices back to this point—that must be it.*

I asked Anna, "What is that area ahead of us called?"

"Museum Island. We're on our way to see the museums located there."

For the rest of the morning and into early afternoon, I followed Anna around three museums. I tried to pay attention to her descriptions, but my thoughts kept returning to the gray pipe. I couldn't understand why the CIA had failed to determine its location in the vacant lot that was our tunnel's target.

After lunch in the museum café, two different people began to follow us—numbers ten and fourteen from Scott's list of individuals who monitored the Tempelhof base. Shift change, I surmised.

As we left the Pergamum Museum at a little after 3 p.m., Anna asked, "Do you want to stop at Alexander Platz for a beer?"

"Sweetheart, are the buildings which contain the East German government located to the west of us?"

"Yes, they are."

"Could you take me on a tour of them?"

On the west side of Museum Island another bridge spanned the Kupfergraben Canal. Casually looking down, I noted another section of that gray pipe suspended beneath it.

Eureka! I've indeed found it.

"Please, show me this area. Tell me what I'm looking at," I said to Anna.

"On the right is Humboldt University where my mother teaches. On the left is the State Opera House." Continuing to walk, she pointed and said, "That complex of buildings contains the Russian Embassy and numerous other Russian organizations. Their collective mission is to ensure that the East German government follows the Kremlin's dictates."

I spotted new cement where the road had recently been cut. It crossed Unter den Linden into the Russia House complex.

Facing west toward the Brandenburg Gate and then turning around and looking back, I thought, *Everything is aligned.*

"Please tell me what you are doing. Are you going crazy?" Anna asked.

"What is this building?"

"The prewar Offices of the German Telephone and Telegraph Administration."

"What's to the left here?"

"Most of the East German government offices."

All of the lines go where they should—absolute Eureka! A glance cooled my excitement. Stasi agent fourteen stood close enough to us to hear everything we said. *He probably speaks English.*

Anna asked, "Shall we get a beer now? You've never been to Alexander Platz. It's the showplace of the East. The best shopping and restaurants are in that area. You'll be surprised; it's much like it was before the war."

I took Anna's offered hand, and we headed east.

The two Stasi agents watched as we took our seats in an outdoor café on a side street near Alexander Platz. Its wooden tables were covered with umbrellas that featured a famous Czechoslovakian Beer *Pilsner Urquell.* We ordered two beers and crisps. I stared at Anna, aware that she was talking. My mind focused on what numbers ten and fourteen would report back to Dieter Holburg and what that might mean to my tunnel-building mission.

I surveyed our surroundings for Stasi agents, and was shocked to see Dieter Holburg walking toward our table. I looked at Anna and smiled, tuning her in as she said, "Twenty people will be at our house for Mama's birthday party this evening. You'll get a chance to meet..."

"—Mind if I join you?" Dieter inquired in German, pulling out a chair and sitting down at our table.

"We would prefer you leave us alone!" I countered. "We are enjoying your city and do not appreciate the interruption."

"*Herr Kapitän* Kerr, your German is improving.. You are to be congratulated, Fraulein Fischer, you're an excellent teacher. Pillow talk helps—no doubt."

"*Mein Kapitän,*" he continued turning to me, "I was surprised to learn that, in addition to the German-speaking men, you have American Army and Air Force men working for you. Fifty, perhaps even more. Yet we never see most of them. I asked myself, are they invisible as they move around Berlin. No, I conclude. They must be building something inside of Tempelhof. You have now almost finished construction under Hanger 1. Are you all going to leave Berlin now?"

I smiled in response. He continued in English, "Or perhaps this is all a—let's see, you call it a red herring. I believe you're just trying to make a fool of me." Standing, Dieter tipped his hat and walked toward the nearby subway station.

Aware that Stasi watchers remained, I fought the onset of a panic attack by sitting rigidly in my chair. Anna sensed my distress, grabbed my hands and whispered, "Breathe in."

Finally, I took one, and then several, sips of beer. I even managed a few chips. My mind raced as I tried to remember every word uttered by Dieter. The security committee's interpretation of each nuance and phrase might be relevant. Collectively, we would have to find a way forward.

CHAPTER 68

Monday, April 24, 1961

THE EMERGENCY MEETING of the security committee was in its second hour before Scott, Kurt, Mark, and I discussed our next moves. At this point, Kurt revealed, "The nuclear-hardened command facilities at Clay Headquarters will be the real thing. It will be used by the senior military and civilian people in Berlin, including the senior Berlin Mission personnel, whose offices are located in adjacent buildings."

Amazed, I said, "So our local commanders are expecting to direct us from a nuclear-hardened headquarters if war comes. Communist forces could easily overrun that facility less than an hour after hostilities begin. And nuclear hardening! Why bother?"

"This is a part of the American government's reaction in-kind policy. They built five nuclear-hardened sites in East Berlin, so we build one big one. No mystery there," Kurt contended.

"Dieter Holburg has some preconceived notions about what we're up to, hence all of our actions from now on need to meet those expectations," Mark concluded. "Now, we need to decide how to react to his meeting with Robert."

Several decisions were made by the group.

1. I would continue to go over to the American Mission building four days a week but would walk from it to the Clay Headquarters building next door. My ride in the trunk of a car each day would commence from there.

    "There are hundreds of Germans who work in various capacities in and around the American Mission building. Robert's movements will certainly be reported to the Stasi," Kurt said to reinforce that decision.

2. Beginning the next week, some of our day-shift personnel would take a US Air Force blue bus to Clay Headquarters, morning and evening, then travel to and from the tunnel building in vans which will operate out of a secure underground parking garage in that complex. Mark assigned Scott and Kurt to make this concept a reality.

3. The remainder of the crew would continue to exit and enter the base through the airport arrival hall entrance or steam tunnel.

We all continued to speculate on Deter Holburg's statement that the Stasi was "close to the truth—very close—a few weeks and I'll have a solution to the mystery of what *Herr Kapitän* Kerr and his crew are really doing in Berlin."

"Sounds to me as if they have a human source who knows and might be persuaded to tell them but hasn't yet," Kurt said.

"It's got to be one of my men, but who? The Chief and Sergeant Loring have been told to keep trying to find the leak," I said.

As the meeting broke up, I turned to Kurt. "The CIA was assigned the task of determining the exact route of the communist communication pipe in our target vacant lot shortly after I arrived in October. We're running out of time. We'll be underneath the vacant lot in less than three months…"

"—We've sent agents who have produced both still photos and even conducted a motion picture survey of the vacant lot," Kurt replied. "You and experts back in Washington have evaluated those films. There are a few clues, but no one, including you, has been willing to decide if those signs of excavation are sufficient to determine an exact route."

"Have they tried everything?" Mark asked.

"There is so much ferrous metal buried in that area, metal detectors have proven useless," Kurt answered. "We're out of ideas. One of our guys even suggested we start digging exploration holes in the middle of the night. Our best intelligence is that it was somewhere in the easternmost third of that vacant lot."

"If we don't find a solution soon, Kurt, I'll be forced to make this an issue with the triumvirate," Mark stated in a deliberate, but calm tone.

Scott stayed behind after the others left. With a broad grin on his face, he said, "Robbie, my friend, I think it's time for you and me to view that vacant lot close up. Perhaps we'll see something the others missed."

"You're suggesting the two of us go into East Berlin and…"

"—Solve this problem here and now," Scott interjected.

"If we go there in uniform, it would be a dead giveaway we're up to something in that specific area. Even if we go over in civilian clothes, we'll be followed."

"So, we go over disguised as East German workers."

"Are you crazy?!"

"When you first arrived, we went on a tour of Berlin and I took you by Bernauerstrasse. Through contacts in the East, I've rented an apartment on that street and stocked it with disguises of all forms. We leave West Berlin by going through the front door of that apartment building and stop by the apartment I rented. We change into clothes appropriate for our mission and we enter East Berlin by exiting through the back garden. Thus, we adroitly avoid the eighty-one checkpoints the East Germans rigorously control. We move freely throughout the city, and we return to the West in the same way. I devised this entrance and escape route to extricate our errant youth from East Berlin. I've been over several times, and I guess I can brag—Kurt's men have also used my apartment on occasion."

"You've got to be joking. If we're caught…"

"—We won't get caught because May Day is the perfect day for such a mission. Dieter Holburg and all of his associates will be at the big celebration. May Day is the largest celebration on the communist calendar. It combines Memorial Day, Independence Day, and Labor Day into one celebration. It's the day when all loyal communists are present to see and be seen by their peers, subordinates, and superiors."

"Yes, but…."

"—We won't get caught. If we are, we'll have our passports and military ID cards with us and we'll talk our way out. It'll be something to tell your grandchildren."

CHAPTER 69

Press Release
Monday, May 1, 1961
General German News Service, the German Democratic Republic's official propaganda organ, released the following day, May 2, 1961:

MAY 1. To celebrate International Worker's Day, a massive military parade was held in East Berlin. Walter Ulbricht, Head of the East German State, his Prime Minister Otto Grothwohl, Defense Minister General Heinz Hoffman, General Ivan Jakubowski, Supreme Commander of Soviet Troops in East Germany, and numerous officials watched from the Reviewing Stand that was decorated with a banner reading: **"FATHERLAND, PEACE, SOCIALISM - WE SHALL BE VICTORIOUS."**

Officers of the Military Academy Friedrich Engels and Cadets of East German Officer schools headed the marching columns, consisting of paramilitary units, and civilians, as well as marching East German troops. There were numerous armored vehicles and guns in the parade, including T-54 tanks, amphibious craft, armored cars, anti-aircraft guns, howitzers, and anti-tank cannons. For the first time, six Russian made surface-to-air missiles on carriers were displayed. This is the type that brought down the American U-2 spy plane last year.

CHAPTER 70

Monday-Tuesday, May 1-2, 1961

ALTHOUGH I DIDN'T feel ready for my first spy mission, I was committed. The interior of Scott's apartment on Bernauerstrasse looked like a poorly organized thrift shop. Rack after rack of clothes for all occasions filled the interior of both the living room and bedroom. The disguises we selected for this mission were poorly tailored, brown and gray, East German-made suits, white shirts with oversized collars, solid color ties, cheap felt hats, a wig for Scott, and glasses for me.

Looking at himself in the mirror, after having me turn around, Scott declared, "Perfect. We look just like two construction workers who are determined to attend the May Day celebration wearing their finest clothes. We'll blend right in with the millions of other underpaid workers of this communist paradise."

With more than a little trepidation, I followed him out the back door of the apartment house and through a backyard garden into East Berlin.

Although the subway ride to the *Ost Bahnhof* (East Train Station) was uneventful,, I felt nervous, sure that disaster was inevitable. As we exited the station, I relaxed a bit until Scott came up beside me and tugged on his ear. Translation: we were being followed. Stunned, I froze.

Scott took off his hat, scratched his head, shook my hand, and bowed slightly. He whispered, "I'll get this guy to follow me. If you don't see me again, I was successful. *Auf Wiedersehen.*"

You're alone—deep breaths—recall your training—SELCH. Review the five. "S" Situational Awareness.....

By taking a random route, I determined that I was probably not being followed. That helped me unwind a little.

Now what, Robbie? Deep breaths. You're a spy who's scared shitless. Do what you came to do and then get the hell out of here!

There must be surface evidence of the route of the communications pipe, I decided.

Go through the acronym—SELCH. The last one: "Hide your Intentions."

Turning around, I surveyed the vacant lot while pretending to gaze at the river and view. Construction debris surrounded a long, continuous almost invisible mound of earth in the middle of the lot.

That could be it. I can almost visualize the trench before it was filled in.

Beyond the mound were the train tracks, more vacant lots sloping downward, two fences topped with barbed wire, and a sentry post to one side of two VoPos—then the River Spree. Perhaps 1500 feet away, I saw our building with its distinctive dome.

Back at the train station, I noticed the sidewalk had been cut to dig what I hoped was the trench for the pipe.

Interesting. This point lines up with the mounded earth, which extends several hundred feet straight ahead.

I retraced my steps, hoping anyone who observed my behavior would assume that I was pacing back and forth as if waiting for someone.

Again, on the sidewalk adjacent to the vacant lot, I tried to see the south side of our building. I knew that the path of our tunnel ran parallel to it.

When I could no longer see that side of our building, I pretended to walk over to the mound to examine some debris. This allowed me to pace off the distance from the edge of the sidewalk to the center of the pile. Thirty-two feet. I moved a large piece of broken concrete to that spot. Since the sidewalk and train station appeared on the public works drawings in my office, I now had two known points of reference.

Back on the sidewalk, I paced off two-hundred-fifty-four feet to the southeast corner of the East terminal building. Since my pace is almost exactly three feet, I made these measurements with reasonable accuracy.

Retracing my steps, I moved the boulder four feet to the north. With any luck, that spot was atop our target—the communications pipe.

Eat your heart out, James Bond. A trained Civil Engineer spy is better than you in this aspect of the game.

Having completed my mission, I returned to the East Train Station, made my way to the subway platform and waited for the next train. I tried to be inconspicuous by standing among other passengers on the platform used for northbound trains.

I sensed I was being watched. Looking up, I saw that a well-dressed man wearing a fedora was staring at me.

How did I give my cover away? I'm dressed like thousands of other lower-class workers on holiday. Perhaps I don't walk, act, or move like a subservient peasant.

I walked out of his field-of-view, then turned and glanced up. His gaze remained on the same spot, obviously lost in thought.

Relieved by his disinterest, I still boarded a different car and took a seat along the side in order to watch the rest of the passengers. No one appeared to be interested in me. I held my copy of the East German propaganda newspaper, *Neues-Deutschland*, in front of my face and avoided eye contact with anyone for the entire trip.

The Bernauerstrasse train station was only four blocks from Scott's apartment and its easy exit into West Berlin. One man followed me out of the station and onto a side street. I window shopped at a small appliance store while he passed me by. Walking on, then turning left into an alleyway, I entered the back garden and used the key Scott had given me to open the back door of the apartment building.

Relieved that I'd made it to a safe place, I rested with my back against the back door and breathed deeply. Suddenly one of the residents opened the apartment door immediately to my right. I was stunned. A massive man in a commanding voice bellowed, *"Guten Tag, comrade. Glücklicher Maifeiertag."*

In response to his greeting me as his fellow communist, and wishing me a good May Day, I mumbled, *"Guten Tag."* With a panic attack imminent, I struggled to negotiate the hall. Lightheaded with my heart thumping, I managed to ascend the three flights. My hand shook so violently it took what seemed like several minutes to fit the key into the deadbolt lock. The door opened. I fell to the floor, managing to kick the door closed with my left foot.

My lengthy panic attack had almost subsided when a German workman in a slouch hat barged into the apartment. I jumped to my feet and thrust the intruder to the side, desperate to flee. I gripped the door latch as the man behind me said in English, "Settle down old buddy. Did you get what you needed, Kemosabe?"

"Yes, I did. What's this Kemosabe crap?" I felt both reassured and stressed.

"You know the Lone Ranger's faithful companion, Tonto, gave him that name. Tonto was always saving his ass, just like I did for you today," he replied, laughing.

Within an hour, we celebrated our foray with pints at the Grossbritannien. During our conversation, Scott revealed, "We weren't really being followed. I just wanted you to stay alert while I completed another mission." He then revealed the purpose of his wardrobe change.

After two beers, I went home to Anna. We had accomplished our objective, but I remained shaken.

I lacked James Bond's nerves of steel.

At the meeting of the Security Committee the next day, Scott and I described our exploits.

Mark Powell said, "Colonel Morgan would have raised hell if you'd been caught, and most of the skin would have been taken off my ass."

"But, sir, it was...."

"You could've at least brought me in on your scheme," he insisted.

"We feared that you'd squelch the idea and we're running out of time," I protested.

Before Mark could reply, Kurt said, "My men have spent countless hours trying to find the communication pipe's route. They weren't prepared to see what was obviously there. A trained eye solved this problem. We should all be pleased!"

Scott handed Kurt a small piece of metal—roundish, dull gray on one side and somewhat shiny with a serrated surface on the other.

"Is this what I think it is?" Kurt asked.

"Yes, it is. The area around the Kupfergraben Canal was deserted yesterday. I borrowed a small boat and managed to get it under the pipe Robert located last week. Climbing on top of the wheelhouse, I used my folding hacksaw to remove that piece."

"I'll send this off to Washington via courier immediately," Kurt said, smiling. "This bit of metal will allow us to determine the Soviet solution to EMP hardening, and it may help us to find a way to negate the protection they believe it provides."

The committee covered other topics and was about to adjourn when I said, "Kurt, I need one of your men to place this exactly five feet above a piece of concrete in the vacant lot. It's a surveyor's target."

"From your description, there are a large number of bits of cement scattered on that mound of earth. How can we ensure he finds the correct piece of concrete?"

"I placed an American half-dollar coin under that particular piece. Once you put the surveyor's target in place, I can use a theodolite to accurately determine the location of their pipe relative to our tunnel."

"I know what to do. We'll find a No Dumping sign and place this on its back. Hiding it in plain sight…"

On Wednesday of the next week, I spent several hours on the roof of our building with my theodolite pointed at the back of the No Dumping sign. After intense calculations, I determined that the sign and, hopefully, the communications pipe were in a straight line, precisely 1846 feet from the entrance to the tunnel.

Feet of Tunnel Completed: 807   Days until Deadline: 149

CHAPTER 71

Monday, May 22, 1961

THREE WEEKS LATER, I traveled to the States and attended a meeting with the triumvirate in Gerald's conference room at NSA Headquarters at Fort Meade, Maryland. My briefing was the primary topic on the agenda, and the first part had gone smoothly. I'd used slides to show how we had completely sealed the section of the tunnel under the River Spree.

In conclusion, I said, "Just before I left Berlin, I walked over a thousand feet from the tunnel entrance past both pressure doors, which are now open, all the way to the TBM. Our air handling system is distributing fresh air throughout the tunnel, and we began normal one-atmosphere digging operations this morning."

"In your memos, you indicated you've determined the exact location of the communication pipe in three-dimensional space," Gerald stated.

"That is correct. We have 782 feet of tunnel to dig. We are currently eleven days ahead of schedule, and the tunneling rate should increase dramatically from this point on."

With obvious pleasure, General Harrison said, "Congratulations, Captain Kerr. You and your crew have done an outstanding job."

After some discussion, I said, "After I leave here, I will visit the probe and telescoping shaft manufacturers, inspect the finished product, and authorize shipment."

"For the benefit of all of us, please again explain the function of both," General Harrison requested.

"The probe is designed to locate the Russian communications pipe by drilling up into the earth from the end of the tunnel. The tip of the specially designed drill bit collects samples of all hard objects it encounters. I was recently informed that the CIA has determined the composition of the heavy galvanization that surrounds our target pipe and will be providing a test kit so we can confirm we've succeeded in finding the correct pipe."

"I understand the probe is a fairly conventional design," Gerald observed.

"Yes. But the telescoping vertical shaft is entirely unique," I explained. "It's designed to allow us to come up from beneath the pipe and surround it without disturbing the surface or making any noise."

"Repeat for the group what you told me earlier about how that is possible," the General requested.

"One at a time, five stainless-steel telescoping sections will be hydraulically lifted up as blades atop the uppermost section remove soil in a windshield-wiper motion. Each section supports the surrounding soil as it moves into place."

I tried to sound confident, but I didn't know for sure if this contraption would work.

During the entire meeting Thomas Lane said nothing. I'd anticipated that he would again vent his animosity toward me and was prepared for verbal fisticuffs. Later I learned that General Harrison and Mr. Scherman had been working for several months behind the scenes to get Thomas Lane replaced as the CIA lead on the tunnel-building program. That effort was soon successful, with dire consequences for all of us.

As the meeting concluded, General Harrison requested that I join him for a brief private discussion. He led me to an office down the hall and closed the door.

Before I could say anything, the General said, "Captain Taylor, I want you to know you're doing an outstanding job. We want to ensure that you keep up the good work. Colonel Morgan has informed me that you have formally requested permission to marry Miss Fischer."

"That is correct, sir. I want the personal satisfaction of finishing the tunnel. I know that it's an essential element of our plan to counter communist expansion into Western Europe. My problem is that I've found the love of my life and want to marry her as soon as possible. We've been together for eight months now."

The general opened his briefcase and took out my Request for Permission to Marry form. "My first inclination is to inform you that if you marry Miss Fischer your security clearance will be revoked. You'll be reassigned to another duty station, probably back in the United States!"

I stood frozen in place, sure that I would be forced into making a gut-wrenching decision, I did not want to make. "Sir, I…"

"—Since our tunnel program has remained hidden, the cover and deception activities centered around you and Miss Fischer have obviously been successful," the General interrupted. "Let me think about it. I'll consult Colonel Morgan and my head of security. Don't assume that I'll approve of your request, but I will evaluate it in light of all of the circumstances, which in your case are unusual." He folded the request up and placed it back in his briefcase. Then he shook my hand, patted me on the back, and said, "It would be a huge change in policy for me to establish the precedent that one of our people can marry a German national born and raised in the East!"

He then turned, opened the door, and left me standing there.

Feet of Tunnel Completed: 1064   Days until Deadline: 129

CHAPTER 72

Saturday-Monday, May 27-29, 1961

A WHIRLWIND OF life-changing activities occurred as Anna and I vacationed after my meeting at Fort Meade. She immediately liked California. As we drove out of the San Francisco Airport, she beamed. "It feels like I'm in a different world. The sun is shining and I feel liberated from the cares of everything in Berlin."

"California has that effect on people."

That evening, my Kerr grandparents welcomed us warmly, but gave us separate bedrooms. We slept in the barn, savoring the privacy after eight days apart.

The next day we drove to my Hunter grandparents' "Home Place." It consisted of twelve hundred acres and a mansion they recently built next to the farmhouse I'd known in my youth. Twenty-seven members of my mother's extended family welcomed Anna to America. We gathered at the picnic tables under massive century-old pecan trees, enjoying Grandmother's delicious fried chicken and produce from their nearby garden.

After lunch, Grandma invited Anna to join the women in the kitchen. Grandfather Hunter took me aside. Checking to make sure we were alone, he put an arm around my shoulder and said, "Robbie, I'm sixty-nine years old now and I'll be retiring soon."

"Grandpa, you're like a force of nature. You'll go on forever."

"Would that were true. No. Every day I feel my age more. Plus, Inez wants to do some traveling, so I need someone to take over here."

"What're you going to do, sell out?"

"I'm going to make you an offer I hope you won't refuse. As soon as you've completed your military duty, come here and be a farmer. I'll give you the maximum allowable tax-free gift of land every year from now on. Also, I'll pay you a part of the profit from each of my enterprises that you manage, and I'll agree to sell you as much land every year as you can afford. You'll end up owning all ten farms I've spent a lifetime acquiring in less than 10 years."

This was the last thing that I had expected to hear from him.

Would Anna be happy here? We'd been so crazy about each other from the beginning, we'd never discussed where we'd live after we married. Working side-by-side on the land, would this be a life she would embrace?

After several moments, Grandpa added, "If you want, you can live in our old house. It's well built, and we'll pay to fully modernize it for you. Your mother will eventually inherit half of our holdings and since you're an only child, I'll be mostly giving you your inheritance early. We'll have to keep books to ensure your aunt and her family receive their fair share."

I hesitated, then said, "Since I plan to ask Anna to marry me at some romantic spot on this trip, the decision is partially hers—perhaps mostly hers."

He nodded. "I understand, Robbie. This is a big step. Don't commit unless you're both sure."

I took Anna on an extensive tour of the animals and crops that grew on this farm. Then, I led her to a teak bench surrounded on three sides by a gigantic climbing rose bush covered with hundreds of tiny white roses. It blocked everyone's view of us as we kissed and held hands. I spent a long time explaining Grandpa Hunter's offer. "They own ten different acreages all located within eight miles of this property. After working hard for a few years, we would be making at least ten, perhaps even fifteen times what I could hope to make as a senior civil engineer."

"Really? That much?" she asked.

"We need to discuss if we'd be happy living here on a farm near this small town for the rest of our lives." Dropping down on one knee I clasped her hands and asked, "Anna Marie Fischer, will you marry me?"

She answered without hesitation. "Yes, I would be thrilled to marry you." She kissed me fervently, then slowly pulled away. "But, Robert, I want to complete my education and then teach art history at a university. Is there a good university this far out in the country?"

"The best is the University of California at Berkeley, which is only an hour's drive away. We'll stop there on the way to San Francisco."

"Perfect. Now, if we live in California, I'll have to know how to drive. There are few cars or other objects around here for me to hit. Will you teach me while we're here?"

"Tomorrow we'll have time," I replied, squeezing her hands.

She smiled.

I intentionally deferred telling her that we might have to leave Berlin after we married—she is so close to her family, and I wanted her to get used to the idea of marriage before I gave her that news.

"I purchased a ring for you. Let's see if it fits, left hand while we are engaged, correct?" I asked slipping it on her ring finger

"It fits perfectly, you did well," She whispered, kissing my cheek.

"You're sure a plain gold band is what you want. No diamonds or emeralds?"

"No, I prefer this. A plain gold band on the left hand while engaged, the right hand when married—in the European tradition." Her eyes twinkled, "And I knew you'd propose while we were on this trip, so I have a ring for you." Removing a ring from the pocket of her skirt, she placed it on the third finger of my left hand.

"Now all of the American girls will think I'm married."

"That's good. I want them to know that you're taken!"

We walked hand-in-hand to the house to tell my grandparents that while we still wanted to tour their other properties and review the books, we were inclined to accept their generous offer. Anna suggested, "We must tell them that our wedding will be in Germany, but we hope that they and all of your relatives will attend."

"Anna be careful…you're going too fast…hit the brake…the one in the middle is the brake…that's the clutch…the middle…" The fence post Anna ran over made a crunching sound and as the barbed wire broke, I heard a twang.

The barbed wire fence in the south pasture now had a hole in it, which I needed to repair before the cows got out.

Several hours earlier, I drove Grandmother's old beat-up 1947 Ford short-bed pickup out to a country lane that ran through a large pasture, thinking Anna would not hit anything. After I briefly demonstrated, I put her behind the wheel. She beamed when I said, "You've easily mastered the foot and hand coordination required to get the truck into gear."

The next step proved to be more difficult. The car died several times as I patiently explained, "You must slowly give it gas as you lift your foot off the clutch or it'll die every time."

I saw her growing frustration, so I took over and demonstrated.

She frowned. "You make it look so easy."

"I've also probably done it a million times. It just takes practice, so be patient," I kissed her and smiled as we again switched places.

"This contraption has got it in for me!" Anna shouted sometime later after the truck died again.

With a determination that was endearing, Anna was soon able to shift gears and drive the truck back and forth around the pasture. She covered several miles. Smiling and gaining confidence, she hit the accelerator instead of the brake pedal when a jackrabbit jumped up from the field and ran across her path. Before either of us could react, she slammed the truck into the fence. Barbed wire stretched across the hood, and one of the fence posts rested on the right fender. "I'm sorry, Robbie. I didn't do it intentionally."

I put my arm around her shoulder, turned her face up, and lightly kissed her, "I know you didn't."

"Stand here to make sure none of the cows get out while I get the fence repair kit from the barn."

She inhaled sharply. "How do I do that? Those huge animals can just run right over me. They might even crush me!"

Laughing, I said, "Anna, sweetheart, you have a lot to learn if you are going to be a farmer's wife. They're afraid of humans. Just wave your arms up and down and say 'shoo cow...shoo cow.' "

"Okay, but don't be gone too long."

When I returned, I asked with a smile, "Did any of the cows attack you?"

"One came over, so I followed your instructions, and amazingly it worked."

As I repaired the fence, Anna sat on the grass with her arms around her knees, apparently deep in thought. "Can I drive part of the way to Los Angeles?"

"You realize that to drive on the highway, you need a driver's license."

"Of course. And I have to pass a test. To do that, I'll need to learn to drive."

Taking Anna in my arms, I kissed her neck, lightly tapped her nose, and assured her, "You did well today. It took me many lessons before I was as proficient. We'll spend a few minutes each day letting you drive the rental car in a vacant parking lot somewhere. When we return to Berlin, we'll get you lessons. Perhaps Scott will lend us his car so you can practice."

CHAPTER 73

Tuesday, May 30, 1961

THE NEXT DAY we checked into the Mark Hopkins Hotel in San Francisco. That evening I took Anna to the Top of the Mark for dinner. With the help of a generous tip, we secured a window table.

"The views of San Francisco and the Pacific to the west as the sun is setting are spectacular," she exclaimed. "Robert, I like everything about America, but I want to be near my family in Berlin."

I saw the conflict and pain in her facial expression. "The terms that Grandpa Hunter outlined are very generous," I replied. "We will be able to afford to fly to Germany several times a year."

"If we can get away. I fear that your responsibilities—no, our responsibilities—will tether us to the farm and the university."

"True, but we'll plan times when we can travel to visit your family—Christmas for sure and one or two other times each year. Also, if we settle on the farm, we'll be living next to my wonderful grandparents, and they'll be involved in our lives. I think they'll help ensure that you have the free time you require to go back to school and help us to raise our children."

"I'll still miss my family."

"Anna, you were absolutely ecstatic when we visited the University of California Berkeley campus today."

"I was impressed, especially since I got to talk to the head of the Art History Department, Doctor Sanderson. She and the university are internationally recognized as the best in my field. They will need to review my transcript, but she seemed confident I could finish my undergraduate studies in one year."

"I'm glad that you are pleased." I felt thankful that she seemed to be accepting the idea of living in the United States.

"I'll fill out the application she gave me; we'll see how they respond. As you know, they also have a combined masters/doctorate program which I could attend."

Over dessert, I took Anna's hand, kissed it, and told her, "This is one of my favorite places, both for food and the view. It's only an hour's drive away from the ranch. We can have the best of both worlds—civilization here in San Francisco when we want it—the peace and quiet of life in the country most of the time."

CHAPTER 74

Monday, June 5, 1961

"I CAN CONFIRM that we have a traitor," Kurt Altschuler announced at an emergency meeting of the Security Committee the day I arrived back in Berlin. "One of your construction crew revealed to a Stasi operative or informant that he was working on a super-secret project which would ensure that the Americans and West Germans win the next war. He identified you, Robert, Chief Weber, and Sergeant Loring as his superiors."

Stunned, I started to ask about their source, but knew we wouldn't be provided this information.

Mark asked, "Robert, do you think that we can still trust your senior people?"

"I noticed the Chief wasn't invited. Now I know why."

"Precisely."

"Several months ago, we asked the Chief and Sergeant Loring to become familiar with the off-duty activities of each man. Now, we don't trust them. Why?" No one responded. "I'll stake my life on the fact that neither of them is the source. Most of the time those two are working in the building or in the barracks. We must rely on them to determine who it is. I'll get on the KY-7 scrambler phone and have them join us ASAP."

Once I returned to the meeting, Kurt said, "We have another matter to discuss. Remember the sample you sawed from the pipe, Scott."

"Sure, I risked life and limb for my country. Did I do good?"

"Yes, it turns out that particular galvanized cast iron pipe is famous,"

Kurt said with a broad smile. "It was made in Russia after WWII and shipped to East Germany as part of their economic support agreement. Problem is, it's unfit for its design purpose of serving as a water main. The galvanized surface is poisonous. Instead of being almost pure zinc, it's almost 6% lead and over 4% arsenic—a deadly combination. The East Germans unsuccessfully tried to sell it or give it away. It sat in a storage yard in East Berlin for almost ten years. It does provide excellent nuclear hardening protection, so the commies finally found a use for it."

Scott beamed as if he had single-handedly completed the intelligence coup of the century.

"That leads me to excellent news," Kurt continued. "Robert, as I told you earlier, when your probe is eventually able to take a sample of a pipe you believe is the communications pipe, you'll be able to easily ensure that you have found it. Here." He handed me a rather large wood box with several vials of liquid marked with all kinds of cautionary labels and an instruction manual.

"What the hell is this?" I asked.

"It's a MAITK," Kurt chortled.

"What?"

"A Metal Alloy Identification Test Kit. Follow the instructions inside the box. The galvanized exterior of your sample will turn orange when you use one chemical and a bright purple with another. If it turns those exact colors, you've got a match with what Scott sawed off of the pipe under the bridge. Instructions, colored test strips and heavy rubber gloves are enclosed."

"That solves one of my primary problems—making sure that I've found the right pipe," I said. "It would be a travesty, if after spending all this money and time, we tapped into one of the main East German water supply lines."

"This is all courtesy of your local friendly CIA agent and the guys in the CIA lab back in Washington."

A little later, the buzzer rang. I admitted my senior NCOs to the tank.

After explaining the situation, I asked, "Do either of you have any idea who the spy might be?"

"Can't be any of the 'Polish Option' people; they've all conformed to their restrictions. Of that, I'm sure," the Chief replied.

"So that leaves how many?"

"Twenty-seven. Nine of the Air Force people and eighteen of my Army guys, including me," Sergeant Loring replied.

"Can we think about it and get back to you tomorrow?" the Chief asked.

"This guy apparently hasn't revealed any damaging details about the tunnel yet, but they'll be badgering him for more information," Kurt said. "Get back to us soon. We can't wait until the men are off duty again this weekend."

"Chief, as long as you and Sergeant Loring are here, please give me a status report," I asked as the meeting began to break up.

"Sir, during the two weeks you were gone we completed almost 200 feet of tunnel, and we're now on the upward incline at about 40 feet below the surface."

"Any problems?"

"We recently started encountering debris from buildings destroyed in the war," Chief Weber said. "The boring machine has moved right through everything so far, but we've had to slow down the tunneling rate."

"We've assigned one additional man to each shift. It's his job is to monitor what the boring head is encountering," Sergeant Loring said. "The master shutoff switch is constantly in his hand."

"How does he determine when to use the switch?" I asked.

"Sound. The noise level increases dramatically when the machine hits hard objects like concrete."

"Keep up the good work, and keep me informed. I'll be over to the building later today for a look-see."

Feet of Tunnel Completed: 1187   Days until Deadline: 115

CHAPTER 75

Wednesday, June 7, 1961

"THE TRAITOR HAS to be one of three men," Chief Weber said. "Unfortunately, all three are some of our best workers."

"Sorry to hear that. Can we spare all three?"

"With a few adjustments, we'll get by," Sergeant Loring replied.

"All three have German girlfriends, despite the fact that two of them are married." The Chief shook his head in disgust.

"Ok. I'll declare that we need to cut staff to save money and send those three home. You two need to see that all three leave Berlin ASAP."

"Hopefully that'll solve our problem," Sergeant Loring added.

"Thank you, Sergeant, Chief," I said. "We need another all-hands meeting to reiterate the importance of maintaining secrecy about tunnel construction."

Feet of Tunnel Completed: 1216   Days until Deadline: 112

CHAPTER 76

Friday, June 16, 1961

I WAS CALLED to Colonel Morgan's Office and surprised that Mark, Kurt, and Scott were waiting there. The Colonel signaled for me to be seated. "I have news from General Harrison on your request to be allowed to marry Miss Anna Fischer. This was not an easy decision. Your outstanding job performance and Anna's integral part in our ongoing cover and deception efforts against the Stasi are viewed as mitigating factors in what would have normally been an easy negative decision. At my request, Kurt and the CIA conducted an extensive background investigation into Anna and her family—we have determined they are not a security risk. Our only concern now is that the communists could use threats against Anna or her family to get you to reveal information about the tunnel. The risk of this happening is viewed as no greater if you are married or maintain your current status. In summary, you have our permission to marry Miss Fischer."

Shocked, I jumped to my feet, grabbed the Colonel's hand and shook it vigorously. My friends gathered around me and offered heart-felt congratulations.

Kurt followed me to the tank. Once we were alone, he said, "It would be best if you could persuade Anna's family to immigrate to the West. That was a condition they wanted to impose, but my investigation indicated that her parents will probably not willingly leave the East. Perhaps you could persuade them to do so."

To celebrate my birthday, Anna invited her entire family to our apartment for a party. Most of the afternoon was spent discussing our wedding.

Before supper I presented a slide show of our recent vacation in California. I started with numerous photos of my grandparent's farms and the old ranch house. "This is where Anna and I will live when we move to California."

The presentation also included photos of Anna and the barbed wire fence as well as San Francisco, Berkeley, Big Sur, San Simeon, Santa Barbara, Hollywood, Disneyland and the beach in Southern California.

Bernard, Emma, Anna and I lingered in the living room after the others left. I mentally struggled with how to introduce the subject of the immigration of the entire Fischer family to the West into the conversation. Then out of the blue, Bernard said, "Two days ago, Walter Ulbricht had a news conference with Western reporters. One asked him if 'the rumors that the East/West Berlin border would be closed soon were true.' Herr Ulbricht replied that 'no one has any intention of building a wall.' "

"I read about it. No one mentioned anything about a wall, so why did he mention a wall?" I asked.

"Many people from the East now believe that the border will soon be closed permanently. Several families from our area have recently left for the West," Emma told us.

"Yesterday, the *Berliner Morgenpost* stated that the number of applications at the reception center in West Berlin has more than doubled." In pleaded voice Anna added, "Papa, don't you think it's time for our whole family to immigrate?"

"Anna, dear, you're lucky. You're already in the West. Perhaps three months from now, when Derrik is out of prison, we'll all go. Even your mother and me."

"Mama, Papa, you must think what is best for the whole family. You don't want your grandchildren to grow up under that terrible totalitarian regime, do you?"

"No. You're probably right. Its just…our home is there," Emma's chin quivered and tears filled her eyes. "And my parents in Dresden still need our help and financial support. They are both so frail."

"We both know you are right." A pensive Bernard observed, "It's in our hearts that we have problems—so many people rely on us."

Supporting Anna's argument, I said, "Bernard and Emma, you are dear to both Anna and me. My parents or grandparents would sponsor you, and you could immigrate to America a few months after you move to the West."

Anna exclaimed, "Then we can all be close to each other. That would be wonderful."

Neither Bernard nor Emma responded further to our pleas that they leave the East now.

Over the next few days, we managed to schedule our civil ceremony for the 3rd of July and reserved the small chapel in the northeast corner of the new Kaiser Wilhelm Church in West Berlin for the next day. Since the 4th of July was an American holiday, all of our friends from the base could attend the church service.

CHAPTER 77

Friday, June 23, 1961

Tunnel building was proceeding so well, it was inevitable that something would disrupt our progress. When we encountered a storm drain, it caused a minor delay. However, it ultimately turned out to be a highly consequential occurrence.

TOP SECRET LUMAR—RESTRICTED
DISTRIBUTION—US EYES ONLY

Memorandum #28 from Captain Robert Kerr   Berlin, June 23, 1961

On Wednesday afternoon, June 21, the TBM cut a clean hole across the top of a storm drain. It did not appear on the public works drawings we'd been given. They were last updated in the 1930s.

During our survey of that drain pipe system, we found an access shaft in the courtyard of an abandoned industrial complex. This system had been designed to drain part of the boggy flatlands of Friedrichshain, the primary industrial area of East Berlin.

Two of our German-speaking Seabees went down into the drain and constructed a semi-circular form. We installed rebar and poured quick-drying concrete into the hole, thus generating what we believe will be a strong, virtually invisible, repair in the drain pipe.

The men disassembled the form, transported it to the surface, and hid it beneath some debris in one of the abandoned buildings. They returned to West Berlin using their American passports.

The tunnel is now only 317 feet from the juncture with the communications pipe.

Signed,

Robert T. Kerr, Captain USAF

**TOP SECRET LUMAR—RESTRICTED
DISTRIBUTION—US EYES ONLY**

Feet of Tunnel Completed: 1529   Days until Deadline: 96

CHAPTER 78

Monday, July 3, 1961

"ROBERT, OLD BUDDY, you won't believe what just happened!" Scott declared over the telephone.

I envisioned all kinds of problems with security at the tunnel site.

Scott continued, "Thomas Lane just left my office. He's demanding that I lift your security clearance and have you shipped out of Berlin ASAP."

"Did you inform him that General Harrison has approved my marriage?"

"He retorted that the CIA director views you as a huge security risk."

"What's he doing in Berlin? He's no longer part of the triumvirate!"

"More bad news. He's the new Senior Deputy Director of CIA Berlin Station. He's Kurt Altschuler's new boss!"

"Oh, shit. Are you kidding me? So, what are you going to do?"

"I'm sending an Eyes-Only message to each member of the triumvirate and General Harrison's head of security telling them that I have no intention to follow orders from the CIA Berlin Station. Thought you'd want to know that your worst nightmare is in town."

CHAPTER 79

Monday, July 3, 1961

"COME ON ROBBIE. Hurry or we'll be late!"

"Wow!"

"You like my new dress!" She twirled around in the living room of our apartment.

"Yes, and what's inside it, too," I replied, trying to kiss her.

"Don't, you'll muss my make-up. Your mother helped me select this floral print dress while we were in LA. We both thought it to be very appropriate for a summer wedding in a town hall."

The Justice of the Peace's chamber at Charlottenburg Town Hall was crowded with fifteen people—my parents, both sets of my grandparents, Aunt and Uncle Gibson, and Anna's parents and paternal grandparents. Anna and I stood before the justice, hand in hand.

He said, "You posted the banns fifteen days ago in accordance with the law. Do you both certify that you are free of any encumbrances that would prevent you from marrying?"

We both answered in the affirmative.

"Are each of you marrying of your free will?"

We both answered yes.

"Does anyone know of any reason that these two should not be married?"

Silence reigned.

"Then please sign the Marriage Certificate."

Neither Anna nor I hesitated. We both knew that after everyone signed the official document, we would be legally married and everything that followed would be celebration.

After my father and her mother signed as witnesses, I took Anna into my arms. We kissed for a long time. I heard the Justice of the Peace clear his throat. Apparently our 15 minutes were up, and it was time for him to welcome the next happy couple.

CHAPTER 80

Monday, July 3, 1961

ANNA LOOKED RADIANT as we posed for a variety of photographs on the front steps of the town hall. My Uncle Jimmy had appointed himself chief photographer for the wedding. At his urging, I kissed Anna again.

We arranged for our group to occupy a long table outdoors under the Linden trees at a nearby restaurant. After much banter in both English and German, everyone ordered their drinks and lunch.

I stood, placed my hand on Gunther Fischer's shoulder. "Anna's grandfather is a man of high principles. Several times in 1938, he preached from his pulpit that what the Nazis were doing to the Jews was morally wrong. The Nazi's answer was to send him to prison for two years. Since 1945, he has been active in the efforts to undermine the communists in East Germany by organizing a Christian youth movement."

My family looked on, speechless. Finally, Grandfather Hunter stood. "I'd like to quote one of the most brilliant men of this or any generation. Almost thirty years ago, Albert Einstein observed; 'The world will not be destroyed by evil men, but by those who watch them without doing anything.' " Raising his glass, he continued, "I propose a toast, to the bravest man any of us has ever met."

"Here, here!" and "Prost!" were heard from all present as glasses clinked.

Bishop Fischer rose. In a somber voice he told us in English, "I'm now 77. Marie and I have had a long and eventful life, but we are finished with the East. I have again been threatened with prison for my activities against the foul communists."

With tears in his eyes, he took his wife's hand. "I will not survive another stay in prison. This gathering gave us a good excuse to come to the West. We will stay with Edger, our son, who is a minister in Darmstadt, until we can find a home. Our suitcases contain few clothes. We packed mostly the photos and other family memorabilia we could not leave behind. I will get a pension from the church and another from West Germany, so we will get by."

Anna turned to her parents and said in German, "Mama and Papa, all of our family should join them in the West."

The Polterabend (broken pottery) party was held in the large private dining room at the Neu Ratskeller. Barmaids in traditional dress served drinks and German food.

After he arrived, Scott shook my hand and gave me a teletype message from General Harrison's Head of Security. "Reference the marriage of Captain Kerr to a German national. The Director of the CIA has been informed that granting of security clearance to members of the military is a DoD responsibility."

I heaved a sigh of relief and said, "I hope this closes this matter, at least for now."

People were soon dancing to the oom-pah band's music.

At precisely 9 p.m., Bernard took the floor, made sure everyone had a drink and proposed, "A toast to the happy couple—long life and happiness."

The entire gathering cheered. Additional toasts in both German and English followed.

"According to my wife, who is an English professor, there is no word for Polterbend in English. The closest we can come is 'evening of the broken pottery.'" Taking a sip of beer, he continued, "Anna and Robert, please stand just here." Now if everyone is ready, smash your porcelain at the happy couple's feet. We heard 'Scherben bringen Gluck'—'Broken crockery brings you luck' again and again as a line formed and people passed by us throwing their cups, plates, saucers, and platters on the floor at our feet.

Papa Bernard then announced, "Just so, such an incredible mess. The bride and groom will show that they can work together to clean this up."

Scott carried in two large rubbish bins. Sophia brought in a broom and large dustpan with ribbons tied to their handles.

"Good luck, Robert. That's a real jumble," Scott shouted in both German and English, which elicited laughter from the crowd.

As our friends and relatives coached and berated us, we cleaned up the broken dishes.

Finally, Papa Bernard ran his hand over the floor and announced "It is clean! May nothing in your house ever be broken and may you both always have good luck."

Everyone shouted their congratulations in both English and German.

Late in the evening, Anna and I were dancing to a slow number when Bernard tapped me on the shoulder. "Anna must go home to our house tonight. We intend to conform to the American tradition that the bride and groom do not see each other before the ceremony."

"We're already married!" I protested.

"Only in the eyes of man," was Bernard's retort.

Conceding defeat, I said, "I have a few things in the office I need to take care of. Anna, you and your parents can lead the tour tomorrow morning, and I'll see you at the wedding," giving her a hug, kiss and a gentle pat on the behind.

CHAPTER 81

Tuesday, July 4, 1961

AFTER I COMPLETED some paperwork, I caught the Chief and Neal Loring in the barracks, and asked them to accompany me to the tunnel building.

Once we reached the basement, the Chief gestured to our surroundings, "As you can see, we've fabricated all of the tunnel sections and started to remove the sand. We've also started to return the equipment we no longer need to our construction yard."

"Next week, we'll move in the lumber, and some of our men will start building the exploitation center walls and ceilings on the other end of the basement," Sergeant Loring said. "We may beat the deadline for this facility by several weeks, sir."

"Plus, our target is just 177 feet on the other side of the tunnel boring machine," the Chief added. "We should finish tunneling in ten days, Friday the fourteenth."

"Hey, why aren't you getting ready for the wedding?" Neal asked, looking at his watch.

"The wedding isn't until 1600. I've got plenty of time."

"Nervous, sir?"

"Not really. We were legally married yesterday before a justice of the peace—today is just a celebration."

"We appreciate your invitation and will be there with bells on, won't we, Chief."

Feet of Tunnel Completed: 1669   Days until Deadline: 85

CHAPTER 82

Tuesday, July 4, 1961

AS WE WALKED down the aisle arm-in-arm without any attendants, I looked over at my beautiful fairy princess. She was radiant. I felt like the luckiest man on earth.

Her mother and my father took their places beside us. Grandpa Gunther blessed us and talked about the sanctity of marriage. He then requested, "Robert Kerr, repeat after me, 'I take you, Anna Fischer....' "

After we read our vows, I took her engagement ring from her left hand and transferred it to her right hand. She did the same for me.

Grandfather Gunther stated, "I now pronounce you man and wife in the sight of God and the church."

I took her in my arms. I kissed her so fervently that many individuals in the church began to whisper and then giggle. Someone even clapped.

Grandfather Gunther announced, "I present Herr Captain and Frau Kerr." We turned to face the assembled friends and family.

Someone had decorated the three Volkswagen buses with ribbons, flowers, and signs that read, "Just Married" in German and English.

I handed Anna an envelope, "This was delivered this morning to our apartment."

She excitedly ripped it open. "It's from the University of California," she began to read aloud. "We are glad to inform you that you have been accepted to the Spring Semester.... And at the bottom of the letter, they say that I have enough credits to graduate in one year."

"Anna, that's wonderful. Just what you wanted. Can we tell Grandpa George and Grandma Inez we accept their offer?" I asked.

"Yes. Oh, yes."

CHAPTER 83

Tuesday, July 4, 1961

OUR MOTHERS COMBINED German and American wedding traditions into a unique wedding reception. Father Bernard served as the master of ceremony. After dinner and the cake cutting, he said, "It is now time for the *Baumstamm Sägen*, the traditional Log Sawing. Anna and Robert please come forward."

Putting his arms around both of us, he continued, "The log represents the first of many obstacles you will have to overcome in your life. The future is uncertain. You will have to face those obstacles together. This log sawing is good practice in working together."

We were handed a bow saw with ribbons tied to the handle. Many people left their seats to get a better view and to offer the advice they knew would be required.

Our first efforts were greeted with good-natured banter:

"Back and forth—just like sex."

"Slow and easy strokes."

"Wait until she is ready."

Finally, Anna said, "When you pull as I push the saw—the blade binds. See, when I push, you must provide only support, then you push back."

Soon we began a rhythmic back and forth motion and were quickly finished—we got a thunderous round of applause.

As the log-sawing debris was cleaned up by the hotel staff, Bernard announced, "It is time for us to start the American tradition of the first dance…"

Much later, Scott's girlfriend, Mia failed to catch the bouquet, because of another guests athletic jump in front of her.

When Anna was blindfolded for the traditional German wedding game of blindman's bluff for single women, Mia won easily. I intentionally threw the garter in Scott's face, so he had no choice but to grab it. Later, I saw that they were engaged in a very animated conversation—I knew what the subject had to be. He seemed to be on the defensive.

Anna and I danced until the band stopped playing at 1 a.m. After convincing the diehards that the party was indeed over, we went to our room in the hotel and romantically began our lives as a married couple.

CHAPTER 84

Wednesday, July 5, 1961

AT A LITTLE after 3 a.m., the phone rang. I almost didn't answer, assuming it was a wedding joke.

"Hello."

"Captain Kerr, this is Chief Weber. We have a huge problem. You need to get over to the base now. I'll notify the other members of the security committee. We'll meet in your tank ASAP."

I had intentionally consumed little alcohol, but the Chief's call still came as a shock.

By the time I arrived, everyone was in my tank.

"What's up?"

"Soon after I returned to the barracks, I got a phone call from William Perkins. He's in East Berlin."

"He's the Air Force linguist, the one who's so fluent in German we've used him primarily as a truck driver," I recalled.

"That's correct. Perkins was stationed at our Signal Intelligence intercept sites at both Hof, West Germany, and here in Berlin before going into the reserves at Fort Meade."

"He's one of the guys who spends most of his time off base on the weekends?" I asked.

"Exactly. All I know at this point in time is that he was drugged and taken to East Berlin. He managed to escape by using a tire iron to open the trunk lid of the car transporting him to the East. He's hiding in a pension in the Herzberge District of East Berlin."

"Where's that?"

"Near Stasi headquarters," Kurt replied.

Mark asked, "Recommendations, gentlemen?"

"It would be best if we could get him out without officially transiting any of their eighty-one checkpoints. They'll have photos of him, and they will detain him if possible," Kurt advised us, his deep concern evident.

"We need to determine immediately what he's told them. Damage control is essential," Mark said.

"Chief, have Sergeant Loring take four men and go over to the building. Increase the number of guards on the entrances and roof, and initiate a full-time foot patrol of the surrounding area," I ordered.

"Yes, sir."

"Immediately inform us of any unusual activity via the KY-7 scrambler phone," Mark ordered.

"Kurt, you've used my apartment on Bernauerstrasse for a few of your operations," Scott said. "What do you think?"

"Unfortunately, I can do nothing without consulting my new boss, Thomas. He'll use this whole situation to get at all of us, but especially Robert. I'm a known entity and shouldn't become involved directly, if possible. This is really a military matter."

"Do you have any other suggestions?"

"Perhaps you and Robert are ready for another spy mission into East Berlin," Kurt suggested.

Scott nodded, "If Perkins hasn't already told them about the tunnel, he certainly will if he's recaptured."

"I'm willing to risk going into the East again if you are, Scott. If we don't, the whole tunnel-building project may come crashing down."

Mark shook his head. "When I told Colonel Morgan of your first excursion into the East, he was fit to be tied. We'll have to get his approval. Given the circumstances, he may well concur we have no choice. There is too little time for him to seek guidance from his superiors."

An hour later, Mark returned from a trip to the Colonel Morgan's quarters. With obvious trepidation, he said, "We have the Colonel's approval.

Just don't get caught. If you are captured, I'm not sure whether you two or the Colonel and I will be in more trouble. The outcome won't be pleasant for anyone."

I hadn't told Scott about my panic attacks. Too late now. I was committed.

Dressed in the same suits we had worn on our last spy mission, Scott and I exited through the back garden of the apartment on Bernauerstrasse. Our obvious objective was to retrieve Sergeant Perkins without getting caught by the East Germans.

This time, we intended to blend in with the East Berliners as they made their way to work on a glorious summer morning. The Bernuerstrasse station was on the same subway line as our destination, the Frankfurter Alle station, so we didn't need to change trains.

We intentionally occupied different parts of the same car. We read copies of *Neues Deutschland* newspaper to look busy and hide our faces.

If we were being followed, Scott would've pulled his ear. I relaxed, taking deep breaths and not actually reading what was in front of me for the almost twenty-minute ride.

By previous agreement, I led the way to the pension where Perkins awaited us, Scott trailing me to assure we weren't being followed and that no one waited outside.

I started feeling light-headed when I reached the top of the subway stairs and stepped out into bright sunlight.

Breathe deep, relax. Situational awareness. Walk purposefully. You're on your way to work. Scott is behind you. Just relax—even strides—forward. You've memorized the route.

Several blocks later, I reached the side street where I would turn left. I looked back but didn't see Scott. Before departing the apartment, he'd said, "If I disappear, just keep going. I'll join you, if and when I can."

Perkins sat on a sofa in the living room of the pension. He greeted me in German, saying, "My friend, please follow me."

Silently, we went into his room, where I handed him the large brief-case. He hurriedly changed into his German suit, which I'd taken from his locker in the dressing room at the base. He then donned the wig, glasses, and hat we'd selected from Scott's mélange of disguises.

"Here is your Green American Passport. Chief Weber took it out of your room. Fortunately, it makes no reference to you being in the U.S. military, but only show it if absolutely necessary and remember you speak no German. If stopped, we're American tourists who need directions to find the West."

As Perkins and I walked to the subway station, I caught a glimpse of Scott. He pulled his earlobe and turned down a side street.

I decided to return to the Bernauerstrasse apartment as soon as possible.

Sergeant Perkins and I boarded the nearest subway train and sat together in silence. I looked at my wrist, remembering I'd left my wedding ring and American-made watch behind.

Intently staring at my newspaper, I tried to act like another bored workman who rode on this same train every day. The guy next to me was a stranger.

At Schillingstrasse station, two VoPos on the platform asked people for their papers. They walked toward our car and boarded just as the doors closed.

Knowing we were trapped, I fought to remain calm. Perkins squirmed and seemed about to burst. I feared he would blow our cover by drawing attention to us.

Several people occupied the subway car. One in particular received prolonged attention. Knowing that if we stayed in that car, our identity would be checked, I stood. Perkins joined me, and we exited the train at Alexanderplatz.

Standing at the top of the stairs on the sidewalk in a strange city, I felt trapped. Referring to the map in my pocket would draw unwanted attention.

Perkins looked like I felt when a panic attack was imminent. At the end of the next block I saw a *gasthaus*. We entered and found an inconspicuous booth in the back. I said, "You do all the talking, order breakfast for both of us," placing a twenty East Mark bill on the table.

While sipping my coffee and studying the map, I whispered, "It's a mile to our destination. We'll try to walk. Relax. We're safe here."

The clock over the mirrored bar read 11:25 when we exited the *gasthaus*.

After getting my bearings, we turned north. I was shocked. The streets appeared deserted, yet there seemed to be VoPos every block or two. With most people at work, we were too conspicuous. I grabbed Perkins' arm and steered him into a tobacconist shop to avoid two VoPos heading for us on the sidewalk.

We purchased two packs of Bulgarian-made cigarettes and a magazine. *"Streichhölzer, bitte,"* I requested. The proprietor gave me a small wooden box of matches. After we had exited the store, I said to Perkins, "Go back and purchase a can of lighter fluid."

Heading back to the subway station, we encountered more VoPos.

We must lay low until workers start heading home this afternoon, I thought.

As we neared Alexanderplatz again, I saw a movie theater. The subtitled, double feature was an old American Western starring a very young Gene Autry, and a Russian film about the 1917 revolution and the sailors on the Battleship Potemkin. We purchased tickets and snacks, then settled in for the afternoon.

While the movies played, I mulled over our next move, deciding on a diversion.

The huge 24-hour clock in the Alexanderplatz subway station read 16:12. Following signs that directed passengers to each of the six subway lines that converged here, we finally found the correct platform. People rushed every which way. No VoPos in sight.

Behind my back, I surreptitiously emptied the lighter fluid into a rubbish bin next to the tracks. Just as our northbound train arrived at the station, I lit a cigarette, immediately threw it and the match into the trash can. Flames erupted. As our train departed, smoke filled the platform.

When our train stopped at the next station, I heard an alarm and saw VoPos leaving our train to board the train which returned to Alexanderplatz.

Perkins exclaimed in English, "Sir, that may have done the trick!" He paled, realizing his mistake.

Glancing around, I determined that no one was watching us.

As our train approached the Bernauerstrasse Station, I stood. Perkins followed. Seeing no VoPos, we exited the train.

Rubbery legs carried me the four blocks to the alley, through the back garden, and up the stairs. As we entered the apartment, I collapsed to the floor. The Chief turned me over, put something under my head, and then placed handcuffs on Perkins' wrists.

"William, it'll go easier for you if you follow instructions. Once the Captain, who risked his life to save you, recovers, we'll leave here. Forget what you've just seen. There is a car waiting for us downstairs."

My panic episode subsided as Scott reentered the apartment.

Vigorously shaking my hand, he said, "I've searched half of East Berlin looking for you. Why didn't you stay on that train? I was in the next car and saw you leave. By the time I returned to Alexanderplatz, you'd just vanished into thin air."

I described our entire adventure.

"Colonel Morgan is fit to be tied. Kurt and Mark have had a hell of a time convincing him not to issue a formal complaint to the Russians over your disappearance."

"Is that all? What about Thomas?"

"And Thomas was apparently livid when Kurt informed him that you were in East Berlin. Kurt indicated that he thought that Thomas was going to explode—he turned red and rushed around the room like a caged animal."

"Going East was probably a mistake. I'm sure this will be my last spy mission. James Bond can have the adrenalin rush. Never again," I vowed.

"And Anna is worried sick—your families were supposed to spend today together."

"Hell, I figured we'd be back before noon."

"You're in trouble with everyone but me, Kemosabe," Scott said. "I figured you were a goner! Dieter Holburg would love to get you into an interrogation cell at Stasi Headquarters. Those guys are masters at getting information by using unique means that include mental and physical torture."

As soon as I could, I telephoned Anna at our apartment. "You abandoned our wedding bed in the middle of the night, and you've allowed me to worry about your whereabouts. Now you're asking me to forgive you! Well, that's not good enough!"

"Anna, please. Colonel Morgan assigned me to a high-priority mission. I'd have called if I had been able to. I'll be there in fifteen minutes, so I can get ready for the symphony concert and dinner this evening with our families."

"Your family was surprised, then disappointed, and toward the end of today were expressing concern for your safety," she said. "I may have to accept your lame excuses, but you can explain to them what you've been up to. I'll get everything you need out so you can dress quickly. That way, we can at the very least pick everyone up on time."

Four days later, Anna and I accompanied my visiting relatives to their gate and said our tearful goodbyes.

Grandpa George reminded us, "I'm planning for you to start taking over the business in nine months. Don't let me down."

I smiled, "Don't worry, Anna and I are committed. Nothing will keep us away."

Little did I realize the challenges ahead of us before we could fulfill that commitment.

CHAPTER 85

Tuesday, July 11, 1961

THE INTERROGATION OF Technical Sergeant William Perkins took three days. Scott came to my office and with the results. "Perkins is a switch hitter."

In response to my questioning look, he continued, "He likes boys and girls in equal measure. He accepted this assignment because he still had friends from the time when he was stationed here. The Stasi apparently penetrated a hedonist club, which sponsored all-night orgies at a bathhouse here in West Berlin."

"What did he tell them?"

"A supposedly married couple accepted him into their open relationship. When off duty, he lived in their elegant apartment. They claimed to be staunch anticommunists, so he bragged that the construction project he was working on would overcome the Russian and East German numerical superiority and save Berlin. He says for months he resisted their efforts to get him to reveal more details."

"Do you believe him?" I asked.

"We'll know for sure if someone snoops around the building, but I believe he's sufficiently frightened to tell us the truth," Scott replied.

"Perkins is the traitor we were looking for a long time. We sent three good workers home but failed to identify the real culprit. Now we got the right guy."

I later heard that Sergeant Perkins received a dishonorable discharge, two years in the brig, and was fined a large amount of money, along with an admonition that he would be severely punished if he ever revealed details about the tunnel to anyone.

Given what ultimately happened to Anna as a result of his revelations, he got off lightly.

CHAPTER 86

Wednesday, July 12, 1961

THE WORST POSSIBLE thing happened. Only three days from our goal, the TBM hit a massive steel-reinforced column.

The top of the tunnel ran parallel to the surface about 30 feet down. The TBM bits we selected were designed to move freely through everything except steel. The column's heavy reinforced rods were over an inch thick.

The construction crew on duty immediately stopped the boring tool and backed it up. I arrived about an hour later.

"How bad, Chief?

"The cutting teeth of the main boring head are chipped and dulled. As the metal pieces passed through the debris removal system, it was also damaged."

"Can either subsystem be repaired?"

"To fix them right, the TBM would need to be disassembled and most of it replaced. This would set us back weeks, if not months."

"We've less than seventy feet to go. We could've punched that out in no time, but now who knows." An idea occurred to me. "Before we give up, let's determine the digging rate of this crippled rig."

"Good idea, sir."

"How long will it take us to remove the part of the column in our way?"

"Sir, one or two days, working 24 hours a day. There'll be so little work-space, only one or two men can work at a time."

"I'll stick around for a while and monitor your progress."

As I watched, the men built a support structure over the work area to prevent cave-ins. Then, a man with a jackhammer started on the lower extremity of the column. Next, one of the men began to use a reciprocal saw to cut the smaller steel rods.

By the end of evening shift two days later, we had moved the tunneling equipment 3.9 feet beyond the column. The Chief reported, "With this tunneling rate, it'll take at least another week to dig the rest of the tunnel."

My weekly report detailed our new problems and the solutions I'd implemented.

The messages from Thomas to the people in Washington were critical of my leadership—even accused me of sabotaging the digging device. Mark and I decided that Thomas' accusation was so outlandish that we'd ignore it.

Feet of Tunnel Completed: 1782   Days until Deadline: 72

CHAPTER 87

Anna

Saturday, July 22, 1961

MY TRIP TO my parents' home that Saturday portended the future. As I passed through the East German border control station at Stadtmitte Subway Station, a tall, portly Senior Transport Police Officer approached me, asked me to step out of line and asked, "Were you born in the East?"

Startled I replied, "Yes."

"You're Anna Fischer, aren't you?"

"Yes," I felt the ground shift beneath my feet as I recognized him.

"I am Gustav Mueller. We used to play together. I lived on Waldenser Strasse near your parents' house."

"Oh, I remember you. You're now a Captain in the TroPos. Impressive," I said, relaxing.

"You have immigrated to the West?"

"Yes, I work in West Berlin."

He kept glancing at my ring, "And you're married?"

"Yes, two weeks ago."

"Oh, too bad, I was hoping you and I could get together."

I shrugged. Since he had tried to get fresh with me at a friend's birthday party six years ago, I had avoided any contact with him. He was taller, big—almost fat—and had the florid complexion of one who consumes copious amounts of alcohol.

"Let me examine your passport."

Complying, I handed it to him. I thought, *Be careful. He is not very bright, and his father is a senior communist leader. Don't make him angry.*

"Your papers are issued to Anna Fischer. You are no longer this person—you are Anna…"

"Kerr. My married name is Kerr."

"That is an English name. Is it not?"

"Yes, I married an American military officer—a captain in the American Air Force."

"But your papers must be correct."

"I was told that I had three months…"

"Please follow me. We have a problem!"

Without further explanation, Captain Mueller ordered a guard to escort me to a police car with sticky seats and the odor of vomit. They drove me to nearby Mitte Police Station.

I was locked in a room, which consisted of unpainted cement walls and floor. Its décor consisted of a metal table and two battered wood chairs. It smelled of unwashed bodies and stale cigarettes.

Thirty minutes later, Gustav Mueller entered the room, approached me from behind, and grabbed me by my hair. He forced my head back and clumsily kissed me. "See what you are missing!"

Jerking free of him, I shouted, "You are one of the most disgusting men I've ever met, you *arschgteige* (arsehole)! As you know, my father knows many people far superior to you."

"Anna, you have always treated me poorly. Perhaps you will change your mind after your next visitor." He pulled my head further back, roughly grabbed my right breast and savagely twisted it. "I'll see you again later!"

More shocked than hurt, I shouted, *"Du bist trantute!* (You are a bag of whale blubber!)"

Petty tyrant, I thought, shaking with anger. *The whispered rumors of beatings, rapes, torture, and disappearances are probably true. Keep your mouth shut for once!*

To my shock, Dieter Holburg entered the room and sat down opposite me. "Ah, so, Fraulein Fischer. Oh, that's right you're married now, Frau Kerr.

There I go again—stay calm. I can't let them see that I'm frightened.

"You are very confident of yourself. But you are now in my custody here in the East. I can do anything I want with you—maybe you can just disappear or perhaps your husband, the handsome young captain will cooperate with us in order to secure your release."

"Kidnapping the dependent of an American military officer off the streets of East Berlin will get you into big trouble. The four powers still control this city!"

"Just tell me what your husband does, and I'll personally transport you to your parents' home."

"He's a weatherman!"

"Just sign this piece of paper, admitting that you traveled to East Germany using false travel documents, and we'll let you go."

"My passport is valid."

"Yes, but it does not have your correct name and marital status. You are now Frau Anna Kerr. Is that not correct?"

"By German law, I have up to three months to make that minor correction in my passport!"

"Not according to our regulations!" Dieter replied as he left the room.

Captain Mueller returned, stood over me and said in a threatening manner, "You are accused of violating Article 37, line 19 of the regulations on entry into the German Democratic Republic—that is intentionally using incorrect or falsified travel documents to enter or leave the DDR. This infraction carries a maximum ten-year prison term for each offense."

"I was told..."

"Makes no difference what you've heard. Now you can either go with me to my apartment where you will experience a real man, or to a jail cell."

"You despicable, miserable...."

"A jail cell it is." He placed a handcuff around my right wrist, attached it to a metal loop on the table, and left the room.

What are these two up to?

An hour passed, and then another.

Eventually, I decided, if they planned to lock me up, I would be in a cell. They wanted to intimidate me into revealing Robert's real work. My family will miss me, call Robert, and learn that I left our apartment hours ago.

I'll just wait out these two schweinehund (bastards)—that's my best course of action.

Dieter Holburg returned and again sat in the chair opposite me. "Sign this document, admitting to a minor violation of our regulations, and you will be released."

"I refuse to sign anything. My father knows numerous influential people. You will both be reprimanded for detaining me on trumped-up charges. I also desire to file charges against Captain Mueller for physical abuse!"

He laughed. "You are our prisoner. You are not in the West. We can do anything we want with you over here. A night in the cells should make you reconsider!" Then, he left.

As time passed, I became less confident that their harassment would end with me being released.

A short time later, the door opened, and a voice I didn't recognize said, "Frau Anna Kerr. Your father, Bernard Fischer, is concerned about you. I have come to take you to your family."

"Who are you?" *Is this a trick to get me into a car and take me to Stasi Headquarters?* I wondered and cringed at the thought.

"My name is Manfred Ehrhardt," he replied. "I am the Chief Secretary to the President of the Council of Ministers for the DDR." He presented me with his card, then continued, "In 1945, your father saved the lives of my two oldest sons. When he called today worried about your safety, I could do nothing until I determined your location. A few phone calls led me here."

He uncuffed my hand and helped me to my feet. "Now, I will take you to your parents' home and will ensure that those who harassed you today are reprimanded."

I told Robert about my passport problem but decided not to tell him that Dieter Holburg had again threatened me. That proved to be a mistake.

CHAPTER 88

Robert
Sunday, July 30, 1961

ON THE PREVIOUS Friday, the crippled TBM finally completed the horizontal part of the tunnel. I ordered that the damaged boring head and shield continue forward until they buried themselves out of our way. Instead of the usual concrete top and side sections of the tunnel, we installed a temporary wooden support structure in this area.

Today, we began the final and most perilous stage of tunnel building. If we disturbed the surface of the vacant lot above us or made a noise discernable on the surface, our tunnel might be discovered. Our entire effort would be wasted, and its discovery would probably cause an international incident.

To help ensure that nothing unforeseen happened, the Chief and I agreed that both of us would spend almost full time for the next two weeks on site.

We had only sixteen days until the NSA crew who would arrive in Berlin to begin tapping into the communications pipe. Today, we had to precisely locate the pipe relative to our tunnel or risk a day for day slip in the already tight schedule. We selected a Sunday morning to minimize the attention our activities might receive.

One of Kurt's operatives stood in the vacant lot which contain the communications pipe. The Chief and a few men located at the end of the tunnel operated the probe. I was on the roof of the building with high-power binoculars. When Kurt's man in the vacant lot saw the tip of the probe emerged from the surface, he communicated its position relative to the No Dumping sign to me via hand signals. Using a field telephone, I directed the repositioning of the probe.

It took five hours, but eventually we were able to locate the pipe itself. The probe took a sample from the pipe. Using the MAITK (Metal Alloy Identification Test Kit) Kurt had provided, we were able to determine that the surface of the pipe contained the expected amounts of lead and arsenic. Although the entire crew was elated by this success, we still had one more task—precisely determine the orientation of the pipe. Numerous additional activations of the probe allowed us to determine that information. A long and productive day finally ended just after 2100 hours.

Feet of Vertical Tunnel Completed: 0   Days until Deadline: 60

CHAPTER 89

Thursday, August 3, 1961

DURING THE FIRST three days of this week, three shifts worked around the clock. They built the terminus room—a ten-foot high, twenty-foot square with a sixteen-foot wide circular opening in the middle. Sergeant Loring's crew was experienced in this building method. I'd only read about it in books—building a form the shape you wanted, drilling numerous holes through the wood structure of the form, and using high-pressure hoses to insert a highly concentrated cement mixture into the earth above and on the sides. The Berlin sand proved ideal for this type of application.

At 0800, I kicked off a meeting with the Chief and his hand-picked crew. "We've empirically proven that the bottom of the Russian communications pipe is only eighteen feet above the center of the terminus room. Our goal now is to assemble and raise a telescoping shaft until it surrounds that pipe. We have just eleven days to complete this task. The purpose of this is shaft is to minimize the potential that the surface of the vacant lot will be disturbed while we tap into the communications pipe.

"The shaft is made of one-inch thick stainless steel. The top section will ultimately be five-feet tall and fourteen-feet across at its base. It's the only section which has a top. Each of the outer sections is slightly shorter in height and wider in diameter."

Pausing to collect my thoughts, I then said, "In the top of the upper most section are two round holes and a long, wide slot. The holes are where the two massive, electric powered, metal blades resting against the wall

TELESCOPING VERTICAL SHAFT

Shown installed around Russian/East German communications pipe

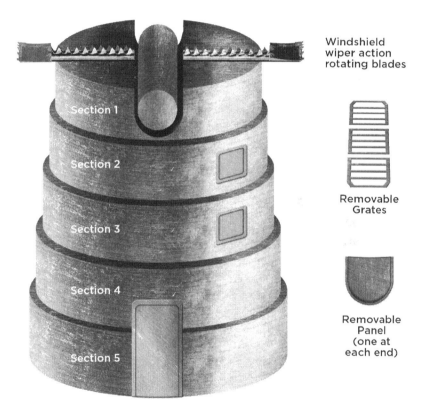

Windshield
wiper action
rotating blades

Removable
Grates

Removable
Panel
(one at
each end)

over there fit. Those digging blades are made of the nickel-chrome alloy called Inconel and should be indestructible. They're designed to sweep back and forth through coordinated 220-degree arcs in a windshield-wiper type motion. They will loosen and sweep soil onto the four-foot-wide opening in the middle of this section. That opening, and the grills which will cover it, run the entire length of the center of this section's top. The excavated soil falls through the grates and onto the floor as the shaft is propelled upward."

I paused for questions. Hearing none, I continued, "On the ends of this section immediately below the grates, there are two U-shaped openings. While the shaft is being extended, those openings will be covered with panels, which will ultimately be removed so the shaft can be extended until it surrounds the pipe."

"Sir, you might explain how that shaft is extended," the Chief prompted.

"As this first section is being assembled, it is mounted onto nine hydraulic jacks. Next, the other four sections are placed around one another. The hydraulic jacks then begin to raise the inner section. Just like a telescope being extended, the bottom of the upper section catches a rim on top of the next section and carries it upward and so forth, until only the bottom section rests on the concrete floor. Does everyone understand?"

I saw a few nod their understanding. No questions, I thought, so I continued, "Our last task will be to make the shaft's top watertight by replacing the grates with metal panels and installing rubber collars around each end of the exposed pipe. Stairs and a metal platform under the communications pipe will provide access to both of its sides for the NSA crew."

Petty Officer Kowalski asked, "We're going to be drilling through another twenty plus feet of earth, so where will that soil go?"

"The soil will be allowed to accumulate on the bottom of the shaft. Our objective is for it to cushion the falling debris. It is a part of our noise-suppression measures. The two middle sections of the shaft have access panels and the bottom two have an opening that will eventually contain a door. This means that we can work inside and remove debris when required. Ultimately, all of the debris will be removed."

The Chief said, "Sir, as you know, we expect to encounter large pieces of concrete, because the building which originally occupied the vacant lot was destroyed in the war. Those grates will allow substantial-sized objects to pass through, but not the largest pieces of concrete debris we may encounter. Unfortunately, jackhammers will create too much noise. Hand labor will be required to break them up so they can be removed."

"Good point, Chief. Before you dismiss the men, there's something else I need to say." The men again turned to me. "I can't emphasize enough the danger of detection and what it could mean. The area above us is only a little over 250 feet south of the East Train Station, the primary departure and arrival point for destinations all across East Germany. A sidewalk is located less than twenty-five feet east of our shaft. We won't be able to anticipate if or when someone might walk by. For this reason, we will restrict digging operation to a few hours in the middle of the night. Both the Chief and I will be in the terminus room anytime the telescoping shaft is being extended. All of us must avoid any unnecessary noise of any form while we are working in the terminus room. The closer we are to the surface, the quieter we must be."

Feet of Vertical Tunnel completed: 0   Days until Deadline: 56

CHAPTER 90

Friday-Monday, August 4-7, 1961

THE CHIEF AND I spent most of Friday determining the exact location of each of the nine hydraulic jacks. The bottom of the two U-shaped openings had to be precisely centered over the number one and number five jacks.

To ensure no miscommunication among members of the crew, we assigned a number to the sections of the vertical shaft. Section one was on the top and contained the blades and grate. Two, three and four were in the middle, and the bottom section, which would rest on the floor, was number five.

It took almost two days of diligent effort for the crew to build section one. The quarter circle sections were placed on the hydraulic jacks. Large flat-head, stainless steel screws married the individual pieces of the almost inch-thick stainless-steel structure to each other. The U-shaped panels were installed next. I marveled at how smoothly and precisely each milled-out surface mated with its neighbor. With the help of an A-frame and slings, the two debris-removal blades and the grates were carefully and silently lowered down onto the shaft, then screwed, bolted or pinned into place.

It only took another day for the other four sections of the telescoping shaft to be assembled around the innermost one.

Feet of Vertical Tunnel Completed: 0   Days until Deadline: 52

CHAPTER 91

Tuesday-Wednesday, August 8-9, 1961

JUST AFTER 2300 on the eighth of August, we were ready to begin rais-ing the telescoping shaft into position. At my signal, the Chief activated the blades whose electric motor made a discernable, smooth whirring sound. Soon we all heard muted thumping and thudding sounds as debris of vari-ous sizes passed through the grates and hit the floor inside the shaft.

Smiling, I felt proud that I'd helped create such a unique mechanism.

We had extended the shaft about two feet when suddenly we heard a loud crunch sound. The whirring of the motor ceased, then resumed almost immediately when the Chief reversed the drive mechanism. A loud, prolonged screech followed before it stopped again.

We sent two men with ladders into the telescoping shaft through the access panel in Section 3. After a few minutes, they handed out a note which read, *Large piece of concrete wedged beneath digging blade. Need support structure, tools & more men.*

We sent in six additional men and tools, as well as material to construct the temporary support structure required to prevent cave-ins.

Trying to clear the obstruction brought with it another problem. Noise. A lot of it.

The Chief grimaced and put his hands over his ears, shouted something in Polish above the din and disappeared into the structure.

Emerging sometime later, he motioned me to follow him to the tunnel. "Sir, immediately above us, the basement floor of the building is buckled downward. Perhaps one of the bombs landed nearby. The grate is open, the safety structure is in place, and we're working to clear that obstruction. I'll stay until they finish. Why don't you go home and get some shut-eye?"

I glanced at my watch. 0254. "Do you think we'll be able to start digging again tonight?"

He shook his head. "Doubtful sir. We'll be lucky if we are able to clear the obstructions before we quit at 0430."

"Okay, see you tomorrow afternoon."

Feet of Vertical Tunnel Completed: 2.4   Days until Deadline: 50

CHAPTER 92

Wednesday-Thursday, August 9-10, 1961

AT JUST BEFORE 2200, the Chief next gave the men their work assignments, concluding, "We'll probably have to stop and dig out the area above the shaft several times tonight. Those of you who are assigned to complete this task, do so as quickly as possible. We need to excavate six to seven feet this evening."

The whirring of the digging blade's motor indicated we were again operational. Shortly before the end of the shift, we'd managed to penetrate four feet of the earth above us, but we had to stop three times to manually remove large obstructions.

After the last stoppage, Sergeant Adams, who was responsible for the clean-out crew, signaled me to follow him into the tunnel. Once we made our way to a spot beyond the zone of silence, he reported, "There is a small stream of water emerging from between two pieces of concrete above us, sir."

I shrugged. "It's rained for three days. With the sandy, boggy Berlin soil, that rain needs to go somewhere. We've had some water seepage before, but it sealed itself before causing a problem. Thanks for the head's up, but we have no choice but to continue, Sergeant."

Adams started to object but nodded his reluctant acceptance. We returned to the terminus room. I was pleased to note that the shaft was moving upward again without difficulty.

All of a sudden, I heard a loud whooshing sound. Water seeped out from under section five. Seconds later, a wave of water gushed out of the opening in section three, flooding the terminus room floor. The men looked at each other, shock and concern on their faces.

Water quickly rose above my ankles. I considered our next move, mentally kicking myself for not heeding the Sergeant's warning! Next, a torrent of water rained down on the work crew from the space between the telescoping shaft and the opening in the ceiling of the terminus room, drenching us all. The water level reached above my knees.

When the flow of water began to abate, I heaved a sigh of relief. Then I heard a loud clap, immediately followed by a deafening metallic ringing as a huge mass struck the outside of the metal shaft with immense force. The lights in the terminus room blinked off. Since the lights on our hardhats no longer worked, the whole area went dark.

"Chief, am I correct that sixteen people, including us reported for duty this evening?"

"That's correct, sir."

"Okay. Can anyone get the light on their hardhat to work?"

When I received only negative replies, I said, "They must have all gotten wet and short-circuited. Each of you needs to sound off, report if you are injured and if you have any means of illumination. I'm Captain Kerr. I'm number one. I'm okay and have no light source."

"Chief Weber, number 2. I'm okay. I tried my Zippo lighter, but wet Zippos don't work."

We soon determined that all sixteen of us were there unhurt, but also unable to provide any light source.

"Does anyone have any idea where the exit from this room into the tunnel is located?" I asked.

The Chief's accented voice said, "I'm standing next to it."

"Each of you move slowly toward the Chief's voice," I directed. "We should be safe once we get a distance down the tunnel. Sound off, Chief."

"Follow me," he ordered. "This way….this way….this way…."

I headed for the Chief's voice and the exit once silence indicated that everyone else had left. I kept my hand extended, brushing the wall to help orient myself as I walked. With the water just up to my ankles, I sensed the decreasing rate of water flow.

After an extended period of time, the Chief finally declared, "Men, I see a pinpoint of light ahead of us."

In a relieved tone, someone said, "Thank God."

A different voice called out, "The lights are on in the level part of the tunnel. They should all be operating from that point all the way back to the building."

The light hurt my eyes when I first entered the illuminated area.

The Chief approached me and said, "All sixteen present and accounted for, sir."

"Anyone injured?" I asked.

"Apparently not, sir." Turning to the men, he said, "Relax while I confer with Captain Kerr."

We walked in the direction of the building. "Chief, do you have any idea what happened?"

"At first, I thought that we'd hit a water main, but the flow now seems to be abating. I'm going to take a wild-ass guess, based on my years of construction experience. That vacant lot above the terminus room is bowl-shaped. When the Russians dug the trench to install the pipe, they used heavy equipment. I doubt they compressed the soil over the pipe itself after they finished. When it rains, water collects in the bowl, flows down and around the pipe, and then penetrates into the debris field below."

"That means the thud and ringing noise we heard after the water began to gush around us was part of an old building falling some distance onto the telescoping shaft?" I suggested, following the Chief's line of reasoning. "Dammit, that means all our work ends in a complete and utter failure." I voice my frustration as I repeatedly used my heel to kick the wall I was leaning against. "Damn, damn, damn. That son-of-a-bitch Thomas Lane will have a field day with this fiasco."

"Captain, it's too early to give up. It's a little after 0400, and we all need rest. Neal Loring and the day shift will be here in four hours. I'll tell him to get the lights and power back on and clean up the mess. You might ask your friend in the East to find out if the appearance of the vacant lot has changed. That information will be essential. Let's meet at around 1300 tomorrow for a look-see into what exactly happened tonight."

Exhausted after arriving home. I showered and fell asleep in Anna's arms without giving the tunnel fiasco, Thomas Lane, or my panic attacks another thought.

Feet of Vertical Tunnel Completed: 7.8   Days until Deadline: 49

CHAPTER 93

Thursday-Friday, August 10-11, 1961

KURT, MARK AND I met with Chief and Sergeant Loring at the building. Kurt smiled and said, "I have only good news. The ground above your work site remains undisturbed, despite what happened last night. The only noise my associate heard was a single, very loud, clunking ring. The area was deserted at the time, so no one else heard it."

Neal and the Chief both gave a thumb's up, then Neal reported, "We have restored power and are cleaning out the debris and water from the tunnel and terminal room."

The Chief smiled. "More good news. A few minutes ago, Neal and I ran the probe up through the grates in the telescoping shaft. We were able to determine that five feet of muck, debris, and chunks of concrete are above us. The next four feet is a large space void of anything except good old air."

"How is that possible?" I asked, amazed.

"The explanation is straightforward, sir," the Chief said. "Water has been accumulating beneath the lead pipe since it was buried three years ago. The building that once occupied this site was destroyed by bombs, but substantial open spaces remained between the layers of debris. Our excavation efforts destabilized the area beneath the pipe. The water carried sand, soil, and small particles of debris down into our subterranean cavern. I think the pipe probably supported the soil above it."

"Why didn't the cave-in impact the area on either side of the pipe?" Mark asked.

"The heavy equipment the Russians used to bury the pipe compressed the soil around the trench. That well-compacted soil absorbed little water, so it was stable compared to the soil beneath the pipe. If I'm correct, then only the soil beneath the pipe shifted position, leaving a long void only a little wider than the pipe itself."

A lengthy conversation ensued, resulting in a universal agreement with the Chief's assessment.

I requested, "Will everyone join me in the office that the Chief and I share in the building?"

Once the door closed, I declared, "If we inform Thomas Lane about what happened last night, he'll raise hell with the triumvirate and bureaucrats in Washington. I suggest we all forget that last night ever happened…"

"—That'll only work if we can report that the tunnel is successfully completed in the next few days," Mark proclaimed.

"Sir, I can assure you that we're close," the Chief said. "Two more nights…at the most three. Then we'll all be able to fend off criticism about any mishaps. Our remarkable task will be finished, and that's what really counts."

"Make it so, Chief," Mark ordered.

A round of handshakes and back slaps followed as everyone except the Chief, Neal, and I departed. I looked at both men, "Chief, I hope you're right. We all have a lot riding on your prediction."

At 2240, the Chief gathered the men around, explained what he thought they might encounter, and gave them their assignments.

Shortly before the 0430 quitting time, the telescoping shaft broke through into the cavern. The Chief and I climbed ladders, stood on the grate and touched the steel communication pipe, which was only a little over five feet above the top of the shaft. Using a powerful spotlight, we determined that the void stretched for at least forty feet in each direction.

Once we could talk, I expressed my concern. "If we leave this cavern as a void in the earth, there may eventually be a cave in, and our little secret could be discovered."

The Chief nodded. "Yeah, that's definitely a problem."

"Do you think we have enough sand left in the basement to fill that entire void?"

"Probably. I'll have the day shift bring back an electric concrete/sand pump and position it with sand in the tunnel."

Feet of Vertical Tunnel Completed: 12   Days until Deadline: 48

CHAPTER 94

Friday-Saturday, August 11-12, 1961

AT A LITTLE before 0400 on the August 12, 1961, the stairs and platform were bolted into place. Then at precisely 0448, just a few minutes after our usual stopping time, the last screw in the collars and panels sealed the pipe inside of the now waterproof top of the shaft.

A happy group of exhausted men dashed into the tunnel before bursting into a boisterous round of shouts, handshakes, back slaps, and hugs. I went around the group calling each man by rank and name as I shook their hands and thanked them for the monumental task they'd completed after so many months of struggles, isolation, and setbacks.

As I was leaving to go home and get some much-needed sleep, Chief Weber and Sergeant Loring intercepted me. "We're having a victory party this evening at 1900 in our recreation area; T-bone steaks, baked potatoes, and all the booze you can drink. It won't be a party without you, sir."

"I'll have to check with my wife but will be there if I can. I'm kind of new to this marriage business—I'll need a kitchen pass to leave the house." This comment received laughter from these two; both had been married for decades.

Although I hated to miss the party, Anna and I had seen each other only in passing for the last two weeks, I wanted to make it up to her, so I offered her a special night out, explaining, "Good things happened at work, and I want to celebrate. How about another night at Chez Orleans, that fancy restaurant at the French Officer's Club?"

"Robbie, I'm glad you've been successful, but I've promised my parents that I'd visit this weekend so my entire family can celebrate a close friend's anniversary. Sorry, liebchen. I told you the other evening, but I guess you were too tired to hear me. You fall asleep the minute your head hits the pillow!"

That night, I crashed back at our apartment at about 0100 after attending our victory party, oblivious to events occurring only a few miles away that would change the world forever. One of the most fateful nights of the twentieth century was unfolding here in Berlin while I slept alone.

Vertical Tunnel Completed   Days until Deadline: 47

PART THREE

"The solemn vow each of us gave to West Berlin in time
of peace will not be broken in time of danger. If we do
not meet our commitments to Berlin, where will we later
stand? If we are not true to our word there, all that we
have achieved in collective security, which relies on these
words, will mean nothing. And if there is one path above all
others to war, it is the path of weakness and disunity."

John F. Kennedy, Speech to the Nation
during the Berlin Crisis, 1961

CHAPTER 95

Sunday, August 13, 1961

THE TENSION AROUND the Wing Commander's conference room was palpable. Whispered speculation passed among the seven United States Air Force officers present. Everyone wanted to know why we had been ordered to report for duty at a few minutes after 0400 on a Sunday morning? Groggy from lack of sleep and a little hung over, I remained sufficiently alert to realize something monumental had occurred.

After being called to attention, Colonel Morgan ordered, "As you were. What we know is that yesterday afternoon, tens of thousands of East German People's Police, military units, and construction reservists were told to report to work. At a little after 9 p.m. last night, numerous phone conversations we intercepted upstairs between individuals in East Berlin contained instructions to implement Operation Rose."

"Sir, have we or our allies determined what that is?" I asked.

"No confirmation yet, but the border between the two Berlins was closed in total secrecy at midnight last night."

"That seems impossible with all of the resources that we, the British, and French have devoted to spying on them and monitoring all of their communications," Mark observed.

"I agree," Colonel Morgan said.

Before he could continue, I asked, "Sir, you may recall the press conference Walter Ulbricht, the East German leader, had with Western reporters last month. In response to a question about rumors that the border between East and West Berlin would soon be closed, he said: 'No one has any intention of building a wall.' Is that what this is all about?"

Colonel Morgan replied. "What we do know is that at midnight, East Berlin Radio announced that all traffic between East and West will be halted until further notice. Then all telephone lines between East and West were severed. Intercepts made by the Army Security Agency over at Andrews Barracks indicate that three Motorized Artillery Divisions—two East German and one Russian—have been ordered to move toward Berlin. Each of these units has approximately 110 heavy tanks…"

Anna had attended a celebration in the East and spent last night with her parents. I cringed. Could she be trapped there temporarily—even permanently?

I missed some of Colonel Morgan's comments, but refocused when Colonel Powell asked, "Sir, are they going to attack us here in West Berlin?"

"We can't tell yet. At midnight, armed sentries were placed at three-foot intervals across all eighty-one crossing points in the barrier that surrounds West Berlin. All American military personnel in Berlin have been ordered to full alert. Most will stay in their barracks or quarters, and everyone has been ordered to stay away from the border."

The on-duty flight commander rushed into the room and handed a message to Mark. He stood and paraphrased the communique. "The Surveillance and Reporting Center at Zweibrucken has ordered us to be prepared to destroy all encryption equipment and codeword-classified materials, starting with the Top Secret files."

"Everyone in this room will remain on the base until further notice," Colonel Morgan instructed. "One of your tasks will be to help supervise the destruction activities should that become necessary. In the interim, the Signals Intelligence Processing Center is now fully manned by analysts. Those of you who are in command of that area are excused to see if you can discover what's going on in the East from their intercepted communications."

As a captain and two first lieutenants stood to leave, Colonel Morgan added, "Please report any developments back to us. The sun is now up. We should know a lot more fairly soon."

Four of us remained in the conference room—Colonel Morgan, Mark, Scott, and me.

Mark received another message, "Gentlemen, this situation is looking more dangerous. A phone conversation that one of our linguists upstairs just intercepted indicates that East German Air Forces are on full alert. Their aircraft are being armed, and pilots have been ordered to report for duty."

Colonel Morgan grimaced. "Well gentlemen, it appears we're in a crisis situation. I know I can count on each of you to do your duty. Now..."

I felt the tension mounting. Looking directly at my closest friends, I knew why.

Mark worried about the safety of his wife and three children, whom he'd brought to this menacing place.

Scott, usually so lighthearted, was glum. He and his girlfriend Mia had quarreled, and she'd recently moved back with her parents in the East.

Anna! My heart rate sped up. *No, not a panic attack. Not here. Not now!* Frozen in place, I slowly breathed in and out to steady myself.

"Colonel, if it's all right with you, I'd like to check my sources and perform a reconnaissance of my own," Scott requested. "Firsthand knowledge may help us with our tasks."

"Please do so, Captain Taylor. While we wait for further developments, you have a task, Captain Kerr. Let's go to your tank."

Once Mark and I joined him in the tank, Colonel Morgan looked at me. "You've completed the tunnel. Now, you must expedite construction of the new Signals Exploitation Center facilities. I need a plan and a revised schedule today."

"I'll start immediately, sir," I replied.

"You understand that the rapid completion of construction may prevent or help us win a war if it comes to that."

"I fully understand. Colonel, while I work, can someone keep me informed of the latest developments?" Pausing, I added "My wife Anna went over to the East this weekend."

"Sorry to hear that, Captain." Colonel Morgan frowned. "We'll keep everyone informed of the latest developments. Several thousand other American dependents are in grave danger as well, including the wives and children of both Colonel Powell and myself."

I struggled to concentrate on the building schedule. My thoughts repeatedly strayed to how I could get Anna safely back to West Berlin.

CHAPTER 96

Anna
Sunday, August 13, 1961

THE PHONE IN the hall started to ring at a little after 6 a.m. that fateful Sunday morning. Papa answered it. I turned over in bed assuming it was a patient who needed his help. Soon after, I heard him call, "Everyone, come downstairs. I have bad news."

Once we gathered around him, Papa announced, "The DDR has closed the border between East and West Berlin. Rumors indicate German and Russian troops are deployed all along the dividing line."

"Does this mean war?" I asked, my thoughts on Robbie.

"Hopefully not," Mama replied as she put her arm around little Andrea, who stood beside her.

An eerie silence followed Mama's words. With tears in his eyes, Papa circled the room, hugging each of us, trying to reassure us all that everything would be all right.

I suggested, "Let's turn on RIAS (Radio in the American Sector). It's operated by the Americans. They never lie to us."

We all sat down in the living room. Stephen dialed the station, which was playing classical music. The next news broadcast came on a short time later. "Our reporters have deployed along the dividing line between East and West Berlin. They have established that East German armed forces have completely sealed the border. Every checkpoint is closed. Construction equipment has been deployed to most of these locations, and work has commenced to seal most crossing points. Only a limited number of checkpoints do not have construction equipment, mostly in central Berlin."

Papa said, "I'm afraid that we have waited too long, and that from now on the West will be closed to us. The totalitarian regime that controls us will begin to exercise more control over every aspect of our lives."

"Stephen will no longer be able to attend school in the West," Sophia said.

"I'm sure he will not be allowed to cross the border," Papa replied.

As I looked around the room, my family's glum faces revealed their concern for the future.

Conscious of the tension in the room, little Andrea crawled up into my lap saying, "Has something bad happened? Why isn't Robert here?"

"Robert's at our apartment in West Berlin, safe and sound," I replied. "All the rest of us are here with you, and we won't let anything bad happen to any of us."

Minutes of silence followed as each member of my family contemplated the loss of freedom and restrictions that they would now be forced to endure.

"Hopefully, the Americans won't let the communists abrogate the four-power agreements on free passage of peoples within Berlin so easily," I offered.

"The members of the Western alliance will move very cautiously. They will not want to start another war," Fredrich replied.

Angelica started to cry, "I was supposed to start school in the West next year. I don't like my current teacher. She spends hours each day telling us of how wonderful life under Communism is."

"We should turn it over to the communist propaganda station, DDR 1, so we can hear what they are saying," Stephen said.

This station also played classical music, but periodically provided some version of the following announcement: "The measures to carry out the decision of the Council of Ministers are taking effect. Our state will no longer allow the West to continue plundering our socialist worker's haven. The East-West border will be closed temporarily. New procedures for passage between the two areas of Berlin will soon be implemented."

I tried to call Robert to assure him of my safety, but the attempt resulted in a busy signal. When I dialed other numbers in West Berlin, they were also blocked.

Turning to Papa, I said, "Apparently all phone lines to the West have been disconnected."

We ate breakfast and continued to listen to the news broadcast, which contained little new information.

"Papa, do you think I can safely return to the West?" I asked.

"I'll try to find out." After two calls he hugged me, saying, "No one knows if the border is open to West German citizens."

I went outside. Everything appeared to be normal—a typically quiet and peaceful summer Sunday morning.

Mama requested, "We all need to go to church this morning to pray for peace."

We all agreed.

"Germany and the world have had too much war already," seemed to be the collective sentiment we heard from others after church.

My father's private conversations with men and women I recognized as East German government employees revealed that they did not know if people with West German passports could return to the West.

I needed to return to the West. Together, Robert and I could find a way to get my family out!

Mama served the big meal of the week, baked chicken and spaetzle. Midway through, Sophia dared to say what we all thought. "We should have all gone long ago. There is nothing here for us. They claim that closing the border will be temporary. Since those communist bastards always say the opposite of the truth, we will probably be stuck here forever."

"I'll make more phone calls and see if I can discern what is happening," Papa said. "One of my patients is a senior official in the Ministry of Interior. He may be able to tell me something."

After the third phone call, Papa turned to me, raised his hands and shrugged his shoulders. "No one knows for sure if individuals with West German identity papers will be allowed to leave."

"I must try to get back to Robert. I'll pack my things and leave soon."

"Perhaps you should wait until we know more."

"No. Papa. I must try now!"

CHAPTER 97

Robert

Sunday, August 13, 1961

ONCE I WAS alone in my tank, thoughts of what could happen to Anna overwhelmed me.

My heart rate accelerated. I gasped for breath. My field of vision shrank, and I felt tingling in my extremities. I stretched out on my desk and I used deep, controlled breathing with my diaphragm to calm down.

A little while later, I used the telephone on the desk outside of the tank in an attempt to call Anna at her parent's home. All I got was a busy signal.

I forced myself to focus on the Colonel's orders, went to the third floor and found the Chief and Sergeant Loring in the mess hall.

Working feverishly, the three of us devised two plans of action for rapid completion of the Signals Exploitation Center, with accompanying schedules. One required additional manpower, and the other necessitated extended hours and weekend work for the current crew.

At precisely 0745, the three of us made out way to Colonel Morgan's office. "We're ready to discuss various construction options, sir."

His nodded. "Be seated. First, I'll bring you up to date on the latest developments. Our signal intelligence intercepts over the last few hours indicate that Russian and East German Air Forces are in an enhanced state of readiness. Over a hundred interceptor and fighter-bomber aircraft are sitting on the ground, armed, pilots in their cockpits, ready to be scrambled on a moment's notice...."

"—What's going on along the barrier between the two Berlins?" I asked.

"Captain Taylor, tell us what you've been able to determine," Colonel Morgan requested.

"As you know, until today the eighty-one crossing points, including those in the underground system, have provided easy access through the fence between the two Berlins for everyone. Shortly after sunrise this morning, East German construction crews began to install concertina wire, new fences, tank traps, and concrete barriers across most of those checkpoints."

"Show them the Polaroid photos you took," the Colonel directed.

Handing us several images, Scott said, "As you can see, concertina wire has entirely closed the Brandenburg Gate crossing point. Apparently, most of the other crossing points between East and West have also been barricaded."

"Are they building defensive positions as if preparing for war?" I asked.

"Only tank traps. It seems as if their objective is to seal the border between the two Berlins. Subway service has been halted, and some underground stations are reportedly being sealed. On the way back here, I stopped at the Potsdamer Platz crossing point. It was closed, but there was no construction evident."

My heart sank.

"Captain Kerr, proceed with your briefing." Colonel Morgan said.

By focusing on the information on those few pieces of paper, I managed to avoid another panic attack. I shut out the reality of my desperate personal situation.

CHAPTER 98

Anna

Sunday, August 13, 1961

AFTER LUNCH, I hugged everyone and made my goodbyes like I was going on a long trip. Mama broke down, sobbing as I walked out the door. Papa accompanied me to the subway station. Once there he whispered, "Anna, if you cannot get over safely, return home immediately. I have friends. We'll get you back to Robert somehow. Don't take any risks."

"Yes, Papa, I understand." Tears welled in my eyes.

"Write often. Your mother worries so about you."

"Papa, you are acting as if we might never see each other again. Surely…"

"—I expect the worst," he said. "We'll be like caged animals, trained to be perfect communists. That is their objective!"

After hugging me for a long time, he walked away, stoop-shouldered, tears running down his face.

My optimism suddenly dissolved. I might never see my family again and wept over our fate. After I thought about Robert and our future together, I managed to regain my composure. I joined a group of nervous people awaiting the next westbound train. Some held packages, others suitcases and some carried nothing. Usually, I changed trains on the way to the subway station closest to our apartment. I decided to stay on this train, which made three stops on the way to the West at Potsdamer Platz.

After we boarded the train, the woman next to me whispered, "I heard this train no longer goes to West Berlin. Is that correct?"

"I don't know. It used to go there."

"We will just have to hope. I was visiting relatives in the East." She tightly gripped her West German Passport.

"Me too." The dull ache in my heart refused to go away. Thinking of being permanently separated from Robert made me physically ill.

The lady next to me touched my arm and smiled. I took her hand and squeezed it.

Millions of families like ours would be separated by this evil barrier. The communists were utterly depraved.

Clutching a cardboard suitcase, the young man on my left cowered. "I came from Dresden yesterday. I had hoped to pass through to the West today."

"I hope you're successful." I feared he'd waited too long.

Across from me sat a woman with three children. She repeatedly looked up, as if praying. "Will my children ever see their grandparents again?"

One stop short of my destination, the train stopped. The conductor repeatedly announced, "End of the line. All out!" Once on the subterranean platform, uniformed transit police shouted, "Westerners and tourists are to go to the Potsdamer Platz checkpoint. If your papers are in order, you will be allowed to proceed. Citizens of the DDR are to go about their business." This message was repeated again and again as if we were deaf and dumb herd animals.

Several apparent emigres joined us Westerners as we trudged almost in a formation toward the West and freedom. The heat of the August sun and tension of the unknown caused us all to perspire.

The young man from Dresden walked next to me. He gasped and pointed to our right. Two tanks with DDR markings had been positioned to ambush any Western forces that might try to tear down the new barriers with force.

Ahead, I saw numerous armed individuals in a variety of uniforms. The young man whispered, "They look like they mean business." He threw his suitcase over a wall as we passed a government building. I stopped, opened my small bag, and threw a wheel of cheese and several sausages Mama had given me over the same wall. There were laws about taking food from the East.

Border guards carefully examined each individual's papers, thus prolonging the process. At the head of the line, an older woman was suddenly seized by the elbow and escorted into a waiting van. The young Dresdener, who stood ahead of me, slipped out of line and went back. I assumed he would try to retrieve his suitcase and think about what was next for him.

I had applied for new identity papers, but they hadn't arrived from Bonn. The passport I clasped in my hand still indicated that I was Anna Fischer, born in East Berlin. I removed my wedding ring and slipped it into my pocket.

Perhaps twenty people stood in line ahead of me. I suddenly felt the earth drop out from under my feet. Unable to move, I clenched my teeth. Captain Gustav Mueller had emerged from a shack and now hovered near the border guards supervising the exit process.

He'll arrest me.

My mouth went dry; I began to tremble. My legs felt frozen in place. Mueller stepped forward to answer a guard's question about something. Finally, out of his line of sight, I slipped out of line undetected and returned East.

At the first available pay phone, I rang Papa's surgery.

"*Doktor* Fischer. May I help you?"

"Papa. I cannot go through the Potsdamer Platz checkpoint. Gustav Mueller is there. I told you what he did."

"Call back in ten minutes."

I paced back and forth, continuously glancing at my watch. Finally, I dialed the number.

"Anna?"

"Yes."

"The Friedrichstrasse crossing point is still open. It's a little over a kilometer from you. Go there. Let us know you're safe if you can. Remember, we all love you."

I hurried down Leipziger Strasse, past rows of government office buildings.

When I reached the Friedrichstrasse checkpoint, people on both sides of the border waved at each other. A young woman stopped me. "Do you see that young man over there in the gray suit?" she asked as she pointed.

"Yes, I see him."

"We were supposed to be married next weekend. We have an apartment already furnished; all my possessions are over there. Everything. I just came to stay with my parents for one night. Now, who knows? Ask him to wait for me."

Hugging her, I promised, "I'll tell him."

Although two people ahead of me were taken out of line, I nervously passed through as the border guard gave my papers and possessions only a cursory glance.

Elated, I wanted to shout at the top of my lungs, "I made it—freedom and Robert."

Approaching the young man in the gray suit, I conveyed the girl's message. He waved to her, tears in his eyes. I gave this complete stranger a long hug. Fate can be so cruel.

Elated, I floated on and off of two trains, and then ran to the door of our apartment house. After several attempts, I shoved the key in the lock, ran up five flights of stairs and joyfully flung our door open. In anticipation of the safety of his arms, I called out, "Robert, I'm home safely. Robbie? Robbie, honey?"

The bed was unmade; his pajamas and evidence of a quick shower scattered about the bedroom. His uniform was gone from the closet. He hadn't left a note. The American military must be on duty, I concluded. I turned on the radio and listened to the same old news.

Huddling in the chair next to the radio, I didn't feel safe. Would the Americans just accept the division of Berlin and Germany?

The world is changing again. Will those I love survive in this new world?

CHAPTER 99

Robert

Sunday, August 13, 1961

AT 1335, COLONEL Morgan called us all into his conference room. "Gentlemen, I may have good news. General Norstad, the SACEUR, has received the assurance of General Ivan Jakubowski, the Supreme Commander of all Soviet Troops in East Germany, that local authorities are only restricting the movement of people who live in East Germany. New travel regulations will be promulgated on Monday. To implement these restrictions, the East Germans will be closing most of the crossing points between the two Berlins."

Kurt, who had just arrived, stood and said. "I can confirm what the Colonel has announced. The information the CIA received from a very reliable source indicates that East German leaders, with Russian approval, are in the process of permanently sealing the border to those living in East Germany and East Berlin. It is their way of preventing young, educated East Germans from fleeing to the West. It's as simple as that."

"Is this only the start?" I asked, thinking that the signing of a separate peace treaty with East Germany might force a confrontation and possibly cause World War III.

"The answer to that question depends on how rapidly we can complete the Signals Exploitation Center," Colonel Morgan answered, pointing his index finger at me. "You committed to having the first part of it operational in four weeks, using your currently available work crew!"

"We can finish our part. The problem is tapping into the tube, install-ing the patch panels, and running all of those signal lines back to the Exploitation Center," I replied. "Those tasks aren't our responsibility."

"I'll begin working on that with my counterpart from NSA first thing tomorrow morning. You need to make certain we're not part of the problem."

"Yes, sir."

"You're all dismissed for the day. See you in the morning."

Mark stood and smiled. "At least there won't be a shooting war here in Berlin anytime soon."

Scott approached. "Being stationed here in Berlin allows us to witness history in the making. Something to tell our grandchildren."

"I'm in, but first I must make sure Anna safely made her way across the border. She may want to go with us." I called our apartment. When I received no answer, I turned to my two friends. "She is not there; I need to find her!"

Mark grabbed my arm. "Give us a minute to change, and we'll help you search for her."

CHAPTER 100

Sunday, August 13, 1961

AFTER RACING UP five flights of stairs, I burst into our apartment. Seeing Anna, I gathered her into my arms. "Oh thank God, you're safely home! Did you have any difficulty getting over the border?"

"No, not really, but now my whole family is stuck in the East!"

"I've been told this isn't the first time the East Germans have restricted travel between the two Berlins."

She nodded. "That's true. But this is the first time they've made such extensive changes to the facilities along the border and closed subway stations. This feels...permanent," she said.

"You're probably right. I would like to see what's happening. Will you go with me?"

"I don't know. The knot beneath my heart only disappeared when I got back here—inside this apartment. I've already seen what's happening on the other side; it's not pleasant."

"Aren't you the least bit curious about what they are doing?"

"Yes, but is it safe to be near the border?"

"It should be. Give me time to change into civilian clothes, and we'll have a look see."

"So, you Americans have decided to do nothing," she snapped, her tone accusatory.

"What choice do our leaders have? War? Armed confrontation? The truth is, our leaders are trying to decide what to do. Mark and Scott are waiting for us downstairs."

An hour later, we approached the Brandenburg Gate. Scott shouted to be heard. "It's so crowded, this could turn into a flashpoint for rioting. Best we move south toward the Potsdamer Platz."

"Why are the West Berlin police keeping everyone back from this point?" Anna asked.

"They know the communists could easily use 'restoring order' as an excuse to invade West Berlin. That may even be their prime objective," I said, as I helped her push through the crowd.

Looking back at the Brandenburg Gate Plaza, I saw that concertina wire stretched all the way across that broad opening. Behind that barrier, a new chain-link and barbed-wire fence was being built. And through the pillars of the Brandenburg Gate, I saw armed troops holding a large crowd of East Germans at bay.

The mostly young male mob on this side shouted insults at the East German troops and construction crews. Pig head, dog, swine, dummy, traitor, stooge, and idiot were common insults. I also heard vile epithets about the East German workers' and soldiers' lineage or sexual preferences.

"The West Berlin police are arresting young men who are carrying cobblestones!" Mark said, in a voice filled with concern. "Let's get out of here."

We followed his lead through the crowd.

"Notice that the VoPos are standing behind the construction crew to impress on them that trying to escape would be fatal," he said.

"Let's hurry," Anna urged, tugging on my arm.

After walking south through the Tiergarten for some time, we viewed the scene on both sides of the Potsdamer Platz checkpoint as people passed through to the West.

"The line of people waiting to cross over has gotten much longer since I was here earlier this afternoon," Anna said.

"Notice all of the people on both sides of the border waving to friends and relatives." Mark shook his head in disgust.

With tears in her eyes, Anna murmured, "Please notice the faces of my countrymen! Families, friends, and lovers know that a long period of separation is in their future. You can see it in their desperate, tear-stained faces and furtive waves."

I hugged her as she wept.

"All of my family except you is now trapped in the East. If I didn't have you…" Her voice trailed off.

To comfort her, I led her away from our friends and the crowd. We sat on a bench in Tiergarten Park, and watched the sun set in the west, intentionally not looking at the human tragedy unfolding behind us.

"I swear to you, I'll do everything in my power to get your family to the West. Somehow, someway, you'll be reunited with them," I promised, unsure how I would ever accomplish such a daunting task.

CHAPTER 101

Monday, August 14, 1961

EARLY THE NEXT morning, Thomas Lane demanded a meeting with the senior officers of my unit. We assembled in my tank. He adopted his usual superior tone. "In my hand, I have a communique from the Director of the CIA to the Secretary of Defense, Mr. McNamara, urging him to dissolve the triumvirate and transfer the entire tunnel building program to the CIA."

"What was his justification for this demand?" Mark asked.

"Captain Kerr's slipshod management of the construction of the tunnel and exploitation center. If he had used his resources expeditiously, we'd have had advanced notice of this travesty!"

Standing, Mark snapping, "You and the other members of the management triumvirate insisted on a 1 October deadline for completion of the first phase of construction. The construction is now almost complete, due to Captain Kerr's diligent management. We're going to be operational several weeks before the 1 October deadline!"

"He should have started earlier and driven his men harder."

"You and the triumvirate received full approval and funding almost nine months before his arrival. If anyone wasted time, it was you! General Harrison told me that a significant amount of that delay involved a CIA attempt to take over the program! And that it was you who masterminded that attempt!" Mark barked.

"NSA and the military have sixteen intercept sites that do nothing but monitor Russian and Warsaw Pact communications, yet they failed to discover East German intentions...I..."

"—Your CIA organization here in Berlin also failed. You have over 200 agents and full-time employees, plus several thousand operatives, who detected none of the preparations for this closure of the border! You're right under their noses and can freely move through East Berlin!" he shouted.

Both men stood toe to toe. Their raised voices and flushed faces made me think this confrontation might turn into fisticuffs.

"The truth is, the entire Western Intelligence establishment—CIA, British MI-6, and the French Deuxieme Bureau utterly failed to detect any unusual activity from behind the Iron Curtain," Mark continued loudly. "You're speculating that if Robert had...."

Colonel Morgan stood and approached the two men, "Mr. Lane, you are a guest in this DoD facility. Let me make this clear to you...everyone in this room takes his orders from General Harrison, and not one of us has any intention of following any orders you give us. Now, please leave before I have a security detail do the job for me."

Thomas turned and stalked to the door where he paused to glare in my direction, as if to say this matter was far from settled.

Scott, Kurt, and I remained in the tank. Kurt said, "Bernauerstrasse is still open. The East Germans have been working so hard to guard and seal the eighty-one checkpoints, they've failed to seal the doors and windows in that almost two-kilometer long street of apartment houses that abut each other and are the border..."

"—That means we have a chance to save people trapped in the East!" I said, thinking about my promise to Anna.

"I've got five people I'm desperate to save. Mia is pregnant with my child," Scott revealed. "I'm sure she'll also want her parents, sister, and her sister's husband to come west, as well."

"Anna cried almost all night. She won't be happy until her family is here," I added.

"Even I have a group I want to save from life under those bastards!" Kurt admitted.

Scott and I looked at Kurt in amazement.

"I have a daughter. I must save her. Her mother is the love of my life, and her grandmother lives with them. I have three people to bring West. Are both of you free now?"

We both nodded.

"Give us a few minutes to get out of our uniforms, and we'll join you on an excursion to Bernauerstrasse," Scott said.

The Fischer house looked deserted. I rang the bell for the surgery. Receiving no response, I rang the front doorbell several times. Sophia's thirteen-year-old son, Stephen, cautiously opened the front door. He smiled broadly as I hurried inside.

"Uncle Robert, it's you!" he exclaimed.

"Is anyone else here?"

"No. I'm alone."

I looked at the clock above the fireplace. 1:17 p.m. *Not much time.*

"When will they return?" I asked.

"Everyone is at work or in school. Grandpa told me he had rounds at the hospital, then house calls and would be home late. Grandma usually is the first one home at about 4 p.m."

On the way here, I had seen a few VoPos and decided to get Anna's family near the exit point on Bernauerstrasse and then take them in small groups over the border. *What now?*

"Does anyone work close by?"

"Not really."

"There is a way over the border. Put some clothes in your rucksack and come with me."

When Stephen returned, he said, "There was room for my Elvis album you gave me. I'm ready.

I'll get him across the border and then come back, I decided.

The familiar street that ended in a wall had been deserted earlier, but now was crowded with trucks, VoPos, and people. A couple carrying suitcases walked toward us. Stephen asked them, "What's happening?"

The man answered, "The VoPos will not let anyone through who cannot prove that they live on Bernauerstrasse!"

The alley we needed to reach was on the next block. The damn VoPos stood between us and it. What now?

As we drew closer, I saw a construction crew hauling concrete blocks and bricks into apartment houses on both sides of the street. Apparently, they intended to seal the doors and windows. I needed to get us to safety.

Leading Stephen back to a side street, I whispered, "We must find a way through."

We began to walk toward Scott's apartment house on an adjacent street. When the three of us had exited the building earlier as a group, we'd hidden a key under a pot in the back garden. As we approached it and safety, two VoPos spotted us. They walked toward us.

Seeing them, I muttered, "Turn around and ignore them. We cannot allow them to question us."

"Halten Sie!" one of the VoPos shouted behind us as we sprinted around the corner and out of their sight.

Stephen dashed through an open garden gate we'd just passed. I followed and secured the latch. I joined him into a nearby shed, as he secured its simple wooden latch behind us. We could hear the two VoPos shouting questions at each other as they searched for us.

A loud thud indicated they'd forced open the garden gate. *"Scheisse— Sie müssen hier sein!"* (Shit, they must be here!)

An old tenant of the apartment house stuck her head out of the kitchen window and yelled, "Why are you breaking my gate?"

"Did you see two people. A man and a boy. They refused to obey our order to stop."

"I have been standing here for some time. They climbed over the fence into the next garden. Be gone with you."

The VoPo's moved toward our hiding place when someone shouted at them, "You blockheads! You've left your guard station. Return to that area immediately. Two people just scrambled over the wall you were supposed to be guarding."

After waiting in silence for several minutes, I motioned for Stephen to follow me. The old woman waved to us as we cautiously exited the broken gate. I silently mouthed thank you in German. I led us north, away from the area. In the middle of the next block, a man held the door of an apartment house open. He signaled us and whispered, "Straight through here and both gardens. You'll end up in the West."

Sensing a potential trap, but having little choice, we followed a cue of people out one apartment house and into another.

Some of those carried suitcases. Most had nothing but the clothes on their backs. All wanted to live free.

We walked down a long hall, passed a row of mailboxes, through an open door and a step down onto a broad sidewalk and street.

"We made it! Bernauerstrasse!" I shouted, recognizing it by the trolley tracks that run down its middle. Elated, I hugged Stephen.

As we walked to the nearest subway, we passed the familiar entrance to number 124, Scott's apartment building. The door was now sealed. A window on the second floor opened and sheets tied together flopped down. Stepping out of the way, we saw suitcases and items tied into bundles fly out of the window. We helped by grasping the end of the sheets as a family of five shimmied to freedom.

Scott suddenly appeared in that same second-floor window. I held the bottom of the sheets again as Scott and a young couple I didn't know descended onto the street.

"This is Mia's sister, Lina, and her husband, Manfred," Scott told us. "My usual luck. On Friday, Mia and her parents left for a short holiday on a nearby lake."

The helmeted head of a VoPo poked out the window. Everyone scattered as he pointed his machine gun at us. He slowly pulled the sheets back into the apartment and closed the window.

"Kurt has an official passport, but his daughter, girlfriend, her mother…"

"—Perhaps we should stay nearby in case he needs us," Scott suggested.

"I'm thinking of going back over," I admitted hesitating.

"—Don't. The situation is getting too dangerous."

Scott and I took turns standing on the street outside, keeping an eye out for Kurt while the three new arrivals in the West ate lunch at a *gasthaus* across from number 124.

When the fire brigade arrived, I rushed into the pub. "West Berlin firefighters have shown up with safety nets. People are jumping from windows and the roofs of buildings."

Almost everyone, including Scott and Stephen, left behind uneaten meals and half consumed beers, intent on seeing this spectacle.

Gazing up at people gathered on the roofs of the three-story and four-story tall buildings, I spotted Kurt atop a nearby apartment house. Pointing him out to Scott, I said, "We need to get the firefighters to help him!"

Just then a VoPo came up behind Kurt. Although we couldn't see exactly what was happening, the VoPo suddenly tumbled off the roof, landed in a heap nearby, and didn't move.

After a group of firefighters with a safety net rescued everyone from the next building, I rushed to them. "Our friend needs your help," I said, pointing to Kurt's location.

They immediately responded. An older woman resisted Kurt's efforts to get her to jump. He picked her up, held her out over the abyss like a doll, and released her.

"Must be his girlfriend's mother," I shouted to Scott over the din of the crowd.

The firemen helped her out of the safety net. She limped and held her arm as we rushed to her aid. Kurt jumped just as two shots rang out. He landed in the net, his head covered in blood.

CHAPTER 102

Monday, August 14, 1961

THE WOUND TO Kurt's head proved to be superficial. With the help of an undershirt from Stephen's backpack, we stopped the bleeding. After much discussion and a significant payment, I persuaded a taxi driver to take us to a local hospital. Several hours passed before Kurt and his girl-friend's mother received proper treatment and could leave the hospital.

When we arrived back at our apartment house, I had Stephen wait while I checked the listening devices in the basement. When the Stasi removed the tape recorders several months ago, Kurt had informed me, "Replenishing those tapes on a daily basis and then transcribing them takes so much time and effort that even the Stasi have difficulty maintaining that type of surveillance for extended periods."

At the time, I'd asked, "Does that mean I no longer need to check every day to determine if the recorders have been reinstalled?"

"No, Robert, my friend. You're stuck. It must remain an important part of your daily routine. We'd remove the boxes, wires, and microphones, but that would tell them we're on to them. We don't want that. It's all part of the game—keep them guessing as to what's really happening in every way possible. Remember, they can reinstall those devices at any time."

Anna had just stepped out of the shower when I rushed into our bedroom, kissed her, swung her around, and exclaimed, "I have a special surprise for you in the living room."

"Whatever it is, it'll have to wait while I dry my hair and get dressed."

"Put on your robe and come now!"

Curiosity got the best of her. Following my instructions, Anna walked into the living room. She almost fainted when she saw Stephen.

"What?" she hesitated, stammering, "Has the border been reopened?"

"No."

She rushed to embrace him. "Did you escape?"

"No. Robert came to get me!"

She looked over at me in amazement. "How…what did….why not all of them?"

We sat in the living room, going over the events of the day. Anna kissed and embraced me frequently. At one point she said, "I don't know how to tell you how much I love you and how eternally grateful I am. You risked your life today to rescue my family. And you managed to get Stephen out. He can continue his education in the West. That's very important to my whole family."

She then began to weep. After she recovered somewhat from her sadness, she said, "Stephen, you can live with us. You will be able to go back to school tomorrow."

Pointing at the radiator and then my ear, I said, "I believe it would be best if, first thing in the morning, we placed Stephen on an airplane for Frankfort."

Anna nodded in agreement. "Your great-uncle from Darmstadt can pick you up. What do you say?"

"I'd like that," Stephen replied. "And great-grandfather is there; I really want to be with him!"

That evening in bed, she held on to me and cried. "It is too bad you could not get them all out."

"I wanted to, but he was the only one at your parents' house. It was too risky to try to find all of the others." I ached for Anna, as she sobbed. I assured her, "When it's safe, I'll try again to rescue your family."

CHAPTER 103

Friday, August 18, 1961

AFTER MONDAY'S EXCURSION East, Scott, Kurt, and I met frequently.

At this first gathering, Kurt revealed, "My lady friend, whose name is Erica, was in her apartment and could have come with her mother. But our daughter, Gretchen, who's only eleven, was at a youth camp for two weeks. Erica decided to stay behind for obvious reasons."

"So, we still have fifteen people to get out of that hell hole," Scott said.

"Before we attempt to get the rest of our people out, we must make careful plans, and the extraction must be precisely timed," Kurt advised. "Being patient is important."

"I've heard people are escaping through the sewers and storm drains, which were built long before the city was divided," I offered.

"The East Germans sealed most of those back in the early 1950s in an attempt to crack down on the tremendous black marketing of goods unavailable in the East," Kurt said.

"As long as the drains and sewers are still functioning, humans will figure a way through those barriers," Scott observed.

"I've heard that people can travel to another country like Czechoslovakia, cross the border into neutral Austria, and then fly to safety from there." I offered.

"Exit visas are now being very tightly controlled," Kurt replied. "But

I've heard that one of the senior officials who issues those documents can be bribed."

"If you need money to make any of this happen, let me know," Scott offered.

"It might take lots of money," Kurt replied.

"I've got lots of money."

I shot a puzzled look at Scott, but I didn't ask any questions. *Was he willing to pay the cost of getting Anna's family to safety, or just his three loved ones?* I wondered.

"As you both know, I've contacts on both sides of the border," Kurt said. "Let's meet again on Tuesday. By then I'll know more."

CHAPTER 104

Friday-Saturday, August 19-20, 1961

ON THURSDAY, PRESIDENT Kennedy announced his response to the closing of the border between East and West Berlin. He dispatched his Vice President, Lyndon Johnson, and General Lucien Clay to West Berlin to "assure its people of our continued commitment to their freedom."

When we heard about their visit, Anna said, "If you asked the average Berliner who they would want to visit during these troubled times, they would almost universally say General Clay."

"Why?"

"He was the military governor of Germany. He organized the Berlin Air Lift, which saved this city in 1948. We all love him. If it weren't for him, we would all be living under communist rule now. He is our savior and one of Papa's heroes." She frowned. "Too bad Papa can't see him."

On Friday, I learned that Gerald Scherman and I would be giving Vice President Johnson a briefing on the construction of our tunnel and the Signals Exploitation Center before he departed on Monday. After I helped to prepare the presentation on Saturday morning, Anna and I stood with over a million Berliners as Johnson and Clay tried to get to the Brandenburg Gate via motorcade. They failed because the throngs brought the procession to a slow walk.

That evening, Johnson gave a speech at the Schoenberg Town Hall, in which he reassured Berliners by saying, "President Kennedy wants you to know, I want you to know, and the entire United States wants you to know that we are pledged to maintain the freedom of West Berlin. Our commitment is firm."

The next day, President Kennedy transferred 1,500 men from the 8th Infantry Division to Berlin in a show of force. No one had any idea how the Russians would react to this significant force movement, because these men would bring their full complement of arms and howitzers with them. This action proved uneventful, although nearly all West Berlin turned out to welcome another visible sign of America's resolve. In my uniform again, I saluted as they passed by.

An elderly West Berliner and his young granddaughter introduced themselves to us as we stood on a sidewalk just before the parade passed by. An obviously well-educated gentleman confided, "Until these troops arrived, I was concerned your commitment to us was just words. Now, I'm sure you will keep us free. On behalf of all Berliners, I want to thank you."

I saluted him. Anna and I both hugged his granddaughter.

As our troops passed by me, I felt proud to be an American. We risked another war, but we'd undertaken the correct course of action.

Walking hand in hand as we neared our apartment building, Anna started to cry. By the time we reached our door, she was sobbing. I picked her up, carried her inside, and placed her on the bed. Using my handkerchief, I dried her tears and gently embraced her. "Please don't cry."

"Don't you understand. Everything over the last week makes me both happy and sad. Very sad, and also very anxious. I just don't know what I would do without you. You're my entire world now, Robbie. My family is no longer free. My poor, broken country—how much longer must we Germans pay for the mistakes of the past? You Americans are committed to a free West Berlin, but those in the East, including my family, are cast adrift on a communist sea."

CHAPTER 105

Monday, August 21, 1961

"SHOW ME WHAT you got. No lollygagging," six-foot-four Vice President Johnson requested after introductions to Colonel Morgan, Mark, Scott, and me. He seemed to fill the small conference room in my tank with his presence.

Gerald started through his slideshow going over each detail—the building outside, the basement, the ramp, the first pressure door.

"What's that damn door for?"

I responded to his question. "For the last hundred and fifty years, every tunnel under a body of water has used increased air pressure to prevent water leaks during the drilling process. The two pressure doors allow us to remove the excavated soil and resupply concrete tunnel structural elements in one section of the tunnel, while boring operations continue in another."

"Got it! Go on!"

Having a famous man at my work place seemed almost surreal.

The slideshow continued with pictures of the boring head, tunnel shield, soil removal and structural element placement.

"Got it! How much is done now and when will the whole shooting match be operational?"

"Captain Kerr will give the next part of the briefing," Mr. Gerald Scherman informed the Vice President. "He's the Chief Engineer on the project."

Take a deep breath. Smile. Relax. He won't bite you.

"Sir, if you would come over to the charts hanging on the wall, I'll show you where we are and what we intend to do over the next few months. As you can see, here is a front view and a side view of the tunnel. The ramp here, the two pressure doors, and the river here. We finished tunneling several weeks ago and have recently installed this vertical shaft," I said, pointing to another set of drawings.

"Captain, who designed that makeshift contraption?"

"I did, sir. With the help of several mechanical engineers."

"Do you think it'll work?"

"The telescoping shaft is an improvised—Rube Goldberg kind of contraption, sir. It's in place now. We finished installing it ten days ago. As we got close to the surface, we encountered debris from the building which once occupied the site, but with effort and ingenuity, my crew managed to get that contraption, as you call it, around the communications tube."

"How'd you manage that?"

"We don't have time for a detailed explanation—suffice it to say that windshield-wiper type blades are located on the top part of the shaft roof." I pointed to the plan on the wall. "They dug the earth as the shaft was slowly extended into place with hydraulic jacks. The excavated debris fell through an opening in the center to the floor of the tunnel. We then used wheelbarrows and shovels to remove that debris."

"And you did that without disturbing the surface of that vacant lot above."

"That's correct, sir."

"Amazing. If it had been detected, the East Germans and Soviets would've raised more hell last week than they did."

"That's the reason we took two weeks to complete this one task."

"I'm glad. Last year, the Soviets made a big stink about the U-2 spy plane and Francis Gary Powers. That'd be chicken-feed compared to the stink they'd make if this tunnel were found."

"Yes, sir, I'm sure it would."

"Now, I know who you are. Captain Robert Kerr. The young genius that took those Washington bureaucrats' scatter-brained dreams and turned them into reality. Congratulations, son. I want to shake your hand again." He extended a giant hand and warmly shook mine.

"Make me a promise, son, don't let the Washington types like Mr.

Scherman here push you into making a mistake. Complete this construction at your own pace. With the delicate situation we're in now, we don't need an international incident because of it. Is that clear?"

I flushed at his praise. "Don't worry, sir, my crew and I can handle it."

This moment makes all of my hard work worth the sacrifice. I'll have to share this with my men.

"Are you finished?"

"By no means, sir. Construction will take most of the rest of the year. We are now building the Signals Exploitation Center, which will occupy the basement and most of the first floor of the building. Also, some barracks, a mess hall, and other facilities. Plus, we'll be remodeling the apartments…"

"—We are going to turn this building into an American housing complex. It'll be occupied exclusively by those who work there," Gerald interjected. "We'll hide a major intelligence collection site in the middle of Berlin, in plain sight."

"Clever. Hope it works," the Vice President said, moving toward the door then turning back to me. "How big a crew do you have working for you now, Captain?"

"Fifty-eight men, sir, all three services. They're a mixture of active duty and reserves called back to active duty."

"I'll make sure that every one of them gets a medal. No make that two medals. Take my word for that."

"Thank you, sir. The men will appreciate your recognition of their efforts."

"Gentlemen, I must go. Running late…seems like I've been late since I got here!" Vice President Johnson said as he shook each person's hand and left the tank. On the way out, he gave me a pat on the back.

Within two hours, Thomas Lane stood in my office raising hell. "You knew that Vice President Johnson was going to receive a briefing on **my tunnel project** today, and you didn't inform me of that fact."

"Mr. Scherman was responsible for inviting people to that meeting…"

"I needed to be there to assure the CIA's interests were protected. Scherman is an NSA guy. He may still be leading the overall effort, but it's mine here in Berlin. Do you not understand that you work for me?" he shouted.

"Well, sir, my actual chain of command is through Colonel Morgan. I suggest that if you..."

"—Listen carefully to me. This is a CIA tunnel, and I'm in charge here. Is that clear?" he again shouted.

I answered with silence. I understood what the real problem was. Lane hoped to use the meeting with the Vice President to gain an advantage— either a promotion or political appointment. From this point on, he redoubled his efforts to make my working life hell. I avoided him as much as possible. His enmity would end in disaster.

CHAPTER 106

Tuesday, August 29, 1961

"THE OFFER OF East German exit visas for money was a trap," Kurt announced to the escape team in my tank.

"How's that?" Scott asked.

"They accept payment, take an individual's passport or identification documents, and ask them to return in three days. When they return, they're arrested. Although usually later released, they are placed permanently on the Stasi watch list."

"Glad we waited," I said.

"The students at the Free University are using three methods of getting fellow students out," Kurt continued. "The first is a real passport made out to the individual carrying it."

"Where did they get those?" I asked.

"They're Belgian passports. The real thing. The father of a student is a senior official, and he provided blank passports and the required seals to make them official. A cover story is even provided for trips across the border."

"Amazing."

"The second is the passport of another individual who looks enough like the person in the photo to pass through."

"That won't work for us. We have some children."

"The third is a sewer recently opened with hacksaws and diligent effort."

"The adults might stand the stench and filth, but not the five children."

"An individual at the Swiss legation is selling real passports for 300,000 West Marks each."

"Seventy-five thousand dollars each," I gasped. "Wow! That's way out of my means, and I've got to pay for ten people."

"Swedish and Danish passports are much less expensive, but then you have the language problem when you try to cross the border," Kurt remarked. "With those Swiss passports, you can be from almost anywhere in Switzerland and have German as your mother tongue."

"As I recall, there are two German-speaking cantons in Belgium," Scott said. "One of my German language professors was born there."

"Kurt, can you find the source of those Belgian passports?" I asked.

"I'll call another meeting as soon as I gather the information."

CHAPTER 107

Friday, September 8, 1961

"MY REAL NAME is Kurt Altschuler," he told Anna. "Finding a way to get our loved ones out of East Berlin has been difficult. We need your help."

"Obviously I'm willing, since Robert explained that my family is among the fifteen people we are trying to help escape."

"Do I remember correctly that your father has a camera and knows how to use it?" I said.

"Yes, he has a prewar 35-millimeter Leica, which he's very proud of."

"Does he also have a tripod?" Kurt asked.

"Yes."

"Anna, if you agree, you'll transport two rolls of black and white film to the East tomorrow, and then you'll return immediately after they're exposed," I explained.

"Everyone will gather at your parent's house for a party," Kurt revealed. "Your parents expect them. Ask your father to take three photographs of each member of his family and each of their guests against a uniform, light-colored background."

"In addition to the film, you'll return with a description of each individual...height, weight, age, hair and eye color," Scott added. "A Belgian passport will then be generated for each of the fifteen, which they'll use to get to the West. Your help is urgently needed, because too many escapees are using Belgian passports. The Stasi is bound to become suspicious and close this avenue of escape."

"You can no longer stay in the East overnight, so you'll be home in time for us to go out have dinner," I reminded her.

After I escorted her down the stairs and into her office, she kissed me. "Robbie, thank you for working so hard to get my family out. I love you so."

"I promised, remember!"

"I hope nothing goes wrong. I'll try to think only happy thoughts about my family."

CHAPTER 108

Saturday, September 9, 1961

THAT SATURDAY, I arranged for my crew to enjoy a beer-baseball morale function. We purchased several kegs of German beer and drank while playing on an athletic field at Clay Compound. It was the first time my entire crew gathered together outdoors since arriving in Berlin nine months earlier.

Kurt awaited me when I returned home a little after 3 p.m. He greeted me, "Anna missed the 2 p.m. rendezvous where she was supposed to hand over the film. Let's call her family to see if they know anything."

"You can make calls into East Berlin? I didn't know that was possible."

Smiling, Kurt picked up the phone in my apartment and dialed the number of Doctor Fischer's surgery. I stood close enough to hear the operator ask, "Authorization number, please."

"Seven—nine—eight—three—six—four."

"One moment, comrade." After a long pause, the operator said, "I will connect you, comrade."

Once Bernard came on the line, Kurt spoke in an officious sounding voice. "Was your operation today a success?"

Bernard paused then rasped, "No. It will have to be rescheduled."

"Your patient should have arrived on time."

"Afraid not. Some of my associates here may know something. I'll check." Bernard replied.

"We'll keep you informed of any progress on our side," Kurt said, ending the call. As he left our apartment, he promised, "I'll have my contacts on both sides of the border check on her, and I'll let you know the moment I learn anything."

"We shouldn't have asked her to courier that film."

"You're right. Her connection to you made her unsuitable for that task." He said patting my shoulder. "Please don't use that code. One of our operatives gave it to me for emergencies. If we use it too often, he might be compromised."

I sensed that something terrible had happened to Anna. I decided to shower and then try to rest while I waited to hear from Kurt. As I walked into the bathroom, I felt dizzy and almost concurrently got tunnel vision. The walls disappeared, but I managed to get into bed. Concentration on my breathing for a long time allowed me to avoid the more severe symptoms of a panic attack. I didn't get up until I heard the phone ring.

I rushed to answer it. Kurt said, "The West Berlin police received reports that a young blonde woman was taken out of line at Friedrichstrasse checkpoint at 9:48 this morning. She protested loudly that she carried a West Germany passport and was married to an American Officer.'"

After I found my green civilian passport, I exited the building, intent on rescuing Anna.

CHAPTER 109

Anna

Saturday-Sunday September 9-10, 1961

IT HAD BEEN almost a month since I had last visited my parents. I carried five hundred West Marks and the two rolls of unexposed East German-made film. Although I wanted to help my family leave East Berlin, I still feared a repeat of my earlier encounters with Mueller and Holburg.

I decided to go through the Friedrichstrasse checkpoint to avoid Gustave Mueller, who seemed permanently assigned to the Potsdamer Platz Checkpoint. I had my hair down and wore a hat in an attempt to hide my face.

Since my last time there, a shed had been built. Inside of it was a maze for people to cue up while waiting for an open position at one of the nine windows.

Finally, my turn came. I handed my papers to a female officer. She examined them, then called over an associate. He left. Two uniformed ToPos (Border Police) approached me as the female officer ordered, "Please go with these officials, Frau Kerr." When I turned around and attempted to return to the West, they seized me.

A shiver went up my spine, and my knees buckled as I protested, "I have a West German Passport and am married to an American military officer."

"You must come with us, Frau Kerr." They escorted me to a police van, opened the back door and, when I hesitated, they shoved me inside. I hit the floor hard.

The van door was closed and locked. It moved east away from the border. There were two smeared and dirty windows in the back doors of the van. Familiar streets passed as we drove through the old government center of Mitte, then past the Alexander Platz, into Friedrichshain and then Lichtenberg.

They're taking me to Stasi Headquarters! I shuddered.

A sign which identified the Ministry of the Interior confirmed my fear. The van stopped at the back of a building. My heart rate and respiration increased. I felt light headed and was clinging to the bench seat when the back door of the van opened. All the rumors of Stasi rape, torture, murder, truth drugs, and brainwashing ran through my head.

"No, please!"

I grasped the bottom of the bench. Two men wrenched my arms free and shoved me out of the van. I stumbled and landed on my knees. My left knee began to bleed. I looked at them asking, "What am I accused of doing?"

I took a handkerchief from my purse to staunch the blood flow. One of the men snatched it and my purse while the other seized my elbow and marched me down a long ramp, through a door and into the basement.

A long row of cells stretched down the hall in both directions. After being thrust into one, I heard the door lock.

If they are trying to scare me, they've succeeded.

I hugged myself and looked around. One low-wattage light bulb hung from a cord attached to the ceiling. An empty bucket sat in the corner. The only furnishing, a three-legged stool. The stench made me gag—a combination of urine, feces, vomit, decaying meat, and garbage. The floor and walls appeared to be covered with some kind of living slime.

The cells were not sound-proof. I heard a man cry, "No, not again! I cannot bear it!" Then a thudding sound, followed by silence.

I shivered violently.

I kept looking at my watch. Precisely twenty-three minutes later, a woman with a mustache, huge breasts, and a massive upper body came into the room. She ordered, "Please follow me."

She led me down the hall to a room with stainless-steel-topped tables and metal chairs. "Remove all of your clothes immediately." When I hesitated, she demanded, "Either you undress, or I will get the guards in here to take them off you. Understand?"

I disrobed, carefully folding each item as I removed it. Finally, I stood before her, one arm across my breasts and the other covering my crotch.

She took a wooden tongue depressor and examined my mouth. "Raise your tongue up and around. Just so, nothing there. Now bend over the table, face down and spread your legs apart as widely as possible. If you cooperate, I'll try to make this as painless as possible."

The metal table was so cold, I struggled to comply. She inserted an ice-cold vaginal speculum and engaged the mechanism, which spread me wide apart.

I gasped, my shiver turning into a spasm. Her touch was cold as she examined me there.

"And so, nothing."

Next, she put on a pair of rubber gloves and examined my anal cavity. She apparently knew what she was doing because it was unpleasant, but not painful. "Just so, nothing in either orifice. Put on this smock and those sandals. You will return to your cell."

"But my clothes!" I protested.

"We will examine your clothes and other items. You will get them back if you ever leave here!"

"If I ever leave here?" I repeated her statement, astonished and frightened.

She glared at me.

Dejected, I dressed and followed her back to the cell. On the way, I pleaded, "My father Bernard Fischer is a doctor. Please contact him for me. You will be rewarded handsomely."

The only response I received was the sound of the door as it slammed. I sat on the stool and began to sob.

A few minutes later, Dieter Holburg carried a chair into the cell and sat down across from me, a stern expression on his scarred face.

"Why did you use false identity papers to enter the DDR on July 22, 1961?"

"My new West German passport contains the correct information. One of the guards took it."

"So, you admit you entered the DDR using an invalid passport?

"Your saying that I…"

"—You admit everything."

"No…" My voice trailed off, my confusion apparent.

"My superiors will determine what to do with you!" He stood, took the chair and bucket in the corner, banged on the door which soon clanged shut behind him.

Within five seconds, the light went out. Soon I felt a cold breeze from a vent high up on the wall. I sat on the stool, afraid I would slip on the slime that covered the floor. My legs ached. I alternately lifted one leg at a time to relieve the cramping and to fight the cold.

I will not let them break me. I will be strong. Papa, Robert, Herr Ehrhardt, they'll get me out of here!

Time passed slowly. My teeth chattered, and my left leg became numb. I shivered uncontrollably, stood and slowly moved around the room, holding my hands out to feel the walls. They were quickly covered with slime. I found the door and banged on it for a while. When I tried to kick it, I slipped and fell into the muck on the floor.

Miserable and filthy, I retreated to the stool and sat on it for an interminable period. The vent was definitely focused on this spot, so I carried the stool over to where I thought the door was and felt the wall. Eventually, I found the door, rested the stool against it and waited for their next assault.

I lost track of time, still dazed and bewildered by what had happened when I heard the key turn in the door and jumped to my feet. The door knocked the stool out of the way. It slammed it into my shins. Entirely at their mercy, I would have done almost anything to get out of that room.

Two men carried in a table, then a straight-backed metal chair. They positioned the stool on the opposite side of the table and gestured for me to sit down. A slight, swarthy, dark-haired man with a slight limp entered the cell and sat down on the chair.

"Frau Kerr, you admit traveling to the DDR using false documents. That is an offense punishable by ten years in prison. I'm sure we can find some other crimes to convict you of. Do you want to spend years in the

DDR prison system? As you can imagine that would be rather unpleasant. Well, what do you have to say?"

"I was only married eight weeks ago, I was told…"

"—Ignorance of the law is no excuse. We could easily plant false evidence in your clothes and convict you of several other crimes."

I did not respond, realizing they would twist every word.

"Our laws require correct documentation. Any variance is a criminal offense."

"But I was told…"

"—We could claim that you were a spy for the Americans or West Germans. Or you could just disappear, like so many others. You are a traitor, so you deserve to die."

I shook my head but said nothing.

"We could use the information you were carrying to arrest your entire family. Your father Bernard, mother Emma, sister Sophia, brother Fredrich, brother Helmuth, and his wife Johanna could all be put into prison as co-conspirators. After we are finished with them, they will confess and implicate anyone we want them to accuse, including you. As for your nephew Stephen, he is already thirteen and has been corrupted in the schools in West Berlin. He will be sent to a reeducation center. Once he is fifteen, he will be assigned a very menial task. Construction crews are a rough bunch, and they will quickly teach him his place."

My head jerked up at the mention of Stephen. My interrogator didn't seem to notice.

"Your other nieces and nephews—Angelica, Hans, Ludwig, and Andrea—they will be sent to orphanages to be reeducated. Do you want this for your family?"

"No," I replied meekly.

"We may let you go if I like your answers. I only have a few questions. Will you answer truthfully?"

I nodded, "Yes."

"What is your husband, the American flier, doing in Berlin?"

"He doesn't know how to fly. He is a weatherman."

"Really, we hear that he is in charge of a top-secret project—this project will help the American and NATO forces win the next war. We outnumber your husband's forces ten to one? What could possibly assist them to overcome such a numeric advantage?"

"You have to believe me. I know nothing about my husband's activities. He spends his days in an office on the second floor of the Tempelhof Airport building. On my desk at the bookstore, I have a photo of him in his office. I've never actually been in his office. It is in an area that only Americans can enter."

"You expect me to believe such obvious lies?"

"But it is the truth!"

"Perhaps if you spend several more days with us, your memory will improve. I will leave you alone to think about it."

The table, chair, and stool were removed, the lights again turned off. For what seemed like hours, I stood cold and hungry, avoiding contact with the foul walls. I needed to urinate so badly, I was in pain. Finally, I struggled over to the opposite corner and relieved myself. This added a new odor to the disgusting stench of the cell.

I was thirsty and cold. I began to sob.

To get out of the path of the vent, I crept over to the corner nearest the door and leaned against the two walls, the stinking muck coating my back and buttocks.

My legs cramped, forcing me down on the cold, slime-covered floor. Soon I dozed, losing all track of time.

The entire back of my thin smock and hair were now soaked with the foul-smelling muck. I had uncontrolled shivering fits and wept for a long time. Ultimately, I became emotionally and physically numb, slumped to the floor and lost consciousness.

Occasionally, I awakened to the sounds of screams and menacing shouts.

All of a sudden, a picture flashed in front of my closed eyes—a picture of Sophia being raped by that huge Russian. My own screams soon added to those of the others in this hell hole.

The walls began to close in. "I have to get out of this cell. I have to, whatever it takes," I screamed as I clawed at the cell door.

CHAPTER 110

Robert

Saturday-Sunday, September 9-10, 1961

"ANNA FAILED TO return from her courier mission. I think she's been taken by the Stasi. We must go East and find her. Let's use our green passports and go over as tourists!" I said as I stood at Scott's apartment door.

"Come on in," he urged. "Sit down. I've talked to Kurt. We both agree that none of us can put ourselves in danger by going to look for her. If we knew where she was and had a chance to rescue her, that'd be one thing. All we know is she was taken out of line at the Friedrichstrasse checkpoint and never arrived at her parents' home."

"You must go East with me." I pleaded.

"We can't. All foreign tourists and American military personnel must now enter and exit East Berlin through Checkpoint Charlie and the adjacent East German Friedrichstrasse Checkpoint. The new Provost Marshall regulations state we must use our military ID and register with our forces before entering the East."

"Is there any other way for us to get over there?"

"None that I can think of. Kurt is your best bet for that."

"I've talked to him. He's working on finding Anna through his clandestine sources."

"I'm truly sorry that we got her involved. Kurt could've gotten the film over there some other way, but using Anna was the quickest."

"Scott, help me. I'm desperate."

"Old buddy, you're better off here in the West. Dieter would like nothing better than to get you into an interrogation room. Remember, we've been relatively successful in foiling his efforts."

"I'm terrified of what's happened to her."

I walked back to our apartment, hoping that if I were exhausted enough, I'd be able to sleep.

Once there, I paced, fearing the worst for my new wife. Finally, at almost 2 a.m. someone buzzed the front door. I went downstairs and found Kurt waiting. He motioned for me to follow him into the nearby park. After assuring himself that we were alone, he reported, "She's disappeared. Between people her father knows and my resources, we'll find her."

A knot formed just below my heart, and I could barely breathe. "Kurt, can we go east—try to find her?"

"Travel now is not a good idea. Since we don't know her location, it would only make matters worse."

"But we must do something."

"Patience is best under the current circumstances. Go to Potsdamer Platz checkpoint every two hours, beginning at 10 a.m. Wave your arms above your head for good news. Wave your hands at your sides, for no news. Bernard will use a similar signal to impart the results of his inquiries."

CHAPTER 111

Anna

Sunday, September 10, 1961

THE DOOR BANGED open, the guards carried in a table, chair, and my stool. Soon Dieter Holburg again sat across from me, his demeanor dramatically different. His smile gave me hope that he might help me. He gestured for me to move closer to him. "My associate who was here before is a dangerous individual. I do not like him. His name is Hans Haeger, and he is cruel to those who are unfortunate enough to come to our attention. I can get you some water and perhaps something to eat—even a shower and clean cell with a bed. Just tell us what your husband does for the American military."

Between sobs I managed to say, "I told the other man the truth. He is a weatherman. His job is to predict when it is safe for American military transport aircraft to fly into and out of Tempelhof airport. That is all I know. We do not discuss his work...it is boring for me to hear him talk about isobars and isotherms."

"Do you know how long you have been here?"

"I have no idea."

"Can you envision days of interrogation with my associate, Hans. He spent time in a Nazi concentration camp. You must have noticed his limp. He learned his lessons well. He usually makes people wish they were dead. They always tell him what he wants to know." He suddenly grinned, "Are you thirsty? Water, perhaps?"

"Yes, please!"

He banged on the door. A guard handed me a large glass of water, which I consumed quickly. I only noticed the bitter taste after I had drained the container. Dieter talked. His words started to fade. My head became heavy and I felt drowsy. Before I slumped forward across the desk, I realized I had been drugged.

I woke up bound to a straight-back chair in another cell, feeling groggy and lethargic. As the fog cleared, I realized I was talking about Robert and his work as a weatherman. And then rambling on about the weather-betting contest in the *gasthaus*. "How could anyone who was not a weatherman know so much about weather forecasting?" I asked. The interrogator stood, slammed his fist on the table, and stormed out.

The other man who had been in the room untied me and removed all the furniture from the room. After he walked out, the lights went off. The floor was relatively clean, so I lay down and fell asleep on the cold concrete. I jerked awake to loud music and flashing lights. For hours as soon as I dozed off, this process was repeated again and again.

Eventually, the guards brought in a fire hose, drenched me with cold water, and forced me to occupy a corner with my back turned to them.

The smock became transparent, and the guards commented on my appearance and stated, *"Sie wurde guter fick sein"* (she would be a good fuck.) I was taken to another room and again seated on a stool.

Dieter Holburg sat behind the desk as I hugged myself, trying desperately to get warm and cover my body—the water had been frigid, and I shivered uncontrollably.

"Anna…Anna Fischer…Anna Kerr?!"

He slapped me to get my attention. "Listen to me. We will let you go back to your corrupt, decadent West if you collect information on your husband for us. All you have to do is find out what he does every day and report back to us. If you agree, you can leave here today. Right now. Or you can spend months, years, or even a lifetime while we repeat these methods until we find one that breaks you. Your choice."

I still felt groggy from the drugs in the water, plus my right bicep hurt. I was battered, bruised, and frightened, but I remained silent.

"Will you help us find out what your husband is doing here in Berlin?"

"What if I agree?" I whimpered.

"We will release you, and you will return to your precious Robert only a little worse for wear. My associates will make it easy for you to find out what he does every day."

"What if I find out that he's actually just a weatherman?"

"If you provide proof then we will not persecute your family or you further. I must warn you, if you agree and then don't help us, we will kidnap you off the street of West Berlin. Also, remember your family lives over here. What do you say?"

"Can I have a shower and my clothes back?"

"Yes, of course."

"I'll help you any way I can," I replied, surrendering to their demands, although I did not believe they would actually allow me to return to West Berlin.

Dieter knocked on the door, and the weightlifter lady took me down the hall to a modern bathroom. I showered, dried my hair as best I could, and looked in the mirror. A changed woman looked back at me—a woman determined on revenge for the indignities I'd experienced.

My watch read 3:35. What day? I wondered, certain that several days had passed. All of the contents of my purse were there, including the money. However, the unexposed film was missing.

After being shown to Dieter Holburg's office, he said, "Please be seated. Here is a confession that you traveled to East Germany using false documents and have agreed to assist the DDR in determining your husband's responsibilities."

With trepidation, I signed the paper.

Handing me the photograph of a hawk-faced, dark-haired woman, Dieter said, "This is Olivia Katz. She is your new best friend. There is a French Cafe called 'Paris in a Cup' near your workplace at Tempelhof. Olivia is an old classmate of yours from the gymnasium. You will renew your acquaintance at 12:30 this coming Wednesday. Then, every Wednesday and Friday you will meet for lunch. She will be the person you report to. If she becomes unhappy with your cooperation, you or your family will suffer the consequences. Dire consequences. Remember, we have your signed confession. Is everything clear?"

"Yes, entirely clear." I replied and then asked, "What day is it?"

"Oh, you have only been here thirty hours. It is Sunday afternoon."

"Really, that seems impossible."

"Imagine how interminable weeks, months or years of life here with us would be. Ah, but you do not have to worry—you are going to help us—remember, we own you now."

"When can I leave?"

"Soon, but first we must give you a cover story…"

CHAPTER 112

Robert

Sunday, September 10, 1961

"I WANTED TO believe that I would eventually be released. Thinking of you kept me sane." Anna murmured, clinging to me moments after she passed through the Potsdamerplatz checkpoint. Most of this cobblestoned open space was in the East, but we occupied the wide sidewalk adjacent to a busy thoroughfare in the West.

I kissed her and held her, caressing her face, neck, and hair. "You're alive and safe, that's what matters."

"We must make certain that your father knows you're here," I whispered in her ear. At my direction, we faced the East, saw Bernard on the hill, and we both waved to him. It was precisely 6 p.m.

After we lowered our arms, Anna's smile became a frown. She repeatedly shuddered. Her chin quivered, and I thought she might cry, so I said, "Maybe it'll help if you tell me what happened and where you've been. Everyone has been so worried."

Anna cringed, pointing East with her eyes. "Do you see that man? The ToPo (Border Police) Captain looking at us. His name is Gustav Mueller. He grew up near me. I never liked him. His father is some senior officer in the SPD—the Communist Party. For years, he pursued me."

Clenching my fists, I wanted to confront the son-of-a-bitch. As I took a step in his direction, Anna grabbed my arm. "Robert, don't do anything rash."

"He's the one who had me detained last month. Yesterday, he decided to again make trouble for me. On his word, I was taken to jail. Once I was in a holding cell, he offered to release me if I'd have sex with him. I spit in his face. He ordered that they lock me in a cell and not list my name on the booking sheet. They just released me a few minutes ago…"

"That bastard, I should kill him."

"You'll just get in trouble, and that won't help my family or me. Understand."

"We shouldn't have sent you to the East. I knew it might be dangerous for you."

"I wanted to help my family."

"Anna, my love…"

"—I'm here and will never go to the East again. We'll need to find another way to get my family out of that hell hole."

When we got home, she told me, "I'm terribly hungry—they didn't feed me anything, but first I must have a shower."

Once Anna was in the shower, I went down to the basement and determined that the recording devices had been reinstalled. I took my clothes off, joined her in the shower and reported, "The walls have ears again." She clung to me at that news.

While we stood in the shower, I asked, "Do you still have the film?" Obviously confused, she eventually mumbled, "Someone must have taken it, because it was missing from my purse when I got it back."

She consumed the scrambled eggs, ham, and toast I made for her in an almost zombie-like state, only responding to my questions with odd sounds and one-word answers. I knew she was hiding something, but I didn't press her further.

Once in bed, she grabbed me and began to weep. Her crying fits were interspersed with restless sleep for both of us. At the time, I thought her emotional reaction typical for someone who had been traumatized. The next day, I learned the shocking details of her ordeal.

CHAPTER 113

Monday, September 11, 1961

"IT WAS A nightmare, Robbie. A terrible nightmare!" Anna sat on an examination table in the base infirmary, gripping my hands and trembling. "This is the only place I could think of that we could talk freely," she told me. I alternately held her hands or hugged her as almost mechanically, she related details of her hours in the Stasi Prison.

Enfolding her in my arms, I said, "What you experienced is terrible, Anna. You suffered at their hands, and it's my fault. Can you ever forgive me?"

"No! Robert, it's not your fault. I tried to act strong, to deny I was vulnerable…that I might be in jeopardy. But I'm not strong…" she began to cry again.

I held her for a long time. Eventually I said, "Anna you're so precious to me. You suffered such awful mental and physical torture. I am so grateful you survived."

"Mostly, I thought about you. You helped me through each second, minute and hour."

She paused briefly. "I must tell you something. They told me that if I don't spy on you, they will make my family suffer. Prison for the adults and orphanages for the children. I'm more concerned for them than myself."

"Somehow, we will make that dirty son-of-a-bitch Dieter Holburg and his Stasi thugs pay for what they have done to you. Our revenge will be getting your family out of East Berlin to safety."

"Until then we must protect them, but how can we do that?"

"Obviously, you will spy on me. I know people who will help us to get even in the process."

"Promise me that we won't endanger my family," she pleaded.

"I promise no harm will come to them. Are you all right? What did the doctor say?"

"I asked him to look me over and take a blood sample. Perhaps someone will identify the drugs given me by the Stasi." She dried her eyes.

"Can I leave you for a few minutes?" I gave her a tender kiss.

She nodded. "I'm still a little shaky, but we must act quickly. My first meeting with the Stasi agent is in two days!"

"Get dressed, and I'll be right back."

"Robbie, if I knew your real job, perhaps we could figure out a way to satisfy them."

I shook my head no. I could not and would not share that information.

For the third time, Anna was admitted onto the second floor of the Air Force Base. In the conference room outside of Scott's office, she again related the details of her entire ordeal to Kurt and Scott.

"Anna, we should never have asked you to go East. They confiscated the film and probably had it developed while they held you," Kurt speculated. "When the film was blank, they decided to subvert you into spying for them. I'm sure our escape plans and your detention are unrelated."

"Hopefully, I didn't tell them about our escape plans," Anna said.

"If they didn't ask, you probably didn't volunteer the information," Kurt assured her. "In actuality, the so-called truth serum doesn't work on most people."

"I'm glad of that."

"Act as normal as possible," Kurt instructed her. "Whatever your regular routine is, follow it. Please return to work."

"Gladly."

"Tell those who work for you that you received some medication and are feeling better. Go to the meeting with Fraulein Katz on Wednesday and

Friday, per their instructions. Report any and everything back to us. Do you have any questions?"

"You're telling me to cooperate with those communist bastards?" Anna demanded in German.

In German, he answered, "You will appear to assist them. We will exact revenge for you. Believe me!"

"How?"

"Our goal will be to convince them that Robert is a weatherman by providing information that substantiates that contention."

"They haven't been convinced yet," Anna retorted.

"Exactly…trust us. We know how to stack little facts on top of each other, which will force them to conclude that there is nothing new to learn. Once they are no longer interested in him, we give them small subtle pieces of false or misleading information, which leads them to make damaging mistakes."

"Good. I'm ready for revenge if my family doesn't suffer. What should I do?"

"Both of you must follow your usual routine. Does the bookstore have a back exit?"

"Yes, it opens into a hallway that ends in stairs which lead to the second floor. There's a guard at the checkpoint at the top of the stairs."

"When you return to the base after your meeting on Wednesday, go through the bookstore, take that stairway, and we'll arrange for the guard to admit you. Robert, Scott, another man and/or I will be waiting in this room each day to debrief you."

"Is that all?"

"No. In the interim, we'll use all of our people to formulate a detailed plan of action. We'll review it with you and Robert on Wednesday afternoon."

After Anna left the room, I kicked the wall hard enough to dent it. *This was all Perkins' fault—the fucking bastard and traitor.* Because he told them that my project would help the West win the next war, the Stasi obviously believed my duties included something new, something vitally important, perhaps even threatening, to their national interest. No matter what Anna or I do, they'll continue to hound us.

In the two months since I'd rescued Perkins, no one had shown the least interest in "the building." The security committee had recently concluded he hadn't revealed the big secrets—what and where. But the East Germans, and probably even the Russians, were now desperate to find out the answers to those two vital questions.

In our meeting, Kurt told Anna that she needed to help us maintain my weatherman cover. Although she often expressed doubt about its validity, she agreed to help us, primarily to protect her family. If she cooperated with the Stasi her family might be safe, but one miscue on anyone's part could prove ruinous, even fatal, for one or many of them, and perhaps even the two of us.

"What are we going to do?" I asked when only Kurt and I remained in the conference room.

"We'll instill doubt in the other side about what the game is, who the players are, and the ultimate objectives. We've managed to keep them guessing for the last year. It's time for you to again be the head of the USAF Berlin weather station."

I looked at him in disbelief. "I know you don't think the Stasi are stupid, right?"

"No. Your project and the new Nuclear Hardened Command Center beneath Clay Headquarters are highly classified programs. We can't tell Anna anything about them or what's really happening, so we have no choice but to help her sell the story that you're a weatherman."

I asked, "What if they figure out she's also working for us and everything is fabricated…" I suddenly realized the truth. My lovely wife Anna was at the center of a game of international intrigue. Additional lies would be layered on top of existing lies in a desperate bid to hide the truth and survive. I managed to say, "We're probably fucked!"

CHAPTER 114

Anna

Wednesday, September 13, 1961

TOO NERVOUS TO sit at my desk, I left the bookstore early and walked to the tea room, hoping the exercise would allow me to calm down. Concerned that Olivia would see right through my façade, I devised a plan of action. I would say as little as possible and be genial and cooperative as she led the conversation.

Arriving ten minutes early allowed me to select a table in a secluded corner. Olivia, a few years older than me, wore a poorly made, manly cut suit coat and skirt. She styled her hair into a severe bun that left no doubt that she lived in the East.

"Anna, Anna Fischer. It has been a long time."

"Anna Kerr now," I responded holding out my right hand.

For the next fifteen minutes, we updated each other on our lives since leaving the gymnasium.

"I live in the East," Olivia stated. "Everything is much better there. The state provides health care plus food, and almost everything is much less expensive. Rents are very low, and the people are much happier."

"I came West to finish my education and am now married to an American."

"Really. Tell me about your husband."

"He is the head of a weather station at Tempelhof, and we live in a nearby apartment. Soon we will go to Califonia to live."

"Really? That is most interesting!" She looked surprised.

"When do you two leave Berlin?"

Had I revealed too much? I wondered. "March or April of next year."

"And so, you have agreed to help us?"

"Yes, but I've already told your associates everything I know."

"Nevertheless, you will help."

"Yes. What do you want?"

"Find out what your husband really does. You and I both know he is not a weatherman!"

"I've lived with him for months, and I know nothing I have not already told your people."

"Get into his office, steal papers, documents, whatever you find."

"There are armed guards fulltime at the two entrances to the second floor. They prevent anyone without a picture badge from entering those areas. That's impossible."

"Make drawings of the base, where the guard stations are located, and where his office is located within those spaces."

"How will that help?" I asked.

"We have plans for the Tempelhof Airport from when it was built in the 1930s. You'll come to the East and help us to locate your husband's office in the area that the American Air Force occupies—then perhaps we can help you..."

"I will never go to the East again!!" I shouted, drawing the attention of everyone in the café.

At this point, Olivia said in a quiet tone, "Anna, I will have no choice but to tell Herr Holburg you were totally uncooperative today. He will decide our next course of action."

"I will make the drawing, but you'll have to bring the building plans over here."

"That is better."

"You told Herr Holburg you have a photograph of your husband at the desk in his office. You will bring that photo and your drawing of the base with you to our meeting on Friday. Understand?"

I nodded. She smiled pleasantly, stood, smiled again, and walked away, leaving me feeling vulnerable and fearful.

CHAPTER 115

Robert

Wednesday, September 13, 1961

THOMAS LANE, SCOTT, and I gathered in Scott's conference room to await Anna's return from her first meeting with Olivia. I'd learned the previous day of Kurt's failure to persuade the Chief of CIA Station-Berlin that he should retain control of Anna's interface with the Stasi. Kurt told me, "Thomas Lane will personally handle every aspect of her case. We can all only hope he doesn't fuck it up as badly as I fear he will."

Too nervous to sit down, I paced the conference room. Scott and Thomas discussed their shared interest in college football.

Eventually, I asked Thomas Lane, "Shouldn't Kurt Altschuler be involved in the management of Anna's interface with the Stasi? He's been in Berlin a long time, knows the Stasi and KGB, and knows best how to interact with them. Plus, he promised a detailed plan of action."

"Captain Kerr, I have the training and experience required to make this sting a success. Kurt has other responsibilities." Thomas gave me a smarmy, superior smile. "Enough said."

"Tell me about your plan." *You bastard!* I thought, wanting to punch him into the next century.

"We'll give them correct information whenever possible—information they already have or can validate. Once the Stasi believe they have a reliable source, we feed them false and misleading data."

Scott entered the conversation. "I thought their primary interest was in learning about Robert's duties. Doesn't that need to be our main thrust?"

"In my mind that is only part of our actions. This situation has exceptional potential!"

The guard escorted Anna into the conference room. She described her meeting and Olivia's demands.

"Make the drawing as realistic as you can, it must be in your own hand," Thomas ordered in a tone one uses with a child. "Bring it and the photo here tomorrow at 2 p.m., and we'll review and copy everything before you hand them over on Friday."

"Robert and Anna, remember your walls still have ears. Act out your roles."

"We understand," I replied.

"We have the results of your blood tests, Anna. Your water had chloral hydrate to make you unconscious. Then they gave you a shot of sodium thiopental, also known as a truth serum to make you tell them what they wanted to know."

"Since I knew nothing about Robert's work, they learned nothing."

"So, you are telling me Robert has never provided details of his actual duties."

"No. Never!"

Thomas, you idiot, you just confirmed Anna's suspicions that I have other responsibilities! Somehow, she may let that fact slip in conversations with the Stasi lady! You're a really dumb spy.

"Is that true?" Thomas queried with a doubtful glance.

Thomas Lane tapped my arm as the meeting concluded, "Join me in your tank. Immediately!" Once there, he ordered, "Make your presence apparent in and around the base several times a day by going out to lunch, down to the hangers, or for a walk. Any place where you'll be seen by their watchers. Don't go to the building unless it's essential for your mission."

"Now that the tunneling phase is complete, I can comply. I've already arranged for my senior NCOs to brief me here daily on their progress and to report any problems immediately by KY-7 scrambler telephone. I'll only go over once or twice a week, or if they have problems."

"Speaking of progress, how are we doing?"

Surprised by his friendly tone of voice, I said, "My construction crew has completed the CIA office and intercept floor spaces two weeks ahead of schedule; the facilities for NSA and the Air Force will be completed in about two weeks and the Army spaces about a month from now."

"But my sources indicated that overall we are behind schedule."

"True, the NSA employees who are responsible for tapping into the communist communications lines and bringing those connections back to the patch panels are almost two weeks behind schedule. The task was more complex than anticipated."

"Enlighten me."

"Originally, we assumed the only reason the Soviets and East Germans encased these particular communications cables in a galvanized pipe was nuclear hardening. Clandestine sources recently revealed there was a second reason which is to allow them to determine when someone has tapped into the cables."

"I was informed of this, but why has it impacted the NSA technician's efforts?"

"The pipe was pressurized to 20 psi with dry nitrogen. If the pressure drops by a detectable amount, say down around 16, 17, or even 18 psi, the bad guys would know that the pipe had been tapped. The upper sections of the telescoping shaft were designed to be watertight, but the bottom-most section stands on a concrete floor and is not. My crew attached one of our pressure pumps to the shaft, and it brings the pressure up to 20 psi anytime it drops by two psi. Since air is almost 80 percent nitrogen, none of the dry nitrogen can escape. The NSA crews must spend an hour in a decompression chamber after each seven-hour work shift, thus, decreasing the number of productive hours in a day."

"But they're two weeks behind schedule."

"My crew and I've helped them in every way we can. They're increasing their staffing levels, but the additional men won't arrive for several days."

"Washington is leaning on the CIA to begin exploiting the high-level diplomatic and military communications between and within Warsaw Pact

Countries," Thomas informed me. "You know that's the real reason for your accelerated schedule."

"Yes, hopefully we'll discover what the next Russian moves will be."

"At least, no one can blame you or your men for the delays."

"Because they are putting in ten to twelve-hour days, my team is almost four weeks ahead of schedule on most activities. Later this week, we'll start building the mess hall, barracks, and other facilities and remodeling the apartments. They have a big incentive—if they finish by the middle of December, they can all return home for Christmas and will not have to return after the holidays."

CHAPTER 116

Friday, September 15, 1961

AFTER HER SECOND meeting with Olivia, Anna debriefed Scott, Thomas, and me. "She looked at the front and back of the photos of Robert in his office and on the roof of the building, and she said, 'These are exactly what we want.' Then, she tried to take me to a nearby apartment with my drawing. I refused."

"We had people surrounding you, but never allow anyone to get you into a vehicle or someplace where we can't assist you," Thomas instructed.

"As you probably know, we went to a nearby *gasthaus*. We spread the plans out on a large table, and I tried to incorporate my drawing into their plan."

"Was that successful?" I asked.

"Not really. You Americans have apparently added to and modified the internal walls, so my effort was probably not of much value to them."

"Good!" Thomas chortled.

"For our next meeting, they want more proof that Robert is the Air Force weatherman in Berlin. They're now demanding the Tempelhof Air Force Base Phone List and Organization Chart."

"Anna, just relax," Thomas instructed. "They probably already have both, and this was likely a test. Their demands will never cease. They are looking for the advantage that information provides. What you give them today may be worthless, but by complying, you're suborning yourself to their will. It's all part of 'The Game.' They operate on the assumption that the next thing they get from you could be exceedingly valuable."

CHAPTER 117

Tuesday, September 19, 1961

ON THE SATURDAY following Anna's imprisonment at Stasi Headquarters, Kurt managed to get two rolls of film to Bernard. The future escapees reassembled to be photographed. Scott and I waited in my tank for him to return with fifteen Belgian Passports.

Kurt entered the tank, threw a thick package onto the conference table, and muttered in disgust, "Gentlemen, we've wasted over a month and almost $19,000 on fifteen worthless passports!"

"Are you sure we can't use them?" I asked, having invested all of my savings in the ten passports for Anna's family.

"Last week, the East Germans announced that a tourist's visa application had to be filled out by each passport holder when they enter the East. It will be date and time stamped at the point of entry. The individual must have this card and their passport in their possession any time they are stopped by a DDR official. That card is reviewed and surrendered when that person leaves East Berlin."

"Are we sure this policy has been implemented?" I asked, hoping for time.

"My sources verified this policy went into effect last Friday. Over the last few days, several people tried to use Belgian Passports. All were arrested after being interrogated."

Scott asked, "Ideas, gentlemen?"

After several minutes of quiet, Kurt cleared his throat. "A daring young entrepreneur who carried out several excursions into the East for me has proposed digging a tunnel for us. We pay for it. He persuades people to dig it, and our loved ones are the first to be extricated. He then gets as many paying customers out as he can."

"Give us the details of what he's proposing to build," Scott said.

"Here's a map he prepared. The tunnel he wants to dig would start in the basement of an apartment house in the British Sector and end up in a crypt in a graveyard adjacent to the border fence. A length of some 375 feet—size perhaps one-meter square. Just enough space to crawl through."

"How much?" Scott asked.

"$50,000—200,000 West Marks. As we all know, Berlin soil must be supported during digging operations, so his cost is lumber to support the earth above the tunnel and to pay the workers."

I don't have any money! Even Grandpa George might have a hard time raising my share in cash!

"This guy's smart," Kurt continued. "He selected the site because a builder just razed a structure next door to his proposed tunnel's entrance. That gives him a convenient place to get rid of the dirt as they excavate."

"Platforms are being erected all along the wall so that VoPos can monitor activity on both sides of the border," Scott said.

"At this point in time, only two fences—one barbed wire and the other chain link pass through this area. It is patrolled by VoPos and guard dogs attached to a line which runs down its center," Kurt continued. "From the window of his recently rented apartment, one can see the large crypt that is his target. I would…"

"—Using my theodolite, I can help him establish the distance to his target," I offered. "And I could help him get his tunnel started in precisely the right direction. Then, by using a piece of taut string, he can keep the tunnel straight and accurately determine the distance covered."

"So that only leaves one problem. Money," Scott declared. "I'll go downstairs to the American Express bank and get 40,000 West marks. I'll then have the balance owed transferred in this week. Kurt, you manage the business end of this endeavor. I'll provide the money, and Robert will provide the technical expertise."

Shocked, I said, "I can't…You may never…"

Scott shook his head, "It's settled! This'll be our joint endeavor with each of us making a significant contribution."

We shook hands, and that became the basis for our new escape plan.

CHAPTER 118

Tuesday, September 19, 1961

THOMAS AND I sat with Scott in his conference room, the gathering place for our Anna-Double Agent Committee meetings.

I looked at the newly modified base phone list and organization chart. Both contained the statements: 'Last Update 1 August 1961' and 'OFFICIAL USE ONLY' top and bottom. It identified me as Officer in Charge of the Berlin Weather Station, and listed Scott as the Public Information Officer.

To my surprise, I saw my organization—Detachment 2 of the 6910 Security Wing—included on the list.

Looking over at Scott, I asked, "Shouldn't the Security Wing be left off?"

"The bad guys already know what we do here. That antenna farm on the roof of this building is a dead giveaway. Having that included gives the list authenticity. Anna's providing verifiable information of little real value."

Day and night, I pondered our current situation, attempting to find a solution that did not involve risk to Anna's family. *Think, Robbie, think.*

Later that day I received a summons for a meeting with Colonel Morgan in his office. Mark, Kurt, and Scott were there when I arrived.

I knew that I was in trouble when Mark said, "Your recent verbal status report to Thomas has been used against us. He claims you admitted that delays in the installation of the patch panels and communications antennas on the roof were caused by your team's incompetence."

"I told him NSA is responsible for those activities, and I'd been informed that they were behind schedule due to staffing, technical and supplier problems."

"Thomas Lane is using this delay in his continued effort to seize control of the tunneling program from the Triumvirate."

"Can't we get the truth to the decision makers?" I asked. "Certainly..."

"—Captain Kerr, you don't seem to understand the big picture," Colonel Morgan said. "This is a fight between the CIA and DoD over who will control the Signals Exploitation Center when it becomes operational. The CIA wants to take credit for all the valuable intelligence that'll be derived from that facility. In a nutshell, it's about congressional approval of future funding and prestige. All of us, but especially you and your wife are caught in the middle. Unfortunately, Thomas Lane and the CIA manage your wife's interface with the Stasi."

"Has this been his objective from the beginning?" I asked. "To discredit me in order to take over the tunnel?"

"I know for a fact someone high up in the CIA has been directing Lane's efforts." Kurt exclaimed, "I hate this political bullshit!"

"The Triumvirate will be here in two weeks," Colonel Morgan said. "Do everything you can to meet the artificial deadline established over a year ago. It's imperative the CIA and NSA compartments in the Signals Exploitation Center be fully operational by 1 October.

"Yes, sir!" I knew that, with some added effort, we could probably meet that deadline.

CHAPTER 119

Wednesday-Thursday, September 20-21, 1961

AFTER HER THIRD meeting with Olivia, Anna returned to Scott's conference room to report she'd had a pleasant but uneventful lunch. "Olivia wants me to search Robert's office and steal papers from his desk, trash cans, burn bags, or file drawers."

Thomas Lane said, "Anna, since your apartment is bugged, you need to start urging Robert to show you his office. In bed tonight, use your feminine wiles to persuade him to show you."

In the pre-Olivia briefing the next day, Scott handed Anna a sizeable manila folder stuffed with papers. "Some of these apparently stained items were retrieved from the trash, and the crumpled ones are from a burn bag."

"We're just going to give them this information?" I asked.

"Everything here is classified no higher than 'For official use only,'" Scott replied.

Thomas requested, "Anna, tell them you nagged Robert to show you his office and he smuggled you upstairs with a friendly guard's consent. When he briefly left you alone, you tucked these items under your clothing. You might want to sprinkle a little powder or scent on it to give it an additional air of authenticity."

She nodded. "I understand."

"And this evening, thank Robert for showing you his office as only a wife can."

CHAPTER 120

Anna

Friday, September 22, 1961

THE 'PARIS IN a Cup' Café had a table in a secluded area. It had become our standard meeting place. After pleasantries and lunch, I surreptitiously handed Olivia a folder containing the papers I had supposedly collected in Robert's office.

"You'll have to excuse me. Please stay here until I return." she said, entering the adjacent women's restroom.

I froze in shock when Dieter Holburg approached that restroom and hung a sign on the door—Nicht in Ordnung—Out of Order. He signaled for me to join him.

When I didn't comply, Olivia returned to the table, "Join Herr Holburg immediately."

I stood and slowly walked toward the bathroom, ready to flee at the first hint of danger.

A smug smile on Dieter's damaged face greeted me. "I must compliment you on the excellent job you have done for us. You are now a full-fledged Stasi operative. Here is your first month's pay. Two hundred West Marks."

"I…I do not want your money."

"You must take it. This seals our contract. You are now one of us."

When I refused to take the money, he grabbed me and stuffed the notes down my blouse, groping me in the process. I shuddered with revulsion at his touch.

"Since you're one of us, I have a present for you. It's a tiny Minox subminiature camera and six rolls of film. Photograph everything in and around the base, including the stairs leading up to the secure areas and those areas themselves, if possible."

"I don't know how to use a camera!" I protested.

"You just point and press here. It is a remarkable new East German invention. It can easily be concealed in the palm of one's hand or your purse. The perfect tool for a spy like you."

For fifteen minutes he showed me how to use the camera and how to reload the film. "When you get to California, you will report to my friend in the Russian consulate in San Francisco. I'm sure they'll find you very useful!"

Shocked, I didn't respond. I turned and exited the café, terrified this nightmare would never end.

CHAPTER 121

Robert
September 29, 1961

IN THEIR NEXT meeting, Anna gave Olivia several rolls of exposed film which showed areas of the base including my office, and the weather station on the roof including the adjacent antenna farm. Members of the Double Agent Committee took the photos, not Anna.

Olivia told her, "My bosses are pleased with the pictures and documents you are providing. Try to gain access to the offices on the upper floors of the base and take pictures of documents out on peoples' desks or in open file cabinets." She gave Anna fifteen additional rolls of film.

After the others left Scott's conference room, Anna turned to me. "I'll have to spy for them as long as my family is in the East. That means even after we move to California."

"Both of us want this nightmare to end."

"Robert, can't we just tell them what you really do?"

"That'd only lead to more difficulties, believe me." I replied.

"Think about it—for my family and for me—please."

"Anna, neither of us could have anticipated what has happened." I attempted to lighten the mood. "I've not enjoyed our pretend sex sessions either, but I won't entertain those bastards! The sex standing up in the shower isn't that bad, is it?" I tenderly kissed her as we held each other.

CHAPTER 122

Saturday, September 30, 1961

BOTH ANNA AND I worked that Saturday. Anna because she had been taking so much time off for her 'treatments in the clinic.' This was her excuse to cover her double-agent activities. I had to complete our briefing to the Triumvirate the following Monday and help the team digging the 'Escape Tunnel' for us.

Just before lunch, Colonel Morgan said, "After you make the changes I've indicated, I'll be satisfied with the briefing we've prepared. I hope it accomplishes our objective of keeping the CIA at bay."

Scott and I grabbed a hamburger at the Officer's Club and then drove in his car to the site of the Escape Tunnel. Kurt met us, and we went up to Gunther Becker's apartment.

The previous Saturday, I'd assisted Gunther in establishing the distance and precise direction that the escape tunnel should take.

"We are here to monitor your progress and to see if you need our help," Kurt told Gunther as we each shook his hand.

A few minutes later we studied a narrow, deep pit at the back of the basement.

"Robert, at your suggestion we have gone down to eight meters below the surface, which is five meters below the basement level. That way, we should clear any subsurface obstructions and listening devices the border guards employ.

"How's it going?" I asked.

"Two people are working in the tunnel now. The further we go, the more time it takes because the soil and the boards must be transported longer distances. We are working four-man two-hour shifts, twenty-four hours a day. As you can see, we have made considerable progress. We are placing the boards on all four surfaces to prevent cave-ins."

"How far have you gotten?" Kurt asked.

"Almost thirty meters. We should be done in another three weeks."

"That means that we won't be able to get our loved ones out until late October or early November." Scott shook his head, exhaling.

"I'm also disappointed in how long this will take," I admitted. "I wish we had a viable alternative. So many things can still go wrong, and there are too many people who know about this escape route. It could be easily compromised."

Scott and Kurt nodded their agreement.

Kurt said, "I'll keep checking for other routes."

Referring to my notes and using my theodolite, I spent most of the rest of the afternoon ensuring the tunnel was headed in precisely the correct direction. A small error becomes magnified as distance increases.

As we prepared to leave, we informed Gunther that his progress was satisfactory.

CHAPTER 123

Monday, October 2, 1961

MY MEN AND I worked hard to complete the construction and furnishing of the large conference room in the Signals Exploitation Center. It still smelled of fresh paint. General Harrison, Gerald Scherman, George Mason (the new CIA representative to the Triumvirate), and Thomas Lane took their seats on one side of the conference table. Colonel Morgan, Mark, Scott, Raymond Keefer (the NSA Construction Team lead), and I sat opposite them. Everyone wore civilian attire and had been transported to the building in the back of construction vans.

After Colonel Morgan completed his introduction, Mark stood. Using slides to illustrate his comments, he said, "The CIA intercept facilities have been fully operational for over a week. So far, they've been able to begin collecting information from several high-level Russian and East German diplomatic and government telephone and teletype communications links."

General Harrison asked, "What percentage of the communications lines have been tapped so far?"

"Only about twenty percent," Mark replied.

"And I understand we are already receiving exceptionally valuable information."

"That's correct," Mark replied. "The Soviets and East Germans are unable to agree on the terms of their unilateral peace treaty. Plus, the Russians are disgruntled about the amount of economic and military aid the East Germans are demanding next year."

"During my last trip to Washington, I went to the Pentagon," General Harrison reported. "Mr. McNamara, the Secretary of Defense, congratulated me on this facility and the information we were already gathering."

Mark resumed his briefing, "The NSA and Air Force intercept facilities are complete and will be fully operational in two weeks. The Army intercept area will come online slowly over the next month. Fabrication of the barracks, mess hall, and recreation facilities, along with the remodeling of the apartments will be completed by mid-December."

Thomas Lane had not uttered a word. It appeared Colonel Morgan's suggestion to have Mark give my briefing was working.

He spent another hour presenting details of various aspects of the program and then took everyone on a tour of the entire facility, including the tunnel. We had spent countless hours preparing backup material to refute anything that Thomas Lane criticized. He said nothing during the entire meeting. I sensed he was up to something, but what?

CHAPTER 124

Tuesday, October 3, 1961

"THE SPY GAME in Berlin is changing," Thomas reported to Mark, Scott, Anna, and me as we sat around Scott's conference table. "Anna, your problem with Olivia and the Stasi is solving itself as we speak."

"That seems impossible." Anna proclaimed, turning to each member of the Double Agent Committee, then hugged me from the next seat.

"Although the border is still ostensibly open for everyone to pass freely between the two Berlins, our spies and operatives have been denied entry or harassed once they are in the East. As we speak, we are implementing alternate means of getting information out of the East. Easterners with the 'right papers' are still permitted to visit West Berlin, but virtually everyone coming West is either an East German Stasi officer or an operative. About five hundred per day have been crossing over—most still return East each evening."

"As I remember, several thousand of their spies used to come over each day, including the thirty or so who watched Tempelhof," Scott said.

Thomas went on, "True. For the past two weeks, the identity card of any Easterner coming over the border has been checked and compared to known spies. They are being followed so we can assess their activities. Many individuals have been detained, returned to a checkpoint, and told not to return.

Scott added, "I've heard that a few have even been arrested on espionage charges."

"Correct." Thomas pointed his finger at Anna. "As your last act as a double agent, you're going to give Olivia a classified document. She'll be arrested for espionage and sent to prison for a long time."

Anna stood. "No! Never! That would only make the Stasi suspicious of me, and they would want revenge. Treat Olivia like the rest. Just tell her to not come back. Otherwise, there's a good chance they will harm my family!"

"But it's imperative that I…we break up a major communist spy ring."

I could no longer control my temper. I stood. "You got it right the first time. You'll do anything to get ahead in the CIA, including the sacrifice of innocent people you've never met, people superior to you in every way, you dirty son-of-a-bitch!"

"Anna, I'm ordering you to give Olivia this document at your meeting tomorrow," Thomas shouted, as he handed a highly classified document to her. The title page read:

TOP SECRET/LIMITED DISTRIBUTION/US EYES ONLY

PLAN FOR BRINGING REINFORCEMENTS INTO BERLIN IN THE EVENT OF ARMED CONFLICT

"This will damn my family to Stasi hell!" Anna screamed, flinging the document in his face. "The Stasi won't believe I was able to get my hands on such a highly classified document! And I don't take orders from you!"

I took Anna's hand, and we walked out of the room.

Anna gave Olivia several rolls of film at their last meeting. Olivia didn't have the film in her possession when she was stopped later in the day, as she exited West Berlin. She returned to the East without being arrested or told not to return.

CHAPTER 125

Wednesday, October 11, 1961

"THOMAS LANE HAS been chastised and put on a short leash by our boss, the CIA Chief of Station in Berlin," Kurt reported. "His responsibilities have been explained to him, and he barely managed to retain his current position. Unfortunately, someone in Washington intervened. We'll still have to deal with him, plus he remains my boss."

"That's a shame," I lamented.

"Today, Olivia tried to reenter West Berlin. She and twenty-nine others were arrested, photographed, fingerprinted, taken back to a checkpoint, and told not to return," Kurt reported.

"That's good, she wasn't singled out for special treatment," I said.

"Anna will need to keep her lunch appointments for the next two weeks, but I suspect no one will ever approach her again at that café. If they do, one or two of my men will be close by to arrest them."

"Anna will be happy to have this all behind her. Thank you, Kurt."

"Whether it's all behind her is yet to be seen. The old days of Berlin being an open city, where our spies and their spies pass freely back and forth is ending. Both sides have assets in place to monitor their respective opponents."

"What you're saying is the spy game in Berlin has changed from overt, open collection of intelligence to covert, undercover operations," Scott said. "The number of people involved has been reduced, and Stasi covert spying activities will be limited to what they perceive to be critical areas."

"That's correct. Despite Thomas Lane's comments last week, they may perceive Anna as a sufficiently valuable resource to assign a covert handler to her."

"I understand what you're saying, but I hope you're wrong. This has been very hard on her."

"This new situation makes the signals intercept facility Robert and his men are building even more vital to the defense of our country," Kurt said.

"Speaking of tunnels, have either of you been over to see how they're progressing?" Scott asked.

"I was there last weekend," Kurt replied. "They got a new guy who's a master digger. He can excavate twenty, perhaps thirty percent more than any of the other men."

"So, when will they finish?" I asked.

"It's taking longer than they thought. Probably another three weeks."

"Next week, we'll start making plans." I said.

Kurt said, "Here are your keys. We completed the sweep of your apartment and found no additional recording devices. We left the original ones in place, but disabled them. Everything should return to normal soon for you and your wife."

"Thanks, Kurt. You are a true professional and a friend. Anna and I are eternally grateful for your help." We shook hands.

"And Scott, once I can tell Anna your financial assistance helped to get her family out of the East, you'll be her hero for sure."

"Anna's an exceptional woman. She has demonstrated tremendous inner strength and fortitude throughout everything," Kurt said, genuine empathy in his tone. "You must be very proud of her."

We all hoped Anna's ordeal with the Stasi was over.

For several weeks I had sensed that Anna's mental health was teetering on the brink. That evening, she was elated when I told her, "Your ordeal with Olivia may be over—Kurt has disabled the bugs in this apartment—Thomas Lane has been reprimanded."

Anna had reacted with joy and adulation each time we heard that people had escaped from the East. Recently a truck had barreled through a fence with a family aboard—an individual swam across a river—a small woman hid in a tiny space in a Volkswagen—a train rammed through a fence with thirty people aboard.

Three days ago, in a public meeting, East Germany's Ulbricht and the Russian leader Khrushchev again threatened a separate peace treaty. Their threat sent Anna into a shouting rage, "This move will give the bastards in the East sovereignty over the road, rail and air access to Berlin, and it will turn the Cold War into a Hot War. I can feel it!"

Then yesterday, three teenage boys were shot trying to escape—one died immediately—a second was allowed to die slowly in no man's land screaming for someone to help him—a third was severely wounded but managed to make it to safety in the West. Anna was inconsolable as she wept. I held her for hours before she calmed down.

This morning I learned my 'early out' had been approved. I told Anna, "As soon as I complete my current task, we can leave Berlin. By the middle of December for sure."

"The Stasi are no longer harassing me, and we'll be in California again in two and a half months! The worst may be behind us!" she exclaimed.

Almost instantly, her elated facial expression changed, "But my family will still be here, exposed to Stasi harassment and worse. How can I possibly abandon them to that fate?" The glum expression on her face left little doubt that she was suffering great mental anguish.

I hadn't told her about our latest plan to extract her family. I didn't want to get her hopes up.

CHAPTER 126

Anna

Wednesday, October 18, 1961

AT THE CONCLUSION of my meetings with Stasi Agent Olivia Katz, my hallucinations began, and I suffered from insomnia.

Twice, I dreamed of lying in a dark, slime-filled puddle when Robert awakened me. "Anna, you're having a nightmare, wake up!"

On other occasions, I felt the ropes that secured me to that chair in Stasi Headquarters as I sat at my desk in the bookstore.

In the middle of the film *Judgement at Nuremberg.* I felt the stress of being interrogated.

The spray of water in the shower became the violent assault of the fire hose.

In the middle of a conversation with strangers in the bookstore, I would panic, and think of fleeing.

Confined spaces like my small office or a foul smell took me back to that cell, again and again.

I fought to overcome those sensations. I kept the experiences from everyone, especially Robert, until that Wednesday.

Robert had to work late, and I was walking home alone when several people started to follow me. Soon I sensed that a slow-moving car was also behind me. Sure that Dieter Holburg was inside it I ran, tripped, and fell, skinning both knees and ruined my stockings. Sobbing, I ran on.

People looked at me as I passed them hurriedly. Finally, I got into the apartment building and sobbed uncontrollably sitting with my back against the front door to keep those following me out.

Soon, a tenant on the ground floor heard me. She came out and helped me to stand. "Frau Kerr, should I call the police? Has someone harmed you?"

"No. I am all right. I tripped."

With her help, I slowly climbed the five flights of stairs to our apartment.

After I cleaned my scraped knee, I lay down on the bed and attempted to fight the delusions that had made me panic. Eventually, I felt safe and was able to convince myself that I'd imagined today's entire episode.

I dozed off for a few minutes, then heard a knock on the door. Since no one had buzzed from the apartment house's front door to be admitted, I assumed it was the lady from downstairs checking on me. I made the mistake of opening the door.

Dieter Holburg and another man forced their way into the apartment. When I tried to close the door, they flung it back into me hard. I ran, attempting to reach the bathroom which had a lockable door. Dieter's associate grabbed me, securing both of my arms in a grip. I struggled to get free, but his strength overwhelmed me.

"We must talk to you," Dieter insisted.

I thought of spitting in his face, but I decided that wouldn't accomplish anything except make him angry.

Dieter's foul breath, and the other man's body odor almost overpowered me. I suddenly remembered being restrained by those Russian soldiers. Sophia lay sprawled on the ground whimpering and I felt so very cold.

Dieter gripped my hair and forced me to look at him. "Have you forgotten your recent stay with us?—The prison?—Your promise to help us?"

His words propelled me into the Stasi cell clad in that thin smock as, yet another interrogation session started. They shoved me onto the sofa, instead of securing me to a hard chair. They loomed over me. Dieter stooped and yelled into my face, "Just because Miss Katz can no longer come to the West does not mean you are not one of our operatives! We need to know your husband's actual job, and we require additional information about the American military. Is that clear?"

I remained silent. Dieter shouted, "Respond immediately!"

I heard my disembodied voice reply, "Yes…help Olivia Katz. Now I know…Paris for lunch."

Dieter gripped my shoulders and shook me hard. "Pay attention! This is Warner Eisenman. He is your new handler, but you will normally only make contact through a dead drop. This is a drawing of the place where you will leave the exposed film or documents you collect. He will leave instructions, including a rendezvous point should a face-to-face meeting become necessary."

He grabbed my hair and forced me to look at the drawing, "This is the Soviet War Memorial in the Tiergarten. Do you know where it is?

"Yes…in the park…near the middle." *I like the park—it's nice. A pleasant place with Robbie….dear Robbie.*

"Each of the two fountains at the rear of the memorial is surrounded by a high hedge and has a single bench. A large tube is fastened to the underside of the bench on the east side. Place your deposit in the container and close the lid. Using chalk leave your initials—AMK—on the leftmost column of the memorial. The letters are your initials—AMK. Understood?"

"Yes…AMK…My initials."

"Mr. Elsenman will erase your chalk marks when he picks up your drops. He will write his initials, WJE when he has something for you. Is that clear?"

When I didn't respond immediately, Dieter slapped my face, "Do you understand your instructions?"

I pressed my hand to my cheek, barely able to focus, "Yes…I understand."

As they stood at the door, Dieter taunted, me, "Remember your family is available if you do not follow orders.

I nodded. "Yes…I'll spy on Robbie."

As they exited the apartment, I heard, "She is so terrified now, she will cooperate from now on."

"The other replied, "I'm sure you're right—she was almost incoherent with fright."

After the door closed, I tried to move, but collapsed into a heap on the floor. I avoided being sprayed with the hose. I was helpful. That was good. Wasn't it? I hated lying in the filth of that cell, but how could I get out?

CHAPTER 127

Robert

Wednesday, October 18, 1961

THE MOMENT I entered the living room of our apartment, I knew something terrible had happened. A coffee table was overturned. A sofa cushion and several throw pillows were scattered across the floor.

"Anna, are you here?" I shouted.

Silence. Moving through the bedroom quickly, I found Anna huddled in a ball on the floor of the bathroom. Almost comatose, she slipped in and out of consciousness.

"Robbie, you've saved me…I'm so happy." Then, she faded away.

I crouched down beside her.

She scuttled away from me, shivering and screaming, "No! Not that! Not again!"

After I picked her up, she settled down and became almost lethargic. Despite clinging to me, she remained conscious. I called Scott, and he arrived within thirty minutes. We rushed Anna to the Army hospital in his car.

The Chief Psychiatrist at the hospital, Colonel Allan Ward, determined that she was suffering from Gross Stress Reaction. He recommended she spend several days in the hospital for further evaluation.

On the third day, I received a summons from Colonel Ward. Anna had sufficiently recovered her memory and wanted to tell me what had happened. I went to her room. Obviously sedated, she was still able to tell me of her latest encounter with Dieter Holburg.

When she finished, I tried to maintain a calm façade. Despite my rage I assured her, "Don't worry, Kurt, Scott, and I will place something of value in the dead drop every week."

Frequent therapy sessions with Doctor Ward helped her begin to deal with her anxieties. She agreed to visit him three times a week until they both felt she could manage on her own.

With the assistance of my superiors and Doctor Ward, we moved into a two-bedroom house in Clay Compound. It resembled a little American city within the confines of West Berlin. Access to the base and housing area was controlled. Anna felt safer, and I reassured her, "Dieter Holburg can't find you here."

CHAPTER 128

Monday, October 23, 1961

SCOTT, KURT, AND I gathered for a meeting of the Escape Committee. Kurt asked, "How is Anna getting along?"

"She's still in the hospital. She may be released on Wednesday. She is so fragile, we must get her family out ASAP," I explained. "This tunnel needs to be finished quickly."

"I understand what you're saying. Mia's letters are sounding more desperate all the time," Scott said, looking distressed.

"Beginning this Friday, we'll have to feed a dead drop with valid information until we can get Anna's family out."

Kurt offered, "One of my agents is a tall brunette who resembles Anna. With a blonde wig, she could pass for Anna from a distance."

"So, she can service the dead drop with information we generate."

"Exactly. I'll not tell Thomas about this latest development. He'll just get involved and screw up everything. I've some ideas about what to give them. I'll take responsibility for generating the material and getting it into that canister."

"Thanks, Kurt, you're a true friend." I shook his hand.

Scott asked, "Did anyone make it to the escape tunnel this weekend?"

"I went over on Saturday," I replied. "They won't be finished until the middle of next week. They've had to dig around a huge water main. Then I helped them get back on the correct track."

"Did you hear about all the excitement last night at Checkpoint Charlie?" Kurt asked.

"No, what happened?" Scott replied.

"Well, as you know, for the past 16 years, American official vehicles and cars with green USA license plates have passed through all Berlin checkpoints without their occupants showing identity documents. Last night, one of our senior civilians and his wife were refused entry by East German Border Guards."

"A confrontation was bound to happen," I said. "If we recognize the authority of the East Germans to demand documentation to enter Russian-controlled territory, we are tacitly recognizing the division of Germany."

"Exactly. That can only be accomplished via an international peace treaty," Scott agreed.

"What happened next?"

"As we were all instructed to do, he demanded that a Russian official be called to authorize his entry. When no Russian appeared, he drove into East Berlin. A block up the street, armed VoPos barred his way and threatened to shoot if he didn't stop."

"And?"

"Almost two hours later, eight armed MPs marched into East Berlin and escorted his car back to the checkpoint. His wife exited the car, and he turned it around. With the MPs walking beside his vehicle, he drove several blocks into East Berlin. To reinforce our rights, for the next several hours, a whole fleet of staff and civilian cars with allied civilian and military personnel in and out of uniform crossed the border and traversed the area where the East German government is located."

I smiled. "Interesting!"

"This morning, the East German News Agency announced that all persons in civilian clothes who enter East Germany, will be required to show their identity papers. This isn't the end of the showdown between the East and West."

CHAPTER 129

Wednesday, October 25, 1961

TWO DAYS LATER, Colonel Morgan's staff received an order to assemble in his conference room. He announced, "Yesterday, strong letters protesting the unauthorized denial of access to East Berlin were sent to the Soviet military leaders here and to the Russian government in Moscow."

Looking each member of his staff in the eye, he continued, "At 0925 this morning, a civilian official was again refused entry into East Berlin. The American officer in charge at the scene told his East German counterpart, 'If this access is denied, then force will be used.'"

The Senior NCO in charge of the Communications Center entered the room and handed a message to Colonel Morgan.

"Gentlemen, a full-blown military confrontation is anticipated within the hour. We have been ordered to full alert. Arms will be issued to each man, including side arms for officers. Change into fatigues, and then report back here."

As I changed into the combat gear I'd been issued when I arrived in Berlin, but had never worn, one thought ran through my mind: *In less than two months Anna and I would be out of this perilous place. But as long as her family was trapped in the East, we could never really leave Berlin! We must get them out.*

Once everyone returned to the conference room, Colonel Morgan said, "Thirty-five minutes ago, ten of our M-48 tanks arrived in the vicinity of Checkpoint Charlie and kept their engines running! The two lead tanks are equipped with the bulldozer blades required to remove the new East German barriers. Numerous jeeps with armed troops joined them. Soon, our forces will begin to escort official vehicles over the border!"

"Sir, have our intercepts revealed anything about enemy intentions?" I asked.

"The Army Security Agency reports that a Soviet tank company consisting of twelve tanks is on its way to the site."

Colonel Powell stood, "On the blackboard is a list of your assignments. Stay within this complex until released to your personal quarters. Any questions?"

"Sir, what about my guys who are working in the building?" I asked.

The Colonel asked in return, "What do you recommend?"

"I want to alert the swing shift to make their way to the building ASAP. We'll load additional arms into our delivery vans. Many of my guys are combat vets—WWII or Korea. If the flag goes up, we'll protect the building and the people working in it."

"Good idea, make it happen," Colonel Powell ordered.

In an all-hands meeting, I told my men everything I knew. "Chief, organize our people into fighting units and distribute the arms. Rotate the men between guard duty and work at their regular work assignments. Eight hours on, eight hours off until further notice."

After returning to Tempelhof, I arranged for box lunches to be made at the enlisted men's mess. Then I found cots and blankets for each man.

I telephoned Anna, who was off work and at our new home recovering from her recent trauma. "Darling, I must remain at work. The East Germans have created an incident along the border, but hopefully there's nothing for us to worry about."

"Will you be home this evening?"

"Don't know for sure, but I'll try. I promise."

We talked for several more minutes. "Remember that I love you and your safety is of paramount importance to me. I'll call every chance I get, and I'll be home as soon as possible." I heard her crying, but I needed to return to my men, so I said, "The Clay Compound is the safest place in Berlin for you until this is over. I love you."

"Love you, too," she managed.

Once back at the building, the Chief approached me. "Sir, several of the men have voiced concerns. We are armed men out of uniform. Either side may decide we are the enemy, or even worse, spies. I'd like to allow several men at a time to go in the delivery vans back to Tempelhof. They'll get their uniforms and eat a hot meal at the mess hall."

"Good plan, Chief."

Back at Tempelhof, I slipped into Colonel Morgan's conference room. He stood at the lectern, "Over the last three hours, our armed troops have escorted several American civilian vehicles on short tours of East Berlin. A senior Russian officer has finally shown up, but he hasn't actually opened the border to our vehicles. If either side fires a shot, this rapidly escalating crisis could result in full-scale war."

Turning to Mark, I said, "I hope all of those guys have cool heads. This is how wars start."

The colonel continued, "Ten Russian tanks are now located in a vacant lot just out of view of Checkpoint Charlie. This is the first time since WWII that Russian tanks have entered central Berlin. Intercepts from numerous locations indicate the entire Russian and East German Army and Air Forces in Germany are on the highest level of alert."

After providing additional details of recent events, Colonel Morgan said, "It's almost 1830. Here are my orders. Those of you with dependent children, go home and assure your families that they shouldn't be frightened. If the balloon goes up, they will be evacuated to West Germany. The evacuation plan calls for transport aircraft from Rhine-Main and Ramstein to bring armed reinforcements to Tempelhof and fly dependents back to West Germany. Your family is permitted one suitcase. Each family will be notified when to report for evacuation. Here is a list of evacuation pick-up points. Please ensure that your spouse knows where to go. Are there any questions about any of this?"

After some discussion, the colonel excused the men with dependent children, instructing them to return to duty at 7 a.m.

Mark paused and said quietly, "Anna can join my family. That way, she won't be alone."

I whispered, "Thanks, Mark. I'll let her know. You're a loyal friend," I appreciated his generosity. Although concerned for his own family, he took the time to think of Anna.

The colonel issued further orders, "You bachelor and married officers without children here in Berlin are stuck with night duty for the duration. Rooms in the BOQ have been arranged for you."

He looked at Scott. "Captain Taylor, you are the senior man. I want two officers here on duty always. They'll help the flight duty officer supervise the destruction of all classified material and equipment if fighting starts."

Once back in the building, I called an all-hands meeting. I shared everything I knew about the events occurring less than two miles away. In closing, I said, "Sometime during this crisis, some idiot may fire a shot which will set off World War III. The Russians and East Germans may even take Berlin, but the important thing is that each of us does his duty to protect and defend the United States so that we can hold our heads up with pride that we've done our collective best for each other and our country. Our primary job is to keep our little project here a secret. Knowledge of it could be used to justify their actions in the arena of world public opinion."

CHAPTER 131

Thursday, October 26, 1961

"THE SITUATION IS starting to look truly dangerous," Scott said during his morning briefing. "Overnight, the Russians moved more tanks into central Berlin; now a total of thirty-three are within 300 yards of Checkpoint Charlie. Ten of our M-48 heavy tanks and five armored personnel carriers are now parked on the street that leads to Checkpoint Charlie."

After the briefing, I returned to the building where Chief Weber told me, "Master Sergeant Loring went over to McNair Barracks and he requisitioned two 50-caliber machine guns and two super bazooka-antitank guns. We've identified defensive positions and we're ready if they come. Everyone, including me, has had a hot meal. I've also encouraged everyone here to write their family back in the States to let them know they're safe."

Back at Tempelhof, I mailed the letters, ate a hot lunch, and then decided to call Mark's house. Doctor Ward had warned me that Anna's reaction to stress could be anything from comatose withdrawal to hallucinations to shouting fits of rage. I wanted to reassure her I was well, and determine how she was managing the fear everyone was experiencing because of this crisis.

Once Anna took the phone, she said, "Robbie, I'm glad you called. I've been so worried. Can you tell me anything more than what the news broadcasts have reported?"

"No. Nothing other than the situation is looking perilous. Are you feeling all right?"

"Being here with Mary and her children helps to me stay grounded in reality. I miss you so."

"Stay with them until I come for you. If they order an evacuation, you will accompany Mary by bus to Tempelhof, and then you'll be flown to Rhein-Main. You'll be able to join your uncle and grandfather in Darmstadt."

"Robbie, is an evacuation likely?"

"No one knows." I said honestly. "I hope not."

We talked for several more minutes, "Hopefully, this crisis will be over soon. I must run. Scott just called me to a meeting. I love you."

"Hurry to me when you can. I love you, too!"

I turned to Scott and asked, "Anything new?"

"Come with me, and we'll see it first-hand. We're going to enforce our rights to enter East Berlin again at 1500 this afternoon."

We drove to Checkpoint Charlie.

"Scott, it seems as if the West Berliners are going about their lives as if nothing is happening."

"What'd you expect them to do?"

I shrugged in response. "I don't know…be concerned for their own safety if fighting starts."

Scott parked the car. We emerged on foot from a side street, just as three American tanks leveled their guns directly on the East German guards. "The guy driving that car is a G.I. in civilian clothes. He's going to enter East Berlin without showing his identity card."

A car threaded its way through the maze of barriers at the East German checkpoint. When asked for his identification, the driver shook his head and waved hands back and forth in obvious refusal. The metal pole blocking entry remained closed.

After a few minutes, an Army full colonel in uniform walked across the border, past the VoPos, and climbed into the car, which was then driven into East Berlin.

When it returned a few minutes later, the colonel got out, talked to an East German officer and then signaled. Three jeep-loads of soldiers with bulletproof vests and rifles with bayonets fixed escorted the colonel and this same vehicle back into East Berlin.

Over the next few minutes, numerous US and British vehicles entered and exited the border. The frustration of the East German VoPos was apparent as one balled his hands and held them rigidly to his sides; another moved his hat back on his head and scowled. A third held his hands out as if to say, "How could you be allowed to do this to us?"

On the way back to Tempelhof, I told Scott, "Our forces are doing everything necessary to reinforce on the Russians and East Germans that, as an occupying power, we are within our rights to enter East Berlin at will without showing identification."

According to press releases I read the next day, the American colonel told the East German Officer, "The United States will never recognize your authority to stop or request identity papers. East Germany does not exist!"

That evening, Colonel Morgan allowed married officers without children to spend twelve hours at home. I called Anna at Mark's house to let her know. I found her in the kitchen when I got home, making one of her delicious meals. We went to bed early and made love like we'd never see each other again.

CHAPTER 132

Friday, October 27, 1961

I GAVE MY men an update at an all-hands meeting. "President Kennedy is telling the Russians and the world that West Berlin is in the vital interest of the United States. The four-power agreement on Berlin remains in effect. If they try to take West Berlin by force, it will mean war."

To my surprise, Jeff Robinson, Chief of the CIA intercept station, found me and requested that I join him in his space.

Once there, he informed me, "We appreciate that you and your men are willing to protect us. However, I have ominous news as a result of a recently translated message. Khrushchev has ordered the Commander of all Russian Forces in Germany to answer all American provocations in kind!"

"What do you think that means?"

"They don't intend to back down as a result of our efforts to enforce the status quo!"

"This could quickly escalate into an all-out war. We're outnumbered ten to one and over a hundred miles behind enemy lines. I really don't like our odds," I said. "Do I need to inform my superiors?"

"They already know. We sent a Critical Warning message to the entire intelligence community. I'm sure President Kennedy and his national security staff are discussing it as we speak."

Fifteen minutes later, the KY-7 scrambler phone in my office at the building rang. Scott said. "You missed the meeting Colonel Morgan just had with the rest of us."

"What was said?"

"This crisis just deepened. Another American civilian and staff car expedition into East Berlin started at 1000 hours. When the Commies refused to admit those vehicles, ten of our tanks rolled into firing position in the street leading to their checkpoint. The Russians answered with ten tanks of their own. The cannons on the two formations of tanks are positioned to fire on one another from very close range."

"So, this is the ultimate confrontation—High Noon at Checkpoint Charlie! Thanks for telling me. I'll cease all construction work and place my men on two-hour shifts in the defensive positions we've established."

All of the radios in the building tuned into General Lucius Clay's 1230 speech on the Armed Forces Network. "The fact that Soviet tanks appeared on the scene proves that the harassments taking place on the Friedrichstrasse were not those of the self-styled East German government but ordered by its Soviet masters. The right of all four powers to move freely throughout Berlin will be maintained at all cost."

Lieutenant Lee, Commander of the Air Force intercept facility told me, "All American forces worldwide have been placed on a higher alert level."

At a little after 1900, I took the plumbing truck back to Tempelhof for my hot meal of the day and to see if Scott had any additional information. He greeted me by saying, "Well, old buddy, just think about those poor guys out there on this cold, drizzly night."

"I'm sure the guys on both sides are hoping no one screws up and starts shooting," I replied.

"One interesting development is the lack of reaction from the communist side. Radio Free Berlin (RFB), RIAS, and AFN Berlin are all providing full details of what's going on, while the East German propaganda machine is silent about the whole confrontation."

"They would usually be spouting anti-American and anti-imperialist rhetoric. Accusing us of being fascists intent on subverting the legitimate regime of Germany," I said.

"That's right. But nothing! Not one a word about the crisis," Scott shook his head. "They know their propaganda isn't believed by most of their own people. East Germans listen to Radio Free Berlin when they want to hear the truth. Perhaps the Soviets have confronted us to save face. If that's true, then this crisis may be solved soon."

"You read Khrushchev's message. I see a different course for this crisis. WW Three. I hope you're right, because my vision of the immediate future is a personal and international disaster!"

CHAPTER 133

Saturday, October 28, 1961

A NIGHT IN a real bed with Anna felt like a luxury when compared to a cot for one. After rising with an aching back, I went to Tempelhof, showered and shaved. In the morning staff meeting, we learned that the confrontation was continuing, as both sides replaced their forces with fresh troops.

A photograph of the previous day's tank confrontation at Checkpoint Charlie covered the entire front page of *The Stars and Stripes* newspaper.

That same photograph adorned the front page of virtually every newspaper across the globe. The world held its collective breath, hoping the Berlin Crisis would not lead to World War III.

As I prepared my weekly report, an NCO came to get me. "Sir, you need to report to the conference room, the Colonel wants all officers and Senior NCOs to attend."

"Good news or bad?"

"Don't know, sir,"

A short time later, the Colonel stood and addressed those in the room. "Gentlemen, I have what I hope is good news. Three hours ago, the CIA people in our building intercepted a message. In it, Khrushchev accuses Ulbricht of intentionally fomenting a crisis in Berlin to force Russia into confronting the Allies. In retaliation, Khrushchev won't sign a unilateral peace treaty with East Germany this year, and he is withdrawing his forces from their current positions."

The nine officers and seven NCOs in the room grinned and shook hands.

The colonel cleared his throat, regaining our attention. "About an hour and a half ago, the Russians moved their tanks. Thirty minutes later we did the same. Our helicopters have determined that the Russian tanks are now deployed on side streets. We are still on alert, and will remain so. Go about your duties."

"Sir, some of us would like to go home this evening. Is that possible?" I asked.

"Yes. Several of the officers who have been home with their families the last three nights will have duty tonight. This includes me. We old guys should still be able to pull an all-nighter, right, Colonel Powell?"

That got a laugh as Mark smiled. "It'll be rough, but we'll manage somehow."

As I left, I shifted my focus to how to get Anna's relatives out of the East. I'd almost forgotten the tunnel into the graveyard. It must nearly be finished, I thought.

After we made love, Anna snuggled against me. "We'll be leaving Berlin in less than two months. As long as I'm here, I feel close to my family."

"Once you get your American passport, we can come for an extended visit without having to worry about the Stasi arresting you. That might take a year or more, but we'll return often after that."

"I can hardly wait for our first visit."

CHAPTER 134

November 2, 1961

DURING THE NEXT week, the last of the troops from both sides of Checkpoint Charlie returned to their bases. The Berlin Crisis was like a major snowstorm. It came out of nowhere, profoundly impacted our lives for a few days, and just as quickly subsided.

The Berlin Crisis proved to be just another attempt on the part of the Russians and East Germans to probe for a soft spot they could exploit. When President Kennedy called their bluff, they folded. Gradually, American forces in Berlin returned to their regular alert status, which always remained one level higher than that of the rest of the American military worldwide.

"Our recent excitement has set us back almost a week," I said to the Chief and Sergeant Loring in my tank office. "Do you think the men will agree to work more extended hours and perhaps most weekends, if it means they can go home before Christmas and not return?"

"Sir, I'm sure that they will."

"Let's look at the list. The appliances and cabinets for the mess hall should be installed this week. The Army intercept spaces will be completed next week. The command and recreation centers are scheduled to be finished in two weeks."

"Sir, those last two activities may be delayed because the lighting, furniture, and other fixtures haven't arrived in Berlin. Their delivery was delayed by recent events."

"When will we get them?"

"Next week, unless the East Germans decide again to disrupt rail traffic into Berlin."

I nodded. "Here's what we'll do. Let's start remodeling the apartments and shift our primary effort into the building of the barracks."

"Good idea, sir. All of the material required to complete those tasks are in the parking garage."

"I want to get out of here as much as you guys do. My early out has been approved. I can leave as soon as we're done."

CHAPTER 135

Saturday-Sunday, November 4-5, 1961

AFTER OVER A month of planning, Kurt, Scott, and I were ready to assist sixteen people to escape to the West. Sophia's husband, Derrik, had been released from prison early and would join his family in their escape to the West.

Construction of Gunther's tunnel had been completed on Friday afternoon, when he pushed one of the limestone slabs that covered the floor of the crypt up and out of the way.

As a part of the planning, we completed a map of the area and viewed the scene several times from as many angles as possible. The barrier between the two Berlins had separated a church from its cemetery. Kurt arranged with the rector for us to use the church steeple positioned adjacent to the fence. This vantage point gave us a clear view of the cemetery and surrounding area.

At a little after midnight, the three of us ascended the ladder to the belfry. Through openings in the stone structure, we saw two pairs of armed VoPos with dogs. They patrolled the well-lit, no man's land between the two fences. Lights atop tall poles along the fences illuminated the area. The gravestones and crypts beyond formed long shadows, which would allow the escapees to approach the vault without exposing themselves.

"Fortunately, the wind's blowing toward us, which means that the dogs between the fences shouldn't be able to detect our escapees," I whispered.

"Hope you're right, because they'll be only a hundred or so feet away from the fence when each group reaches the crypt," Kurt said.

"My task will be to keep an eye on the VoPos below us at the fence," Scott said. "I'll wave and point if either group becomes interested in anything in the cemetery."

Kurt had managed to acquire six sets of the two-way communication devices the East Germans had developed for the Stasi. When he told us about this successful acquisition, he bragged, "We'll use their technical capability against them by keeping each of our groups apprised of what's happening and to direct their actions, if necessary."

I mounted my thirty-power binoculars on a tripod and focused on the area around the crypt. I could see most of the cemetery and part of an adjacent street.

"The workers' girlfriends should arrive soon," Scott said after glancing at his watch.

Two of the diggers agreed to work on the tunnel in return for having their girlfriends, who were trapped in the East, come through first.

"There they are," I whispered as I watched two female figures dart between gravestones and then crawl the last few feet before disappearing near the crypt.

Looking down at the luminous dial of my watch, I determined that Bernard, Emma, and Fredrich should arrive in twenty minutes. This arduous and gut-wrenching task could well be completed in a little over an hour. Breathe deeply. Good air in....bad out.

Fifteen minutes.

Ten minutes.

Five minutes.

Two minutes.

Suddenly, I thought I detected movement on the street. Repositioning the focal point of the binoculars, I saw silhouettes pass through the illumination of a street light.

Anna's family is too smart to expose themselves like that, I thought.

One of the silhouettes stopped. I saw the submachine gun in his hand.

I stood and motioned my companions away from the opening. "Kurt, use your gadget to tell everyone to go home. The bad guys have arrived in force."

"Are you sure?" Scott asked quietly.

"Certain. Whoever is on the street is armed."

"Crap."

Kurt was crouching down so that his voice wouldn't carry out to the VoPos below. In German, he whispered, *"Abbrechen! Sofort abbrechen!"* (Abort immediately!)

Rushing back to the thirty-power binoculars on the tripod, I watched submachine gun armed men in uniform and civilians carrying pistols swarm into the cemetery. Gunshot fire erupted in the vicinity of the crypt. Soon, men surrounded it.

The three of us looked at each other, defeated by the reality that we'd tried again and failed.

I sighed, whispering, "I'm glad that I didn't get Anna's hopes up by telling her about tonight."

The others nodded their agreement, knowing that their loved ones on both sides of the border remained vulnerable.

The next day, Kurt, Scott, and I met Gunther at his apartment. He was distraught—the man that was handing out flashlights and directing people into the tunnel was killed. He confessed, "I screwed up. A friend recommended one of the workers, who had a girlfriend trapped in the East and was desperate to get her out."

"You accepted him into your group?"

"He worked harder than any of us. Turns out he crossed over the border to visit his girlfriend in the East two months ago. He was arrested, and only released after he agreed to try to stop people in the West from building tunnels. They held his girlfriend in custody to assure his cooperation."

"Let me guess the rest," I said. "His girlfriend was one of the two they allowed through as his reward."

"Exactly," Kurt replied.

Once the three of us were back in my tank, I hurled a glass ashtray across the room so hard, it shattered a wood in/out basket. Then I shouted, "We've lost over a month and all of Scott's money. And we're no closer than the day we started."

"Don't worry about the money," Scott said. "We are all feeling angry and desperate. In our communications, Mia sounds more distraught each day. I can afford to purchase Swiss passports for everyone."

"That's over $800,000. Anna, her family, and I could never repay you."

"Don't worry about it. I can easily afford it!"

"How?"

"My family's wealthy."

"I've enough savings to afford my share," Kurt said.

"The Fischer family's share is still over half a million dollars," I protested.

"Don't worry about it, Robert. I'm only in the Air Force because I like it. Anna's family's is so exceptional, just knowing I was able to help them to freedom will be my reward."

I stared at him speechless.

Hugging Scott like a brother, I said, "We'll all be eternally grateful for your generosity. I accept on their behalf. Thank you."

"Kurt, as soon as you've completed the agreement with the Swiss diplomat, I'll have a letter of credit for the full amount sent to a Swiss bank," Scott said. "Pay me back at your leisure."

Kurt's eyes brimmed with tears. "Thank you."

The challenge we faced as we tried to rescue our loved ones had fostered a profound sense of brotherhood among the three of us.

CHAPTER 136

Friday, November 10, 1961

"I'VE GOT A foolproof way of getting everyone out of East Berlin," Kurt said after joining Scott and me in my office at Tempelhof. "As I told you on Wednesday, the man in the Swiss embassy selling passports was recalled to Bern after the East Germans and Russians complained about his activities."

"Tell us about your new alternative!" I urged.

"One of the senior officials at the Austrian Embassy decided to get rich. He's selling authentic Austrian passports, and we could be his first customers. Our people can travel freely within East Germany using their own travel papers. So, sixteen people divided into four groups will travel to Dresden on the same train. Using the Austrian passports, they will take another train through Prague to Bratislava."

"And Bratislava is right on the Danube River, very near Vienna," I smiled feeling hopeful. "The Czechoslovakian border guards are slack, and their chief in Bratislava is on the CIA's payroll," Kurt said. "Plus, to make certain nothing goes wrong, I'll travel with them playing the part of my paramour's husband."

"How soon can we pull this off?" Scott asked.

"It'll take about a week to get the passports back after we pay the Austrian Embassy guy here and give him the photos. The passports are generated in Vienna."

"How much?" I asked.

"Eighty thousand West Marks—$20,000 for each passport."

"Let's make it happen, my friends," Scott said as we shook hands and discussed the details of money transfers and potential travel dates.

Thus, our next escape plan was finalized.

CHAPTER 137

Wednesday, November 15, 1961

AFTER SEVERAL HOURS of paperwork, my brain felt fried. I looked around at the tan walls and gray furniture of my office in the tank aware that this space would soon be occupied by someone else. Anna and I will be flying back to the States in five weeks, staying first with my parents for a few days, spending Christmas in Rutherford, and then flying to Hawaii for a week in the sun. My almost six-year stint in the Air Force would be over.

Someone high up in the Kennedy administration had told the CIA to stop trying to take control of the Signals Exploitation Center in the building. Since then I hadn't seen Thomas Lane. My buzzer on my Tempelhof tank rang. To my surprise, Thomas, Kurt, and a man I didn't recognize stood outside.

"This is James Joerger, who's on his first overseas assignment," Thomas said by way of introduction. "He's Kurt's new protégé."

Joerger looked to be my age, thin, and under six feet tall. He had unruly, long blondish hair and a ruddy complexion. During our handshake, his grip felt weak. Throughout our meeting, he only made furtive eye contact with any of us. He lacked the usual self-confidence of a CIA agent.

Kurt started us off. "What I am about to tell you is strictly 'need to know.' In Berlin, only the four of us will ever know. For the last ten years, one man and his wife have been at the center of one of the most productive parts of our espionage efforts against the East Germans and Russians."

Thomas said, "That's an amazingly long time in the spy game."

"A little over three months ago, one of their sources was arrested and tortured." Kurt looked directly at me. "Eventually, the Stasi learned enough to guess the identity of the couple."

"How can I help you?" I wondered if my confusion was apparent.

Kurt seemed to be trying to convince me of something, but what? Then I realized—he was attempting to manipulate Thomas into taking an action.

"Two days ago, one of the messages the CIA received and translated in the building was from Stasi Headquarters to Ulbricht's office. It was an arrest warrant for our couple and their family," Kurt said. "The document instructed the arresting officers to closely monitor the agents' activities for the next few days. If possible, they are to be arrested with evidence against their sources and their Western handlers. It instructed them to attempt to identity of the rest of the espionage ring and their contacts in the West…"

"—Captain, I recall that you severed and repaired the top of an East German storm drain during the construction of the tunnel," Thomas interjected.

"Yes, that is true. As far as we know, the storm drain repair is almost invisible from their side."

"Is there any reason we couldn't get eight people out through the tunnel by reopening that hole?" Kurt asked.

"It's certainly feasible. Are the people in Washington willing to risk compromising the existence of our tunnel and facilities that some have called the 'greatest intelligence coup of the century' to rescue them?"

"At this point in time, we only have permission to assess the feasibility of such an operation," Kurt said. "We have managed to get one or two people across to the West at will, but extracting all eight safely would be tough, especially since three young children are among the group."

Was Kurt encouraging Thomas to use the tunnel so it would be open and available for our sixteen? I wondered.

Thomas added, "The East Germans have had months to detect and eliminate all of the easy ways to get people to the West. This is a potential solution. We haven't much time to improvise another scheme."

I went over to a flat storage cabinet, opened the third door down, moved a few drawings around, and withdrew a top and side view of the storm drain and our tunnel. I spread it out across the conference table.

"This is our tunnel. It hit the storm drain here. The path of that drain goes from the River Spree all the way back to this area, which was once the manufacturing hub of Berlin. Now, it's primarily damaged and abandoned buildings."

"What are these smaller pipes?" James asked.

"These side drains bring the water down from the streets." I pointed. "Here's the vertical shaft that provides access to the drain system from the surface. It's located in the abandoned industrial complex I sketched in here."

I retrieved a map of East Berlin. "That complex is located here, about a half a mile from where the tunnel and drain meet."

"How would you make a hole in the repaired tunnel flooring and storm drain?" Kurt asked.

"Jackhammer is the quickest, but it makes a lot of noise," I replied.

"Won't the noise attract attention?" Thomas wanted to know.

"The whole area is covered with ruined and vacant factories and warehouses," I stated. "If we scheduled the extraction for Sunday, when the area is deserted, we'd have to be awfully unlucky for someone to even detect noise emanating from a drain grate on nearby streets. I seriously doubt anyone could determine the location of the noise source, or what caused it."

In the East, it doesn't pay for an ordinary citizen to become too curious," Kurt said to validate my statement.

"Who'd run the jackhammer?" Thomas asked.

"My senior NCO, Chief Weber. He helped to build the tunnel and knows about the storm drain. We still have an electric jackhammer in our basement storage area at the building."

Each man thanked me, shook my hand, and left.

If they have us open the tunnel, perhaps we could use it too. No that's impossible. Or is it?

CHAPTER 138

Thursday, November 16, 1961

THOMAS LANE ORDERED Kurt to spend every waking hour searching for alternate ways to extract the American double agents and their family from East Berlin. For the first time in several days, he joined us in my tank late the next day.

"That son-of-a-bitch at the Austrian Embassy is threatening to give the photos of our sixteen escapees to the Stasi unless we pay him an additional million West Marks!" Kurt exclaimed in disgust.

Scott and I were shocked.

"That's $250,000 on top of the $230,000 we've already paid him!" I exclaimed.

"I'm willing to pay him, but I'm concerned that we'll never see those passports," Scott said with obvious concern. "He may just continue to make demands."

"If he gives the photos to the Stasi, our loved ones will be in immediate danger, probably even arrested," Kurt's voice cracked with emotion. "Bernard and Emma Fischer and my beloved are sufficiently well-known to be identified immediately."

"We must act quickly," I replied. "Tell Scott about the double-agent extraction."

Kurt nodded, "Since I determined the CIA would need to immediately extract eight people from East Berlin, I've urged Thomas to use Robert's tunnel and the storm drain for that task. I initially viewed it as an option. Now, it's our only possible route."

"When?" I asked.

"This morning we received permission from Washington. The Secretary of Defense plus heads of the CIA and NSA approved the tunnel extraction for our double agent and his family this Sunday afternoon."

"And then we'll use it to extract sixteen additional people," Scott shouted. "Thank God!"

"A dream opportunity that will be entirely under our control." I exclaimed joyously as we all rose to our feet in unison, shook hands and embraced each other.

Kurt nodded. "It doesn't leave us much time to make our plans and notify our escapees. Here's what I'd suggest…"

CHAPTER 139

Saturday-Sunday, November 18-19, 1961

THE CHIEF AND I spent most of Saturday morning transporting tools, form building material including fast drying concrete mix in bags, a ten-foot extension ladder, a mixing tub, cans of water, waterproof boots, flashlights, a hoe to mix the cement, and miscellaneous items into the tunnel. We reviewed each activity to be certain that we had everything we needed.

The Chief said, "So at 1600 tomorrow, Kurt and I'll go down into the storm drain and construct the form. You'll then fill in the hole."

"After an hour, you two will tear down the form and be extracted from East Berlin by the CIA and U.S. Army. You both speak German like natives, so that process should go smoothly."

"We should be back by 6 p.m.," the Chief agreed.

"There are only probably a million things that could go wrong," I added.

"Sir, I think we need to be armed just in case. I took a semi-automatic grease gun for me, plus two .38 caliber pistols for you and Captain Taylor out of the arms locker."

"A prudent move, Chief."

The Chief and I met Thomas, Kurt, and James Joerger at the main entrance to the building at 0700 Sunday morning.

At our excavation site, I handed out gloves and ear protection. "If you think a jackhammer is loud, you should hear it in a confined space like this."

Soon parts of the tunnel flooring were loose. Working as a team, we removed pieces of concrete and cut the rebar, piling the rubble nearby.

When I suggested to Thomas that he might help he replied, "I'm equivalent to a two-star general. I don't do grunt work."

Two hours later, we lowered the step ladder down into the hole and removed the rubble which had fallen through.

Thomas looked at his watch. "Our visitors should arrive at the rendezvous site in about forty-five minutes."

"Are you going to return to ensure that the tunnel is sealed?" I asked,

"Kurt, you're in charge after James and I leave. You've sufficient help. If there's a problem, Captain Kerr can get additional subordinates to help reseal the hole."

"Weren't we going to limit the number of people who know about this operation to us five?" Kurt asked.

"Once we get our double agent and his family out, the need for that level of secrecy ends. You're in charge. Call the safe house if anything goes wrong."

Thirty minutes later Kurt looked at James. "It's time." They both donned rubber boots. Kurt lowered himself down into the drain. James handed down a box of flashlights, a box of rubber boots of various sizes, and then joined him.

Almost half an hour later, we heard children's voices. One sang, "Splish-splash, *Ich nahm ein bad.*" (Splish, Splash I was taking a bath). Another child giggled.

James stuck his head up through the hole in the tunnel. "They're behind me."

Thomas moved toward the hole and helped each person up into the tunnel, giving the adults cold, perfunctory handshakes.

The group consisted of an older couple in their sixties, a couple in their early forties (the double agents, I assumed), a man in his thirties, and three boys who ranged in age from a pre-teen to a preschooler.

"Are we in the West yet?" the older gentleman asked.

I said in German, "Not yet. Soon."

Once they were seated on electric carts, they received blindfolds. In English, Thomas explained, "Please put these on for the trip to the West. Once we arrive at the surface, you'll be told when to remove them. Soon, you'll be in a safe house in West Berlin while we arrange transportation for you to the United States, where you'll be given asylum."

Kurt translated.

Washington had insisted that our visitors be blindfolded to avoid any knowledge about their route to freedom.

The small convoy departed with Thomas and James driving.

An hour later, Scott arrived in one of the carts. Per our plan, he and Mark had hidden in the back of the van that brought boxed lunches for the men on duty that day.

He exhaled, the nervous strain evident on his face. "We'll bring Mia and her parents through in thirty minutes. Wish us luck."

I gave him a thumbs up. More than luck would be required, I feared.

Kurt looked at Scott, "We'd better leave now. It takes almost 15 minutes to get there, and we need to make sure they weren't followed before we contact them."

CHAPTER 140

Sunday, November 19, 1961.

SCOTT SUCCESSFULLY BROUGHT Mia and her family through to safety. Confident the second group would arrive soon, I sat in the driver's seat of one of the carts. I heard the faint footfalls coming from the tunnel entrance. No one should approach from that direction, I thought. Scott said he'd stay with Mia and her parents until summoned. Kurt was due to return with his female friend and daughter via the storm drain; the Chief is with them.

"Scott, is that you?" I called quietly.

No response.

"Scott?"

Stepping out of the cart, I fingered the .38 at my side. Just as I unbuckled the strap on the holster, Thomas appeared and pointed a pistol at me.

I strained to catch my breath. *No way, not a panic attack, not now, under no circumstances, I vowed, clenching my fists tightly.*

My resolve stiffened: *That son-of-a-bitch will not win this time!*

"Ah! Captain Kerr. Slowly unbuckle your belt and allow your weapon to drop to the ground."

As I complied, he moved closer.

"Where are Kurt and Chief Weber?"

"In my office changing into their suits," I replied.

"How soon will they be back?"

"Very soon. Why are you here? And what's with the gun?"

"Despite specific orders, I knew you, Captain Taylor, and Kurt

Altschuler would try to get people out of East Berlin. The temptation was too great."

"As soon as the Chief and Kurt get back, we'll reseal the tunnel according to the plan. You're welcome to help me mix concrete." I tried to hide my growing anxiety.

"I took a photograph of Captain Taylor as he led two women and a man into the elevator of this building. You're probably using one of the apartments upstairs to hold the escapees until they've all arrived."

"You're imagining things."

"When does your wife's family arrive at the storm drain entrance?"

"I don't know what you're talking about." I feared he could hear the nervous edge in my voice.

"You know exactly what I'm talking about!" Thomas taunted.

As he bent over to move my weapon out of reach, I thought, it's now or never. I lunged at him.

He retreated with my gun and holster in one hand and signaled with his weapon for me to move back. For a fat old fart, he moved quickly.

"Why do you care if we use the tunnel? Your double agent has been extracted.

"I care very much. My leadership at the very highest levels have made it clear my future is dependent on my taking control of this facility for the CIA. Your unauthorized use of the tunnel is prima facia evidence of NSA and DoD's inability to manage such an essential national intelligence asset. In addition, Kurt, Scott, and you have done everything possible to humiliate and belittle me—so each of you will suffer as your loved ones languish under the yoke of a totalitarian regime or suffer equally while you're in prison!"

Thomas Lane's decibel level increased with each word until he raged, "My recent reprimand as a result of your wife's unwillingness to follow my orders was particularly galling!"

"My wife isn't under anyone's chain of command. What you were suggesting would have put all her family at significant risk, and you knew it!" I shouted as anger replaced my fear.

We glared at each other, "So, what are you going to do if you do succeed in subduing all four of us?"

"I don't need to capture you four. With my testimony and a few more pictures, your superiors will arrest you. You'll each be convicted of conspiracy, numerous violations of established security procedures, misuse of government property, and failure to follow orders. You'll likely get thirty years!" His smug expression betrayed his eagerness for revenge.

"Sending us to prison won't help the CIA gain control of this facility."

"To the contrary—it'll prove that NSA and Air Force can't maintain the security of this building. My small camera has proven very useful," he smirked, patting his pants pocket.

As I again moved toward Thomas, he waved his gun. "If you take another step, I'll kill you. On occasion, my plan included eliminating you," he sneered, "so don't tempt me."

I halted. Footfalls in the tunnel became audible. This time, it had to be Scott.

"Stay where you are. I'll shoot you if you make a sound or move," he whispered as he knelt down behind the cart.

I had to warn the others, but how? Then it hit me. Force Thomas to fire his gun. I heard voices and splashes of people coming through the storm drain. Thomas didn't appear to have heard them.

I lunged at him, my foot caught in the hoe and I plunged forward and hit the tunnel floor hard.

He fired his weapon. Realizing I hadn't been hit, I looked around for a weapon and grabbed the first thing I saw—a claw hammer from the pile of tools.

Thomas stared at his pistol, stunned that his first shot failed. He hesitated. I buried the claw hammer in his wrist. His gun skittered across the floor. My second blow with the hammer flat on the side of his head knocked him unconscious.

Scott rushed to my side, collected Thomas' gun, and returned mine to me, "You okay, Kemosabe?"

Kurt scrambled up the ladder, gun in hand, and surveyed the scene quickly, "There are handcuffs in the briefcase over there. Cuff him."

I complied, then checked his condition, "His pulse is steady. He'll survive and be madder than hell when he wakes up. He threatened to send us all to prison for thirty years and even threatened to murder me."

Kurt's daughter entered the tunnel and screamed when she saw Thomas, who was bleeding from both his wounds. She hid her face against her mother's body as Kurt directed them to one of the carts.

"I'll take these two up to the penthouse and return. Chief, why don't you come with me? We need to determine if anyone accompanied him."

The cart left after our guests donned blindfolds.

Scott asked, "Is there any place we can put him while we complete the extraction of Anna's family?"

"We built a locked storage room at the far end of the tunnel for the NSA technicians to use," I replied.

Scott nodded and grabbed one of his legs. I grabbed the other, and we dragged him into the storage room and locked the door.

On our way back to the storm-drain entrance, I asked, "We don't have to worry about him escaping from that room, but what are we going to do with him after we're finished?"

"The fat's in the fire now, old pal. If we release him, he'll raise hell. He's right, we could all go to prison. Perhaps Kurt has an idea."

When he returned, Kurt said, "Thomas has balls. He apparently came alone. Perhaps he intended to only take pictures and observe our indiscretions, but he got carried away."

"If we release him, we'll all pay dearly, and what about the Chief? He helped us. Will Thomas ruin him, too? We need to take care of the bastard," Scott swore.

Taken back, I implored, "Cold blooded murder—are you suggesting…"

"—I have a plan that may solve many problems concurrently." Kurt interjected.

I stared at them in disbelief.

"Rest assured I'll do nothing that will incriminate us," Kurt promised.

"Let's just get our loved ones out of East Berlin, seal the tunnel, and then release him," I suggested.

"You're willing to condemn us to life in prison so that Thomas fucking Lane can take his revenge on us and look big in the eyes of his superiors?" Scott demanded. "Well, I don't give a damn what happens to that son of a bitch. Kurt, take care of him any way you see fit."

"Chief, you've been to the rendezvous point twice. Did you see anything suspicious on your way there?" I asked.

"Sir, that area of derelict factories and warehouses is as quiet as a morgue on this cold, rainy Sunday. Anyone in their right mind is inside keeping warm."

We descended into the storm drain, walked in silence, and ascended the built-in ladder to the surface. The Chief pushed aside the manhole cover. We quickly scrambled out, replaced the cover, and hurriedly moved into a nearby building.

After ensuring that everything was still quiet, the Chief whispered, "We can now walk casually to the rendezvous point."

A cold drizzle started. We turned up the collars of our overcoats up as water dripped from our hats. At the end of the first block, we turned a corner and were both startled when a man moved out from an overhang and stumbled into us. We both recoiled in shock. I struggled for my .38.

The Chief put his hand up to stop me. *"Wer bist du?"* (Who are you?)

"Hans Schmit," the man replied swaying back and forth. I realized he was just another drunk wandering the streets of East Berlin, not an uncommon sight in communist countries.

Chief Weber extracted a twenty East Mark note from his jacket pocket. "Hans, my friend, go to a nearby *gasthaus*, get warm and drink your fill."

He grasped the bill in his dirty, gnarled hand and staggered down the street toward the East Train Station.

The Chief grinned. "We don't have to worry about him reporting us to anyone."

After covering the two blocks down an adjacent street and a couple of turns, we entered the courtyard of a massive abandoned complex of manufacturing buildings, up a nearby set of steps, and into an abandoned warehouse. My eyes slowly adjusted to the mottled light. I could see most of Anna's family—Papa Bernard, Mama Emma, Fredrich, Helmuth, and Johanna with their two children.

I signaled silence as I hugged each of them. At the Chief's signal, we exited the compound, traversed a maze of streets, and descended one by one down into the storm drain.

Everyone donned rubber boots and walked through the storm drain, except little Andrea. I carried her the whole way. Once up the ladder and into the tunnel, Bernard whispered, "Are we really in the West?"

"Not yet, but soon," I replied.

Hugging me, Emma asked, "When can we see Anna?"

"Anna knows nothing about this, but you'll be reunited soon," I said.

"You haven't told her about your efforts to get us over here?" Bernard looked shocked.

"No. The Stasi traumatized Anna. She's receiving medical care, but she's still fragile. Once she knows you're all in the West—she'll be perfect again."

"Climb into these carts and put on the blindfolds. This gentleman and I will transport you to the West. Soon I'll go back for Sophia and her family."

The Chief drove one cart, and I took the other. I led them into the basement elevator. Once the elevator door closed, I said, "You can now remove your blindfolds."

Mark greeted them at the door of the penthouse, "Welcome to West Berlin. You are now free."

Everyone sighed in unison and broke into smiles. Bernard encouraged his family to participate in a group hug. Emma said, "Robert, confirm that we are really free."

"Yes, you're in West Berlin."

Everyone knew each other from the photo sessions at the Fischer's home. Hugging, backslapping, and joviality ensued as the adults all seemed to talk at once, elated to be free, and unconcerned about the future.

The three children retreated to a corner to talk about their journey through the storm drain and tunnel.

I said, "It time for me to get Sophia and her family. We should be back in less than an hour." I tapped my wristwatch.

"Attention everyone. I doubt you had time for lunch, so please enjoy this buffet," Mark said. "There is room for everyone around the table in the next room. Enjoy."

I translated for Mark before departing.

CHAPTER 141

November 19, 1961

"CHIEF, WHY DON'T you go up to the apartment and have lunch?" Kurt suggested. "We'll find you when it's time to seal the tunnel."

As the Chief's footsteps faded, Scott turned to us. "That bastard Thomas Lane deserves to die."

"This is one of his usual schemes to take advantage and dispose of some people he views as enemies," Kurt said. "You two don't realize this, but his enmity toward me is monumental. I'm good at what I do, and he's an incompetent politician who will stomp on anyone to get ahead!"

"You think he knew that we'd attempt to use it to get our families out?" I asked.

"I'm sure of it," Scott replied. "And Kurt's correct. If we allow him to live, we'll all suffer."

"You're saying…" My voice trailed off.

"They'll throw the book at all of us. Maybe the Chief, too," Scott speculated.

"We can't just commit murder." I protested that course of action.

"I have a solution," Kurt said. "When I was upstairs, I contacted someone in the East. In an hour, he'll call Stasi Headquarters and report a clandestine meeting between a CIA operative and a double agent at our rendezvous point. My contact will be believed. Let's let the Stasi take care of Mister Thomas Fucking Lane for us."

"That way we aren't committing murder, per say," I said.

Scott nodded. "I also like that distinction."

Kurt said. "I'll take Thomas Lane on a little tour of East Berlin. It's proven fatal for many others. While he's there, he'll be confronted by the Stasi. If they don't kill him, he'll take the coward's way out by using his own gun."

"How are you going to manage that?" I asked.

"That sniveling bastard may need a little help from me," Kurt said, "and I may even have to improvise at some point along the way, but my objective is to destroy his credibility and reputation in the eyes of his contemporaries and the world!"

CHAPTER 142

Sunday, November 19, 1961

THOMAS, CONSCIOUS WHEN we opened the door of the storage locker, yelled, "You'll all pay for this!"

Kurt grabbed his hair, jerked back his head, and stuffed a gag into his mouth, which he secured with electrical tape. He then yanked Thomas to his feet, shook him violently, and warned, "You're going to the East, so you can experience what the real spy game's about. If anything happens, I'll use the first bullet on you. If we all survive this last extraction, then we'll release you. You have your official passport in your pocket. Perhaps you can convince the East German border guards to honor it."

Both of us covered Thomas as we walked back through the tunnel, down the step ladder, and through the storm drain. Kurt stopped when we arrived at the storm drain's metal-runged ladder. He seized Thomas by the throat. "Do you believe if you try anything that I'll kill you and leave your body down in this drain?"

Thomas nodded.

"When I uncuff your wrists, you're going to climb up this ladder. Robert, go first and keep him covered."

He removed Thomas' shackles. As he started to climb, Kurt shoved his gun between his buttocks "One wrong step and my bullet will travel up your body. It might even make it to your heart assuming you have one. Now climb."

After the three of us exited the storm drain, Thomas' hands were shackled behind his back. We moved hastily and in silence toward the rendez-vous point. Halfway there, Kurt handcuffed Thomas to a lamp post inside a fenced area.

A block further on Kurt pushed open the door to the meeting place where Sophia, her husband Derrik, and two of their children were located. Our trip back to the tunnel proved uneventful.

In the penthouse, the sixteen escapees joyfully hugged and kissed each other.

As the jubilant celebration unfolded around me, I wondered what would happen when Thomas Lane ended up dead in East Berlin. He wasn't supposed to leave the tunnel! Kurt, Scott, and I will be at the center of a massive shit storm.

Worry about the future filled me, but too much still needed to be done to secure the tunnel. I announced to everyone, "Scott and Mark will now take you to a safe place. I must remain here for a few hours. Anna and I will join you as soon as possible."

CHAPTER 143

Sunday, November 19, 1961

"CAPTAIN, IT'S ALMOST five. We've waited over an hour for Kurt to return, and now the sun has set," the Chief said as we stood near the exit from the storm drain. "We better get a couple of men down to help seal the tunnel and use the darkness to extricate ourselves. Face it, sir, Kurt's not coming back."

"Wait here, and I'll check. It'll only take a few minutes."

The earlier rain storm had passed, and the cloud-free night sky and almost full moon allowed me to easily navigate the maze of ruined buildings.

As I neared the rendezvous point, I spotted a body in the middle of the alley. I moved forward, ever so slowly, adhering closely to the side of the building. I had to make sure the body was not Kurt.

Once close enough, I could see he was wearing a leather trench coat. Stasi. I kept my weapon pointed at him.

The man rolled over, jerking his gun into firing position. I swerved to the left and fired.

Gunfire shattered the silence of the night.

The individual on the ground convulsed and then slumped. I secured his weapon, then felt a stinging sensation. I'd been hit in the bicep.

Crawling into the shadows, I checked the wound to my right arm. Only a flesh wound, but it bled profusely and hurt like a son-of-a-bitch. I tied my handkerchief around my arm to staunch the flow of blood and then shrugged back into my sweater and coat.

After crawling over to the open gate, I heard labored breathing to the right. The moonlight revealed four bodies on the ground. Only one was still breathing. I crawled in his direction.

I kept my gun at the ready. The man turned his head toward me. Kurt! I dropped down beside him and cradled his head. "I need to get you to a hospital. Where's Thomas?"

"Dead…perfect angle…look like…he shot himself…coward. I took… Stasi bullet…bad," he gasped, then coughed up blood and passed out.

I located Thomas' body, confirmed his death and that the weapon was still in his hand. The other two dead bodies appeared to be Stasi.

Rushing back to the storm-drain entrance, I yelled, "Chief, come with me. Kurt needs a hospital!"

Using a plank we found in the debris, we transported Kurt to the drain entrance. The Chief picked Kurt up, threw him over his shoulder, and carried him down into the drain. I closed the manhole cover. Using the plank again, we conveyed him to the hole in the tunnel, up the ladder, and onto a cart. Unconscious, he looked stark white. His extremities were cold to the touch. The Chief and I exchanged a glance. I shook my head.

We drove to the garage and placed Kurt into the back of a delivery van. The Chief drove the van to the roll-up door and told the two guards, "There is a severely wounded man in the back of this van. Take him to MEDDAC Emergency immediately. Then bring the vehicle back here and resume your duties."

CHAPTER 144

Sunday, November 19, 1961

RESEALING THE TUNNEL as soon as possible was now our overriding task. I called Scott. "We found Kurt. He's in bad shape. Plus, we need some help here."

The Chief retrieved the first aid kit from our office, cleaned my wound, applied a pressure bandage, and declared, "You'll probably live."

Scott arrived thirty minutes later. After a brief discussion, he tried to lighten the somber mood. "I agree we must seal the tunnel, but I don't understand why you have all the fun!"

"Because you need to leave this building ASAP," I said soberly. "That'll support your cover story that you only came here to conduct a surprise security inspection."

He nodded. "Thanks for mixing the first batch of concrete for me."

The Chief and I put on our suits, top coats, and stocking caps. We wore rubber boots. Our street shoes and Homburg hats stuffed in the backpacks we'd discard once we exited the storm drain.

"Do we look like prosperous West German businessmen?" I asked.

"When the East Germans line you up in front of the firing squad, your attire makes little difference" Scott quipped. "This'll be your fourth mission to the East. You're pressing your luck, old buddy!"

"The Chief is smart and speaks the language like a native. I bet you a beer that we'll be back in the West before nine tonight."

"I want to lose that bet, so you're on."

We descended the ladder, then shoved it up so Scott could lift it up into the tunnel.

"Okay, send down the plywood and two by fours." I requested.

Scott complied silently.

We inserted our pin-light flashlights into our stocking caps. "Chief, why don't I hold the plywood against the opening while you position the boards?" I proposed.

As soon as it was all in place, we heard pieces of rebar and concrete hitting the plywood. At 1953 hours, precisely sixty minutes after the first fast-drying cement had been placed in the hole, we removed the plywood and boards.

"Let's carry the form material to the storm-drain entrance in one load if possible," the Chief suggested.

We placed the boards on top of the plywood and quickly transported it all through the manhole cover and up to the surface of the still-vacant courtyard. We hid everything—the form material, our backpacks, stocking caps, and flashlights—amidst the debris that filled the nearby buildings.

I said quietly, "Let's get ourselves back to West Berlin."

The plan Thomas Lane had approved called for a mid-afternoon extraction of the Chief and Kurt. Today, Kurt implemented a three hour delay in the start of this part of the plan. We were now over two hours behind that revised schedule. We walked a memorized route and arrived at the East Train Station. A few minutes later, a West Berlin taxi pulled up. A man dressed much as we were got out.

Per the plan, we got in. The Chief told the driver, "Take us to Stadmitte Subway Station."

The driver announced, "I only accept West Marks!"

"We have West Marks." The Chief handed over prearranged identification in the form of a mustache added to the portrait on a fifty West Mark note.

He glanced back at us and smiled. "Glad you two made it safely. We were beginning to worry."

When we arrived at our destination, the taxi driver turned to us, "Your limousine will arrive in ten minutes at the meeting point. Good luck, gentlemen." He smiled and gave us our change.

The Chief and I stood on the appointed street corner until a U.S. Army, olive green Ford staff car pulled up.

We remained silent during the four-block drive to the East German's Friedrichstrasse Checkpoint. When the vehicle entered the maze designed to prevent drive-through escapes, my chest tightened. *I will not have a panic attack—I vowed and clinched my teeth together.* The East German border guards casually raised the metal pole and waved us through.

My heart beat wildly, as we covered the half block to the wooden shed that was American Checkpoint Charlie. On the way, I said to the Chief "No matter what, I'll never go back to the East again. It isn't worth the adrenalin rush of success."

At Checkpoint Charlie, an individual in an Army Major's uniform climbed into the front seat. He looked at us, "I had orders directly from General Clay's office to raise hell with the East German Border Police if they failed to recognize the right of you and your vehicle to exit East Berlin."

"Major, we're glad your help wasn't required. This part of the extraction worried us the most."

"We've got the East Germans buffaloed. Since the events in October, they automatically wave any staff car through their checkpoint, no matter the circumstance. Probably the only advantage we gained because of the Berlin Crisis."

"There is one more, Major. They now know it means war if they try to take Berlin by force."

"True. Okay, where do we drop you two?"

"The arrivals entrance to Tempelhof Airport."

The Chief located our resident Air Force Medic. I declined his suggestion that I go to an Emergency Room. He cleaned my wound and gave me a shot of penicillin and a container of painkillers. He also agreed to forget he had ever treated me.

CHAPTER 145

Sunday, November 19, 1961

ANNA WAS IN bed asleep when I finally arrived at our new home. I snuggled in close, wrapped my arms around her and held her tightly.

She stirred sleepily, then sat up in bed. "Robbie, what has happened? Are you, all right?"

"I'm fine, but have I told you recently how much I love you?"

"You told me as you left this morning."

"Well, I love you even more now."

"Where've you been?"

"East Berlin."

"Stop joking. That's just another of your little stories."

"Get dressed and I'll show you the proof."

"Come to bed, silly. It's late, and we must go to work tomorrow."

"Woman, just do as I say!" I kissed her nose and gave her a playful swat on the butt.

Fifteen minutes later, we left our new home. I drove northwest into the British sector of Berlin in Scott's convertible. Anna bombarded me with questions and displayed a touch of annoyance. "Where are we going in the middle of the night?"

"To a mansion Scott rented in the Charlottenburg District."

"Why would Scott rent an estate there? That's where very wealthy Berliners live."

"That's true."

"How can Scott afford a mansion? He's just an Air Force Captain like you."

"Well, it turns out that Scott's family owns a big part of Texas, so he can easily afford such luxury."

"Robert Kerr, you'll immediately tell me where we're going and why?"

"No, that'd spoil the surprise."

"I don't care. Tell me now...."

I smiled at her. "The mansion's in the next block. Sure you can't wait?

"No—tell me! Tell me NOW!"

"Your entire family is in West Berlin, and they are waiting in the mansion to be reunited with you."

"That's impossible. How?!....who?!....when?! She sputtered, shaking her head in an attempt to clear her mind. "Robert Kerr, you sometimes lie in jest. Are you kidding me? This isn't a nice trick!"

"Well, if you are going to cast aspersions on my character, we'll just go back home."

"Robert..."

"We're here," I said. "Take my hand." I slipped my free arm around her waist. "I don't want you to faint or fall down and hurt yourself."

"What you're saying can't be true. People get killed trying to escape! Why are you doing this?"

I led her through massive front doors into a vestibule and then a large living room. All the adults sat on three sofas and two chairs arranged around a roaring fire in a massive fireplace.

Bernard saw Anna. He jumped up and headed for her. Clearly overwhelmed, she started to weep. All conversations stopped as everyone else turned to us.

Bernard reached her first, then other members of her immediate family surrounded her. I stepped out of the way. Following a group hug, she embraced and kissed each individual, touching them as if to assure herself they were indeed alive and well.

"I have spent long hours worrying that I would never see any of you again," she declared. "Now you're all here! Give me a few minutes to get used to this—I can't believe my eyes. You are all here and safe!"

I handed Anna a handkerchief. As she dried her eyes, she cried out, "The children, where are they?"

Bernard embraced his daughter. "We just put them to bed. They had a big day, but we will get them up."

Soon she was hugging each of the children. The last, little Andrea insisted that Anna pick her up. After a sloppy kiss the little girl said, "I missed you and Robert. I was able to bring the Barbie doll and all of her clothes with me in my backpack."

After the furor died down, Anna drew me into her arms. We shared a long, ardent kiss. "How did you manage this, darling?" she asked.

"You won't believe it, but I really can't tell you. It must remain a secret."

At this point, I introduced her to Kurt Altschuler's daughter, Gretchen, her mother, Erica, and grandmother, Rachel.

I took Bernard and Anna to one side. "Do they know that Kurt was seriously injured?"

"Scott called the military hospital. Kurt didn't make it," Bernard said. "Erica is grief stricken. While they were in the tunnel, Kurt apparently gave her a large manila envelope. It contained a letter and his Will, which named Erica and their daughter as his heirs. Fortunately, his assets and CIA pension will ensure that they will never have to worry about money."

"I'm relieved. Over these past few months, he became like a brother to me."

Emma joined us. She asked Anna, "I heard that the Stasi mistreated you, dear. How are you feeling?"

"The Stasi threatened to send you all to prison, and the children to orphanages, which was why I was so frightened. They tried to force me to spy on Robert. Now that you are all here, I feel wonderful."

Anna grasped her parents' hands. "Robert won't tell me how you escaped. Tell me, please."

Bernard answered, "We met him in an abandoned warehouse near the East Train Station, where he led us to a storm drain which we walked through to a hole. Then we climbed up a ladder into a tunnel, rode in a motorized cart blindfolded, had lunch at an apartment somewhere near the River Spree, and were brought here in a plumbing van."

"That doesn't help me understand at all." Her confusion showed as she looked at Emma.

Emma shrugged. "Papa's right. That is all we know."

"Mama, were you able to bring any of your nice things with you?"

"We have the clothes on our backs, our identification papers, and a few photographs. Everything else is at home," Emma's lips trembled.

"I was told that I should not even bring my doctor's bag, so it is still back in my surgery."

Bernard took Emma in his arms. "We have each other. Family is the most important thing in life, and now our family will be together... and safe."

Looking at her parents, Anna asked, "Have you decided where you want to live?"

Sophia, standing nearby, noticed her parents' hesitation. "The man came by the house late last evening to tell us about the escape plan, so none of us has had time to think about such things."

"Did you know that this is our third escape attempt?" Bernard asked.

"Actually, I believe Scott, Kurt, and I developed a total of six escape schemes if you include Bernauerstrasse," I said.

"Robert promised he would not give up until you were free, but he didn't tell me how he planned to make that happen."

"I just didn't want to get your hopes up if we failed," I slipped my arm around her, and gave her a squeeze.

Anna whispered in my ear. I shouted to be heard over everyone. "Attention. Anna has an announcement."

"Now we can all live in America and be together. I want to be near all of you, so you must come to America next month when Robert and I move there! Robert says we can sponsor you and you can probably leave here soon." She waited expectantly for their excited agreement.

After a brief, almost tense silence, Bernard came over, and took Anna's hand, "Although we are grateful that Robert helped us to escape from the East and we would like to visit America, your mother and I will probably decide to live in West Germany."

"And this is a decision Sophia, Derrik, Fredrich, Helmuth, and Johanna will make for themselves and their families," Emma added.

I saw the disappointment in Anna's eyes. She mutely nodded her understanding.

CHAPTER 146

Monday, November 20, 1961

THE CELEBRATION FINALLY subsided at a little after midnight. Several hours later, the phone in the master bedroom rang. I heard Scott answer, "Hello." He fell silent for a moment. "Impossible. Thanks."

A moment later, he banged on our door. "That was Mark. A recent intercept at the building indicates the Stasi received extrajudicial authorization to conduct a raid on this house and kill all its occupants. They may arrive at any moment."

"How could he possibly know where the Fischer family are staying?" I asked.

Anna joined us. After explaining the situation, she retrieved her father. Once the four of us were together, Scott asked, "Bernard, do you have any idea how the Stasi discovered our location?"

His shoulder slumped as he replied, "After we arrived, I called Saint Hedwig Hospital in East Berlin from the telephone in the hall. I needed my patients to be assigned to other doctors. It took a few minutes to give them my instructions."

"They've probably traced the call to this address. We can expect the Stasi any minute!" I concluded.

"Why do they want to kill my family and me?" Bernard asked. "I don't understand."

I explained. "Three Stasi agents were killed last night, and they found a small leather case with your calling cards at the scene."

"They think you're a CIA operative, and they want revenge," Scott added.

"I do carry a case for my business cards."

"Is it with you?"

He went after his suit coat. "It's usually in the inside breast pocket of this jacket, but it's gone." Obviously both embarrassed and worried. "How could I have been so stupid,"

Cool-headed Scott took control of the situation. "Get everyone up and dressed. Turn off the lights and lock the doors. I know someone I can call. He will quickly get people here to protect us."

The West Berlin Police connected Scott to his friend, Herr Captain Hans Bauer. He held out the phone so I could hear the conversation. "Hans, buddy, I have a huge problem and need your help. Don't ask me how I know, but the Stasi have been authorized to conduct the extrajudicial murder of twelve members of Doctor Bernard Fischer's family."

"They live in the East. I can't help you."

"They managed to escape yesterday."

"Wonderful news. Bernard Fischer has done so much for the people of Berlin. He personally treated my older brother, when as a teenager he was wounded in the struggle to save Berlin from the Russians."

"He and his family are going to be very dead if you don't help."

"We're in a large home at 23 Gardes-Du-Corps Strasse," I said loud enough for Bauer to hear.

"Patrol cars should start arriving within fifteen minutes," he replied. "Get everyone to the safest place inside of the house."

"Got it!" Scott replied.

"I'll be there as soon as possible to direct our operations."

"Everyone into the basement," Scott directed. "It has a metal door and a deadbolt lock. I'll stay up here to welcome the police when they arrive."

"I'll stay with you," I exclaimed. "We've been in worse danger recently."

While others hurried downstairs, I felt the onset of my first panic attack in months. Through the difficult moments while we completed the tunnel, tried to free Anna's family from the East, and the last twenty hours, I'd experienced no panic attacks. Why now?

The first sign, a rapid intake of breath. Next, tunnel vision, then my extremities began to tingle, and I became dizzy. Although I made it to one of the couches in the living room and initiated my deep breathing exercises, I knew that this would be a severe attack. Scott, aware of my problem, rushed to my side. With dead-panned look he said, "Not an appropriate time to be lying down on the job, Kemosabe!"

"I know," I whispered, impressed by his sense of humor given the circumstances.

"What can I do for you?" he asked, this time more seriously.

"Keep the bad guys at bay until I recover."

"Easier said than done, my friend."

Minutes later, the first police cars arrived. My symptoms eased slowly, and I was on my feet before those hiding in the basement returned.

CHAPTER 147

Anna

Monday, November 20, 1961

SCOTT, ROBERT, AND I rousted everyone out of bed, told them to get dressed and go down to the basement quickly. At Robert's insistence, I accompanied my family and helped barricade the door as Scott instructed.

Ten minutes later, I heard police cars arrive. I relaxed a little, confident we would be safe. Soon we returned to the first floor.

Captain Bauer, a muscular, handsome, almost six-foot-tall blond, arrived about thirty minutes after Scott's original call.

He tried to reassure us about our safety. "I have a squad of specially trained men whose primary job is to protect VIPs. These men are the best—everyone thoroughly vetted and trained. They'll all be here soon. Our presence should deter the Stasi from taking any action."

"Do you plan to protect us here?" I asked.

"No, it's best that we get everyone out of here. Those bastards might try something drastic in this normally quiet residential area. We don't know how they will cross over the border or how many might be coming."

"Do you have a suggestion?" Scott asked.

"The Hilton has a VIP area in an isolated wing with restricted elevator and stair access—ideal from our viewpoint," Herr Bauer replied.

Scott made a quick phone call. "The whole wing was unoccupied. It's ours now."

"Who's paying for the hotel?" I asked.

"Don't worry about it!" Scott replied. "Let this be my parting gift for a wonderful family I really admire. I'm protecting Mia's family as well as Kurt's, whom we are all now responsible for."

By four a.m., twenty members of the Berlin Special Police Squad had arrived and surrounded the mansion. As usual, Berlin weather again changed for the worse. Bitter cold and the usual cloud cover, rain intermingled with a heavy mist. The officers wore dark-blue rain slickers with **POLIZEI** emblazoned on the back.

Robert summoned the adults into the living room. "For your safety, the police are taking everyone to the Hilton Hotel. We will leave as soon as the police announce it is safe."

At Captain Bauer's direction, seven dark-green Mercedes police vans pulled into the driveway of the mansion, engines and heaters running. Armed police spread across the front entrance, around the convoy of vans, facing out, MP-28 submachine guns at the ready. Sophia's family, Erica's three, Scott's four, and Helmut's family were escorted to the middle four vehicles. Next, Captain Bauer directed, "Herr Doktor and Professor Fischer, Fredrich Fischer, Captain and Frau Kerr, please go to the second van. I will drive that vehicle."

Captain Bauer addressed his team, "While you are inside your vehicle have your arms at the ready in order to exit and defend the convoy should that become necessary. Squad leaders, take your teams and occupy the leading and trailing vans." With hand signals, he directed other individuals to be drivers or to sit in the front passenger seat of the remaining vans.

The vans had bucket seats in front with three bench seats in the back. Robert and I sat just behind the driver. We watched as six policemen got into the first vehicle. Another sat in the passenger seat in front of us, alertly assessing the surrounding area.

Captain Bauer took the driver's seat, turned on the two blue flashing roof lights, and glanced back at us. "That is my signal for the convoy to proceed to the hotel."

The other vans and police cars also activated their flashing blue lights. The lead van followed a squad car as it turned right out of the driveway onto the street. Bauer put our van into gear and followed. We had just reached the entrance to the driveway when a fast-moving, black Opel sedan rear-ended the lead van.

Knowing that the men in that van and car were probably injured, policemen from other vans, including Captain Bauer and our front seat passenger, quickly ran to the scene. I saw their struggle to open the doors of the wrecked van. Then I heard someone shout, "Gasoline is leaking from one of the vehicles! We must get everyone out before these vehicles catch fire." A policeman rushed to our van, grabbed the fire extinguisher from the center console, and ran back to the wreck.

I had a feeling I couldn't quite explain or shake. I didn't believe this was an accident. *We were in danger.* I stood, moved forward, and leaned over the front seats for a better view of the situation. Captain Bauer had left the engine running and the lights on. Despite the heavy mist and darkness of the night, I saw no unusual activity on the street ahead. The van's head-lights and nearby streetlights illuminated the area.

"Anna, what are you doing?" Robert asked.

Looking toward the accident, I realized all the surviving policemen were occupied in the rescue operation. I heard the rat-a-tat-tat of machine gun fire at the back of the convoy. I shuddered with dread. *The wreck was planned, and we are all in danger. Again!*

Several policemen raced toward the rear van as Robert said. "Captain Bauer has deployed all his available men to assist the crew in the rear van. They'll be able to stop the attack."

I felt a renewed sense of danger. Between the fire and the attack in back, no one was providing protection for our van. We were the primary targets!

I didn't fret for long. A large Mercedes sedan with tinted windows and its lights off approached from the left. I watched it move slowly towards us, then stop on the opposite side of the street.

Three men exited the Mercedes and surveyed the scene. Signaling each other with thumbs up that they were safe, one of the men opened the street side backdoor. A short man in a leather trench coat stepped out of the vehicle and placed a homburg hat on his head. Horrified, I looked into the face of Dieter Holburg!

A slender man with an intense expression opened the trunk of the Mercedes, pulled out a machine gun and handed it to another man. *They were here to kill us; the attack in the back was just a second diversion.*

No time to warn the police or even Robert. I saw what was happening. I needed to do something to save my family. I started to crawl into the driver's seat.

Robert shouted, "Anna, what are you doing? Sit back down, please!"

I lunged forward. The gear shift and parking brake between the seats acted as a barrier. Finally, I got my feet over them and fell into the driver's seat, my head hitting the side window.

All four men from the sedan held weapons and were in the process of installing magazines or placing bandoliers over their shoulders.

I silently put the van in gear.

Dieter made hand gestures, instructing his men to spread-out. Less than twenty feet separated us. *I must hit them with the van and stop them from shooting my family.*

I slammed my foot down on the gas. The van lurched forward, tires squealing. I caught Dieter and the man beside him by surprise. It took only a second or two for the van to cover the space between us. The Stasi *schweinehunde* (pig-dogs) tried to dive out of my path. Their car blocked their way. The impact of the van drove them back into the side of the sedan, crushing their evilness.

The windshield in front of me displayed smeared blood, body parts and a familiar, but now squashed, face an instant before the glass exploded. That was the last thing I remembered.

During the ambulance ride to the hospital, I regained consciousness and focused on Robert's face, "Is that bastard dead?"

"Yes, Dieter Holburg and three of his underlings are very dead," Robert replied.

"Good." I collapsed back onto the stretcher.

Once at the hospital, the doctors determined I'd suffered a concussion and they decided to keep me overnight for observation. Frederick suffered a broken arm, but my parents and Robbie got off with only bruises and slight contusions.

CHAPTER 148

Robert
Monday, November 20-Friday, December 1, 1961

A CASCADE OF events happened during our remaining days in Berlin. An intercept at the building revealed that Anna, I and her entire family were on the Stasi extrajudicial "Kill on Sight List." As a result, Anna's entire family was immediately granted visas to immigrate to the United States.

Since they had left the East with only the clothes on their backs, most of Wednesday was spent acquiring clothes, suitcases, and even small toys for the children in preparation for their long journey to America.

On Thursday, the Hilton served a delicious Thanksgiving dinner—turkey with all of the trimmings in the large dining room of the Presidential Suite. At the end of the meal, I distributed visas and airline tickets to Anna's family. "You'll leave on Saturday and stay at my Hunter Grandparents' home while you get settled."

At the funeral service for Kurt Altschuler on Friday, I attempted to give a stirring remembrance speech for a man I'd learned to love like a brother. "Kurt Altschuler was a consummate European gentleman, who adopted America when he could no longer live in Germany. He spent the war years battling the Nazis behind their lines. Then, in 1946, he voluntarily came to Berlin to battle the corrupt communist regime in East Germany. After a fifteen-year struggle, he gave his life in that fight. We all salute him for his valor and courage. May he rest in peace." The other military men and I saluted as taps played and his coffin was lowered into the earth.

Scott then announced in a subdued tone of voice that, "Mark Powell, Robert Kerr, and I commissioned a headstone for Kurt Altschuler's grave which will read as follows:

KURT ALTSCHULER

BORN BERLIN, GERMANY: JANUARY 25, 1918
DIED BERLIN, GERMANY: NOVEMBER 19, 1961

HE GAVE HIS LIFE FOR THIS CITY AND
THOSE HE LOVED

FATHER OF GRETCHEN ALTSCHULER

To Be Born Free is an Accident
To Live Free is a Privilege
To Die Free is a Responsibility

On Saturday, a police convoy transported Anna's family to Tegel Airport for the flight to America. Even though she would be reunited with them in less than a month, the emotional farewell at the gate lasted so long, the airline staff threatened to leave Bernard and Emma behind if they didn't board the airplane immediately.

For the next month, Anna and I occupied "safe" VIP quarters at Tempelhof AFB. Armed guards escorted us on the few times we left the base.

On Monday, Scott and Mia were married by the same justice of the peace. Anna and I served as their witnesses. It was a lovely ceremony. Mia beamed like any blushing bride, despite being five months pregnant.

In rapid succession, Scott reported that he had married a foreign national from East Berlin, his security clearance was revoked, and he resigned from the Air Force. On December 1, we went to Tegel Airport as all five members of Mia's family and Scott headed to a large cattle ranch near Fort Worth, Texas.

The CIA acquired a copy of the East Berlin Police forensic report on the 'Shootout at the Warehouse.' It indicated that Thomas Lane, Deputy CIA Station Berlin had "died at his own hand."

The newspaper *Newes Deutschland* reported his cowardice with great fanfare and indicating that "a number of other American spies and saboteurs were also injured in the gunfight with heroic Secret Police agents. Those Enemies of the State have managed to escape the scene and are now the subject of a massive manhunt." The three Stasi agents who died that night were never mentioned.

CHAPTER 149

Saturday, December 2-Monday, December 18, 1961

IN EARLY DECEMBER, Colonel Morgan told me the CIA was urging the Air Force to investigate the circumstances which had led to the death of two of their agents in Berlin. "Your departure from Berlin will be delayed indefinitely while the circumstances of their deaths are investigated. Be prepared to face a General Court Martial. I must inform you that the charges they are contemplating are very serious and could result in an extended prison stay."

After a two-week emotional roller coaster, while the investigation focused on my role in the incident, I received a person-to-person phone call from Texas. Scott Taylor said, "Robbie, old buddy, I've been able to save our collective bacon. They were threatening to call me back to active duty and prosecute you, Mark, the Chief and me for our roles in the deaths of Lane and Altschuler. Vice President Johnson assured my father he has squelched the investigation because of National Security. He has also cleared the way for you to be separated from and depart Berlin next week, right on schedule. Call me collect immediately if you aren't officially informed of this today or tomorrow. Mia and I will join you and Anna in Hawaii right after the first of the year. Good luck, Kemosabe."

"Thanks, Scott. I'm eternally grateful."

On December 18th, the Chief, Sergeant Loring, and I walked through the now completed tunnel and Signals Exploitation Center with the officer and NCOs who would take responsibility for maintaining what we had built.

At the end of a party in their recreation room that evening, my crew of hardened veterans and I choked up and even cried as warm handshakes, back slaps and extended hugs were exchanged between our brothers-in-arms from the other services.

General Harrison presided over a parade and awards ceremony in Hanger 1 at Tempelhof the following day. Each man received the two medals Vice President Johnson had promised, the Outstanding Unit Award and Distin-guished Service Medal. During the ceremony, I mused over what this small group of dedicated Americans had accomplished in less than a year.

CHAPTER 150

Wednesday, December 20, 1961

MARK AND MARY Powell stood on the tarmac as Anna and I ascended the metal stairs into our Pan American DC-6B. We could have flown a jet out of Tegel, but I decided to leave Berlin the same way I arrived. Much had changed. I had arrived a lonely single man and am now leaving with a lovely wife. The two of us and my relatives will soon gather with her family for a joyous Christmas celebration in California.

Anna took the window seat, and I sat beside her as our aircraft lifted off the runway at Tempelhof Airport. With layovers in London and New York, it'd take us almost twenty-four hours to reach San Francisco.

Because of the direction of the wind, the aircraft took off heading east. Once airborne, it began to slowly ascend and turned to the left to avoid East German-controlled airspace.

"I'm glad we're going to fly right along the dividing line between East and West Berlin," Anna observed. "This route will allow me to see familiar sights one last time. I…" She broke off and began to cry.

I put my arm around her and gave her my handkerchief. She dried her eyes and smiled at me, then took my hand for comfort.

As the aircraft banked, the distinctive roof of the Signals Exploitation Center building, which housed the entrance to the tunnel, came into view. In my mind's eye, I could see the tunnel as it passed under the River Spree and into the ruined industrial area in the distance.

The aircraft completed its turn to the west to eventually enter one of the air corridors over East Germany. Anna said excitedly, "I can almost see the house I grew up in. It's just over there in that clump of Linden trees. I'll probably never see the house my family loved again, but I'm taking all of those happy times and wonderful experiences with me to my new life."

"And there is Museum Island just ahead."

In less than a minute, Anna observed, "And there is Unter den Linden. Oh, and there is the Brandenburg Gate, and over there is the burned-out Reichstag Building."

"You can see that the slab wall they've been building in front of the Brandenburg Gate is almost finished," I said. "And the watchtowers are now almost continuous in this sector. The barriers to freedom are becoming more formidable each day."

Five minutes later, our aircraft passed over the continuous barren strip of land and the barbed wire fences that separated West Berlin from East Germany.

Anna squeezed my hand tightly and asked, "Will all those people below us ever be free again?!"

"I'm confident that someday Europe will again be free."

EPILOGUE

ANNA AND I took over Grandpa Hunter's farming operations. I devoted full time to the farms while Anna attended art history classes at the University of California Berkeley. She received her bachelor's degree in one year and entered their two-stage integrated master's and doctoral program (MA/PhD) program in the fall of 1963. She became a professor there and was chairman of the Art History Department for years.

Once we returned to the states, Anna began therapy sessions for Gross Stress Reaction, which is now known as Post Traumatic Stress Disorder. She has done remarkably well in gaining control of her new life, but still must cope with infrequent, but all too real, flashbacks.

Occasionally, I experience a panic attack. Therapy didn't help my affliction, so I just learned to live with it. Fortunately, farming is not very stressful.

We've raised four children and now have fifteen grandchildren.

Anna's entire family moved to the states and settled along California State Route 29, which runs from near our farm to San Francisco. We joke that the extended Fischer/Kerr/Smith/Altschuler family are on it so often, we were responsible for it being in a sad state of repair.

All the émigrés became American citizens. They have prospered, purchasing their own homes and assured that their children received university educations.

The Berlin Wall eventually fell, and Germany was reunited. Scott, Mia, Anna and I have remained close and are going to make our fourth trip to Berlin soon. Tempelhof Airport has been turned into a memorial to the airlift and a recreation park. The many American bases and facilities we knew so well, including the Clay Compound, are now abandoned—uninhabited reminders of that bygone era.

In the mid-1960s, the apartments on Berneurstrasse were torn down and replaced with a section of the Berlin Wall. Recently, an area along that wall has been turned into a memorial for those who died and suffered as a result of the Berlin Wall and communist oppression. One of the few remaining parts of that graffiti-decorated Berlin Wall has been preserved there. This is always the first stop on our tour of Berlin.

AUTHORS POSTSCRIPT

By 1960, when our story begins, most of the ninety-six mile-long barrier that separated West Berlin from East Germany was a chain link or barbed-wire fence. The part of the Wall that was concrete slabs or blocks was less than ten miles long. Even in 1989 when "The Wall Fell," the wall part of this barrier was only forty-three miles long.

An estimated 560,000 people left East Germany over the 28 years between 1961 and 1989. Over sixty percent were elderly individuals who were allowed to go to West Germany primarily so the East German government could stop paying them their old-age pensions. Over 120,000 escaped while visiting another country; most of those defectors were athletes, government officials, artists and business people who saw their opportunity to escape and took it. Another five percent were ransomed by the West German government. How much more corrupt could a country be than to sell its own citizens for cash!

What of the rest? The over 30,000 people who managed to escape over the barrier that separated West Berlin and West Germany from the East? Each of them had a harrowing story to tell. Over two-thirds of those escapes occurred between 1961 through 1970. By the 1980s, only one percent of the people leaving East Germany escaped over the now virtually impenetrable walls and fences that surrounded Berlin and the entire Western border.

By one estimate, every day from August 12, 1961 until November 9, 1989, seven people were **Captured Trying to Escape East Germany**. Those over 75,000 people spent an estimated average of five years in Stasi prisons. Many were convicted of espionage and summarily executed. An estimated 810 freedom seekers were murdered at the walls and fences surrounding East Germany and East Berlin during those bleak 28 years.

ACKNOWLEDGMENTS

When people found out that I was writing a novel about the early 1960's and the Berlin crisis, everyone said, "This era and topic have not been covered in modern fiction." So, I worked hard for over two years to get this book ready for publication. I hope you enjoyed it.

They say "write what you know." So, I did. I lived in Germany in the 1960s and was a US Air Force Signals Intelligence Officer. We monitored communist countries communication 24 hours a day, 365 days a year. I made the decision to issue reports which ultimately got President Lyndon Johnson out of bed at least five times.

During my training as a signals intelligence officer, we learned about Project Gold/Stopwatch. Even though this was almost eight years after the fact, this project was still classified Top Secret codeword.

I owe a debt to a great number of people. An early draft of this novel was completed in late 2016. Marni Freedman, a writing coach read it and for the next nine months made valuable suggestions on how to improve the story. During this time, the novel evolved into the romantic thriller you've read.

My mentor and primary critic was Karen Black. She is a published author, who believed that I had a "good read," and patiently helped me through the many versions of this novel

Members of the Scribblers, a North San Diego writers group, heard me read numerous excerpts from the book and provided valuable feedback. Terry Badger, leader of the Scribblers, and also a published author, served as a late Beta and proofreader.

Early Beta Readers who made significant contributions to this novel are my ever-patient bridge partners, Diana Glimm and Sue Compton.

Other Beta Readers include my sister-in-law Katy Phillips, my wife Margaret Liles, Ingrid Hoffmeister, Sarah Vosburgh, Jean Jantz, Nick Durutta, Augie Houser, Dale Barden, and Raymond Curtiss. All of their comments helped me improve the story in a myriad of ways.

Laura Taylor line edited the entire manuscript. It reads much better and is substantially shorter due to her efforts. My son, David Liles performed a final edit and made many valuable suggestions for changes, additions, and deletions. Proof readers of the final manuscript included: My niece Ann Phillips, my nephew Mathew Phillips, Kathy Allman, and Zan Rose. Victor Pitcock, a fellow cold war and signals intelligence warrior read an early draft and recently proofread the Nook ebook version of this novel.

Finally, I must thank, the publishers at Acorn—Holly Kammier and Jessica Therrien—for agreeing to publish this book. They have patiently taken me through the myriad steps required to get a book published. I hope their faith in me and my book are rewarded.

Proof

Made in the USA
Columbia, SC
14 August 2018